PENGUIN BOOKS

War Brides

Helen Bryan is the author of *Martha Washington, First Lady of Liberty* (Wiley, 2002) which received an Award of Merit from the New York Colonial Dames in 2003. *War Brides* is her first novel. She lives in London where she is a barrister.

War Brides

HELEN BRYAN

PENGUIN BOOKS

PENGUIN BOOKS

Published by the Penguin Group
Penguin Books Ltd, 80 Strand, London WC2R 0RL, England
Penguin Group (USA) Inc., 375 Hudson Street, New York, New York 10014, USA
Penguin Group (Canada), 90 Eglinton Avenue East, Suite 700, Toronto, Ontario, Canada M4P 2Y3
(a division of Pearson Penguin Canada Inc.)
Penguin Ireland, 25 St Stephen's Green, Dublin 2, Ireland
(a division of Penguin Books Ltd)
Penguin Group (Australia), 250 Camberwell Road,
Camberwell, Victoria 3124, Australia (a division of Pearson Australia Group Pty Ltd)
Penguin Books India Pvt Ltd, 11 Community Centre,
Panchsheel Park, New Delhi – 110 017, India
Penguin Group (NZ), 67 Apollo Drive, Mairangi Bay, Auckland 1310,
New Zealand (a division of Pearson New Zealand Ltd)
Penguin Books (South Africa) (Pty) Ltd, 24 Sturdee Avenue,
Rosebank, Johannesburg 2196, South Africa

Penguin Books Ltd, Registered Offices: 80 Strand, London WC2R 0RL, England

www.penguin.com

First published 2007
2

Copyright © Helen Bryan, 2007
All rights reserved

The moral right of the author has been asserted

Set in 12.5/14.75pt Monotype Garamond
by Palimpsest Book Production Limited, Grangemouth, Stirlingshire
Printed in England by Clays Ltd, St Ives plc

ISBN 978-0-141-02712-8

As always, with love for Roger, Cassell, Niels
and Michelle, and now for darling
Bo Hackworthy Bates Bryan-Low, too

Acknowledgements

A book has a long journey from the initial glimmer of an idea in the author's mind to the finished product resting on the bookshelf, and I am grateful to many people who helped *War Brides* along. First of all, I want to thank my agent Kathryn Green, of the Kathryn Green Literary Agency in New York, for her enthusiastic encouragement and practical support. I was fortunate that someone with Kathryn's experience in publishing liked *War Brides* as much as I did, and she was an invaluable source of advice about the best way to shape and focus the book without losing anything essential. Thank you, Kathryn. I cannot imagine having a better agent.

It has been a pleasure to know and work with everyone with whom I've come into contact at Michael Joseph. Louise Moore – then publishing director, now managing director – makes authors glow with the warmth of her enthusiasm for their work, and her own passion for history informs any discussion of historical fiction. Commissioning editor Clare Ledingham refined the book with painstaking care, and a sure touch. Copy editor Hazel Orme perfected it with equally painstaking care and precision, and because Hazel is extremely know-ledgeable about the period we were always at risk of drifting off into long discussions about the way women in England lived in the 1930s and 1940s. Among other things, we discovered a shared appreciation for pre-war elegance – the hats, the gloves, the dressing-cases – and I am grateful for her practical input on catching escaped bulls. Thanks are due to assistant editor Claire Bord, for keeping everything on track, seeing manuscripts went to the right people and generally making sure that what was meant to happen happened.

Like many writers, I am technology's hostage, and I am grateful to H. Jassim and his brother Sirwan Jassim, resident geniuses of BJ Computers in Camden Town, who made many house calls to rescue the computer, the manuscript and me from technological crises and meltdown. Without them the book would have disappeared into cyberspace.

Finally, I want to thank my dear husband Roger, who not only gave me a room of my own and the time to think of nothing but writing in it, but understands when I get a blank look on my face that means I am 'thinking' and dinner will be late again. And while a room in which to write is the greatest imaginable luxury, happiness comes from the family on the other side of the door when I emerge – Roger, our daughter Cassell, our son Niels and his wife Michelle who, despite busy lives, are never too occupied to be supportive or show an interest in my efforts.

Introduction

War Brides probably began to take shape long before I was aware of it. I was one of the American post-war baby-boom generation, whose early years were touched, though in my case gently, by the war's long shadow. My husband and I both had fathers who had served in the US Army, as did most of our uncles, except for one in the navy and one who became an air-force pilot. Women played an active role too. An aunt by marriage was an army nurse, and my mother was an officer in WAVES, 'Women Accepted for Volunteer Emergency Service'. As a child, I was fascinated to learn that this wife, mother, housewife and pillar of her church had once worn a pistol on her hip as she escorted telegrams and urgent communications across Norfolk Navy Yard. Because my husband's father was posted to Europe shortly before he was born, his mother gave birth in a military-base hospital in Alabama, then made a long, arduous journey home to her family in Wisconsin, struggling with a screaming baby on a series of trains packed with servicemen. Stories of how anxious families at home had waited and coped with everyday life, living for letters and working extra hard, were part and parcel of our childhood as much as the family photographs of relatives in uniform propped up in the sitting room.

As a bride in 1944 my mother had walked down the

aisle of her local Episcopal church wearing bedroom slippers beneath her satin bridal dress – shockingly louche by the standards of her Virginia town, but shoes were rationed and that was what brides did then. But everyone had enough to eat, despite rationing imposed by the US government, and the European war was far enough away from the United States to make a German invasion seem unlikely. It was only later, when I studied history, that I learned more about the war and its horrors, the grim and terrifying realities, hardships and privations people had faced across Europe, and when I moved to England to live I began to grasp the war's impact, how dark and long its shadow really was. I had lived in London for years by the time an American acquaintance visited shortly before the fiftieth anniversary of VE Day. He went dutifully to the Imperial War Museum, Churchill's War Rooms and Eisenhower's underground headquarters. By the end of the day he was shaken. He emerged from the last saying he wanted to shake the hand of every English person over the age of sixty. I know what he meant.

The family photographs of uniformed men and women were yellowing and mostly consigned to closets and drawers to make way for wedding pictures, then new babies and holiday shots when I began to add to my information about how women coped during the war, not sure at first what I would do with it. The preoccupations that were common to women of the 1930s – falling in love, marriage, looking after husband and family, struggling in many cases to make ends meet or forced by circumstances into genteel spinsterhood – remained the same as the war engulfed everybody in the next decade. In terrible times, and despite the heavy burdens imposed by war work, rationing and the threat of invasion, many women fought a desperate battle for normality, with the kind of personal courage never mentioned in the history books. Elsie, Frances, Alice, Tanni and Evangeline had soon invented themselves, and hung about, waiting for their stories to be written.

But if I could pinpoint a starting place for the book, it lies in the character of Manfred, who gives the book its uncomfortable edge in reality. All of the other characters in the book are imaginary and, so far as I am aware, there is no de Balfort family in Sussex. If there are living de Balforts anywhere, I apologize for any unintentional connection with Manfred. Characters must be called something. But Manfred was a real person, although it is unlikely his identity will ever be known. I learned about him from an older family friend, who served in British Intelligence during the war. John did not like talking about his experiences there. A deeply civilized, kind and intelligent man with a great sense of humour and devoted to his family, he was never the sort to nurse a grudge but, even so, on many occasions he spoke of a German collaborator in the south-east who, Intelligence knew, was sending vital weather reports to the Germans on the French coast to enable them to carry out bombing raids on clear nights. That the traitor, spy or collaborator, whoever he was, was never caught and brought to justice clearly rankled, after fifty years, with him enough to make me wonder about the war's deep scars and unsettled scores. Although the real Manfred is almost certainly dead now, I am sorry that John, may he rest in peace, will not read this book. In lieu of real justice, I like to think he would have been satisfied that Manfred was exposed and punished at last, if only on the printed page.

Prologue: London, Spring 1995

In the departure lounge of the Atlanta airport on an early May evening, Alice Osbourne Lightfoot, the trip's organizer, smiled at everybody and said, 'Hey! How you doin' this evenin'?' as she ticked off their names on a list of the London-bound party. A line from the Introduction to *The Canterbury Tales*, memorized in her schooldays, went round and round in her head – about how in spring 'Thanne longen folk to goon on pilgrimages'. Still do, even if the reasons we make pilgrimages are different now, she reflected.

Alice was the last to board the plane. Carefully she stowed an old-fashioned dressing-case in the overhead locker and took her seat among a group of elderly ladies at the front of the economy cabin. The women were wives of the remaining members of Joe Lightfoot's Eighth Air Force unit, college friends from the Georgia-Tennessee-Alabama area who had joined up together in 1941 and served in Europe. Those still able-bodied enough were making the trip back to England for the fiftieth anniversary of VE Day and a reunion with other air-force units, at their old base in Norfolk, from which they had flown B-17s and B-24s on dangerous daytime missions over Germany. Alice had volunteered to organize the trip, and because she was British-born, and had a natural tendency to take charge, the other ladies looked up to her as their leader.

After take-off the ladies slipped off their shoes and soon were doing what southerners call 'visiting' over their dinner trays. Mostly they talked about their families, and liver-spotted hands passed pictures of grandchildren back and forth across the aisle. 'Bet you're lookin' forward to goin' home, darlin',' they said to Alice. 'Wonder if England's changed much since you left.'

'Home! Honey, Alice's *home* is *Atlanta*. She's lived in America for fifty years!' Alice's friend Rose Ann protested from the next seat, 'I declare, Alice!'

'Shame you aren't gonna be at the reunion and the wreath-layin' and the dinner with us, specially after the hard work you did, fixin' this trip for Joe and the boys, but since y'all are havin' your own service, 'spect your old friends'll be right glad to have you! 'Spect y'all got a lot of catchin' up to do!'

'Oh, yes, we do, and I'll be real glad to see them,' Alice responded, in the north-Georgia drawl that had crept into her voice over the years. 'Oh, yes,' she repeated to herself. A lot of catching up indeed. Alice had never been one to shirk, and after what Elsie had written about Frances, it was her duty to go back.

As the flight wore on the women ignored the growing racket at the other end of the plane, where their husbands were drinking too much whiskey, telling war stories and dirty jokes, patting the stewardesses' bottoms and calling them 'sugar'. After dinner some, like Alice, took out knitting or crewelwork. Others tried to sleep. At last Alice yawned, wound up her knitting, switched off the overhead light and pulled on the eyeshade from the airline's toiletries bag.

*

As Alice's plane boarded, another London-bound flight took off, from Ben Gurion airport. Because it was almost midnight the cabin crew served the meal quickly, then dimmed the lights. Soon Tanni Zayman's teenage grandchildren were dozing in their seats on either side of her. Chaim and Shifra had left Tel Aviv wearing thin T-shirts emblazoned with the names of their favourite bands. Now the plane was chilly. Tanni asked the stewardess for blankets and draped one over Chaim, sprawled with his feet in the aisle, his *kippah* askew, and another over his sister. She thought how sweet they looked asleep, but she was glad of a reprieve from their constant sibling bickering when her own thoughts were in turmoil. The thought of returning to Crowmarsh Priors left her too agitated to sleep.

Down the dark aisle a baby wailed. Tanni shifted in her seat as the old panic gripped her. She shut her eyes and took calming deep breaths.

She had opened Elsie's letter as she sat by Bruno's hospital bed. As she unfolded it, the invitation and first-class plane tickets to England for Tanni and Bruno had fluttered to the floor. 'No!' Tanni had exclaimed, when she saw what they were for. Even after all this time, the idea of returning to England, let alone the village, even with her husband Bruno by her side, made her feel sick. And after his recent heart operation, travel was out of the question for Bruno.

Her exclamation had woken him, so she blurted out what the letter said, then protested shakily that she wouldn't think of going anywhere while he was in hospital. Propped up on pillows, Bruno was pale, on a drip, and should have been resting quietly. Instead he was surrounded by books, papers and university business smuggled into the hospital past the nurses who had forbidden him to work. Now he gave her one of his penetrating looks over the top of his glasses.

Tanni always found those looks — as if he knew something she did not — rather irritating, but the flash of arrogance passed as Bruno patted her hand, then held it while he considered.

The doctors had assured Bruno that many women suffered severe post-partum depression, though less had been known about it in the 1940s, he reminded himself, and Tanni's amnesia about the period after the birth and death of their baby all those years ago was nature's way of shielding her. Aside from that brief interlude, she had had a full and happy life as a wife and mother, now grandmother. He thought it was safe for her to accept Elsie's invitation now, and said, 'I know it's hard, but think of our obligation to our friends, however long it's been. And with what Elsie says about Frances, you know you must go. But not alone — why not cash in my ticket and take the two youngest with you? You need a break from worrying about me, and in a few months Chaim will be in the army. Anyway, with all their brothers and sisters, there's never been money for him and Shifra to travel. Imagine how they'd love a trip to England. Go! Take the children, see your old friends. Spend a week in London afterwards, take the children to the museums and the theatre. Let them go to those street-markets where the kids "hang out", as Shifra informs me is the correct term, these days. You could even take them to Oxford, show them my old college. They can punt on the river like I used to. Shop a little, enjoy yourself.' Bruno's eyes strayed back to his laptop screen. He was in the middle of writing an academic article. 'Besides, you can go to Foyle's for me. I have a long list of books I cannot get here, and –'

'But, Bruno, I don't want to go! I can't think of leaving you! It's out of the question!'

'So there aren't enough people to look after me? One goes out of the room, and two come in! Thank God the operation went well, no problems, and I'll be home in a few weeks – if the hospital doesn't kill me first. Doctors, students, they come in at all hours, one minute bringing terrible food I don't want, the next, when I'm asleep, waking me up to check my blood pressure. The physiotherapist turns up when I want to read . . . Don't look like that – I was joking. It's all right, my dear. Go already! I'll ring Elsie myself and tell her you will come.' He stroked her cheek, pushed his glasses into place and turned back to his article.

So, reluctantly, Tanni had agreed, and invited her grand-children so that she couldn't back out at the last minute. She wouldn't disappoint them for the world. But now that she was actually *en route*, awake and alone in the dark, her misgivings returned, heightened by the fretting of the unseen baby somewhere behind her.

Just then fifteen-year-old Shifra opened her brown eyes. She smiled at her grandmother and shifted to put her head on Tanni's shoulder. 'I'm so excited about going to London, Bubbie. My best friend Rachel at school went and saw *The Rocky Horror Show*. She says it's brilliant. I told Grandfather about it and his secretary got us tickets for a surprise from him. I've saved up my pocket money so I can go shopping in Camden Lock – Rachel told me where the best stalls are. And I'll get to see where Eema was born! And . . .' Her eyes closed, even though the baby was now howling lustily down the aisle.

Shifra's soft curly hair tickled Tanni's cheek. She was the youngest of her large family and Tanni still thought of her as 'the baby' although in the last year she had grown tall and was losing her childhood chubbiness. Tanni had been little older than Shifra when she had stepped off the train and seen Crowmarsh Priors for the first time, not looking forward to a holiday but married and a mother. Had she ever been as young and carefree as Shifra, with her rock music and the colourful friendship bracelets teenagers gave each other? Bruno was right. She had to make this trip. What would she have done without her friends all those years ago?

People around her were yawning now and sitting upright, stretching cramped limbs. The flight attendants were coming down the aisles serving tea and fruit. Shortly afterwards the captain announced their descent into Gatwick, and her grandchildren craned their necks for their first sight of England as the plane circled over the early-morning traffic on the M23.

The plane's shadow swooped over a big silver Mercedes with a plump little woman at the wheel. The Mercedes was travelling down the motorway towards Sussex at reckless speed, darting between lanes of lorries. Lady Carpenter, the third member of the group, pressed a purple-kid pump hard on the accelerator. To the dismay of her family she insisted on driving herself, even though at seventy-one her concentration at the wheel wasn't what it had been – but since her husband's death she had controlled the family fortune and did as she pleased . . .

The fourth member of the clique was already in Crowmarsh Priors. She had been there for so long that only a handful of people remembered where she had originally come from. Some who did were still living in New Orleans, white-haired widows who had been at the French convent with Evangeline Fontaine many years before. Now they passed the afternoons rocking on the porch of the old people's home that had once been the Fontaine mansion, fanning themselves and talking about the same things they had discussed for fifty years, including the night they had attended Evangeline's coming-out ball in this very house, before the Fontaines had fallen on hard times and had to sell the place. 'It was a real shame, when it had been in the family for so many years. Something to do with the war, I believe, why they lost all their money. That was after Evangeline ran off . . .'

Evangeline Fontaine's elopement had been a scandal at the time and still was.

'That's right – she ran off just before the war. I forget the name of the boy – nobody knew him from Adam or who his people were. I wonder what became of her,' said one. 'It was a shocking thing to happen in one of our old families.' The others rocked and agreed.

'They hushed it up, and nobody's seen Evangeline since.'

'I reckon she's dead,' one or the other of the old ladies would finally remark.

'I reckon she is,' another would say. 'Most folks we knew are.'

In Crowmarsh Priors, Evangeline Fontaine Fairfax was awakened by a fleet of catering lorries that ground to a halt on the village green. Soon cheerful young Australians were shouting directions and g'day at each other. Lorries banged open and marquee poles clanked as they were unloaded. Evangeline pulled back the bedclothes and scrabbled for her slippers with blue-veined feet. She pulled on a frayed satin robe, drew back the curtains and squinted in the bright morning sunshine towards the Channel.

She glanced at Elsie's letter, propped on the dresser between a jumble of photographs in tarnished silver frames, one of her late husband in his naval uniform, another of herself holding their son, Andrew, as a baby, then Andrew graduating from university, and with his wife and children at their home in Melbourne.

She picked up an ivory-backed hairbrush engraved with a P, and poured a tot of sherry from the bedroom decanter into her toothmug. She took both back to the bed and sat down. 'Well, hey, Laurent, hey, Richard, hey, Frances. Fifty years and they say that sorry old war business is over and done with. Folks who weren't there say that, leastways. Maybe today we finish it. Here's to y'all,' she said aloud. The southern accent had thickened now and the once soft voice was husky. She drank some sherry, then brushed her hair while she planned her outfit for the big day ahead. 'Yes, indeed, y'all watch.'

1. Crowmarsh Priors, Boxing Day 1937

At twenty-two, Alice Osbourne was the sort of girl people called a 'brick', sensible and responsible; they were inclined to add that she was pretty when she smiled. She was tall, like her father, the late vicar of Crowmarsh Priors, and her features, brown hair and air of bookish distraction were also his. She was nothing like her mother, whose early prettiness had faded after years of 'delicate' health and disappointed hopes that her husband would rise higher in the church than an East Sussex country parish.

A serious, stolid, only child, Alice had few friends among the village children, except Richard Fairfax, who was two years older, also an only child, whose father had been at Cambridge with the vicar. Alice spent long afternoons with Richard and his nanny, playing in the Fairfaxes' garden in good weather and inventing games in the cellars where Richard's father kept his wine when it rained. The Reverend Mr Osbourne coached Richard in Latin and Greek, and after he was sent away to school, Alice saw him only during the holidays. Each time they met he seemed handsomer, and by the time they had reached their teens, he had become a god in Alice's adoring eyes.

With Richard away and her mother usually indisposed, Alice's main companion and confidant was her father. She was happiest on Saturdays when they rambled across the Sussex Downs, sometimes as far as the coast, and the vicar, who had a lively imagination, indulged his love of local history. He enthralled Alice with stories of the Roman legions who had fortified the coast, pointing out coves where the Vikings might have landed, and where eighteenth-century smugglers had had a network of tunnels and caves to bring in contraband – silks, lace and brandy – from France. On the way home for tea one or other of them would begin 'The Smugglers' Song':

If you wake at Midnight, and hear a horse's feet,
Don't go drawing back the blind, or looking in
    the street,
Them that asks no questions isn't told a lie.
Watch the wall, my darling, while the gentlemen go by!

They took it in turns to recite verses, then joined in the chorus after each:

Five and twenty ponies
Trotting through the dark –
Brandy for the Parson.
'Baccy for the Clerk;
Laces for a lady, letter for a spy,
And watch the wall, my darling, while the Gentlemen
    go by!

Then they would race each other back to the vicarage for tea, and Alice would muffle her laughter in case Mummy was resting.

When Alice was sent to boarding-school she missed those outings, and during the holidays they happened less frequently. Gradually it fell to Alice to take over her mother's job of preparing the altar for Sunday service on Saturday afternoons, Mrs Osbourne's only concession to the duties of a vicar's wife. She still saw Richard when he came home, but she felt awkward and tongue-tied in his presence, although he never seemed to notice. He and his widowed mother Penelope often came to the vicarage for sherry after the service on Sunday morning, when he would chat to Alice and call her 'old thing'. She felt embarrassed later when her father teased her gently about her 'beau'.

When Alice came home from school for good, it was clear that the vicar was less well than his chronically ailing wife. Dutifully she followed his advice, trained as a teacher in Brighton, then came home to take over the infants' class at the Crowmarsh Priors school and nursed her father through his last illness. Meanwhile Richard was at naval college and Alice heard eventually that he had been appointed naval attaché to someone important in London. Penelope took a keen interest in her son's career and passed any news of him to her.

As Richard rose in the navy, Alice's world shrank. The first Christmas after her father died was a sad little observance. 'I don't know what your father would have said if we didn't keep *Christmas*,' said Mrs Osbourne, mournfully, pouring the last of the vicar's port for them to drink with the lopsided Christmas cake Alice had baked. Later Alice went to bed feeling too miserable for words.

Next morning, Boxing Day, dawned clear, crisp and bright, and Alice, cheered by the weather, got up with a sense of purpose. As soon as the holidays were over she and her mother had to vacate the vicarage for its new occupant. They were moving to a small Edwardian cottage on the edge of the village and there was a great deal to be done. Today Alice planned to pack up her father's study. After breakfast she left her mother drinking her tea by the range, briskly tied an apron round her waist and was on her knees tossing papers into boxes when she heard the front-door knocker. 'Bother!' she muttered, and struggled to her feet. She wiped her dusty hands on her apron and opened the door to find a tall, blond man on the step.

'Alice!' Richard Fairfax exclaimed, and kissed her cheek.

'Richard! Oh! I . . . um . . . I thought you were away.' The unexpected sight of him, not to mention the kiss, had made her head spin. How mortifying that he should find her wearing her oldest skirt and the moth-eaten cardigan she used for housework.

'Got leave in time for Christmas with Mama. Thought if you were free we might go for a walk as it's such a lovely day – we'll have lunch at that little pub, you know the one. And there's something I want to . . . Do say you'll come, old thing!'

Fancy him asking her to lunch! It was the first time a man had invited Alice to do anything. 'Oh! How lovely! I'll just . . .' Alice untied her apron, glancing with dismay at her clothes.

'Come as you are, old thing.' Before she knew it Richard had bundled her into her coat and scarf and they were going down the path.

Now, an hour later, Alice, who would normally have looked subdued, cold and red-nosed in her old tweed coat, was arm in arm with Richard Fairfax, glowing with happiness. The wind had turned her cheeks pink and made her eyes sparkle. Darling Richard! The only man, apart from her father, whom she could ever possibly love. As soon as they had reached the top of the downs he had spoken the words. She'd thought she had imagined it, had stopped and stared up at him blankly.

He had taken her hands in his and blurted out, 'Dear Alice, I said, "Will you marry me?" Rather a sudden proposal, I'm sure, but we've known each other since we were children, and all through naval college I've thought of you. I used to look forward so much to coming home because you would be there. I can't imagine you *not* being there, so I thought that, now I'm in a position to marry, you might say yes. Mama has been hinting how much she'd love to have you as a daughter-in-law. Dearest Alice, please say you'll marry me!'

'Oh, Richard! Oh, yes! Yes, of course! With all my heart!' she had exclaimed, breathless with disbelief at the turn of events. Even Mummy would be pleased.

'Now, darling,' Richard said, untucking her hand from the crook of his arm, and reaching into his pocket, 'of course you shall have a new engagement ring, if you prefer, but Mama wondered if you might consent to wear hers. It is rather special.' He held out a velvet jeweller's box.

Tentatively Alice took it, undid the clasp and opened it. Against a satin lining with the jeweller's name in faded gold script, a magnificent diamond flanked by sapphires in an old-fashioned setting blazed at her. She caught her breath. 'Oh!' She had never seen anything so beautiful.

Richard's father had been dead for years, but how could Penelope bear to part with it?

Richard was waiting anxiously.

'Oh, Richard! I should *love* it . . . Does your mother truly mean me to have it?' she added.

Richard chuckled. 'Mama was delighted when I said I intended to ask you to marry me, and I'm to tell you there is other jewellery you shall have too. Apparently I'm supposed to have it all reset for you. And she hopes we'll live in the house here, which I thought you would like as it means you'll be near your mother.'

Penelope Fairfax had been as effusive as her brusque nature allowed when Richard broached the subject. 'My dear boy! It's high time you were married. A naval officer needs a wife to keep the home fires burning, that sort of thing, but the *right sort* of wife is *terribly* important in the Navy. I'm happy to say that Alice, unlike most modern girls, has her feet on the ground, not like those foreign hussies in that rackety crowd the de Balforts have taken up with.'

'Mama, they're hardly hussies! Hugo made friends travelling after university and naturally he has them to stay. Poor old Leander probably enjoys having some young people about. But you're right, except for the shooting, the crowd does run to foreigners, and some of them are a bit fast for my taste, not my sort any more than they're Alice's. There's something so . . . so wonderfully English about Alice!'

'Thankfully she doesn't take after that mother of hers. No, Alice is a brick. Of course she will have the Fairfax jewellery, and I shall be happy to give up this house to you both. Alice's mother will be company for her when you're at sea, and I've so much committee work in London that it'll be far more convenient to stay in the Knightsbridge flat. I've been longing to move there for ages, actually.'

Penelope held up a hand imperiously as Richard tried to protest. 'At my time of life, after a busy day of trying to make cabinet ministers see sense, I prefer peace and quiet, a nice cocktail, little dinners with friends, perhaps the opera or the theatre. I've always found it rather quiet in the country. I need to be *doing*, Richard. And you'll be needing the nursery floor before long, darling. Before you know it, there'll be nannies and prams in the hall, so chaotic, but darling Alice will manage splendidly . . .'

'Yes, Mama definitely approves.' Richard slipped Penelope's ring on to Alice's finger. Alice held out her hand and they both admired it glittering in the sunshine. 'Bit large for you, darling, I think. I'll take it to Asprey's, at the end of my leave, so they can reset and adjust it to fit.' Reluctantly Alice watched him replace the ring in the box. He grinned and gave her a squeeze. 'Don't look so glum. I'll make sure they do it beautifully, I promise. The minute I come back we'll name the day.'

Back? 'Are you going away again?' asked Alice.

'There'll be rather a lot of back-and-forth, but as the wife of a Navy man you'll get used to it, darling. And I'll always come back to you. The thought that you'll be waiting for me makes me unspeakably happy.'

Alice gave a little shiver of pleasure at the word 'wife'. I'm going to be *married*! she thought incredulously. 'Where are you going?'

'I've been seconded to a mission to Washington. President Roosevelt, you know. The situation in Germany. Then I'll be travelling round the United States, meeting industrialists with businesses in Europe. We leave next month, probably come back from New Orleans. We needn't have a long engagement, need we?' he asked, drawing her into his arms.

Alice nearly swooned at his kiss. 'No,' she murmured giddily, into his shoulder, when he finally stopped kissing her and she could speak again.

They walked on briskly to keep warm, until they reached a summit where they could see the coast and the sea sparkling in the distance.

'I love it here,' said Alice. 'Father and I used to . . . If only he were alive to marry us. He would have been so happy.' Her voice had wobbled. 'We used to come up here,' she went on, 'and he'd tell me stories about what used to go on round the coast. He'd heard there had been a smugglers' tunnel that opened in a grave in the church-yard.'

'Is it true?'

'Hard to tell. Father had an old book about smugglers in his study, privately printed, I think. It even had a map, but it wasn't very clear. He once used it to try to find the tunnels. There were some scary stories about a smuggler called Black Dickon who had a gang. Mummy got quite cross when she overheard him reading to me about his gang. They were hanged, and their ghosts came back to lure Customs men to their death on the cliffs. I had night-mares about it for a while.'

Richard put an arm round her and they gazed out to

sea, at the sunlight dancing on the waves. 'I shan't let you have nightmares, but keep an eye open for that book. I like those old stories about the coast too. We'll tell them to our children, and leave out the frightening bits. Now, old thing, let's go and have lunch. I'm starving, aren't you?'

Holding Richard's hand, Alice tried to remember where she had last seen the book. She vaguely remembered putting it into a box with some of her father's papers. She would find it and give it to Richard as a wedding present. Some of the stories *were* grim – her father had said that Black Dickon was supposed to have been hanged on the spot where the pub stood now. She shuddered.

As they went in woodsmoke from the pub's fire tickled Alice's nose. She could smell chicken roasting on a spit, and Richard called for champagne. She hadn't known you could get it in a country pub. He must have brought it in specially. The publican beamed and led them to a table with a vase of Christmas roses in the saloon bar. 'You arranged this beforehand, didn't you? Oh, Richard, what a wonderful surprise!'

Richard smiled and squeezed her hand under the table. They raised their glasses to each other. I shall remember this day for ever, she thought. With such happiness before her, she knew that nothing bad could ever happen to her again. She and Richard would live happily ever after. She banished all gloomy thoughts of smugglers.

2. New Orleans, March 1938

In the shuttered dining room of the New Orleans mansion, Celeste Fontaine surveyed her luncheon table, beautifully laid for thirty. Her brow creased with irritation and she snatched a placecard bearing the name 'Maurice Fitzroy' from its silver holder, tore it in two and slipped a card that read 'Lieutenant Richard Fairfax' into its place beside 'Miss Evangeline Fontaine'. She was upset to have to rearrange her seating plan at the last minute, but Maurice had telephoned to say he was unavoidably delayed by plantation business and would join them for coffee. So rude of him. Or was there more to it? Maurice was too old-fashioned to be rude. She straightened a lopsided flower arrangement. It was such a strain to entertain during Mardi Gras.

Everything went wrong. The coloured servants spent every night in the Quarter, drinking and carousing. Next morning they had headaches and were good for nothing. But Celeste's husband, Charles, had insisted they invite an important English delegation, who had met with the President in Washington, to today's luncheon. The day had begun disastrously: the cook had claimed that her rheumatics made her too sick to get out of bed. Celeste had swallowed her pride and telephoned her mother-in-law in the country to borrow her cook, Inez. Now Inez was in the kitchen, grumbling, clattering pans and bossing the maids at the top of her voice. Suddenly Celeste smelt food burning, heard a slap, then a shriek and glass shattering. A maid sobbed loudly in the pantry.

She shut the glass dining-room doors behind her, praying that the commotion would calm down, and hoping there wouldn't be repercussions if the Englishman sat next to her niece. Lieutenant Fairfax was a pleasant young man, nearly at the end of his week-long stay in New Orleans; if Maurice was annoyed, Celeste would tell him that she couldn't have left the place next to Evangeline conspicuously empty.

Eighteen-year-old Evangeline, débutante of the year, was the guest of honour at today's luncheon. Her coming-out ball tonight – the last night of Mardi Gras – would close the Season. Given that all New Orleans expected it, when the ball ended at midnight her father would announce Evangeline's engagement to Maurice. In the circumstances, Maurice's absence at lunch was awkward – it didn't take much to start people gossiping in New Orleans and the last thing Celeste wanted was to provoke comment or speculation about Evangeline. Well-brought-up girls should never be the subject of gossip, and a few vague but worrying rumours about Evangeline had reached her ears. Celeste hoped fervently that they had not reached Maurice's. He would not have been amused.

More than twice Evangeline's age, Maurice was a long-time intimate of Evangeline's father. He was the last of his family, sole heir to its fortune and a vast estate; the Fitzroy plantation, Belle Triste, was one of the oldest and handsomest in the state. In terms of wealth, family – it was believed that the Fitzroys had royal antecedents – and social position, Maurice had been New Orleans's most eligible bachelor for many years. At the very least, he needed sons to keep alive the family name, but he was a proud man, formal and unbending, deeply conscious of his position as heir to the fortune of one of the oldest families in Louisiana. Gossip had it that he had thought none of the local girls good enough, and in his younger days had sought a bride in Europe. If so, his search had come to nothing. The only daughter of the prominent Fontaine family could not have a more suitable husband.

Maurice had unbent enough to let Celeste know that Evangeline had caught his eye when she was still a convent schoolgirl. Romantic, Celeste supposed. He clearly worshipped Evangeline, scarcely taking his eyes off her, hanging on her every word, lighting her cigarettes, holding her chair and claiming every possible dance at balls. But Evangeline was thoughtless and giddy, flirting and dancing with her younger beaux and running about the Treme with her friends as if she was not on the verge of marriage.

Celeste sighed. Marriage was a sacrament and, in her experience, often a crown of thorns. But it was the custom among the first families of New Orleans that a girl married young, unless she entered a convent, and from then on her happiness depended on clever management of her home and husband. Otherwise . . .

Half-way through luncheon, Celeste frowned down the long table at Evangeline. The girl was pushing Inez's special *étouffe* round her plate, eating nothing, pale and listless, half asleep. Modern young people stayed out too late at night. Although she was childless, Celeste had strong views on how girls should be brought up, and she disapproved of the way Evangeline had been raised.

Young girls should be trained from an early age to attend to their duty rather than selfish enjoyment. Unfortunately Evangeline was the youngest child and only girl in a family of five. She had been spoiled by her parents, and doted on by her four older brothers, who had let her hunt, fish, swim, climb trees and who knew what else? It wasn't ladylike, but her parents had laughed. Eventually her father realized she was growing up into a hoyden and told his wife to see that Evangeline was taken in hand. They had to think about her position in society and her marriage prospects.

The nuns at the school had done their best to reverse the damage, but since she had left the convent last summer and begun her Season, all of their good work had been undone. As a débutante Evangeline had plunged into frivolity and overindulgence. She thought of nothing but shopping, fittings, parties and nightclubs. At tonight's splendid ball she would wear a Paris gown and, Celeste happened to know, a Fitzroy family ring on her right index finger; it had been given with her parents' approval. But despite everything, Evangeline looked bored.

Celeste disapproved of débutante Seasons. She and Evangeline's mother had been brought up in the old-fashioned way. Between school and marriage, they had been kept at home, learning how to run a household and keep a husband happy. They had been taught to supervise servants, arrange flowers, plan menus, even cook. There had been no gadding about.

Celeste shuddered to think how Evangeline would

manage when she was married. Overnight she would become mistress of two grand houses, the Fitzroy home at Belle Triste and the mansion in New Orleans. Maurice would expect them to run like clockwork, of course, and there would be a baby every year. Well, Celeste had tried her best to fill the gaps in Evangeline's domestic education. But just look at the girl!

Down the table Evangeline smoked cigarette after cigarette between sips of wine, not making the slightest effort to talk to the Englishman or to anyone else. To the servants Celeste signalled discreetly that they should pour no more wine for Miss Evangeline, and should bring in the next course. Then, the good wife and hostess, she turned back with a look of rapt attention to what the men were saying. When she heard it was politics, business and what people were saying in Washington *again*, her expression of interest didn't falter but she groaned inwardly. The European branch of the Fontaine business was in trouble, she knew. Yet Evangeline's family were lavishing so much money on tonight's ball. She didn't want to think deeply about that. Let the men deal with business. It was all they were good for.

At the other end of the table her husband Charles's face was red from too many pre-lunch cocktails as he engaged in a heated discussion about the government, the situation in Germany and how it was affecting the Fontaines' business in Marseille. To her intense discomfort he was slurring his words . . .

Evangeline studied the dregs in her wine glass, careful not to look up and catch her aunt's eye. She could feel

Aunt Celeste watching her like a hawk. Did she suspect what might be wrong? The anonymous notes had begun to arrive two days ago, appearing in Evangeline's handbag, in a box of flowers, even on her breakfast tray this morning, in the folds of the napkin where her maid, Delphy, couldn't have seen it. Just a few crudely written, misspelled words.

I BEEN WATCHIN YOU NIGGER'S HORE.

Someone close to her had been spying. Who? It hardly mattered. In New Orleans the consequences would be swift and terrible. Today's note had said:

YOU AND THE NIGGER CANOT RUN ANYWHERS TONITE.

What could she do? Evangeline cast a sideways glance at the Englishman on her left. If she had had less on her mind she might have been flirting with him. He was good-looking, in a fair, English way, and tall, with an air of command. She had danced with him a few times in the past week, and soon he had wanted as many dances as she would give him, but she found him serious-minded, hopeless at the kind of silly banter and frivolous compliments New Orleans girls expected from men. He bored her. But Maurice had watched him with narrowed eyes.

Almost from the moment they had sat down to lunch, her uncle had demanded Richard's attention. Evangeline listened intermittently to their conversation, then concentrated on her own worries. She heard that Richard and his fellow delegates had failed to persuade the President to take an interest in developments in Germany and they were going home. Well, Evangeline didn't blame President Roosevelt: Germany was so far away, why should he? Richard was sailing for England early next morning. If only *she* could escape to England. They had been so careful . . . but someone knew.

The untouched *étouffe* was replaced with a salad that glistened with mayonnaise. Ugh! Feeling queasy again, Evangeline cut some lettuce into small pieces and wondered again what on earth she was going to do. For the hundredth time, she calculated how many days, how many weeks it had been since she'd last had the curse.

This morning Delphy had found her throwing up when she came to draw Evangeline's bath. 'Too much champagne last night,' Evangeline had said, burying her face in a wet towel. Delphy had raised her eyebrows sceptically. She was in the kitchen now: what was she saying to the other servants? Servants' gossip meant everyone knew everything in New Orleans.

Evangeline's eyelids drooped. At night either she lay awake, imagining she heard footsteps creeping up to her bedroom door, or slept, and endured a recurring nightmare. In it she was hunting after dark with her brothers on Grandmère's plantation upriver. When she was little the boys had shown her how to shine a flashlight to blind the rabbits: they would be transfixed, ears twitching. Unless they jumped fast and disappeared into the dark, the hunters fired and they dropped. Most weren't fast enough to get away. Killing rabbits had upset her at first, but the boys told her that that was hunting: the rabbits destroyed the vegetable garden and Inez used them in jambalaya, so she'd got used to it, and had shot plenty herself. But in her dream it was her and Laurent in the darkness, sensing hunters approaching from somewhere. Then the two of them were trapped in a blinding beam of light. Knowing what would happen next but rooted to the spot, powerless to run as the hunters took aim, she would wake as she heard the click of the trigger . . .

Evangeline's palms had grown cold and clammy. Her glass was empty – damn! Alcohol was the only thing that steadied her jangled nerves, calmed her uneasy stomach. She had been afraid to tell Laurent about the notes. And she was afraid to tell him about the other thing, which she hardly dared admit to herself. But she had to do something. And Laurent was smart, he knew many things she did not, things no girl suspected. He had known of a secret place where no one could find them, had shown her what to do that first time. He had taught her wonderful, dangerous games for the two of them to play, and even though she knew they were committing a mortal sin, Evangeline now lived for their next intoxicating time together.

Laurent would take care of everything, would know what they should do. Evangeline could think of no way out – unless they ran away. But where to? And how could they run? With so much happening today, she didn't even know how she'd manage to see Laurent. After lunch she would be expected at home, to dress under the eye of her mother and Delphy. Tonight was the big parade, when she and the other débutantes whose fathers were in the same 'krewe', one of the Mardi Gras organizations, were expected to play the traditional role of girls from prominent families and perch decoratively on the krewe's float. They would wave and smile and throw doubloons or beads to the crowd. Afterwards, at her ball, she would be surrounded by people at every minute. But she had to do something. Before her parents found out – before *anyone* found out. Especially before Maurice found out. Before it was *too late*.

A snippet of conversation startled her. 'What did Uncle Charles just say?' she whispered to Richard.

Richard smiled at her. 'That your family company is sending a new employee to the Marseille office next week.'

'Smart as a whip, that boy, best Jesuit education, no real future in New Orleans,' Uncle Charles said, a little too loudly. Everyone looked at their plate.

Richard Fairfax asked why such a smart boy should have no future in New Orleans.

'Ha! He's Creole, that's why, *gens de couleur*. Part-coloured, Lieutenant Fairfax. But smart, like his daddy.' Charles Fontaine smirked and Aunt Celeste gasped.

Evangeline felt as if someone had emptied a pitcher of ice-water over her. France! No! Laurent wasn't supposed to go until he was twenty-one and that was two years away. He couldn't leave her alone! Holy Virgin, she had to tell him at once.

'Y'all have the coloured problem in England?' Uncle Charles asked.

The servants' black faces were impassive as they removed plates.

Aunt Celeste's glass was trembling in her hand.

Evangeline felt faint. She would never see him again. And if Laurent didn't save her from Maurice . . . She realized, with terrible clarity, that for the first time in her life demanding what she wanted would not be enough. She and Laurent were doomed. Never mind that Uncle Charles had sent him to the Jesuits, that Grandmère doted on him and the family looked after him: his mother had been a quadroon so he was coloured, and no coloured boy could so much as look at a white girl, lest he end up swinging from a tree. He couldn't save her from Maurice or anyone else. He couldn't even save himself. She had to warn him to leave for France immediately. Maybe afterwards she could follow him. But wait . . . Richard was English. England was near France, wasn't it? Evangeline played with the ring Maurice had given her. She didn't like it but her mother had said it would be rude not to wear it. She thought distractedly of Sister Bernadette's geography lessons.

Suddenly the dining-room doors swung open and, with great fanfare, the servants brought in the traditional King Cake.

Was there no one in New Orleans to whom she could turn?

Evangeline had heard that the coloured girls went to an old woman named Mama La Bas, who did mojos and spells, *gris-gris* and black magic, but you had to be careful. Use the spell wrong, they said, and it would turn against you. It would be a terrible sin to go to a woman like that. The Church taught that voodoo was an instrument of the Devil. For courage she picked up the full glass in front of Richard and drained it as conversation resumed. Everyone began to talk at once, but not to Richard.

'Hasn't been in the South long enough,' said someone, audibly.

'Doesn't understand the situation. Coloureds were slaves two or three generations ago. They're like animals, you have to be firm with them,' said another.

To Richard's immense relief, Evangeline rescued him from the awkward moment. She laid her hand, sporting an old-fashioned rose-diamond ring, on his wrist, leaned close and said, in a conspiratorial murmur, 'I want to tell you a secret, but, first, have my brothers shown you a good time in New Orleans?'

Richard, entranced, felt her breast pressing against his arm, and smelt her perfume. Her long eyelashes fluttered on her cheeks. '*Quite* the most splendid time,' he enthused.

'I'll bet André and Philippe took you down to the Treme,' she went on, gazing up into his eyes. 'That's where the speakeasies and good-time houses are.' She smiled, lowering her eyelashes again. 'The nuns at school warned us it was a mortal sin even to imagine what goes on down there. But you must have noticed all the beautiful Creole girls. Well,' her head was nearly on his shoulder now, 'here's the secret. Uncle Charles kept a girl down there in a little house, but she died. Bet the boys took you to hear her son, Laurent Baptiste. Uncle Charles is Laurent's father. Laurent was smart in school, like Uncle Charles said, but what he really likes is music. He plays the piano and the saxophone and, oh, lots of instruments, better than anyone – ragtime, swing and jazz – but the only places he can play are in the Treme.'

Richard was mesmerized. She was so close he could feel her breath on his cheek. 'Anyhow, he's the family member Uncle Charles meant. And he wouldn't normally

28

have been rude enough to mention it but he forgets himself when he, um, talks business.'

She sat up straight as her aunt shot her a sharp look, but let her fingers slide down to brush his thigh, as if by accident.

'Good Lord, Miss Fontaine! I . . . er . . . Your uncle was talking earlier about – I had no idea the fellow was related to the family. He looks, well, like a white man.' Flustered, Richard remembered the good-looking lad with copper-coloured hair at the piano. He had saluted Evangeline's brothers, saying, 'Don't let on to Grandmère I was in here again. Beats the office, don't it?' The sleeves of his immaculate broadcloth shirt were rolled up and the jacket of a well-cut suit was folded neatly beneath an expensive Homburg on the chair beside him.

Evangeline shrugged. 'You won't see a white man playing the piano in the Treme. This is New Orleans. Everybody knows the relationship between us and Laurent – it's quite a common situation really, even in the older families, so nobody ever talks about it. It's just there. In fact, Laurent and my brothers practically grew up together although officially white and coloured people don't mix. When Laurent's mother died our grandmother took a liking to him, and raised him at her plantation upriver. Then Uncle Charles sent him to the Jesuit school for Creole boys. We used to spend the school vacations together at the plantation. Grandmère thinks the world of him, but being coloured, Laurent knows his place, which is why most of the family accept him. Mama and Aunt Celeste, of course, pretend he doesn't exist. And boys like him, if they don't have big mouths, usually end up doing some kind of job for the family. I thought you should know so you won't mention what Uncle Charles said when you're talking to Aunt Celeste. She and Uncle Charles never had children, so Laurent, and others like him, are always a sensitive subject to the ladies. Now, try some King Cake.' A servant was bending over Evangeline with a silver tray and she put a slice on Richard's plate.

'Watch out for the gold baby,' Celeste called, down the length of the table.

'I beg your pardon?' Richard, picking up his fork, was startled.

Before Celeste could tell him Evangeline hurried to explain: 'King Cake is a Mardi Gras tradition. There's always a little gold baby inside. It's for the Baby Jesus and brings good luck to whoever gets it. If you find it in your cake you have to give the next party, but since Mardi Gras is almost over,' Evangeline wrinkled her nose, 'and my ball is the last of the season, I guess you won't have time to give a party before you go back to England.'

She dropped her eyelashes again, thinking. For a *gris-gris* to work on someone you needed a hair or something else from them, something with which they had been in close physical contact.

'Tomorrow morning, Miss Fontaine. Dawn tide, worse luck.' Evangeline, with her teasing chatter, soft voice, pretty frocks, flowers and pearls, reminded him of a butterfly. He was enchanted. He remembered Alice and felt obscurely guilty, but seized the moment anyway: 'Your uncle tells me I'm to attend your ball tonight. I say, you will dance with me, won't you, before I go? I leave shortly after midnight for home.' If the predictions were true that war was coming he would never see Evangeline again, so he wasn't betraying Alice by asking an exceptionally pretty girl to dance. If only – He bit something hard, and spat it into his hand and put it on the side of his dessert plate, just as Celeste rose and announced they would take coffee on the veranda.

Evangeline groped for her bag and stood up. 'Oh, look, you got the gold baby!' she exclaimed. 'I hope it brings you luck.'

Richard pushed back his own chair. 'Miss Fontaine, it will only bring me luck if you save me the first dance,' he said boldly, remembering the tingle he had experienced when she touched his arm, her breath in his ear. He wanted her to touch him again.

'Of course I'll dance with you, Lieutenant,' Evangeline said, her hand brushing his, 'on condition you give me the gold baby. I've never found one in my own cake.' She raised her eyes to his and held out her hand. It had been in his mouth, and there must be some spit on it. Surely that would do for Mama La Bas.

'A fair exchange,' said Richard. He picked it up and dropped it into her outstretched palm.

'Here's Maurice,' said Evangeline, as a tall, middle-aged man with heavy dark brows and a stern expression made his way towards them. Maurice Fitzroy ignored the other guests and their greetings, and stared coldly at Richard, who was struck by the man's resemblance to a Spanish painting he had seen once, of the Grand Inquisitor. He hoped what they said about Maurice being as good as engaged to Evangeline wasn't true. The man struck him as a brute.

Evangeline snapped her purse shut and excused herself. In the hallway, she stopped the butler, who was carrying a tray of liqueurs to the veranda: when he went back to the kitchen, could he please tell Delphy she needed her for a minute?

At four o'clock that afternoon, in a shuttered room off Congo Square Mama squatted on the earthen floor, sucked her pipe between toothless gums and waited to hear what her visitor wanted. Her feet were bare, tucked under stained calico petticoats, and each bore a flat white scar where the big toe had been. The air was fetid with tobacco, herbs, chickens and decay. Candle ends flickered on a makeshift altar covered with small figures made of cloth, human hair, animal bones, beads, feathers and dried snake-skin. She had been born a slave and had once had another name, but so long ago everybody had forgotten it. Now she was just Mama La Bas. It meant 'the Devil's wife'.

Her rheumy eyes blinked. The high-yellow girl, Delphy, who worked at the Fontaines', had yet to get to the point. Mama guessed the problem concerned a man, and knew that men always meant trouble. 'What you got to pay me?' she asked finally. Delphy knelt in front of her, fumbling to untie a knotted handkerchief. Finally she removed something from its folds and placed a ring in Mama's pale palm.

The old woman's sight was blurred but the spirits had given her eyes inside her head. Her fingers told her the gold was soft, the ring old, the stones precious. She traced a cluster of diamonds, felt the familiar pattern and a shock went up her arm, as if a cottonmouth had sunk its fangs in it. 'This here ring come from a Fitzroy. Bad, bad thing. Uh-hunh. Stones make a pattern, family crest. I born on the Fitzroy place. Ise a chile, me an' my sister polish they damn silver every day. Had the same damn crest on it. Ole Miz Fitzroy whup us with the poker if we din' shine it bright enough.' Mama spat. 'She whup us anyhow. Hard. Hard as she could. Sometime she git that poker hot first. Oh, I know this crest well's I know the Devil hisself. My, my, my. Never 'spected to have this ring in my own hand. Whut you doin' with it? You stole it?'

'No, ma'am. Young lady I work for sent me to 'change it for *gris-gris*.'

'You messin' wid evil here, girl, tradin' this ring what bring bad luck. Ev'n if I didn't know it belong to the Fitzroys, I can still feel the evil inside it. I tried to run away once. Miz Fitzroy made them hold me down, cut off my toes herself, so's I couldn't run away no more, couldn't hardly walk. I only eight.

'I'se cryin' 'hind the barn, toes bleedin', hurt so bad, still do hurt so bad and they ain't even there. Ole uncle born in Africa come creepin' over when it get dark, give me a poultice for my toes, tell me if I go steal him a chicken he show me how to make a bad curse, case I lookin' to curse somebody. You got a bad whuppin' if you stole a chicken but I crep' out on my hands an' knees an' took that chicken and then Uncle showed me what to do. I cursed 'em good. Some time helped the *gris-gris* along a little. Just one Fitzroy lef' now, son's youngest

33

boy, Maurice. He bad too, real bad like the rest of the family, done kilt two niggers workin' for him already, beat 'em to death hisself. They say he get worked up while he beaten 'em, like he really enjoyin' hisself. His granmama like that too, when she beat us. Maurice,' she rocked silently for a minute, 'ain't gwine have no chillun. He gwine die crazy as his daddy. The family gone die out. I done fixed that already. Not to say I cain't do more. But first . . . hee hee hee.' Mama reached over on the altar for a strange little figure with stitched crosses for eyes, human hair and a crude knitted penis. It was stuck all over with pins. She twisted another pin through the torso.

'Yes, ma'am, but Miss Evangeline cain't wait,' Delphy stammered. 'Mr Fitzroy fixin' to marry her. But she scared of him, tell her mama and daddy she ain't gon' live way out there by herself with an old man at Belle Triste. Her mama and daddy shoutin', what a lil' girl fresh out of school know? The Fitzroys old family, the richest folks in town, she gon' marry him or they put her in the Irish convent till she git some sense. They say her daddy gambles, owe the Fitzroys money. They say Mr Fitzroy give her that ring, tell her it belong to his granma, so it the most valuable ring he can give her, show her and every-body else she his. Other folks say he like Miss Evangeline 'cause her mama give her daddy four boys before Miss Evangeline born. Miss Evangeline bound to give him some sons. She give me this ring to give you, get some help quick, before he kill her. 'Cause there's another problem.'

'You think I ain't heard? Ever'body done heard! Word all round in the Treme 'bout her and her uncle Charles's boy, that Laurent Baptiste, one his granma ole Miz

Fontaine think so cute. Everywhere he go, Miss Evangeline not far behind. Just cousins. He down here in the Treme playin' that music of his, Miss Evangeline an' her friends just happen to walk in, hear her cousin playin'. Ole Miz Fontaine make him a nice *garçonniere*, off by the river so he kin do what boys do in private. He there, here come Miss Evangeline to pay her granma a visit. Sneakin' down to that *garçonniere* at night. Miss Evangeline,' Mama spat again, 'a damn fool. Laurent too. Don' they know nothin'? They's talkin' in the Treme already 'bout kissin' cousins. Soon's white folks start talkin' too, lookin' bad for Laurent. Trouble comin' for ever'body. You seen niggers hangin' befo', girl? I has. Seen worse'n hangin's. You tellin' me Maurice Fitzroy got his eye fixed on her? That boy gon' disappear soon. They gon' find little pieces of him all over the bayou if the alligators ain't et it all. Her too maybe. But he mean, he find some bad way to pay her back for the shame she bring him.'

The girl lowered her voice and looked at the ground. 'She know. But it's real bad. She *enceinte*. And she scared to death.'

'Don't care how scared she is, I won't get ridda no more babies. They come back, hauntin' in the night. Cryin' in the corners. Cain't get no peace.'

'She ain't studyin' to get rid of it. Laurent Baptiste goin' to France. Just now they's a man from England visitin' the family, think Miss Evangeline lookin' mighty sweet, but he goin' home tomorrow. England a long way off from here. She got to act quick. She want a *gris-gris* make him take her with him, get married on the ship. She say the captain can marry 'em.'

'Unn-uhn! This a *mess*! Where Miss Evangeline at now?'

'Her aunt's. Big party. Her mama busy with the ball tonight.'

'This here Englishman, he there too?'

'Yes, ma'am.'

'His name?'

'Richard Fairfax.'

Mama shook her head, muttered something and sighed. She sat for a minute, working her gums on the pipe, then got up and shuffled to a corner behind the altar. She fumbled in the gloom among her scraps and chicken feathers. She took up bits of this and that, and mixed a concoction in a dirty jelly glass. She spat into it, poured it into a brown medicine bottle and corked it tight. 'Whut you got the man touched? No good unless you got that.' Delphy took the gold baby from the handkerchief and handed it to Mama. 'Been in his mouth,' Delphy explained. Mama crooned to it tunelessly for a minute, spat on her finger and touched its head. 'Richard Fairfax,' she said, and dropped it into the mixture.

She held up the vial. The gold baby gleamed in the murky liquid. 'This what she need. He got to drink it. It strong but you put it in a julep – enough good whiskey and he can't taste it. For twelve hours after she can make him do anything she want. This *gris-gris* powerful, but you tell her, got to be quick, only work for a few hours.' Mama pocketed the ring. She wouldn't sell it: she would make an offering to her mother's spirit.

Celeste's veranda was filled with lunch guests saying goodbye. Among the cars lined up at the kerb the

Fontaines' chauffeur paced impatiently by the car. 'Miss Evangeline, yo' mama say it high time for you to git home and git ready, Delphy or no Delphy. You leave Delphy behind if you have to and come on home. Yo' mama got enough to worry her with this ball already.'

'Just one more minute.' Evangeline saw Delphy slip in at the servants' door. 'Aunt Celeste, may I have a piece of your stationery?' Evangeline scribbled a hasty note to Laurent and spoke quickly to Delphy: she would dress without her help. She watched her maid slip out of the servants' entrance with the note and a worried expression.

There had been a rainstorm but the evening had cleared. As dusk fell, flambeaux were lit and fireworks burst, sparkling across the darkening sky. The colourful floats belonging to the krewes were lined up, and the city's prettiest and most prominent girls were gathering up their long skirts and trains, climbing aboard and tripping up rickety wooden steps in satin slippers to their flower-decked 'thrones'. A stray firework shot across the front of a float and they shrieked. Then they smoothed their hair and fluffed their dresses, and the bolder girls pulled illicit compacts from tiny evening bags – 'painting' was strictly forbidden by parents and the nuns at school – and furtively applied lipstick and powder. When they were all seated and arranged, members of their fathers' krewes handed up their bouquets, bonbons, beads and gilded doubloons for them to toss into the crowd.

Evangeline Fairfax's coming-out ball was the last before Lent, and the girls were in a fever of excitement, whispering that Evangeline's father had hired a train to bring from New York a famous dance orchestra, hundreds of live lobsters packed in ice, caviar, a chef from Delmonico's, and an entire hothouse of orchids. As they waited for the float to move, the girls fished tasselled dance cards from their bags and compared them to see who had begged what dance with whom in advance. Between giggles and cries of 'He said *what*?' 'I knew he was sweet on you!' and groans – 'But he *always* steps on my feet!' – the girls cast sideways glances at Evangeline, who wasn't saying anything and didn't look happy.

The other débutantes stopped chattering to whisper about what was wrong with Miss High and Mighty. She had a real grown-up dress from a real Paris couturier, cloth-of-gold, beaded with tiny purple and green crystals that sparkled in the torchlight. It was low-cut, too. The girls thought it was a wonder she'd been allowed out of her house in anything so daring. 'Lo and *be-hold*!' muttered one, cattily.

Evangeline didn't need powder and lipstick: her cheeks were just flushed enough to highlight her perfect, creamy skin and her dark eyes glittered in the torchlight. The other débutantes felt eclipsed and dull by comparison. Even though everybody knew the Fontaines' business had lost a fortune in France and they had heard the gossip that Evangeline's father had been gambling heavily, she still got to wear the prettiest dress, have the biggest ball and now rumour had it that she was as good as engaged to Maurice Fitzroy and would be the first to get married. Evangeline was always first.

'Maybe she'll go to Paris for her honeymoon,' sighed one girl.

'If she does she ought to stay there!' snapped another girl. 'You wouldn't catch me stuck way out at Belle Triste with nothing but Maurice Fitzroy and the alligators for company.'

Belle Triste, Maurice's two-hundred-year-old plantation, was named for a giant swamp oak heavily draped in hanging moss that guarded the gateway to the drive and looked like a woman in mourning veils. Long ago a Fitzroy had shot somebody or somebody had shot a Fitzroy. Everybody had forgotten exactly what had happened but there had been a duel and a widow who had never shown her face in public again. An air of gloom, or something, clung to the place.

'Sssh!'

'Well, I wouldn't,' she went on. 'They might be rich but everybody knows there's been something wrong with all the Fitzroys. They get sick or go funny in the head. Some people say it's a curse. Didn't Maurice's father have fits and nobody ever saw him because he had to be locked up in the cellar with a nurse? And what about his aunt who used to wander off into the bayou and one day never came back? They say a slave dropped her on her head when she was a baby – it was revenge because they'd cut her toes off.'

'Mama says it came of marryin' cousins too many times 'cause nobody else was good enough.'

'Hush! She'll hear!'

In a lower voice: 'And they say Maurice goes wild sometimes, crazy, even. He gets this sort of fixed look and turns real mean for a spell. He might have killed two of his hands in one of his rages!'

'Well, my daddy says if the coloured hands get out of line somebody has to teach them who's boss.'

Evangeline clutched her seat as a firework burst over her head, and the krewe's band exploded into 'When the Saints Go Marchin' In'. The float set off with a lurch that made the girls shriek. As the float swayed above the masked crowds, she fought down the nausea that came in waves. The dress her father had insisted her mother order was too tight in the boned and beaded bodice. The couturier's fitter had brought it from Paris and adjusted it more than once. Each time she had been sure she had it right, yet a day later Evangeline would complain that it was too tight and she couldn't breathe. And tonight everything smelled so! The odour of hot bodies, the cloying jasmine wet from an earlier rainstorm, gunpowder from the fireworks, beer, horse dung, sewers, the levee, all mingling with the greasy clouds given off by oil drums where oysters were frying for po' boy sandwiches. 'Po' boy for sale, git yo' po' boy sandwich while they hot! Befo' the parade start!'

Around the float, a sea of heads bobbed, masked and unmasked heads merging into a sinister hybrid. What a lot of Loup Garou masks this year, Evangeline thought dizzily. Every time she raised her eyes the lupine, part-human caricature of the werewolf who lived in the bayou leered up at her, torchlight reflecting off human eyes in the slits.

Someone knows . . .

A few feet away, the whispering switched to a fresh scandal. One débutante's unmarried cousin had been found to be 'in the family way'. During a pause in the music, Evangeline caught the words 'her family . . . a paper . . . The judge signed it, it's official, she's crazy and degenerate . . . kept under lock and key . . . baby taken away . . . disowned . . . Never come back.' Crying, pleading and begging to stay at home, the girl had been bundled into a car and taken away. Probably to the convent they had all heard of, in a distant country parish, run by a strict order of Irish nuns who kept leather straps hanging next to their rosaries.

'And that's not all. Guess what our cook says someone told her! Laurent Baptiste! They say it was a white girl! In his *garçonniere*!'

'No! That can't be true! Who was it? Did they see who it was?'

There was a smothered snicker. 'Now that's really crazy! He's coloured.' As they gossiped the girls tossed doubloons and sweets and strings of beads, waving gaily.

Someone knew.

It was easy to spot Richard Fairfax in the crowd. He seemed intoxicated – by the balmy night, the procession, the bands, the excited crowd . . . or the strong mint julep Delphy had given him before he had set off for the parade. 'Richard!' Evangeline called now. She smiled radiantly as he turned, waved and tossed him a handful of doubloons. Richard caught one, kissed it and swept her a bow.

'Don't forget our dance,' he called.

'Well,' said the girl on Evangeline's right, sourly, 'you have another admirer. That English officer's certainly good-looking. Doesn't Maurice get jealous?'

'Oh, you know,' said Evangeline, the smile now replaced by her usual bored look, 'I have to be nice. He's staying with Uncle Charles, who invited him to Mardi Gras and to my ball. He's leaving soon.' She prayed for the parade to end.

'Evangeline looks funny, like she's feelin' sick.'

At the Fontaines' house the band had been told to play non-stop until the supper interval. Among the dancers and flirting couples Maurice Fitzroy was a brooding presence – withdrawn and drinking heavily, people noticed. Several were asking where Evangeline had got to. She had been dancing too much with that English fellow and then disappeared. Now everybody was looking for her. Her mother was trying to extricate herself from a circle of old ladies all eager to talk to her about their own engagements and complain about 'girls today'.

'It's the excitement,' Solange Fontaine said soothingly to Maurice, glancing over his shoulder for her daughter, drawing him into the circle of ladies so that she could make her escape. 'A girl doesn't get engaged every day.' But she thought Evangeline was taking an inordinately long time to freshen up.

Maurice frowned. 'Excuse me,' he said. 'My overseer is signalling to me from the door. Forgive the intrusion, Madame. It's evidently an important matter for him to disturb me at your home.' He withdrew, leaving Solange with the old ladies.

In her bathroom, Evangeline straightened her clothes and pressed a cold cloth to her head. She had left Richard asleep in a guest room – the julep must have worked, but she was overwhelmed by the sense that her life had veered out of control. She was going to have a coloured baby and had just seduced another man. She would go to hell – and the Irish convent – unless the rest of her reckless plan worked. Now she had to slip down to the garden where her note had told Laurent to meet her. She would tell him that she knew he was going to France and that she had found a way to join him. Then she had to get back to the ball. The band was playing but they would stop for supper at any minute and her parents must be looking for her.

Evangeline opened the door and peered down the landing. No one was about. She gathered up her beaded skirt and crept down the back stairs to the basement. She groped for the handle of the garden door, opened it and whispered Laurent's name. There was no answer, so she moved out into the shadow of the house and peered into the darkness. At the end of the garden, down by the swamp oak with the hanging moss, figures were moving. A white evening shirt gleamed in the darkness. There was a pause in the music, and over the hum of conversation indoors she heard the crack of a whip and a scream of pain. Then footsteps hurried through the basement and the door slammed open.

André's breathless voice said, 'Come on, Philippe! God knows why but Maurice is having one of his crazy fits. He's brought his men to horsewhip somebody.' Then her brothers, in evening dress, were running from the house towards the shadows.

'Of all nights!' gasped Philippe.

Evangeline slipped back into the basement and felt about for the old shotgun the gardener kept for killing groundhogs and snakes. She reached into the ammunition box, willing her shaking hands to steady so that she could load the gun. Outside, someone was shouting and pleading, then came the crack of a whip and another shriek of pain.

She ran out, as fast as she could in the hampering dress, and down the lawn. The agitated men didn't notice as she pushed aside the hanging moss curtain. Something bloody lay on the ground – no, *someone*. He was bent into a strange position, obviously badly hurt. Laurent! Maurice was behaving like a madman, lashing the bullwhip across Philippe's shoulders now as he bent to help his cousin. Philippe's evening jacket was slashed to ribbons and as the whip descended again, he staggered and fell.

André was trying to wrest himself free from two rough-looking men who had pinned his arms behind him. 'Have you gone crazy?' he shouted. 'Why the hell are you taking it out on Laurent, when it was the Englishman Evangeline flirted with?'

'Here's her note,' snarled Maurice, his face twisted with rage. 'My overseer's been watching them for weeks, found it on Laurent's desk at the office this afternoon – real careless of him. At Belle Triste the Fitzroys gave slaves a good whipping if they stepped out of line and after that they got cut. I'll teach this one a lesson, cut him first, then hang him right here in your garden where your whoring sister can watch!' A blade flashed.

No one saw Evangeline beneath the hanging moss as she jammed the heavy shotgun hard into her shoulder, as André had taught her, swung the barrel at the white expanse of Maurice's shirtfront, and squeezed the trigger.

The old shotgun fired with a violent upward kick, recoiling into her face and bruising her shoulder. It felt as if her nose exploded and something warm and wet ran over her lips. Through a haze of pain she fired again, blindly. Maurice was on the ground now, making a horrible noise. Someone jerked the gun away from her.

Suddenly Solomon, the butler, appeared, and took charge. The two rough-looking men were gone. Evangeline saw André bending over Laurent again, and Philippe was wrapping a handkerchief over a bleeding hand. Back in the house people gathered at the lighted windows, peering into the garden.

'What's happening out there? Y'all all right?'

'We've got to keep people away from here. Get that damn band playing,' Philippe ordered thickly. 'Solomon, you'll have to help me with Mr Fitzroy. He's hurt bad.'

No one saw Evangeline stoop and snatch a crumpled piece of paper from the ground.

Solomon mopped his brow, then stepped out from under the tree and called, 'Y'all can go on back inside now, ladies and gentlemen. If I done told these chillun once I done told them a thousand times ain't no firecrackers allowed in Mist' Fontaine's garden. Like to blow somebody up lightin' them all at the same time. Crazy chillun! Y'all folks rest easy now, just chillun gettin' overexcited, the way they do at Mardi Gras. We pickin' up the rest of the firecrackers befo' somebody get hurt.'

The band struck up and most people moved away from the windows.

A few guests still hovered on the terrace, peering curiously into the garden. 'Maurice is a regular hero,'

André called, 'protecting those piccaninnies from the blast of the firecrackers!'

'Piccaninnies and firecrackers! I declare, niggers got no more sense'n monkeys . . .'

'André, is that Evangeline out there? What's that girl up to now? Tell her her mama's looking for her.'

'We'll do that.'

Philippe was giving terse orders, panting hard. 'Bandage Laurent up the best you can and get him down to our dock. We've got a ship sailing for Marseille tonight. Get him on it. He's in bad shape, unconscious but, thank God, we got here before Maurice used the knife. What was that about Evangeline and a note?'

'I don't know, I always thought his Fitzroy craziness was waitin' to bust out and now it has,' André said. 'He's bleeding like fury.' He looked up and took in the spectacle his sister made – dress torn, eyes wild, nose gushing blood. 'What in hell are you doing out here, Evangeline?' He turned to Solomon. 'Get her upstairs before anyone sees her and starts another scandal. Mama's going to have a fit.'

Somebody dragged Evangeline up the back stairs. Then Delphy's voice said, 'Miss Evangeline? I got a poultice for yo' face. Get it on befo' yo' mama see you. She on her way. André talkin' to her, 'splainin' this and 'splainin' that to her, drawin' it out so's we got time to git you outta this dress and cleaned up 'fore she git here.'

Delphy worked fast, unclasping jewellery, snatching off stockings and muddy satin slippers, wrapping the blood-stained clothing in a sheet and hurrying off to dispose of it. Evangeline locked the door behind her. She flung open her closet, pushing aside frocks, ballgowns, tea-dresses, and dancing slippers until she found her riding boots, a pair of old trousers and the dark jersey with holes in the elbows that she wore when she went fishing at her grand-mother's. Delphy was back, hammering on the locked door. 'Let me in!'

'Is he all right?'

'Is who all right?'

'Laurent.'

'They carried him off real smart. He goin' to France tonight. He alive, just barely. Broken ribs, broken nose, bleedin' hard, but sound like he gon' live. Doctor with Mr Maurice now. He rantin' and ravin', cain't move his arms or legs. Mist' André drug him in the study, empty the decanters all over the floor till everything smell like whiskey, like they drinkin' heavy before whatever was doin' with the fireworks and all. Yo' papa done collapse in the dining room, yo' mama runnin' back and forth between him and the boys. Oh, Lord, Miss Evangeline! Yo' plan, it ain't gon' work! Got the Devil in it.'

'Hush! It has to work. Tell the boys they have to keep Mama busy a little longer, let me get away.'

'Miss Evangeline, Englishman got blue eyes, light hair. That baby born, he bound see where it come from. And they so many people downstairs, runnin' around crazy as chickens, and yo' fam'ly and all on their way to see you. You cain't git out the house! Ain't gon' work!'

'Hush, I said! I have to think a minute. Go get me some more ice. Just keep everybody away!'

Evangeline tucked her trousers into her boots, snatched up a dark silk scarf to tie over her hair, turned off the

47

bedroom lights and opened the window. As children, André and she had scrambled in and out of her room from the veranda roof but tonight the ground looked far away and she felt dizzy. Her nose was badly swollen, it was hard to breathe and she was sure her collarbone was broken. How would she manage? She gritted her teeth.

Downstairs the band had stopped playing and Uncle Charles was making an announcement, asking everyone to leave at once. There was a buzz of shocked voices and people began to depart, their cars disappearing down the drive, until the only person left was the tall, fair-haired man waiting in the shadows by the gates. Evangeline saw a pinprick of light as he lit a cigarette and smoked it.

Richard reminded himself that she had said she had to wait till the house was closed up for the night. He watched Solomon close the doors, but the sound of the bolt driven home filled him with despair. What if she couldn't get away? If she didn't come he'd die. He was on fire with longing for her. She'd promised to marry him, and he'd said they needn't wait for England, the captain could marry them once they were out to sea. Where was she? He thought anxiously of the tide. 'We don't want them to have time to follow us,' she had said. 'Meet me at the gate.'

Evangeline quelled another wave of dizziness, aware that she had little time left. Delphy wouldn't be able to keep her mother away from her for much longer. There it was, another pinprick of light, another cigarette. It was now or never. Summoning the last of her strength, Evangeline climbed out of the bedroom window on to the sloping roof. Mustn't look down. Remember, she told herself, you've done this many times. It's easy. Slowly she dragged herself to the end where a fig tree grew against the house. Thankfully it was bigger than it had been when she was a child. Nearly fainting from the pain in her right shoulder, she used her left arm to let herself down the tree. She dropped to the ground in the shadows, then skirted the drive, a shabby figure in worn clothes with a swollen face. Just before she reached the gates she glanced back to her home, with its ornate iron balconies and sweeping garden, only a few lights showing through the shutters, which were closed now. Then Richard grabbed her hand and they hurried to the river and his waiting ship.

Three hours later the captain performed a hasty marriage service on the bridge as the sun rose, wondering how on earth the girl had come by her blackening eye and swollen nose. He had never seen a shabbier girl or a happier groom. Then the ship rolled. The bride turned green and rushed to be sick over the rail.

3. Crowmarsh Priors, October 1938

As she unlatched the churchyard gate on Saturday afternoon, Alice Osbourne saw the handlebars of Nell Hawthorne's bicycle poking up from the weeds where she had propped it against the war memorial, with its long list of the village's Glorious Dead, killed in the Great War, and its motto declaring how happy were they who had died defending their country. She was shocked by how high the weeds had grown, and how unkempt the churchyard looked. Jimmy, the butcher's boy, was supposed to keep it tidy, but since the death of Alice's father, he hadn't bothered. Ivy had crept over the gravestones, while stinging nettles and brambles had taken hold at the back.

Alice felt fragile and insubstantial, as if she was recuperating from a long illness. Six months ago Richard had returned from America, and a stunned, appalled Penelope had rung her from London to break the news. 'Darling, so terrible, I hardly know how to tell you.'

'Oh, please, Lord, not Richard. Don't let anything have happened to him! His ship?'

Penelope's voice sank to a whisper. 'No, Alice. He's . . . he's come back from the United States. He's, well, it's just . . . I'm so very sorry.'

'You frightened me out of my wits. Thank God he's all right!'

'He's married.'

'But . . . that's impossible.'

'To an American.' Penelope had sounded as if she were being strangled. 'Alice, he's bringing her to Crowmarsh Priors to live. Apparently the girl's expecting. Alice, I'm so sorry!'

'But, Penelope, Richard and I are engaged.'

'Engaged,' she whispered, as she put the receiver down on Penelope's protests that the news was true. There must be some mistake. Alice had thought it was a cruel, wicked joke.

She did not entirely believe it until one afternoon, a week later, she had seen Richard's roadster pull up in front of Penelope's house. He had jumped out to open the passenger door. Alice's heart was in her mouth as she saw him take the hand of a slender, dark-haired girl, help her out and up the front steps as if she were made of spun glass and might break. Then he swept her into his arms and carried her over the threshold.

Alice soon learned that they had met in New Orleans, eloped and been married at sea. Jimmy had told Mrs Osbourne, who repeated it to Alice over tea in a long, querulous lament. 'Mrs Richard' had indeed come to live in Crowmarsh Priors for the time being. 'It's all so shocking! How will Penelope Fairfax ever hold up her head again? I don't know what your father would have said,' she concluded, as she always did. It took all Alice's self-control not to bite into her teacup, swallow the pieces and choke to death on her own blood.

The next day Richard had called on Mrs Osbourne and Alice at their cottage. Alice answered the door and the colour drained from her face. Unable to listen to whatever he had to say she had turned on her heel, leaving him to her mother, and fled out of the kitchen door. She walked aimlessly until it was dark. In the morning Richard had left the village, but his wife had stayed behind. Alice had come face to face with her in the butcher's. She had dark hair and pale skin, and would have been beautiful but for a degree of puffiness around her nose and the trace of a bruise under one eye. Like rotten fruit, thought Alice, bitterly.

Ever since, Alice had got through the days somehow, going automatically about her daily routine at school, but when she came home her mother couldn't resist a tirade about Richard's behaviour. Alice would run to her bedroom in tears. Now she was struggling to hang on to her dignity, painfully aware that the village knew she had been jilted for a sly baggage who dressed like a stable-boy and spoke with an odd accent.

The future stretched bleakly before her. She would begin, Alice thought, by dealing with the mess in the churchyard. She let herself into the vestry, breathing in the comforting, familiar smell of beeswax, old vestments, communion wine, polish and mice. It was a glorious breezy autumn afternoon and the downs beckoned, but Alice enjoyed having the vestry to herself after Nell had finished the cleaning. She undid her tightly knotted headscarf, which made her head look oddly small, and ran her hands through her hair. It stayed flat and lank, but Alice no longer cared what she looked like.

She put down a freshly ironed altar cloth, and took her flowered pinny, with its limp ruffles, from its hook. She tied it on over the drab brown tweed skirt and the twin-set her mother had discarded, spread out some newspaper and took down the brass and silver polish from the shelf. Nell had set out the altar candlesticks and the collection plate, while the silver communion chalice and wafer plate were in their baize bag, beside a box of fresh candles.

She shut her eyes, imagining her father putting the final touches to the next day's sermon, trying it out in the pulpit to be sure that it lasted exactly twenty minutes, no more. Since his death Alice had continued to prepare the altar for Sunday because no one else in the village had offered to do it. In any case, she had nothing better to do on Saturday afternoons. There was a new vicar now, Oliver Hammet, but he was unmarried. Alice sighed. Mr Hammet meant well, but he was young and this was his first parish. It would have been better if an older man had been appointed. Village gossip had it that Lady Marchmont, who regarded Crowmarsh Priors as her personal fiefdom, had had 'a quiet word' with the bishop about Mr Hammet, who was her distant cousin. When she had been assured that he was 'doctrinally sound, very sound', she had demanded that he be given the parish. As usual, she had had her way.

Alice unfolded the rags she had boiled at home and briskly rubbed polish on to the metal. The problem with Jimmy and the churchyard was the tip of the iceberg. The new vicar was a Cambridge man, as her father had been, but he was not practical. He reminded Alice of a distracted owl, a tall, kindly one with glasses. He was wrestling inefficiently with his timetable – his pastoral duties, the parish council, the churchwardens and the

Mothers' Union. He delivered his sermons in a nervous rush.

Alice had done her best to help without interfering. She had offered Mr Hammet tactful but timely hints about the Mothers' Union, the Dorcas Society and the Sunday-school classes and had mentioned her father's twenty-minute sermon limit. He had thanked her profusely, seeming genuinely grateful for her help, but Alice's efforts hadn't made much impact on his chaotic habits. At the vicarage he lived in a muddle of misplaced objects – sermons scribbled on the back of envelopes, his list of parish-council meetings forever missing. She and Nell had found a lost box of hymn books propping up the leaky cistern of the downstairs cloakroom; they were soaked.

After that, Nell had knocked on his study door and told him firmly that he would be wanting someone to keep the vicarage in order and she would see to it. In his mild way, Oliver Hammet had said, 'Of course, quite, yes, please, most grateful really, Mrs Hawthorne, quite happy, whatever you charge,' and waved a despairing hand at his study.

Nell told Alice that she had never seen the like: it looked as if a tidal wave of books and papers, church pamphlets and schedules had struck. It overflowed the study and the parlour and was gradually creeping across the dining room into the kitchen. She was always unearthing biscuit tins, half-drunk cups of tea, clerical collars, apple cores and odd socks. Mice had made a comfortable home in the pantry. 'The state of it!' she exclaimed now, clattering into the vestry with her bucket and rolling her eyes. 'I gave it a good bottoming last week, everything dusted, polished and tidy as you please, and in no time it's a heathen mess again. It wouldn't half give your mother the vapours. It's a blessing she can't see her old home. He needs a wife and the sooner he finds one the better.' She rinsed her bucket, shaking her head.

This was becoming a sore point with Alice. The villagers kept dropping broad hints about Oliver Hammet's bachelor state, and hinting that perhaps she would soon be back at the vicarage, eh? It made her feel quite desperate. She could hardly follow Nell's example and tell him that the village understood he needed a wife to keep him in order. Fortunately Mr Hammet was absent-minded at the best of times, and if he noticed his parishioners' matchmaking hints he gave no sign of it.

Nell stowed her bucket, mop and cleaning basket in a cupboard, took off her apron and hung it up. 'As for that garden, it wants weeding. You used to keep it so lovely.' She left an opening for Alice to say that perhaps she could spare an hour or two. 'Right under his study window, where he has to see it every time he looks up.' Alice kept determinedly silent.

Mind you, thought Nell, it was no good getting Alice in the vicar's line of vision these days. She wondered if she dared suggest that the girl's hair could do with a good wash. Or something. It was so flat today. But Alice looked so dismal that Nell decided friendly advice would only depress her more. 'Here,' she said instead, handing over a basket. 'I've taken some of the windfalls. Your father always said if they were left to rot they'd attract wasps and anyone who wanted them was welcome to them, especially seeing as how your poor mother was never up to using them, not so much as making a bit of jelly. I don't think Mr Hammet had noticed the apple tree before I mentioned it but he said, "Oh, of course, very good of you, Mrs Hawthorne, please help yourself." So I did.'

'Thank you,' said Alice, wishing Nell would go home.

Studiedly casual, Nell continued, 'Loads this year, never seen so many, and this morning Albert says to me, he says, "Why not take some to the Osbournes? Miss Alice has a fine way with pastry, always makes such tarts for the Harvest Home, her bein' such a practical young lady. Maybe she could make an extra tart for the young vicar, seein' as how he's got no one else to do it for him."'

'Thank you, Nell, you're very kind but . . .'

'Mind, it's the way to their hearts, my girl. My Albert's a devil for pastry. All men are.'

Alice gritted her teeth. She wished Nell, Albert and everyone else in the village would mind their own business. She had no more intention of taking apple tarts to the vicarage than she had of sprouting wings and flying over the downs.

'Cheerio, then,' Nell said, and left Alice to her polishing.

Alice wondered how she could convince Nell that she wasn't in the vestry to catch Oliver Hammet's eye. It was just so nice – after the bustle of the infants' school all week, then looking after Mummy and listening to her complaints, trying to keep her cheerful at home – to be on her own with the soothing tasks that reminded her of happier times.

The day was so warm that she flung open the window. The late-October sun slanted in from the west, across the fields and the downs beyond. A wasp buzzed somewhere. No children shoved and fought, no querulous voice demanded a handkerchief, comfits, lost glasses, lavender water, a cushion. There was no small, ugly house piled with boxes of Father's papers and maps waiting to be put away. Alice shut her eyes and imagined that she and her father were about to set out for their Saturday walk.

In her mind's eye they had just reached the first stile when the heavy oak door to the church creaked open, then slammed, jolting Alice out of her reverie. Perhaps whoever it was wanted the vicar and would go away. Then her heart sank. She had heard the thud of a cane, the unmistakably firm footsteps of authority.

A moment later Lady Marchmont burst into the vestry, holding a wilting green bundle. 'Alice, my dear! Knew I'd find you here. I've brought the last of the Michaelmas daisies for the altar. You might as well put down that candlestick and find some vases at once. I told Mrs Gifford to wrap the stems in damp newspaper, but she hasn't the foggiest notion about flowers.'

'How kind. They'll look lovely,' said Alice, putting down the brass and dutifully producing two tall vases from a cupboard. She held them under the tap, then stuffed in the straggly stems.

'Take them round to your mother after Evensong tomorrow. Cheer her up, I expect. No sense leaving them for the vicar. Wouldn't know one end of a flower from another.' Lady Marchmont lowered herself heavily into a chair. Oh dear. 'And how *is* your poor mother today?'

Alice smiled thinly. 'As well as can be expected, thank you.'

'Humph! You're looking tired, my dear. All that teaching – children can be so fatiguing. And for what? They should either be taught at home by a governess, as I was, or if they're of the lower orders be put to an apprenticeship and learn something useful. What they're expected to do with all this arithmetic and geography and whatnot, when it's becoming impossible to engage a decent housemaid, I do not pretend to know. Now, Alice, I've something serious to say to you.'

Lady Marchmont leaned forward, both hands on her cane. Alice wondered what would happen if she leaped out of the window and ran – far from her mother, Lady Marchmont, the Hawthornes, the infants' school, the village matchmakers, apple tarts, everyone and everything. Instead, trapped, she cleared her throat and waited for the onslaught. Oh dear, oh dear. Lady Marchmont, please don't say anything at all. Please go away and let me have a little peace and quiet in the one place where I'm perfectly happy just doing what I'm doing. If I concentrate on missing Father, I won't have to remember how it felt to be happy, when Richard kissed me, or how we stood with his arm round my shoulders looking out to sea, and him asking how soon we could be married when he returned.

She longed to scream at the top of her voice, 'I don't want to remember that Richard married someone else!' Instead she snatched up the gleaming wafer plate, which she had just finished, and pushed a polish-soaked cloth hard against it. Round and round. Harder and harder.

Lady Marchmont didn't notice. 'I'll come straight to the point. I very much admire the way you've behaved over this wretched business. You've behaved admirably.

Admirably! Who could have believed it of Richard? To marry that hussy! No better than she should be, I daresay, being American. And Roman Catholic, Penelope tells me, which is even worse. But what's done is done. Water under the bridge. Alice, you will marry someone else and be perfectly happy. You'll make an excellent wife, and you simply must buck up and stop moping.

'Your mother, of course, has her health to worry about, and perhaps she's not entirely able to deal with things, but one always feels an interest in a deserving young gel. So, I have a piece of news that will interest you. Young Hugo de Balfort is back at the Hall from his travels at last – for good, so Mrs Gifford tells me, and she had it from the butcher's boy who . . . Well, never mind. Poor Leander's health is failing, you know, has been for some time. Naturally he wants his son at home to see to things before they fall into rack and ruin. Anyway, the boy will inherit a handsome property, a shambles now but nothing that can't be put right, provided he does his duty and marries money. Entailed, of course, and as he's the last of the de Balforts, he'll need to marry soon and provide an heir.'

'Quite,' murmured Alice, relieved that there was no question of her penniless self featuring in any match-making scheme Lady Marchmont had for Hugo de Balfort, who, in any case, she hardly knew.

'The boy should have buckled down immediately after Eton to getting the place back on its feet, but Leander had very old-fashioned notions about the Grand Tour. He said that in his day no gentleman could call himself educated unless he'd done it. De Balfort tradition, he said.

Humph! If you ask me it was the foreign ideas he picked up on his own Grand Tour that convinced Leander he could improve Gracecourt with his cock-eyed schemes – Chinese pagodas and such nonsense. Poor Venetia saw her fortune evaporate with his extravagance. Continentals think one must always be improving things to make them pretty. They have no sense of solid English . . .'

Alice murmured something that sounded like agreement and stopped listening. Lady Marchmont was off on one of her tirades about foreigners. She decided that when she had finished in the vestry she would walk to the de Balforts' home farm for a small pot of cream to go with the scones she had planned for her mother's tea-time treat.

Lady Marchmont had hardly paused for breath. 'I did warn him . . . but to get back to the point, some young friends of Hugo's are staying, down from London for the shooting, though one can't imagine there's much shooting left – the gamekeeper must be nearly eighty. A few pheasant hanging on, I dare say. There's to be a luncheon party next Saturday, after the morning shoot. Naturally one is invited. Since Leander is such an old friend I said I should like to bring a young companion – so much easier at my time of life – and he, of course, remembered your father and they'll be delighted to see you . . .'

Alice was horrified. She could think of nothing more humiliating in her present situation as a jilted fiancée than being dangled in front of Hugo de Balfort's friends like bait on a fish-hook. 'You are *too* kind, Lady Marchmont, but I really don't think –'

'Nonsense! They're several girls short.'

'But Mummy will –'

'Mrs Gifford will stay with your mother and see she doesn't need anything. So, that's settled.'

'But I hardly know Hugo de Balfort and, anyway, they're rather a smart set at the Hall, all cocktails and tennis and fast motors, Lord This and Count That and some Italian artist, not to mention a German singer. I should be absolutely terrified!'

Lady Marchmont waved a hand dismissively. 'One need never mind foreigners, my dear. The clergy are considered quite the equal of the landed gentry, and your dear father was on friendly terms with Leander. He could hardly avoid knowing the de Balforts because the church is on their land and they were his parishioners, so he wouldn't disapprove of his daughter having lunch at the Hall. A gel will never get married if she doesn't meet any suitable men.'

'Still, I would *much* rather not.'

'Stuff and nonsense,' said Lady Marchmont, rising imperiously to her feet. 'Your father would insist on your going, if he were here. And so do I. Gels need to be out and about, seeing other young people, meeting young men, not moping about in the gloom or running themselves off their feet at their mother's beck and call. I intend to call for you in the motor at a quarter to one next Saturday.'

'But I've nothing to wear,' Alice wailed, nearly in tears of frustration and anger.

'And,' Lady Marchmont continued, ignoring Alice to turn a critical eye on her dull skirt and jumper under the pinny, 'for goodness' sake, put on something blue. It suits your eyes. And perhaps you ought to rinse your hair with vinegar. It does wonders for your light brown shade, which one hardly notices otherwise. Just wash it, even. It seems to have gone rather . . . flat. One more word of advice, Alice. Remember to stand up straight, my dear. You tall girls forget the importance of posture. *Posture*, Alice! *Posture!*' She patted Alice firmly on the back for emphasis. 'Good day to you, my dear. I'll see myself out.'

The vestry door slammed. The Michaelmas daisies drooped dispiritedly over the necks of the vases. In the silence Alice picked up the brass candlestick she had been working on earlier. The polish had dried to a film. 'Bother and damnation!' She stamped her foot. 'Hell! Oh, *bloody* bother! Bloody hell!' She rubbed the candlestick furiously. Her elbow hit the basket of windfalls, knocking it off the shelf. A cascade of overripe apples hit the floor, to roll and bounce squashily at her feet.

It was the last straw.

Alice bent down, picked one up and hurled it through the open window as hard as she could. 'Damn Lady Marchmont!' she cried. She picked up another and flung it after the first. 'Bother bloody Hugo de Balfort!' The rest followed. 'Bother his friends! *Bother* Nell Hawthorne and her apple tarts! Pastry be damned! Bloody, bloody, bloody bother!'

As the last apple flew outside Alice burst into tears. 'Damn New Orleans, damn Richard, damn his new wife! Bloody damn everything to hell!'

4. Austria, November 1938

With her long legs tucked under her skirt and a little girl snuggled at either side, sixteen-year-old Antoinette Joseph settled back in the cushions of her bedroom window-seat, opened a beautifully illustrated *Fairytales of the Brothers Grimm* and began to read aloud to her younger sisters. The book had belonged to their mother when she was a child. She put one arm round four-year-old Klara, the other round Klara's twin, Lili. Tanni, as the family called Antoinette, had read 'The Sleeping Beauty' to the twins so many times she could have recited it by heart. She let Klara turn the pages for the pictures.

The autumn sun streaming through the window was warm on their backs, and as the princess 'fell into a deep, deep sleep', Lili dozed off, sucking her thumb. Tanni put her finger to her lips, winked conspiratorially at Klara, then shifted Lili until the child's head lay comfortably in her lap. Klara tightened her arm round Tanni's waist and her eyelids drooped too. They often dozed during the day because none of the three slept properly at night.

Tanni often lay awake with her goosedown quilt pulled up to her chin, listening to her father pacing in his disordered library on the floor below. If she heard her mother sobbing from her parents' bedroom down the hall, she put a pillow over her ears. She always took it off again because in the room next to hers Klara had nightmares and Lili had begun to wet her bed. When they cried out Tanni would get up, wake Klara or change Lili's sheets before they could disturb their mother. Then she took them back to her own bed, where she reassured them they were safe at home, safe with Tanni, and hummed lullabies until they slept again. Then she would lie awake, thinking.

Her father was anxious and preoccupied, these days. He never played with the twins as he once had with Tanni. They never had any fun. Tanni thought wistfully of visits to the cinema or the zoo, and strolls with her parents along the river promenade where an orchestra played in good weather, followed by a visit to the *konditorei*, a magical place of gold mirrors, marble-topped tables, glistening cakes and cream-topped ices in tall glasses. The twins had never been inside. The *konditorei* had been the first establishment in the town to post a 'Jews not welcome' sign in the window. Now those signs were on all the shops and restaurants, the cinema and the zoo. *Judenrein*.

Lili and Klara did not understand what being Jewish had to do with ices, walking in the park or looking at animals. 'But *why* can't we go?' they would wail. Tanni didn't understand either but the town's hostility was almost palpable. Not only did it keep them away from all the nice things in town, it now oozed like an evil smell under the solid front door of the Josephs' house, once a happy home, beneath the windows, and over the garden wall.

Her father's wealthy patients no longer came to his surgery, and the few people who still sought treatment did so furtively because they could not pay. Dr Joseph's consulting room was in upheaval, the heavy curtains down, the shelves empty, his precious collection of instruments and medical texts tossed anyhow. Throughout the house packing cases stood open, partly filled, waiting for china, books and the paintings, which had been taken down and leaned against the walls. The Persian carpets were rolled up and tied with stout twine. Dr Joseph's chess set was scattered. The heavy silver on the dining-room sideboard had grown dark with tarnish and dustballs gathered in the corners. The two maids had left, taking Frau Joseph's pearls, her scent and a gold bracelet. Dr Joseph had refused to call the police, even though the jewellery had been part of his own mother's trousseau.

Tanni's mother no longer sang or played the piano. Neither was she 'at home' to her friends on Thursdays. She no longer had her hair washed and dressed each week at the salon. Now she was short-tempered and anxious, her hair dull and straggly; her pretty Viennese frocks hung unworn on their padded hangers. Lace-trimmed boudoir robes had been crammed into drawers, out of the way, and the once-tidy rows of shoes, handmade to Frau Joseph's own last, were jumbled. Their owner dressed hastily each morning, in old skirts and frayed blouses, and sometimes, Tanni was astonished to notice, laddered stockings. 'It is best not to call attention to oneself by dress,' her mother whispered apologetically, putting on her oldest hat and taking up the shopping basket. A morning trip to the market was the beginning of Frau Joseph's new daily regime. She and her housekeeper, Frau Anna, who had nursed Frau Joseph as a baby, then Tanni and her sisters, now shared the housekeeping, cooking and laundry. Frau Anna was elderly and stiff in her joints so Frau Joseph tried to spare her the hardest tasks.

With her mother so busy, it fell to Tanni to care for her little sisters. Her father called her their 'little mother'. Sometimes when he did he even smiled as he used to. Her father, Tanni realized one day, had a great deal of grey in his hair now.

Klara opened her eyes. 'What does *Kindertransport* mean, Tanni? Mutti and Papa whisper it to each other all the time so it must be important, but when I ask, Papa tells me to run along.'

'*Kindertransport*,' echoed Lili, waking and looking up sleepily at Tanni. She echoed everything Klara said. She adored her twin almost as much as she adored Tanni. Lili had been born second, Dr Joseph had explained to Tanni, and that meant they had to take special care of her because she was not as quick or as clever as Klara. And, indeed, where Klara's eyes were bright and lively, Lili's were placid and guileless.

Tanni was wondering how to answer Klara, and wishing she could curl up and have a good long sleep herself, then wake to find everything normal once more, when all three girls heard a commotion downstairs in the hall, and an alarming wail from their mother. 'No! Dearest Frau Anna, don't leave us! What shall we do without you?'

The girls scrambled off the window-seat and flew to the landing, where they peered over the banisters at the crisis below, unable to believe their ears. Despite their parents' protests, Frau Anna was insisting she must leave. Frau Anna, who had been with the family since her own husband was invalided while fighting in 1917, who looked after them, made wonderful dumplings and tortes on their birthdays, and who had seen the rabbi's handsome son, Anton, slip Tanni a small, beautifully bound volume of poetry. Frau Anna had winked as Tanni blushed.

Frau Anna leaving them?

'My husband says an Austrian mustn't work for a Jewish family,' she sobbed.

'At least you must take a half-year's wages. It's all we have at the moment, and I'm sorry it's not more,' Tanni's father urged. 'Money is worth less and less every day, so buy what you can quickly.' Tanni knew Frau Anna and her husband had become very poor. There were so many poor people.

Wiping her eyes, Frau Anna took the money, kissed them all and left.

'It will pass,' Tanni's father said to her mother, patting her shoulder as she too wept disconsolately. 'It is only temporary, darling. We are all Austrians and our town is too far out of the way for the troublemakers to take much notice of it. Only a few rabble-rousers have disturbed us. Things are worse elsewhere. What, after all, are a few baubles and a housekeeper? We will sit tight, and in the end Chancellor Hitler will call them to order. Then, you'll see, we shall go on as happily as before.'

That did not calm Frau Joseph. She and her husband began one of their urgent whispered discussions, their not-quite arguments. Tanni listened intently and heard '*Kindertransport*! You must! At once!'

Frau Anna's departure was the worst of all the horrible things that had befallen them. Tanni left the little girls and fled to her refuge, climbing up in the fig tree, to cry alone.

A few minutes later, she heard them calling. 'Tanni? Tanni? Where did you go?'

Perched high in the fig tree, long legs drawn up till her knees were folded under her chin, Tanni hugged herself, brooding, biting her nails and trying to hold back the tears. Just now she didn't want to be found. Through the last of the leaves she watched Lili and Klara bobbing here and there as they ran about looking for her. Lili's little plaits, which Tanni had done that morning, were coming undone as she trailed through the overgrown shrubs behind her sister.

'Tanni, stop hiding! Play with us. Push us in the swing! Please, Tanni,' called Klara.

'Swing,' echoed Lili. 'Want to swing.'

But Tanni was too bewildered and out of sorts to play or be anyone's 'little mother' at the moment. She needed someone to talk to, a friend. Her mother had her father and the twins had each other. She had no one. Now she gave in to a few bitter tears of self-pity, then told herself not to be silly and dried her eyes.

From her treetop hiding-place she could see over the high garden wall, with its stout locked door, to the river rushing below and the old stone walls of the town on the opposite bank, its church towers and domes shining golden in the late-autumn sunshine. From here the world looked as it always had. She felt calmer. She was a princess, like the ones in the fairytales, surveying her kingdom from the castle tower.

Below her a window opened in the house. 'Tanni! Please come to the sewing room for a moment,' her mother called, in the direction of the fig tree.

Tanni wanted to stay where she was but she climbed down and went, dragging her feet along the way.

Frau Joseph and Frau Zayman, the dressmaker, had been closeted in the sewing room for days, working furiously. From time to time the three girls had been summoned and measurements taken, garments basted or tucked. Tanni squirmed, as she stood in her shabby old petticoat, which was far too small for her now and increasingly tight across the bosom. Something about the atmosphere in the sewing room stopped her asking for a new one.

'Only sixteen and so tall already,' sighed Frau Zayman, increasing the measurement for Tanni's hemline. 'It seems like yesterday I made your school pinafores.'

'But I am old enough for the *Gymnasium*, Frau Zayman. It's Klara and Lili who need school pinafores, except they don't go to school. I am nearly grown-up. Can't you make the hem a bit longer? My dresses should be longer than a schoolgirl's.' To her surprise Frau Zayman nodded and stretched the tape further. Tanni noticed that Frau Zayman's eyes were red-rimmed as if she, too, had been crying over Frau Anna's departure. She twisted around to see if the tape-measure was far enough down her calf.

'Hold still, Tanni,' snapped her mother, running a pin into her hand.

School was a sore subject. Jewish children were not allowed in Austrian schools any longer, so their worried parents kept most at home. With no one but Lili and Klara to play with, Tanni moped around the house, missing her friends, her music lessons and even geography, which she used to hate. Her schoolbooks and tennis racquet lay on her desk and her satchel gathered dust in the corner. Her father had told her sternly to study by herself, but he was too distracted to notice that she did not. Instead, when she wasn't playing with Lili and Klara, Tanni would lose herself in the book of poems Anton had brought her, and dream of love . . . Anton's handsome face.

Now, while Frau Zayman fussed with the tape-measure, her spirits fell further. What was the point of having a new dress? They never went anywhere and Anton, now excluded from the university, rarely left his house. He would never see her in it. Worst of all, Tanni was not allowed to attend the annual *Kinderball*, which was held in mid-December. The young people's dancing classes were one of the few activities not specifically closed to Jewish children, probably because the mayor's sister made her living teaching ballroom dancing and deportment. Fran Joseph knew that Tanni longed to go to the ball, but she had stopped Tanni attending the classes months ago when she had decided there had been too many ugly incidents for her daughter to go out.

Frau Zayman continued measuring. 'Such a little waist the girl has. You should eat more, Tanni.'

Tanni's mother muttered something about how difficult it was to buy food, and Frau Zayman flushed. For the first time Tanni noticed how thin Frau Zayman looked. She had once been so plump and sturdy, like her son Bruno. 'You've made new winter clothes for Lili and Klara. Such pretty little coats with brass buttons! But what are you making for me with all this measuring?' Tanni tried to take an interest, forcing back the tears that never seemed far away. 'And why are those carpetbags on the floor? I thought they were kept in the attic.'

'Curiosity killed the cat,' said her mother.

'Then what colour? Can't I at least see the material for my dress, Mutti? Please don't make it pink like the last one. Pink with ribbons is for babies, for Klara and Lili. They're only four and they look adorable, like little bonbons. What I would like is . . .'

'What?' said Frau Zayman, holding the tape-measure round her bust.

Tanni thought about the sort of clothes a girl might wear to be fallen in love with by someone like Anton, who had been at university in Vienna. He must have seen many elegant ladies there. Before the cinema had closed to Jews, Tanni had seen a film in which a glamorous American actress had danced into happily-ever-after with a dapper hero in evening dress and a white scarf.

Eagerly she told Frau Zayman, 'Something gorgeous and grown-up and long, in dark blue velvet and silver, perhaps, with feathers at the neck and a little train. High-heeled slippers. A little silk bag for my lipstick and cigarettes. I would have a jewelled cigarette holder, that I would hold just so.' She tossed her head so that the mane of curly hair bounced, then struck a pose copied from the film: her eyes rose soulfully, she held aloft an imaginary cigarette-holder and sashayed across the sewing room, puffing a cigarette and blowing smoke into the air. 'The mysterious but charming Miss Joseph! All the young men of Vienna are madly in love and fighting duels over her.' Tanni kicked an imaginary train as the American actress had, looked back over her shoulder and fluttered her eyelashes. Her mother laughed and nearly swallowed a pin.

Tanni stopped prancing. She pined for the dancing classes she could no longer attend. She adored dancing and Anton had almost always chosen her as a partner because they were both tall for their age. He danced wonderfully well. He said all the men in his family did, but that those who were very Orthodox danced only with other men at weddings and on religious holidays – they thought it sinful to dance with a woman. His father's side of the family had abandoned such old fashioned notions. They, like the Josephs, were modern Austrians.

Tanni had imagined herself at the *Kinderball* – hair up, flowers on her wrist – waltzing round and round in her first proper ball dress with Anton, who had promised to come even though he was too old. They never missed a step, and everyone else stood back to applaud them. Then Anton spun her outside under the stars and asked her to marry him.

She hadn't seen him for ages because, except for her father, the family hardly left the house or its high-walled garden except on high holy days when they hurried to services at the synagogue down the street. Even then they went quickly. Their neighbours would mutter, '*Juden*,' and spit at them as they passed.

The atmosphere in the sewing room, which had lightened briefly, settled heavily again. 'Have you had a letter from Bruno lately?' Tanni asked Frau Zayman. It was impossible to know what to say to the grown-ups. Everyone was so moody and on edge. 'What has he seen in London? Has he met the King and Queen and the princesses? Has he visited the museum of wax people? Do tell us.'

It was a conversational gambit that usually worked. Frau Zayman could talk for hours about her beloved Bruno, and what he had written in his latest letter from England. Bruno was a plump, solemn boy, six years older than Tanni and much shorter. He was terribly clever and Frau Zayman, widowed when Bruno was small, had scrimped and saved to send him to England to study. Tanni knew that her mother ordered new dresses they didn't need to help Frau Zayman with Bruno's expenses and her father purposely ripped the linings in his coats or tore his pockets so that she could mend them.

Frau Zayman said Bruno had been offered a teaching post at Oxford, a prestigious award to an outstanding foreign scholar. Then, uncharacteristically, she fell silent. Tanni intercepted a meaningful look between her mother and the seamstress. Now what had she said that was wrong?

She tried again: 'I want to go to London like Bruno some day,' she announced brightly, 'and do all those exciting things. I shall see the Zoo and the Crown jewels and the soldiers riding their horses outside Buckingham Palace.' Why was her mother's best lace cloth cut in pieces on the sewing-table? 'Can I help with the sewing, Mutti? Frau Zayman showed me how to make the tiniest stitches you ever saw, and I would be so careful you'd be amazed –'

'I think,' interrupted her mother, stitching part of the tablecloth to a length of white material in her lap, 'we may see Bruno today. Be waiting to open the garden door to him quickly when he comes, Tanni.' Usually the girls were forbidden to let anyone in. From the garden door, steps led down to the river and a small landing-stage for fishermen's boats. Once they had brought fish to sell to the cook, but now no one called on Jews. Was Bruno coming by boat? Why not by train, as he normally did?

Her father rapped at the door. 'The rabbi is here with the contract,' he said, as he opened it. 'Really, my dear, that is nonsense!' he exclaimed, exasperated to see what his wife was doing.

'One moment, Herr Doktor!' Hastily Frau Zayman helped Tanni to pull on her dress over her petticoat and fastened the buttons at the back.

'Leave us for a moment, Tanni,' said her father.

Tanni didn't move. Her mother shook out the voluminous white thing she was sewing, then continued to stitch faster than ever. 'It's important. Men don't understand,' she insisted.

Tanni intervened: this was no time for her parents to quarrel. 'I know I'm to open the garden door for Bruno, but why is he coming, Papa, when he has a new teaching post in England? When everything here is so –'

'He is coming to tell us about it. And now I must speak to your mother and Frau Zayman, Tanni. Run along and –'

'But you already know about it! Why should he come back to tell you?'

'Go,' ordered her mother, head bent, sewing furiously. 'Your sisters are calling you.'

'But I want to stay and help sew.'

'Go!' said the Josephs, simultaneously.

Tanni stamped her foot and flounced out. Before the

twins saw her she ran back to the fig tree. Nothing made sense. Tears rolled down her cheeks again. After a while she realized she was hungry. She picked one of the figs that still clung to the tree and ate it, although it was a bit withered. She found a better one for Bruno, who liked figs. Below, wasps buzzed over the fruit that was split and rotting on the ground because no one had made jam this year.

The sun was setting, and the high branches where Tanni perched caught the last of its warmth. A breeze rattled the dry leaves. She could smell woodsmoke on the chilly air. The late-afternoon shadows lengthened. Once, the maids would have lit all the fires at twilight as the delicious smell of supper filled the house. Her mother would have bathed, put on a velvet gown and waited in front of the fire for Dr Joseph to come in from his surgery. When he had kissed them all, he would join her mother in an aperitif before Frau Anna served the soup and cutlets. After supper Tanni and her father had played chess while her mother practised a new piece, or read a novel ordered from Vienna.

There was a sharp knock, then a loud pounding that shook the garden door and interrupted Tanni's reverie. Tanni started, then began to climb down the tree. The door was overgrown with morning glory and ivy and it took a moment to push them aside. The banging was louder, more frantic.

She tugged. 'Just a *minute*, Bruno! Don't be so impatient. The door is stuck. There!'

Outside, she was startled to find an elderly man with stubble, one of her father's patients, who gasped for breath and spat as he talked. 'Hurry,' he wheezed. 'Soldiers are coming! They say they're setting fire to synagogues and Jewish shops, looting and breaking windows – shooting, even! You must get your father! They talk of driving out the Jewish devils. They are beating some to death!'

A breathless Bruno appeared behind the old man, his spectacles crooked. 'Tanni, it was not supposed to happen till next week but we must hurry. You know we are going to be –'

But a shocked Tanni had no time for Bruno now. Who was calling them 'devils'? Had the old man gone mad? Had the whole world gone mad as well as the Joseph household? She stood motionless, holding Bruno's fig.

'Go!' shouted the old man, and gave her a hard shove. 'Run! Tell your father!' His face twisted with fear. Across the river came the unmistakable sound of gunfire. 'They are coming! Soldiers!' he howled.

Terrified, Tanni dropped the fig and ran.

She burst into the sewing room where the rabbi was rolling something up as her parents and Frau Zayman watched. She had no idea why he should be in the sewing room. 'Papa, there is a crazy old patient of yours who arrived with Bruno. He's raving about Jewish devils,' she panted. 'You'd better come. And Bruno is here but even he isn't making sense.'

Dr Joseph and the rabbi hurried out. Tanni's mother and Frau Zayman undid the buttons at the back of her dress again, pulled it off and slipped another over her head. Tanni's head whirled. Did they think of nothing but fittings? Her mother and Frau Zayman tugged and fastened, ignoring Tanni's protests. Exasperated, confused and frightened, she stamped her foot and hit at the folds of fabric, crying, 'Why are you bothering with dresses at a time like this? What is happening?'

'Keep still. This is your wedding dress,' her mother said.

'WHAT?'

Something was draped and pinned on her head, blurring her vision. Lace. The tablecloth. 'Hurry!' her mother and Frau Zayman urged, turning her, tugging at buttons. Tanni was blinded by lace and confusion.

'Hurry,' said Frau Zayman.

'At once!' thundered her father, beyond the door.

'Mutti?' Everything was a blur. They were pulling her along.

'Bruno may take his wife to England,' Tanni's mother said, in her ear as they went. 'Listen to me. This way you will be safe. You are too old for the *Kindertransport*.'

Tanni heard Lili's voice asking why Tanni was dressed like that. Was she a princess?

'Like a ghost,' interjected Klara, 'with the tablecloth over her face.'

'A bride, darlings,' someone said. 'Tanni is a bride.'

They told her to stand still, just here, among the packing-cases in her father's study. Beneath the haze of her veil Tanni saw that she was standing under a wedding canopy contrived from a velvet curtain. Where had it come from?

Frau Zayman asked where the two witnesses were.

'There,' said the rabbi, pointing to the old man and Anton, whom he had brought with him for the purpose.

Anton was staring at her in anguish, and Tanni wanted to escape to her perch in the fig tree to stop this happening, but beneath the wedding canopy she was hemmed in by Bruno, Frau Zayman and her parents.

Lili and Klara were staring up at her. 'What's a bride?' demanded Klara. 'I want to be a bride! Can I be a bride too, Tanni?'

'Some day you can,' said Tanni, responding automatically from habit.

'Bride,' said Lili, and smiled adoringly at her sister. 'Tanni looks pretty.'

'Walk round Bruno seven times *quickly*!' Frau Joseph ordered. Obeying, Tanni gazed at Anton from beneath her veil. They could hear shouting in the street, coming closer. In Dr Joseph's study the candles flickered and the rabbi muttered rapidly. They lifted the veil off Tanni's face. Something wrapped in a napkin was thrust under Bruno's foot and Tanni heard glass break. The twins squealed.

'Ssssh,' said Tanni, the little mother.

'*Mazeltov*!' cried her mother and Frau Zayman in unison, voices faltering. Other glass shattered in the street. The shouting and the sound of heavy boots grew louder.

'We must go. We must try to protect the synagogue!' said the rabbi to Tanni's father. 'Hurry!'

He and Anton ran out of the house, and Tanni's father bolted the front door behind them – but not before Tanni glimpsed a mob followed by uniformed soldiers rounding the corner shouting, 'Jews *out*!'

'Hurry,' urged her father again, and shepherded his family to the back of the house.

But Tanni pulled away and ran back to the window.

'Anton!' she screamed. 'Oh, Papa, the rabbi and Anton! The soldiers have caught them! Please, please, help them! What is happening?'

Her father grabbed her and dragged her towards the garden door. When they reached it, her mother snatched her from him. 'My beloved child,' she said, hugging Tanni hard. Then she kissed her and bent to prise Klara and Lili from Tanni's knees. 'Darlings, be brave and do as I say.'

'Be a good wife. Be safe.' Frau Zayman's eyes were huge and frightened in her white face.

The crowd was howling outside as more glass broke, more shots were fired.

Tanni's mother thrust the carpetbag Tanni had seen on the sewing-room floor into her hands. 'Your trousseau. We prepared some clothes – a bride must always have a few things, but we thought there would be more time. Go safely to England and be ready to look after your sisters when they come.'

'Tanni and Bruno must leave while they can! Go!' Dr Joseph shoved Tanni into the garden. Behind him her mother called, 'We will all come to you in England as soon as –'

'Papa, let Lili and Klara come with me now.'

'No room in the boat,' hissed the old man. 'Come!'

Her father was pulling open the door in the garden wall. 'Child, they will come to England soon, God willing. They have papers for a children's train, the *Kindertransport*. It will be better if you are there, ready to look after them. Promise to take care of them whatever happens. Give me your word, Tanni. Now go!' ordered Dr Joseph, pushing Tanni and Bruno through the door. Somewhere nearby an ominous crackling grew louder. Clouds of smoke billowed overhead. There was gunfire and more glass shattered. A cheer went up. *'Juden raus! Alle Juden raus!'* A woman screamed. Above the noise Tanni heard pounding on the Josephs' front door.

As Dr Joseph shoved Bruno after her, Tanni looked back. Her mother was huddled over the twins, gazing towards the front door. More glass smashed. Frau Zayman waved her handkerchief helplessly. 'Tanni! Tanni! Don't leave us! I'm scared!' Klara cried. Lili blew kisses with both hands.

Tanni was frantic. 'I can't leave them!'

'Go!' her father shouted, and gave his eldest daughter a last hard push. 'The mayor will protect us – I attend to his crippled son! Go!'

'I promise, Papa,' Tanni cried, but the heavy door had already slammed, and the old-fashioned iron lock clunked into place. Immediately afterwards there was a splash from below as the heavy key was tossed over their heads into the river. With the old man shouting at them to hurry she and Bruno stumbled down the dark path on the river-bank, acrid smoke choking them.

A small boat was waiting. It rocked wildly as Tanni tripped and fell over the seat, banging her shin. There was water in the bottom and the skirt of her wedding dress was soaked. As the boat slipped away from the shore, she began to shiver and clutched the carpetbag to her as Bruno and the old man rowed. Above them orange flames roared into the sky. There was a crash as the roof of the synagogue collapsed.

Panting, Bruno and the old man pulled hard on the

oars. After a while the boat caught the river current and went faster. Behind them the town walls, the flames, chanting and gunfire grew fainter. Soon there was just the night, the dark river and the red sky, the sound of oars slapping water, and the cold. Tanni's wet feet were numb. What was happening to her family? To Anton? She wanted to throw herself over the side and swim back.

When Bruno saw that her teeth were chattering and she was hugging the flimsy veil round her shoulders, he put down his oar and made his way across to her. He took off his coat, draped it round her shoulders and kissed her brow. Tanni looked at him blankly. Bruno was her husband.

5. Crowmarsh Priors, March 1939

As he waited for the afternoon train from London to Brighton, the Crowmarsh Priors station master, Albert Hawthorne, sat at the desk in the tiny office and picked up yesterday's papers. He skipped the stories about Slovak separatism in Czechoslovakia, 'Cabinet Optimistic over Relations with Berlin' and someone named Goering holidaying on the Riviera. Someone or something called the Baldwin Fund wanted to 'get them out'. Jews, it looked like. Foreigners, anyway. He skipped that too.

He paused loyally to read the caption beneath the picture of the King and Queen in the royal box at the opera house with the French president and his wife. Albert didn't hold with the French. The King looked strained and unhappy – all the responsibility of being a king, Albert guessed – but by his side the plump little Queen was beaming beneath her tiara and had one gloved hand raised cheerfully in a wave. He whistled softly at a picture of the new model Daimler, and decided to wait until after the train had come through to study the cricket scores in the Test match against South Africa.

He turned the page. A big headline – 'Police Arrest Friends of Duke and Duchess of Windsor' – caught his eye, with a photograph of people in evening dress splashing through the fountains at Trafalgar Square. The men's evening dress was askew and they appeared to be brandishing champagne bottles, while the women were soaked and looked as if they had nothing on. Right at the front a pretty girl was shrieking with laughter, hanging on to a tall, fair-haired man with one hand and holding her wet skirt up so high with the other that there was a shocking view of her legs. In the background the police were closing in. The caption read, 'Admiral's Madcap Daughter Arrested Again!'

Albert read on. There had been a society ball at the Savoy, and afterwards a party of revellers had gone to the Café de Paris. Which, according to the police, they had left at dawn, reluctantly – some had banged on the doors, demanding to be let back in. When they were turned away they had stopped taxis, thrown out the occupants and forced the cabbies to drive to Trafalgar Square, where a number were subsequently arrested. 'See the editorial on page ten, "Scandal of a Modern Debutante".'

It was the kind of story Albert relished. It confirmed his view that the upper classes were no better than anyone else and that the country was going to the dogs. He tut-tutted as he turned to page ten.

There are only three occasions on which a well-bred girl should be mentioned in the papers: when she is born, when she is married and when she dies. After reading of the shocking behaviour and events of last Saturday in Trafalgar Square, as reported on the front page, Miss Falconleigh's escapades raise issues of public concern. This paper feels it is pertinent to question whether her father is competent to command in the Admiralty when, evidently, he cannot within his own domestic circle . . .

An unmarried girl's reputation is priceless, easily jeopardized by thoughtless behaviour and any departure from decorum. Normally girls of Miss Falconleigh's age and position in society are strictly chaperoned to guard them from any whiff of scandal. Typically they are not allowed to travel alone with young men in taxis, and nightclubs remain forbidden to any respectable girl, even in our reckless age. Miss Falconleigh, however, has openly cavorted about Town and, we regret to say, has been photographed leaving many of London's least salubrious nightspots and most scandal-ridden private parties. Her escorts have included a number of well-known playboys, Argentine polo players, and personal friends of His Royal Highness, the former Prince of Wales.

Her only chaperonage, if it can be called such, has been that of Lady 'Baby' Penrose, a former finishing-school chum of Miss Falconleigh, who, though married, is possibly not the most vigilant of matrons as she is only a year older than Miss Falconleigh. It is to the credit of neither that she shares Miss Falconleigh's taste for notorious establishments. The sad fact is that Miss Falconleigh has been in one public scrape after another since she was presented at Court. That in itself is shocking and reflects badly on her. Allowances may be made for the fact that she lost her mother very young, but why did her father neglect to ensure that some respectable older female friend of the family oversaw Miss Falconleigh's entrance into society?

Albert was so engrossed in his newspaper that the London train was pulling into the station before he knew it. Crowmarsh Priors was only a small country station with few passengers coming and going, but his duty was to be on the platform, hat on, whistle at the ready, when the trains pulled in. As he straightened his cap he was reminded that his wife, Nell, would enjoy the newspaper's advertisements for the new spring hats, so he'd best remember to take it home.

He wondered who the sole female passenger was when she stepped down on to the windy platform. No ladies from Crowmarsh Priors had gone up to London today. If they had Albert would have known. So she couldn't be Mrs Richard Fairfax, who sometimes boarded a train to Town, although she was a slender, well-dressed young woman of about Mrs Richard's age. Far smarter clothes than Mrs Richard's, though. Probably for the de Balforts at Gracecourt Hall, although their visitors usually dashed down in smart motor-cars at the weekend and never arrived by train on a Tuesday.

The young woman had a gloved hand clamped to her head to hold on her bit of a hat. Her hair flew about wildly, as she struggled to hold down the skirt of her costume when the March wind blew rain splattering across the platform. Albert couldn't help noticing she had shapely legs and pretty ankles. He reminded himself that a right-thinking man with a wife and growing daughter had no business ogling strangers' ankles.

On closer inspection he saw that the young woman was a girl, really, for all her finery. She had turned to direct the removal of an extraordinary amount of luggage from the train to the platform. As the engine steamed impatiently, Albert counted five large trunks, an assortment of grips, a smart handbag and a handsome crocodile dressing-case.

The guard nodded to him that all the bags were off, and rolled his eyes as he gestured at the mountain of luggage on the platform. He reached back into the train and tossed out what Albert was waiting for: a bundle of the newspapers that passengers had left on their seats, tied with string. The guard was a tidy man who would have thrown them away but Albert thought it a shame to waste them. 'Cheerio, then,' he called. Then he waved, shouted, 'All aboard,' in his loudest station-master's voice, and blew his whistle, even though, as usual, no one was getting on.

As the train chugged away he fetched the ancient baggage cart and rolled it towards the newcomer and her luggage. Her back was towards him as she gazed in the direction of the village where smoke was curling above a few slate roofs and brick garden walls into sodden grey skies. A row of Georgian houses with fanlights, and polished brass on the doors, faced the village green. Mrs Richard Fairfax lived in one of those. There was an old flint church with a Norman tower, surrounded by a grave-yard, and behind it the vicarage. Directly across from the church an imposing Queen Anne house with tall windows was visible behind wrought-iron gates set into a brick garden wall. Albert could also identify the pub, a green-grocer's, a butcher's and he knew where the red pillarbox stood. The drizzle had driven everyone inside, except Jimmy, the butcher's boy, whizzing past the station turning on his bicycle, and the cows in the next field, who had placidly chewed the cud, regardless of the wet.

A delicate flowery scent drifted to Albert's nose. Unaware that he was doing so, he straightened up. 'Let me help you with that luggage, madam ... miss,' he amended. Up close she was just a slip of a thing. Her full lower lip was trembling and, Albert thought with disapproval, it was rather too scarlet for nature. Paint! And where there was paint, there was powder, he thought darkly. No respectable girl should get herself up like a hussy. Then he noticed the smooth cheek, the defiant little nose and determined chin. The girl's dark blue eyes met Albert's. She blinked back tears, and his heart melted.

'Is this Crowmarsh Priors? All of Crowmarsh Priors?'

'Indeed it is, miss.' Albert nodded fondly at the village. To a Sussex man like Albert Hawthorne, there wasn't a better spot in England.

The girl cleared her throat. Something about her was familiar, Albert thought. He was sure he had seen her recently ... Then it dawned on him. The paper! She was the girl in the fountain! But now, on the platform, she looked ladylike and she certainly had expensive luggage ...

She clutched the fur boa draped over her shoulders and stared defiantly at him. 'Perhaps you could direct me to Glebe House.'

Albert was astonished. She was staying with old Lady Marchmont! Whatever for? Lady Marchmont was a widow, had no children and never had people to stay. Perhaps the girl was a relative. She certainly didn't strike Albert as the sort who came as a paid companion, like the whey-faced creature with spectacles and thick lisle stockings who had arrived to keep poor, bedridden Lady de Balfort company during the last years of her life. Albert shook his head. Lady Marchmont would eat a paid companion for breakfast.

How a pretty girl with such a determined look about her – not to mention rouge – would get on in the forbidding atmosphere of Glebe House he didn't like to think. He was just wondering if he ought to warn her what to expect when he heard the sound of footsteps hurrying across the station's gravel forecourt. A tall, dishevelled young man in a clerical collar dashed on to the platform. He stopped just before he collided with the girl and Albert, and gasped, 'Hullo, Albert!' and snatched off a rather unfortunate hat. He apologized breathlessly for being late, and said he hoped he had the pleasure of greeting Miss – Miss – er, Lady Marchmont's goddaughter, whom he was supposed to meet.

The girl's sapphire eyes widened as dismay battled with amusement on her pretty face. Her eyelashes fluttered tremulously as she gazed up at the odd young man, who started apologizing all over again, stammering incomprehensibly about urgent parish business, the brasses, the late vicar and the Mothers' Union.

Albert guessed that he would have babbled for the rest of the afternoon had not the girl cut him short. She moved her crocodile case to her left hand, then held out the right. 'How do you do? I'm Frances Falconleigh,' she said sweetly. 'So kind of you to take the trouble to meet me. You must be Oliver Hammet, the new vicar. My godmother wrote to me about you.'

'Not at all,' began the vicar, flushing and hanging on to the girl's gloved hand. 'Not at all! Welcome to Crowmarsh Priors! So glad . . . Not at all . . . Really, it's quite a pleasure. Too delightful!'

Frances gave a strangled giggle. 'You're a perfect angel

to look after me when you're so frightfully busy. I don't know what I should have done without you!'

'Delighted to be of service,' Mr Hammet stammered. 'Ahem! Er, do allow me to take that, Miss Falconleigh. I'm sure it's far too heavy for you.' He released Frances's hand to take her dressing-case.

'Thank you!' she cooed.

Albert looked from one to the other, his moustache twitching. The little baggage!

Mr Hammet blushed again. 'Er, not at all. My pleasure entirely. Do take my arm. I'm actually a sort of cousin of Lady Marchmont's, distant, of course, very distant. Albert, do you think you might possibly see to the rest of Miss Falconleigh's, er, things?' He gestured towards the luggage mountain.

'Right you are, Vicar. I'll get Jimmy to bring them round on the cart to Glebe House,' said Albert. Mr Hammet was too busy gazing at Miss Falconleigh to reply – the cat had got his tongue.

Frances Falconleigh shifted from foot to foot. 'I should have been utterly stranded, if not for you,' she breathed, with a devastating glance at her rescuer, and tugged his elbow to bring him back to reality. 'And I expect Aunt Muriel will be wondering if I've arrived.' She steered him firmly towards the station steps. 'Mustn't worry her.'

'No, indeed. You had better hold my arm quite tightly – the gravel's a bit tricky,' said Mr Hammet, as Frances's high-heeled shoes slid on the path and she clutched his arm tight to her bosom. The feathers on her hat hid her face, and he didn't see – although Albert did – Frances mouth, 'Damn!' as her ankle twisted.

Albert watched them go, torn between disapproval and amusement. The girl was clinging to the vicar like a limpet.

He returned to his abandoned newspaper to check the photos he had seen earlier. Sure enough, she was the daughter of Admiral Tudor Falconleigh. Very high up in Whitehall.

Albert shook his head and went back to the editorial. When he had finished he asked himself what the country coming to.

An interesting visitor for Lady Marchmont, he thought.

6. London, August 1939

When Tanni and Bruno had landed at Southampton on that grey January morning, they had done their best to neaten their travel-worn appearance, but had seen at once that they were making a far from favourable impression on the lady official at Immigration. She had been cold and stern, reading their documents and passports as though they must be false. Finally she had sniffed disapprovingly and handed them leaflets in English, printed in large type. She tapped one with her forefinger, then said in clipped, precise tones, slightly louder than necessary, 'You are in England now. However you may be accustomed to behave where you come from, you are strongly advised to adapt at once to the ways of your host country. We have prepared a list of things you should and should not do in order to fit in. "The English",' she read, '"are naturally reserved, keep themselves to themselves."'

They did not like it, she went on, when foreigners, especially refugees, dressed garishly or wore outlandish costumes. They should do nothing to call attention to themselves. They should dress normally, be modest, polite and self-effacing, never complain or criticize anything about the country that had so generously allowed them in. Above all, they should not put themselves forward for jobs that local people wanted. Tanni and Bruno must make every effort to adjust quietly and remember to be grateful. 'I hope, Professor,' she said thinly, 'that you appreciate how very fortunate you are to be here.'

Tanni had been tired and numb from months of travelling, crowded trains, waiting for papers and permits to be issued, more crowded trains, more waiting for documents to be stamped, long stretches of walking and finally the rough Channel crossing. She had not understood all the words but the hostile tone was clear enough. She glanced at Bruno, then nodded meekly. She could tell that he was masking fury at the way they were being treated.

He put a reassuring arm round her shoulders. 'My wife is very tired,' he said, then whispered, still in English, just loudly enough for the woman to hear, 'All will be well.'

'Now, Mrs Zayman, if you will step over there for a medical examination,' barked the woman. They didn't check all the newcomers for disease, just those who looked worst. Fortunately a doctor was on hand to examine them today. If the girl, this so-called professor's wife, had tuberculosis or some foreign disease she would be quarantined. 'Step over there,' the woman ordered, pointing to a curtained-off area where several other wan-looking women were waiting.

Two hours later Tanni had come out from behind the curtain, flushed and confused. Bruno, who had been sitting on a bench, stood up.

'Bruno,' Tanni whispered in German, 'the doctor says I'm going to have a baby.'

He looked at her, stunned. Her lower lip was quivering.

'Bruno, a baby! I want my mother! I don't know what to do!' Tanni's eyes were wide and anxious. Bruno looked for the Immigration woman, but she was lecturing another new arrival at the top of her voice and fortunately hadn't heard Tanni speaking German.

'Don't worry. Both of our mothers will be here soon,' he whispered. 'We'll all look after you, *Liebling*. Everything will be fine.' He had no idea what to do either but he had to prevent Tanni worrying. 'They'll be here soon,' he repeated firmly, putting his arm round her again. 'They're probably on one of those awful trains, or waiting for a slow official to stamp the passports, but soon we'll all be together in Oxford. The twins will go to school and your father will have patients again. Our house will have a garden where our mothers can sew, and you and the baby can sit and listen to the bells of the colleges. We'll all learn to ride bicycles, even Mutti. Everyone rides them in Oxford. You'll see. Everything will be fine.'

Tanni felt better and smiled at him. 'Our mothers on bicycles! Imagine! I hope the garden in our new home will have a fig tree.' Bruno said he wasn't sure they grew in England but he had seen cherry and plum trees in Oxford. So, Tanni imagined making plum jam in her Oxford kitchen while the baby crawled on the floor and Bruno returned home to admire her efforts and kiss the back of her neck, sending those delicious shivers down her spine.

But it hadn't happened as Tanni had imagined. Bruno had taken her to the Whitechapel boarding-house where he lived when he was in London, and where they were to wait for the others to come. But the days had stretched from weeks into months, and in March the Germans had marched into Czechoslovakia. Bruno had volunteered to translate for the British intelligence service. Someone higher up made a phone call and he was now on leave from the university. He had said they had better remain at the boarding-house because it was the address Tanni's parents, the twins and his mother had.

For Tanni, life had grown more and more confusing. Her body felt as if it belonged to someone else. At first she was sick and terribly sleepy. She would drag herself down the passage to the lavatory to vomit until she was dizzy and shaking. Then her shape changed and she blew up until she felt like one of Lili and Klara's balloons. As her waist expanded she unpacked the sewing-kit her mother had tucked into her carpetbag and let out two frocks.

Bruno had scoured the Whitechapel markets for lemons, the only thing she wanted to eat. He watched, amazed, as she cut them into slices and ate them, peel and all. He was happy about the baby but was uneasy about leaving Tanni alone. She understood little English – when people spoke to her she just smiled politely. Bruno was torn between his new work, which ate up so much of his time, and his longing to be with his wife. He was very busy and often out until late at night. When Tanni snuggled up to him in bed, and giggled about how large she was getting, he could feel the baby kicking. He had become more and more anxious for his mother and the Josephs to come. When Tanni had gone into labour a month early, they still hadn't arrived, and didn't come even when Tanni screamed and cried for her mother, paying no attention to the midwife who told her sharply not to make such a fuss.

Once she was back in the boarding-house with the

baby, the days and nights merged into each other until Tanni felt she had always been imprisoned in the dingy room during a dusty, muggy London summer. Time slowed as one day dragged wearily into the next. Bruno was away more and more, and as she didn't like to worry him she told him everything was fine. Really. When he wasn't at home she went back to bed after a grim breakfast of cold toast and marmalade and stayed there, covers pulled up to her chin, moving only to feed or change the baby. Often she did not bother getting up for 'tea', as the landlady called the evening meal. If she was hungry she nibbled biscuits from the tin Bruno had brought her.

It became an effort to do anything, even today, when the landlady knocked sharply on Tanni's door and said, 'Mrs Zayman! Letter for you.' Tanni held her breath and sat very still in her chair. She hoped the woman would think she had gone out. It was too hard to make the effort of speaking English to her. The landlady had a thick Irish accent, and if Tanni asked her to repeat what she had said, she would raise her voice and broaden her accent. No matter how hard Tanni tried, she never seemed to do the right thing in England.

Even the prospect of a letter failed to rouse her. She no longer cared about letters. When she didn't open the door at once the landlady slipped something underneath it. Tanni heard the rustle of paper, then the woman grumbling as her footsteps retreated down the passageway, which smelt of boiled cabbage and drains. The envelope lay on the floor for some time before Tanni looked at it. When she did, she saw it was on thin blue paper, with German stamps and official markings. Her heart skipped a beat when she recognized her mother's handwriting. She put the sleeping baby down and got up slowly. If she moved too fast she felt dizzy. She was sore and tired, though it was nearly four weeks now since she had given birth.

She reached down and picked up the envelope. It was dated months earlier, in April, and looked as if it had been opened, then clumsily resealed. Tanni reached for her sewing scissors and slit the envelope. She took out a thin sheet of paper covered with tiny cramped handwriting on both sides.

My Beloved Child,

I hope this finds you and Bruno well, and that you have received my other letters but it is hard to know, so I will write again to let you know that, after the terrifying night when you left, we are safe and well. Just before the mob in the streets broke down the door we were saved by the mayor and the police chief, who managed to divert the crowd – you remember Papa looked after the mayor's little boy, and pulled the police chief's wife through pneumonia? But we were saved at a terrible cost. The best they could do for us was to direct the mob to another Jewish house. My only comfort that terrible night was in knowing that you were going to safety.

We had a letter from Bruno that you are to be a mother yourself. Happy news indeed. I long to be there to look after you, but young as you are, all will be well, I am sure. If you feel sick in the mornings a piece of preserved ginger, sucked slowly, will help. Frau Zayman advises drying out some day-old bread in the oven, with a little salt, to keep in a tin by your bed. Eat a piece before you get up. Papa says to take a few spoonfuls of brandy-and-water if you feel very unwell, and that you must try to have fresh milk and plenty of fruit.

Long before the baby comes we expect to be with you in England! But many things have happened to delay us.

Soon after you left our house was confiscated. We were given only a few moments to get our clothes and a few belongings. There was no time to sell the piano or pack the silver and paintings or Papa's books, so we have lost those too, but they are only things and we must not allow them to become a matter of regret. We are safe and well, if somewhat crowded, living now in Frau Zayman's little flat. Except for her arthritis, we are all well thank G–d and I have become very clever at cooking potatoes. We are more fortunate than some, as the Germans have begun to transport those without exit visas for resettlement on the Polish border. We have our exit visas and are only waiting for the girls to leave first. Meanwhile we must wear a yellow star on our clothing, even Lili and Klara, and must not be on the street after dark. From time to time people are arrested.

We long to be away. People queue all day and night for exit visas now. Papa, Frau Zayman and I obtained ours with the mayor's help, and will follow when the little ones are safely on their way to you. They should have left on the children's train to England in January, but at the last minute both had scarlet fever quite badly and in the end we feared to let them go. We had to cut their hair because of the fever. Lili was very slow to get better and we debated whether to send Klara alone but thought it best not. Papa has been promised they will have a place on another train soon.

They say it is much safer for the children to go separately from us as the Kindertransports *are sure to get through. I confess I do not like it. I could hardly bear to part from you, even with Bruno to take care of you, and the thought of* parting from Lili and Klara even for a few weeks, when they will be at the mercy of strangers, is almost too much. Only knowing that they will soon be with you keeps me calm and sensible. We wait from day to day for news that their train is leaving. Lili and Klara's two little suitcases are packed and ready in the hall, complete with a favourite doll we managed to save for each. Frau Zayman cut down an old coat of her own to make them warm dressing-gowns for England. I am impressing upon Klara every day that she must be brave and a good girl, like her big sister, a good little mother for poor Lili on the train until they are safely with you. The girls are so excited and happy to think of being with you at last. They miss you dreadfully. They ask if you have enough to eat in England, and I tell them I am sure of it. Food is scarce here and they are often hungry. We struggle to pay for the little we can find, mostly yesterday's bread and old potatoes, sometimes a few cabbage leaves. Most shopkeepers will not sell food to Jews. I saw Frau Anna the other day. She has grown thin like many others, and looked at us with an expression I did not like. I shall be glad to leave. Papa, Frau Zayman and I have packed our few things, a little money and some bits of jewellery I managed to bring with me. We shall go the moment the girls are off.

The paper runs out, only room to send you our blessings and love. Be well and don't worry: we will all be happy and cosy together in England soon. Try to be brave until then. We send you a photograph of us all, taken by Frau Zayman's kind neighbour who had a camera. He took this one last picture before he sold it and his developing equipment for food. The girls also send you a little drawing so you won't forget them. Klara wrote a message with only a little help from Papa. Love, my dearest, Mutti.

A blurred snapshot of a couple, two little girls with shorn heads and a drawn elderly woman fluttered to the floor, wrapped in a second thin sheet of paper. At first Tanni thought they had sent the wrong photograph, but then she traced the familiar features of her parents in the gaunt couple, her sisters' faces on the little bald heads and Frau Zayman's in the old woman. She was shocked by their appearance. Then she saw something written on a scrap of the same thin paper. She picked it up. There were two little stick figures in dresses, round heads topped with a fuzzy halo of short hair, topped with enormous bows. 'Dear Tanni do you miss us our hair will grow back in England lots of love and kisses from Klara and Lili.'

Tanni checked the date on the letter: 3 April. It was late August now. Over four months ago. Suddenly she was overcome with relief. By now they must be in England. She could understand why they hadn't found her. The twins had probably arrived first and, not under-standing English, had been unable to explain that they had lost Tanni and Bruno's address. Her parents and Frau Zayman would have arrived too and tried to contact her, but she had missed them because she had been ill and Bruno had been away. They must have come to the house and asked for Professor and Mrs Bruno Zayman, and the short-tempered landlady had pretended not to understand and sent them away. Tanni felt a surge of responsibility. It was up to her to find her family and bring everyone back together. All she had to do was find out where they had gone and she would see them soon.

Her spirits sank as she considered the practicalities. She had no idea how to set about finding them in England.

She wished Bruno was at home, but he had been away for three days and she never knew when he would return or for how long. When he did come he was preoccupied and she didn't like to bother him. The baby woke and began to cry. She had wanted to call him Johan, after Bruno's father, but Bruno insisted they give him an English name, John, and call him Johnny. She struggled with the English pronunciation.

Tanni sighed, unbuttoned her dress, lifted Johnny out of his cot and settled back into the old armchair to nurse him. There was so much she needed to ask her mother about babies, like how to get Johnny nursing properly. Her nipples were sore, but if she moved him from breast to breast, he stopped feeding and howled. The landlady complained of the noise so Tanni winced, bit her tongue and endured.

As Johnny sucked, Tanni looked about, seeing her surroundings through her fastidious mother's eyes. The room smelt of nappies. Her few dresses and Bruno's spare suit hung in a small wardrobe. There was a layer of grime on the window. Bruno's books were piled beneath it, with her comb and brush and a leaflet about bathing babies on top of them. She often felt like lying down on the unmade bed and waiting for the grime to cover her too, but now the thought of her parents galvanized her. She could see dustballs under the bed. Her mother would be shocked, and Tanni decided she had better give the room a thorough clean.

First, though, she should visit her aunt, who was married to a rabbi in Bethnal Green. Tante Berthe Cohen could advise her on what to do next. She was a small, round, kindly woman, a distant cousin on her mother's side, and Tanni's only friend. She was much older than Tanni's mother, always busy, and had lived in England for twenty years. Rabbi Cohen had known Bruno's father and, although Bruno was not in the least religious, he had performed the *bris* for Johnny. Tante Berthe had supported a nervous Tanni through the ceremony and provided honeycake and wine afterwards.

Now that she had something to do Tanni perked up. When Johnny finished nursing she put him down, washed herself as best she could in the sink in her room, then her hair and combed it dry. She sponged Johnny and changed him, then put on her cleanest dress and her hat. She had lost so much weight that the dress was far too big. She must get out the little sewing-kit again to take in the seams. She would do that after she had tidied the room and aired the bed, but before she did any of it she would speak to Tante Berthe.

She wrapped Johnny in a crib sheet, picked up her handbag and shut the door quietly. Hearing the wireless in the sitting room, she tiptoed past to avoid alerting the landlady. Outside, she wondered if it was too hot for the baby, or whether she should have wrapped him in another layer. Could small babies get a chill even on a hot day? It was so hard to know. If only her mother were there. But soon she would be, Tanni thought, and her heart lifted. What a lovely sunny afternoon it was. She hummed a little song to Johnny as she walked along.

The Cohens lived many streets away, in a small neighbourhood in Bethnal Green where the women all wore headscarves and the men had long curls under big hats, black suits and white shirts open at the neck. There were children all over the place and everyone spoke a language Tanni didn't understand. She remembered Anton's description of his Orthodox relations, and her heart contracted. No, she mustn't think of Anton now: she was a married woman and a mother.

When Tanni reached Tante Berthe's street she saw two smartly dressed ladies with clipboards, wearing hats, kid gloves and polished shoes. They looked out of place among the other women in the street, who were mostly in black, with long skirts and thick stockings, their hair covered. The two elegant strangers reminded Tanni reassuringly of her mother. As she drew closer she heard them speaking in the kind of clipped, precise English she had learned at school. She smiled shyly at them, as a large family of black-clad children walked past with their father, who averted his eyes. One of the ladies muttered, 'There are so many of them! However do their parents tell them apart? And they still won't consider evacuation. The parents don't even speak English properly. Quite, quite stubborn. The children should be forcibly evacuated if you ask me.'

'Frankly,' said her companion, 'one sometimes quite understands why the Germans —'

'I know! Come along, Penelope, we're wasting our time.' Both ladies climbed into a black car with a driver.

Tanni hurried on to the Cohens' narrow house. Sweetpeas bloomed cheerfully in the small front garden and starched white curtains hung at the front windows.

Rabbi Cohen was busy in his study but Tante Berthe welcomed Tanni warmly, kissing her and making a fuss of Johnny. Then she led Tanni down the passage into a crowded little kitchen that smelt of baking. Several women were crowded together in chairs round a pile of papers on the kitchen table. They looked up as Tanni came in, and Tante Berthe introduced her. The women all had kerchiefs wound tightly round their heads and stared at Tanni's hat, a fetching one Frau Zayman had concocted from the felt of Dr Joseph's oldest grey Homburg, trimmed with scraps of ribbon and some left-over veiling. But they smiled when they saw Johnny, reaching to stroke his cheeks and shifting their chairs to make room for her.

Tante Berthe brought tea in glasses with lemon, a plate of almond cake and a bowl of dark cherries. Tanni sat politely quiet while the others talked, sipping tea and eating a piece of cake, thinking how delicious it tasted. She was anxious to show her aunt her mother's letter, but the other women were debating something in the language Tanni didn't understand. She stopped listening and waited for a chance to speak. Meanwhile she took a second, then a third piece of cake, licking her fingers with enjoyment. Tante Berthe beamed and pushed the cherries towards her.

Finally there was a break in the conversation, so Tanni wiped her cherry-stained fingers on her handkerchief, then took the precious envelope from her handbag. 'Tante Berthe, I need your advice. I had a letter from my mother,' she began in German. Her aunt said something to the other women, who nodded. With Tante Berthe translating for those who did not speak German well, the letter was passed round for all to read, with the photo and Klara's carefully printed note.

'My little sister,' said Tanni, proudly. 'She's very clever. But my mother wrote in April and the letter only reached me today. The twins are five and speak no English. Lili has always been a little slow and Klara has to look after her. They must have lost my address before they reached England. I don't know where my parents and Frau Zayman have gone. Since Bruno is away I can't ask him what to do. I thought you, Tante Berthe, and the rabbi would know how I can find them all.' Johnny woke and whimpered, and Tanni put him on her shoulder to jiggle him quiet, wondering how soon she could get him home to feed him. 'I can't wait for them to see Johnny.'

Tante Berthe's kind face was grave. 'My dear . . .' She hesitated, her eyes darting round for permission to speak. The women exchanged glances. One after another they nodded stiffly. 'It may be that they have not reached England yet. As your mother says, these are difficult times. We know that many Jews, like your parents, want to leave Germany and Austria, but doors are closing to them everywhere. We are part of a committee trying to help Jews in Europe, and we know how difficult . . .'

'Yes, but my family have left and are here now.'

A younger woman named Rachel burst out impatiently in English, 'Difficult? Pah! It's impossible! Things are very very bad in Austria, bad in Poland, worse in Germany. It is hard to obtain a permit to leave, even with a huge bribe. And few people can pay a bribe now. The Nazis have confiscated Jewish property, and people who were not poor before are poor now. So many countries turn their backs. They close their doors to poor people. It is a little easier for children, but even for them there are difficulties.

My husband liaises with the *Kindertransport*, finding homes for the children arriving in England. They are efficient people. If your sisters had arrived you would have been informed, so I do not think that they can be here. We are getting word that the Nazis have arrested many, many people in Austria for resettlement . . .'

'They call it resettlement,' interjected another woman, 'when people are forced out of their homes to slave for the Germans in labour camps, herded like animals, even children and the old . . .'

Tanni struggled to follow the English. Surely no one would ever send Papa to work in a labour camp, she thought uneasily. He was a doctor and highly respected. As for Mutti and Frau Zayman, what earthly use would they be as labourers? 'Mutti didn't say anything about camps, just that people were being moved. But if the letter was written months ago, they must be in England now. My parents made definite arrangements for Klara and Lili on the *Kindertransport* in April, and they had exit visas to follow as soon as the twins left.'

More worried looks were exchanged across the table.

Johnny broke the silence: he started to cry in earnest. Tanni patted his back and her smile faded. She looked from one woman to another, and her voice rose, as she said, 'You see, I promised Papa – it was the last thing I said! Bruno and I were running away and there was no room for the twins in the boat. He made me promise to look after the little ones in England. It is my responsibility to find them. I was so ill with the baby that I . . . I forgot a lot of things,' Tanni admitted guiltily. 'It was my fault if someone couldn't tell me the girls had come. There must have been a letter or a phone call but I was in bed and too tired to get up and they must have thought I had gone away – but now I've recovered I *must* find where they are. We were all supposed to go to Oxford to live when my parents came. Maybe they couldn't find us in London and went to Oxford to look for us.' Tears welled up. 'My fault . . .' Her lower lip trembled and tears spilled.

The older women tutted. The poor girl looked awful – such dark circles under her eyes and so thin that her dress was hanging off her. Tante Berthe rose and put her arm round Tanni's shoulders. 'Of course it's not your fault, Tanni,' she said. 'The time after a baby is born can be very hard.' The other women nodded and murmured agreement. 'Take Johnny home, my dear. We will try to find your family. If your sisters were indeed with the *Kindertransport* we should be able to trace where they are.'

'And if they were not? So many children, so many . . .' said Rachel, her head in her hands.

'Hush,' muttered another. 'The poor girl is upset enough.'

'And Mutti, Papa and Frau Zayman?'

More looks. 'We will begin with the *Kindertransport* – it is easier to trace – and we will do what we can to find your parents and Bruno's mother,' said Tante Berthe, patting her hand. 'Meanwhile, Tanni, my husband says it is important not to speak of anything we have said outside this house. Not one word. If we are to help Jews else-where we must be discreet. The English –'

'The English are as bad as the Germans!' huffed Rachel. 'You have no idea how careful we must be to avoid attracting the attention of the authorities. Each of our members keeps different information in her head. No one knows everything so that if one of us is interned or questioned she cannot jeopardize the work of the whole committee.'

'Shush, Rachel! Enough already. But, Tanni, take care not to speak in German, even to Bruno. They listen everywhere, and if war with Germany comes they will intern people who appear to be enemy aliens.'

'Intern?' asked Tanni. 'What is that?'

'Detained in a camp, like a prison.'

Relief at the prospect of help was now submerged under fresh worry. Tired now and anxious to get Johnny home to feed him, Tanni rose, thanked Tante Berthe and made her farewells. She walked home as quickly as she could, Johnny howling most of the way, heavy in her aching arms. What if they were put in one of these camps? Would they take Johnny away from her? She hugged him tightly, unable to bear the idea.

When she entered the house the smell from the kitchen of something frying in hot, stale fat turned her stomach. The landlady intercepted her in the cramped passageway. 'There's a lady waiting to speak to you. She's in the parlour.'

Tanni went quickly into the gloomy little room. A woman in a smart costume and hat stood up and her heart leaped. Suddenly everything was all right. Her mother had found her, after all. 'Mutti!' she exclaimed. 'Oh, Mutti, I –' She stopped mid-sentence and her heart plummeted. It was not her mother. Instead it was one of the well-dressed ladies she had seen on the pavement on the way to Tante Berthe's.

'Mrs Zayman?' the woman said uncertainly, checking her clipboard. The girl with the baby looked impossibly young to be married, much less a mother although, judging by what she had seen in Bethnal Green so far, if she was Jewish, who knew?

Tanni nodded, too stunned with disappointment to speak.

'How do you do? My name is Penelope Fairfax, and I am a member of the Women's Voluntary Service. The government expects that we will soon be at war with Germany and, for safety's sake, we are evacuating mothers and babies to the country. It is expected that the Germans will bomb or gas London and the other cities.'

Tanni stared at her. What on earth did she mean? 'War?' She repeated the unfamiliar English word.

'I'm afraid so. Now, Mrs Zayman, just sign this form and we can send you and your baby to live in a safe place in the country.'

Tanni struggled to understand. 'Away from London?' she asked. How could she possibly go somewhere else? What about Bruno, her parents and the twins? How would she manage without Tante Berthe? Her head swam. She fought back panic and tried hard to make herself understood in English. 'Excuse me, please, but I cannot go. My sisters, my parents, my mother-in-law, they are arriving. I must be here in London. We are to go to Oxford when they come. I cannot –'

'Nonsense, Mrs Zayman.'

Cannot indeed! They seemed to think there was room for every Tom, Dick and Harry in England, Penelope thought crossly. Already the billets on her list were over-crowded and goodwill was stretched to breaking-point. Also, it was getting late and she had eight more families on her list for whom she needed signatures of consent. She looked closely at the girl and her baby. Foreign, but both looked clean. No sores or coughing, the girl's husband working for the War Office. The baby, unlike most of the scrawny London urchins on her list, was well fed and healthy. With the current shortage of billets, Penelope feared it was only a matter of time before one of her colleagues decided that, as she stayed mostly in her London flat, her own large house in Crowmarsh Priors had plenty of room for evacuees.

She decided quickly to billet this girl and her baby with Evangeline before she was landed with some much nastier children. Her dozy daughter-in-law needed something worthwhile to do. With darling Richard away on active service Evangeline had too much time to mope. It was time the girl pulled her socks up and got on with things, now that she had recovered from her miscarriage. Whatever could have possessed Richard to elope with the American floozy and break poor Alice's heart? Penelope bit her lip in annoyance. She could never come up with an answer to that question.

She had tried, she honestly had, for Richard's sake, but languid Evangeline was hopeless as a naval wife, and darling Alice would have been wonderfully sensible and active, a real asset to his career. 'Evangeline reminds one of something rather exotic, like – like an *odalisque*!' she had exclaimed once, unburdening herself to a friend. 'Or a cat,' she added, after a moment. 'She's as secretive as a cat.' And, what was worse, Evangeline was remarkably careless about her dress, never making an effort, wearing any old thing, even Richard's cast-off shirts and pullovers. It came of being American, Penelope supposed. They were an uncivilized lot.

'Too dreadful, darling!' said her friend, sympathetically. 'How fortunate they live in the country and not somewhere like Plymouth, where his superior officers would notice.'

'As would their wives!'

Penelope decided to write Evangeline that evening. She would tell her firmly that it was time she pulled herself together, for Richard's sake. She must think of her duty and prepare to take in an evacuated mother and baby.

An indignant wail recalled Penelope to the dingy parlour and her list of billets. 'Really, Mrs Zayman, it gives us no end of trouble when mothers are so awkward about signing.' Penelope made her tone sharper. 'And I had better tell you, for your own good, that the government is talking of internment for German and Austrian nationals, so if I were you I should sign at once, unless you would prefer internment.'

'Internment?' asked the girl, jiggling the howling baby.

'A camp, where people have to stay during the war.'

'But if I sign this paper I am not going to a camp?'

'Quite!' snapped Penelope, holding out a pen. Her head ached. 'In fact, you will be going to a rather lovely house in Sussex, much better than you might have expected. Count yourself lucky.'

*

Two days later Rabbi Cohen took Tanni to Victoria station, promising that the ladies' committee would notify her as soon as her sisters were found. 'Don't worry, Berthe and Rachel will see to it.' He said Bruno knew where she would be and approved of her going. He and Tante Berthe had talked it over and decided it was a good idea for her to go, especially if it meant she wasn't at risk of internment. He reminded her, in a kindly but serious voice, that she was a wife and mother, that she must try to manage and make the best of things because Bruno's work was very important and some day she would understand. For now she must look after Johnny, stay well and safe, and keep her spirits up. Tanni nodded and promised. 'Good girl,' said the rabbi.

7. East London, Late August 1939

The man who collected rent from the shabby two-up, two-down houses on North Street, near the London docks, made his rounds on Monday, washday, when housewives were certain to be in. Those who had the money ready watched closely while he counted and noted it in his little book, then closed the door behind him with relief. Those who hadn't the right amount wondered desperately what excuse they could use to put off payment till next week.

When Mrs Pigeon went to the door to answer the knock, her face was creased with anxiety. The children in the room behind her held their breath. Their dad must have found where she'd hidden the rent money again. When he laid hands on it he quickly disappeared to the pub or the dog races, leaving the children to whistle for their dinner. He would come home late and shamefaced, unsteady on his legs, and there would be a loud argument, sometimes the sound of a slap. Next day their mum would turn the house upside-down, rooting for something to pawn to Uncle. There wasn't much left.

When she opened the door they stared open-mouthed at the person on the step. 'That's never the rent man!' exclaimed one child. It was a lady, dressed like the Queen in the photos of her in the papers: a smart costume, a hat with little brown and red feathers sticking up at the back, hair nicely dressed under the veil. She had gloves on, a handbag, polished shoes and shiny legs. On North Street women wore thick brown cotton stockings, knotted above the knee and house slippers, even outdoors. The lady sounded like people on the wireless.

The children craned for a better view, while their mother stood solidly, blocking the doorway, an apron wrapped over her faded housedress, holding Violet on her shoulder. The lady had called before but, after what had sounded like an argument, Mum had always shut the door in her face before the children got a glimpse of her. This time, the lady quickly wedged a polished shoe inside the house.

'Mrs Pigeon, this time you really must listen! It's not a question of whether war is coming but when, possibly a matter of days. Registration is vital for all London children so that they can be evacuated to a safe place, out of reach of the enemy. But because you refused to register your children, your neighbours followed your example. There are nearly forty children in this street alone. Once the war starts it will be dangerous, if not impossible, for them to travel. Think of your children, the children on this street, Mrs Pigeon! The government believes the docks in the East End will be the Germans' first target in London. That's very near North Street. Any bombs in this area are likely to hit the gasworks, and if it explodes everything here will disappear in a fireball. The Germans are also expected to use poison gas. It is vital to get the children to safety in time, Mrs Pigeon, before they burn to death –'

'Oi, *Mum*!' There was a chorus of wails, and Mrs Pigeon turned to quell her brood with a frown.

The lady seized the initiative while Mrs Pigeon's back was turned and handed Violet a boiled sweet, which Violet popped into her mouth. People often gave Violet a sweet and Violet had learned that the best way to get another was to smile angelically. 'What a lovely little girl! And a little girl with such pretty blue eyes must be a very good little girl. What is your name, dear? Do you know your name?' The lady held out another sweet.

Violet took it, stuffed it into her cheek with the other, and smiled beatifically on cue. 'Vi'let.'

The lady made a note on her clipboard. 'And do you know how old you are, Violet?'

Violet stuck a grubby finger into her mouth to poke the sweets and shook her head. Probably three, the lady wrote. 'Do you have brothers and sisters, Violet?'

Violet nodded. 'Can you tell me their names, darling? I'll just stay here while I write them down.' Mrs Pigeon turned back, her face like a thundercloud. One of the children nudged another. They waited expectantly.

Violet removed a wet finger from her mouth and confided, 'Elsie's cookin' 'er clothes. We'se 'avin' 'em for our dinner. Mum says ain't nuffink else to sell.'

Mrs Pigeon sighed. She put Violet down. Without giving an inch at the doorway, she began to name all of the children and their ages. 'There's me eldest, that's Bert, who's seventeen, an' 'is brother Terence, who's sixteen. They was taken on at the docks like their dad was before 'is accident. Bit of luck that was, with jobs so scarce nowadays. Me 'usband's leg got crushed under a load and never mended properly, so with 'im poorly I 'ad a right job to manage until the lads found work. But they're good lads, steady, bring their wages 'ome. We can't do without them wages, missus. My Elsie there's fifteen, finished school and all she 'as. She'll be goin' out to work. My 'usband's got 'er a place in the glue factory. She starts next week. We can do with her wages as well, keep a roof over our 'eads, all these mouths to feed. Agnes there, she's a sickly child. We've 'ad the doctor out twice this year for 'er and I don't know 'ow she's to go nowhere. She can't 'ardly leave the chair. Them's the twins, Dick and Willie. They're eight an' full of mischief. That's Jem,' Mum finished, as a baby started to cry. 'My youngest.'

'Mum!' There was a chorus from the dingy room behind her.

'You lot best keep still if you know what's good for you!' she warned. She sounded sullen, as she did when she was forced to do something she didn't want to think about, like the time she'd had to pawn her wedding ring to Uncle for the rent money. She turned back to the door, and although she and the lady lowered their voices, they sounded as if they were arguing.

Elsie frowned at the visitor, sympathizing with her mother. Everyone knew not to call on a Monday, with all of them wrapped in bits and pieces of Mum's old aprons and other scraps to keep them decent while their clothes dried. Elsie herself, in a ragged grey petticoat, stirred the washpot with the broom handle, shoving the rags stained by her monthlies under the grey suds before her brothers saw them and asked what they were. Dick and Willie, each in a pair of Mum's old drawers they had to hold up with one hand, were fighting over a broken ha'penny top with the other. Their noise had woken Jem, who had been sleeping in a drawer on the dresser. Agnes was huddled under a blanket in the armchair, whining that the steam and the smell of boiling soap made her cough, but everything made Agnes cough and mostly the family took no notice.

Violet hadn't been given another sweet and began to shriek for their mother's attention. The lady said, 'Good morning, then,' and Mrs Pigeon shut the door hard.

She turned round with a strange look on her face. 'Bloody Germans! Bloody la-di-da. Blackout, if you please! Blackout curtains, they say! Curtains! And nuffink in the 'ouse but potatoes for dinner – and few enough of them – and the lads and your father home to I don't know what for their tea. Willie, stop larkin' about and get Jem for me, there's a good boy.'

'Cor! Mum said "bloody"!' Astonished, the twins stopped fighting. Their mother was a stickler for what was 'proper'.

Willie picked up the baby and made a face. ''E's weed over everything, Mum.'

Mrs Pigeon put down Violet, whipped off the wet nappy and wrapped the baby's damp bottom in her apron.

'Who was that lady? What's that paper say, then, Mum?'

She held the paper up to the light. Her lips moved as she laboriously spelled out the words. 'Ev-a– somefink. What's that when it's at home?' she muttered. Violet whimpered and reached up to be carried. Mrs Pigeon put Jem on the table in the middle of the room and picked her up again. The baby began to howl. 'Oh, for pity's sake! Agnes, stop coughin' for a minute, do! 'Ere, Elsie, you're the clever one, read us what it says.' She handed

Elsie the paper and began to look for a clean nappy. Violet's blue eyes stared at Elsie over her mother's shoulder.

Mrs Pigeon put Violet down again, then unbuttoned her top to feed the screaming baby. 'Read it to me,' she commanded. 'Agnes, you peel them potatoes *naow*!'

Violet stuck out her tongue at the baby.

'Why can't Elsie ever do it?' wheezed Agnes, but dragged herself to the tiny scullery under the stairs and came back with a tin basin and the potatoes.

'Because the less Elsie 'as to do wiv the dinner the better it'll be, as you well know, my girl. Them potatoes'd be peeled to shreds. Besides, she'll be the only one of us can make sense of whatever it is, seein' as 'ow you've been too bad to go to school and the twins can't no more read than Jem.' Mrs Pigeon tapped the piece of paper the lady had given her. 'Tell us what it says, then, girl.'

Elsie sat down, smoothed the paper on the rickety oilcloth-covered table, and read out slowly,

'Government Eva-evacu-a-tion Scheme
'To ensure the safety of London's children the government has ordered their evacuation to areas outside London considered not to be at risk from the threat of German bombs. Schoolchildren up to the age of fifteen should be registered at their schools, which will oversee their evacuation to locations in the countryside. If your children are not registered and you wish them to be evacuated, the teachers or schoolkeeper will help you. If you do not wish your children to be evacuated you must not send them to school until further notice.'

Mrs Pigeon didn't say anything so Elsie read out the notice a few more times, mimicking the radio voice of the lady in the hat. Hoity-toity. 'Evacuation'. The word had an important, official ring to it.

'Oi, Mum, wot's the lady in the 'at say it was?' asked Willie, none the wiser.

Big square woman though she was, Mrs Pigeon looked smaller suddenly, her shoulders drooping. Her thin hair was straggling down from beneath the knotted kerchief she tied it up in on washdays. When she finally spoke her voice sounded as if it was coming from a distance. 'It means – it means goin' away, like. They say there's goin' to be a war and the 'Uns'll come bombin' like they did in the Great War. Awful, that was.' She rocked Jem. ''Orrible. The fires round 'ere burned and burned. I remember 'ouses and shops an' all collapsed with people still inside, whole families trapped. And the smell, people burnin' . . . and the screamin'. 'Orrible it was. They couldn't get 'em out, you see. She came round 'ere twice before, askin' 'ow many of you was under fifteen. "Well, I can't 'ardly bear to think of it 'appenin' all over again," I says to 'er. "It can't," I says to 'er. "But it will," she says, certain as anyfink. "I fink you can count on it, Mrs Pigeon."

'And she says I'd go with Jem and Violet as they're so young, but it might be they'd have to put us in a different place to the rest of you. But that'd mean leaving your dad and the boys 'ere. An', Elsie, I said you was fifteen, 'cause you are, nearly, but that's too old to be evacu-wossname. I don't know what to do for the best.'

Elsie discovered something on the back of the notice.

'Mum, there's even a list. It says 'ere, "Children must bring their gas masks in case." Ugh! 'Orrible! I 'ate wearin' it! And they need two changes of underwear, a nightdress or pyjamas. What's pyjamas, Mum? And a bar of soap, toothbrush, toothpaste, a towel, a comb and brush, 'andkerchiefs, a warm coat and jumper, a change of socks or stockings, a spare pair of shoes.'

'Each,' said her mother, blankly. Elsie did the mental arithmetic to work out how many bars of soap, how many combs and brushes, how many jumpers would be required, and put down the impossible list with relief. 'That fixes it, then, Mum. None of us can go. We don't 'ave spare shoes or them other things.'

There was a moment's silence. Mrs Pigeon looked at the circle of anxious faces. There wasn't one she felt she could do without for a minute.

"Ow 'ot is fire, then?' asked Willie. 'We can keep a bucket of water by the door.'

'I ain't afraid of no fire,' said Dick, stoutly. 'Nor the 'Uns.'

'Fire,' said Violet, and stuck her finger into her mouth.

A bell clanged in the street and a cart rumbled past.

'Wish we 'ad some sausages, though,' said Dick, who was always hungry. The others nodded.

Mrs Pigeon looked up. 'Them potatoes want boilin'. Agnes, chop up that bit of cabbage left from yesterday. That bell'll be the cat's-meat man. I'll get us some bits before them cats 'ave it all. We want a bit of cheerin' up. We'll 'ave it wiv onion gravy. And we've some mustard powder – we could do wiv a bit of mustard to perk us up. Elsie, you mix up the mustard.'

'No! Elsie makes it lumpy, Mum.'

Mrs Pigeon sighed wearily. 'Elsie, wrap a towel round you and get that washin' out on the line. Jem's no dry nappies left.' She untied her kerchief, extracted a precious shilling from the rent money, which was hidden there, and reknotted it tightly on her forehead.

Out in the street, Penelope Fairfax repinned her hat and bit her lip in frustration. She had personally called on Mrs Pigeon more than once because the woman's neighbours had asked, 'And what do the Pigeons say about it all, missus?' and refused to evacuate their children until they knew.

At the thought of the Pigeons, Penelope wrinkled her nose. The smell in the house had been terrible, not quite masked by the fug of boiling yellow soap. Those two scrawny little boys had scabies, she was sure of it. The child with the cough didn't sound at all well, and Penelope had been relieved when Mrs Pigeon wouldn't let her in. The one they called Violet was a pretty little thing, though. Lovely eyes. Unusual to see a child like that in North Street. She probably had lice in her hair like the rest. Or intestinal worms. Or both.

Endless numbers of children had to be evacuated from cities all over the country and the billeting authorities were desperately short of places for them. Penelope thought guiltily of her own spacious house in Crowmarsh Priors. She would have been happy to turn it over to Richard and darling Alice, then move to London, but had felt obliged to remain in the country to help Evangeline – what a name! – settle in, especially as the girl was expecting a baby. But it had been impossible to share a house with her daughter-in-law, whose lethargy got on her nerves, and she didn't care to share it with the likes of the Pigeon children either, thank you very much. The very thought of them running amok among the chintz and antiques made her shudder. She congratulated herself on having had the foresight to send the foreign girl and her baby down on the train last week. Now if the authorities learned about her house, she could say that Evangeline had her hands full already with evacuees.

Penelope paid no attention to the slip-slap of carpet slippers behind her on the pavement until she felt her arm clutched from behind. A breathless Mrs Pigeon, anxiety etched into her face, gasped, 'Oi, missus, I didn't like to ask in front of the kiddies but what'll become of 'em in this eva-wossname? I don't know what to do for the best, wiv their father only working casual down the docks, on account of 'is leg, and the two eldest can't leave their jobs, but I don't see 'ow I'm to leave 'em be'ind to fend for themselves, only lads they are – and there's me oldest girl, just fifteen. Leavin' 'er alone at that age wivout 'er mother ain't right.'

Penelope sighed. 'Mrs Pigeon, as I've told you already, the government is quite clear that children will be safer outside London. As I explained, they will assemble in the usual way at their schools, and their teachers will accompany each class as they are moved out of London and taken to their billets. You really must put your children first and think of what is best for them, as I'm sure you'll agree. Just sign this form while I see about the arrangements.'

Wearily Penelope checked her list. The available billets were already overcrowded and it was clear that many people who had signed up for 'one little girl aged five or six, clean and well behaved' would have to be persuaded to cope with 'six boys, aged between two and fourteen' or 'three girls and four boys, ages unknown'. But duty was duty. 'You have three who could go to the country-side – that would be Agnes, and the twin boys. We've room for three in, er, Yorkshire, on a farm – wonderful place for children. You could be evacuated with the two youngest, though it might not be to the same place as the other three as spaces are short. However, there is a billet near Scarborough.' Penelope knew perfectly well that the elderly couple had specified 'room for one quiet, nicely behaved little girl' but they would have to take in Mrs Pigeon, Violet and Jem. Perhaps they would warm to Violet, so long as she didn't howl.

Mrs Pigeon looked blank.

'I'm sure your husband and the two elder boys will fend for themselves somehow. Now, your eldest daughter – Elsie, is it? She's left school. Rather difficult as she falls between the cracks, so to speak. Hmm. Normally we can only billet schoolchildren but it's just possible that your Elsie would do as an under-housemaid for a friend of mine in the country. A certain Lady Marchmont. She's widowed. Quite the backbone of the village.'

Mrs Pigeon had no idea about Yorkshire and this Scar-place, but at the suggestion that Elsie should take up a post as a housemaid, her face lit up. 'Elsie go into service? Why,' she said thinking fast, 'before my 'usband got 'er the factory job we used to talk of Elsie doin' just that!'

She crossed her fingers behind her back. 'Course Elsie don't 'ave no trainin' but, if I say it meself, she don't 'alf take to trainin'.' She crossed her fingers tighter. Once Elsie was in the country, surely they'd have to keep her. If there was a war.

A similar thought was passing through Penelope's mind. She knew Muriel Marchmont well – so well, in fact, that the old lady had taken it upon herself to keep Penelope informed about what Evangeline was or was not doing. However, her last letter had mentioned that she and Mrs Gifford were at their wits' end since the last housemaid had left to be married. It left an opening of sorts for an untrained girl like Elsie. On the other hand, if that lank-haired girl stirring the washpot knew one end of a duster from another, Penelope was Queen Mary.

Mrs Pigeon sensed hesitation and seized her advantage. 'Elsie'd be out of 'arm's way there. She's a good girl, mind you, is Elsie, but round 'ere you don't like to leave 'em on their own at fifteen just when boys try to give 'em ideas and they get their 'eads turned. It'd be a load off me mind to 'ave her there,' she urged, 'so's I can think about what to do wiv the others. But . . . maybe she wouldn't suit the lady.'

'There's going to be war, Mrs Pigeon. We will all have to make sacrifices,' said Penelope crisply, noticing the time. She was overdue at Headquarters with her lists. 'If I speak to Lady Marchmont personally, I'm sure she will do her bit. I shall register Agnes and the twins at once, and let you know tomorrow where you and the two youngest are to go.' She thrust a form and a pen into Mrs Pigeon's hand. 'Kindly sign here. Now if you will excuse me I am late.' She snatched the signed form from Mrs Pigeon and dashed for the waiting WVS car.

'When are they to go?' Mrs Pigeon called.

Penelope turned briefly. 'On Friday, end of the week. Remember, at school first thing, packed and ready. And don't worry, Mrs Pigeon, we shall all pull together and it will be fine. Cheerio.'

Mrs Pigeon's shoulders slumped. She'd done it. She hoped everything would turn out for the best. Her Elsie would be settled in a respectable household, away from that sly boy Bernie who followed Uncle everywhere. She had spotted him hanging about in the street outside their house and suspected he was watching for Elsie. Mrs Pigeon had learned a thing or two during her marriage, and she could tell that Bernie was a wrong 'un.

And if Elsie went off to be a housemaid they'd have to feed her. That was something. Which made her remember her hungry brood at home. She hurried after the cat's-meat man.

8. Crowmarsh Priors,
November 1939

Two months of living on and off in the middle-of-bleedin'-nowhere-Crowmarsh-bleedin'-Priors with the local police constable and his new wife had convinced Bernie Carpenter that the country was worse than prison. He had never imagined that a place so dull and quiet existed. He missed Bow and Shoreditch. He missed the excitement of the dog track and the bookmakers who deferred to Uncle, the dance halls to which he accompanied Uncle and stood by importantly holding the satchel while they filled it with notes, their protection money, and nodded to 'Uncle's boy'. He missed the dance hostesses with painted faces and silk stockings, who all knew Uncle and smelt nice. They brought Bernie ginger beer and tousled his hair and said they were waiting for him to grow up. He missed the markets where stall-holders shouted their wares and tossed him an apple while Uncle checked the stolen merchandise hidden under the carts. He missed 'smash and grab', too, the night-time excitement of breaking into a shop or a house and scurrying off with a bag of valuables, listening for the lookout to yell, 'Fire!' when he spotted the police. But, most of all, he missed the dark little room under the pawnshop, the smell of ink, the presses and making pound notes, doing the watermark over and over again, practising with the tints on different currencies that had foreign writing and funny old codgers in beards, while Uncle looked critically over his shoulder and showed him how the smallest details made all the difference. 'That'll do' was high praise – Uncle never wasted words. 'You've got the gift, lad.'

Since he'd been in Crowmarsh Priors – he didn't know where it was exactly or he'd leave – they'd come to fetch him each day and he was driven ever so far to somewhere else in the country. Once he got there, though, he had to admit it was a bit like old times, which was nice. The geezers there didn't give much in the way of praise, but he wasn't stupid. Way he saw it, if they were depending on a sixteen-year-old boy to forge their notes, passports and other gear, and paying him to do it, as well as giving Constable Barrows money for his board, maybe it was their way of saying he had the gift. They talked funny, posh, like, saying one thing and meaning another, but they weren't a bad lot. He'd almost stopped nicking their cigarettes, lighters and the odd bit of money.

But there was nowhere to spend it, was there? He wandered aimlessly round the village, not knowing where to put himself.

When he spotted the scrawny girl from North Street polishing the door brass at the big house on the edge of the green, he could hardly believe his eyes. What in the name of Moses was the Pigeon girl doing there? He stepped behind a giant laurel bush beside the gate and watched her. She rubbed her eyes and swiped the back of her hand across her nose, like she'd been crying. She must have gone into service at the big house. He couldn't believe his luck at seeing a familiar face. Specially her.

And her old dragon of a mother wouldn't be around to stop him talking to her.

For days after he had seen her, Bernie hung about outside the gates of the house as often as he dared, waiting for her to come out. They must have kept her hard at work because she rarely appeared. Instead he saw a large old lady with white hair and a walking-stick who stuck her nose in the air like she could smell something bad. Occasionally he saw a pretty girl coming or going. She had the sort of brownish red hair that Uncle liked, and she dressed like a film star, in furs, little hats and high heels. The gentleman from Gracecourt Hall called for her most days, with a roadster full of friends, and they would speed away, laughing, down the drive. Just the sort of girl Uncle would see set up well in St John's Wood or even Kensington.

Thinking about Uncle made him sad. Constable Barrows had told him, not unkindly, that Uncle was ill in prison, too ill for anyone, let alone a lad, to visit him. However, when Bernie had asked him who the big house belonged to, the policeman had lost his genial expression, grabbed him by the collar and said, 'One word of warning, you little weasel. Don't think of trying anything at Glebe House. None of your shenanigans there. Lady Marchmont'd have your guts for garters. Put you in handcuffs, I will.'

So he'd had to bide his time. Eventually he saw her again. Only the top of her head was visible as she crouched in the tall weeds in the churchyard behind the old stone tomb that had on it the fellow in armour with his legs crossed, his sword and shield on his stomach.

The sound of her blubbering had brought Bernie up short. She had on a black dress, too big for her, a huge white apron and a little white frilled cap on the back of her head. Talking to the dance-hall hostesses was easy because they started it, teasing him, like, leaning close and patting his leg. But what did you say to a girl? He kicked a loose stone. 'Ow,' he said loudly, hoping she'd look up. She didn't.

Nothing else occurred to him so he kicked another stone that ricocheted off the tomb. This time she must have heard, because she hiccuped and turned her head. Her nose was running and her eyes were red. There was a red welt on her cheek, as if someone had slapped her.

'Cold day for cryin', innit?' he remarked.

'Bugger off,' she muttered, and wiped her nose on the hem of her apron, which was wrapped twice round her little waist.

He grinned. He had to watch his language around Constable Barrows and his wife.

Inspiration struck. Constable Barrows's young wife, brimming with enthusiasm for housekeeping in her newly married state, had been horrified by the state of Bernie's paltry belongings, spread out in the spare room, and had furnished him with a pile of her husband's old shirts and handkerchiefs, freshly washed, starched and ironed. Now he felt for the handkerchief in his pocket. ''Ere, you'll be wantin' this.' He moved closer and held it out to her. 'Go on, it's clean.'

'Was it you washed it?' she asked ungraciously, but took it. Her hands were red and chapped. She gave a great shuddering sigh as she mopped her face.

'Go on, blow,' he encouraged her, and she did, a great honking sound.

'I seen you before,' he said, squatting down beside her.

'I know,' she said dully. 'I seen you too. You're the lad what's livin' at Constable Barrows's.'

'No, afore that. I mean North Street. You're one of them Pigeons, ain't you?' She nodded. ''Ere, let's get off the ground. We can sit on this.' He hauled himself up on to the knight's tomb. It leaned a bit but it was dry. He held out a hand. She got up, brushed down her skirt and apron, then repinned her crooked cap. 'Come on. Mind that skull sticks out at the end.' He scooted over to make room for her, then took out a packet of Woodbines and offered her one. 'Smoke?'

'No, fanks.' Up close her face was heart-shaped and pale, except for the mark on her right cheek.

Elsie watched him strike a match expertly on the side of the tomb and light his cigarette. Up close his profile was lean and sharp-featured as he drew on the cigarette like an old man, holding it between thumb and forefinger. A shock of brown hair fell untidily over his forehead, almost down to his nose. There was something restless and alert about him – even sitting still his eyes darted about. He reminded her of the ferret her dad had once brought home, having bought it from a man in the pub. It had escaped when he took it out of his pocket to show the children. Mum had screamed as it scampered across the floor, then chased it into the street with her broom.

'You're Uncle's boy,' she said, remembering the day Mum had summoned the pawnbroker because she had to sell her wedding ring. Many people living on North

Street made furtive trips to Uncle's narrow little shop, but Mum hadn't wanted to go there in case anyone saw she was pawning her heavy gold ring, the last badge of her respectability. Instead she had sent word asking Uncle to call on her. When he came the children had been banished upstairs but Elsie had crept down and seen Uncle and the lad who carried his case. The lad had caught her eye and winked as she peeped round the corner of the stairs. She had grinned and winked back before Mum saw her and ordered her back upstairs. After that she had seen him in North Street, but Mum had always made sure he didn't talk to her.

'Well, s'pose I am.' He looked down modestly.

In North Street Uncle was a celebrity, with expensive suits, a motor and soft-spoken good manners. He raised his hat to the ladies, bought rounds of drinks in the pub every Saturday night, wore cologne you could smell a mile off and was said to keep a fancy woman. No one would have dreamed of grassing on Uncle when the police came looking for stolen property or investigating a bookmaking racket. But forgery was his main business. Uncle was an artist, it was said, not just your common criminal. The local lads envied Bernie his luck in being chosen as Uncle's apprentice. Even the Italian gangs in Clerkenwell, the worst of the worst, respected Uncle.

''E's looked after me since I was a little 'un. Me dad was gone in the Navy, and then me mum died. They was going to send me to the 'ome, but 'cause I used to run errands for 'im, penny a time, Uncle said I seemed like a likely lad and 'e took me in. Told 'em me dad was 'is bruvver.'

'Was he?'

'Not really, but they don't care, long as they're not bothered. Uncle treated me proper, never lost 'is temper. But 'e'd keep me up all night learnin' the trade. I'd copy things an' all, pound notes, five-pound notes, till you didn't know which was real an' which weren't. The thing you got to remember is, never make 'em perfect. It's the imperfections marks the genuine ones. 'E said I were a good learner.' He cleared his throat. 'A credit to the profession, 'e said I was, a great credit...'

He stopped. Elsie was gazing at him, wide-eyed. She was a little thing, but it felt nice to be making an impression on a girl.

'Why ain't you wiv 'im now, then?'

A shadow passed over Bernie's face. 'Uncle's in prison again, ain't he? That's why. Sick, too, wiv 'is lungs, somefink. Fevers. Coughs up blood. That's why I'm doin' the work 'stead of 'im.' His thin chest swelled. 'They say they've never seen anybody good as me – keep me at it, too, they do, I can tell you.' He wasn't supposed to talk about it – had been warned never to talk about it or else – but he wanted to keep her looking at him in that admiring way.

'What work? Who says they never seen?'

'The government, I fink.' A note of uncertainty crept into his voice.

'The *wot*?'

'Truf is, I dunno exactly. They can't be some kind of gang, can they, if they come straight to the police station? I were in the station at the time, 'eard 'em askin' for Uncle. Copper says Uncle's dyin' in prison, "where 'e" –

copper nods at me – "looks like joinin' 'im in no time, 'cause Uncle taught that little sewer rat all 'is tricks. 'E's been caught nickin' from shops, runnin' for the Italians, smash an' grab. Couldn't make none of the charges stick," the copper says, "but 'e's Uncle's lad, all right. Only a matter of time before we gets 'im sent to an approved school." 'Earin' Uncle's so ill, they looked at each other and swore a bit, said what was they supposed to do now? One of 'em asked the coppers, innocent, like, did they think Uncle 'ad taught me *all* 'is tricks? The coppers laughed, said I knew as much as Uncle about anyfink criminal.

'The one what 'ad asked said in that case they'd no choice but to give me a try. They showed the coppers some bit of paper and the coppers looked like they didn't believe it. Then one grabbed me off the bench, mad as 'ell. He tells me to be'ave or 'e'll cuff me to kingdom come. Then the geezers put me in their motor and we drive up west in London, to a big buildin' with secretaries an' offices an' all. First thing, they 'ad a row with some other bloke, who said not to credit the coppers and 'ow old was I anyway and stop wastin' their time. Finally, to settle the argument, they takes me into a room. Uncle would've thought 'e was in 'eaven – engravin' things, paper, presses, like you never seen. Gave me some pass-ports, some foreign notes and official-lookin' papers, said could I copy any of those? I were at it all night but it were easy. Next mornin' they came back an' took 'em away. They come back, they says, "By George! Bank of England couldn't tell the difference!"'

Elsie was staring, eyes like saucers. He puffed out his

chest a little. 'They goes off to get a cup of tea, and quick, like, I grabs the five-pound note they'd given me to copy, thinkin' I'd done them enough of a good turn, and skipped out. They sent the coppers after me. Blow me if they didn't find me in Berwick Street market. One copper says to the other, "They bleedin' want 'im back!" In the end they sent me to live with Constable Barrows, supposed to keep me out of trouble. Now they come and get me, I does the work, they pays me, takes me back to Constable Barrows. They don't care what else I do, long as I keep workin' for them. The look on the copper's puss! But can't none of them coppers do anyfink about it. Blimey.' He chuckled and straightened up. 'Uncle would say I landed on me feet.'

Elsie regarded him steadily. He would swagger when he walked, she was sure of it. She also knew instinctively that if Mum knew he was talking to her she'd have her broom out, smacking him into the street same way she'd chased out the ferret. Elsie perked up. For the first time since she'd arrived in the country, her homesickness eased a little. 'What's your whole name, then?'

'Bernard Carpenter – Bernie, really. I know yours already. It's Elsie.'

''Ow old are you, then?'

'Nearly seventeen. Older 'n you. But not so pretty.'

Elsie tossed her head. 'Sauce! Well, I'm fifteen. What's it like at Constable Barrows's?'

He lit another cigarette. 'It's all right. You know. They 'aven't been married long so they're still lovey-dovey. And Mrs Barrows don't 'alf feed you! We 'ave a cooked break-fast with an egg an' all an' dinner an' then a big tea wiv proper bread and butter, sometimes scones and jam and last Saturday tinned pilchards! Then,' he added as casually as possible, 'on Sundays we 'ave a roast dinner wiv beef an' roast potatoes an' Yorkshire puddin', an' there's bread and drippin' for Sunday tea.' He drummed his heels on the tomb, a faraway look in his eye. 'Bread and drippin's me favourite. You gone into service, then?'

'Evacuated to be 'ousemaid for Lady Marchmont.' Elsie sighed and rubbed her right cheek.

'I seen the 'ouse. The old bat in the uniform looks like she's suckin' a lemon.'

'That's the 'ousekeeper, Mrs Gifford. She's a 'oly terror.'

'And the old lady who acts like she's the Queen. Is the girl 'er daughter?'

'Oh, that's Miss Frances. She's Lady Marchmont's goddaughter, whatever that is. She got into trouble in London, 'ad 'er picture in the papers, an' they made 'er come 'ere to keep out of trouble, but she's taken up wiv the crowd at Whatchmacallit 'All. She sneaks out at night when Lady Marchmont's gone to bed. Then they drive to Brighton and go to nightclubs. I go down to unlatch the window very early in the morning so she can climb back in wivout 'er ladyship knowin'. She's got ever such pretty things to wear.

'But Miss Frances is a good sort, the only one's been nice to me, asked me about me family, if they was still in London. When me older brothers wrote last month and said they'd enlisted, I wanted to send a letter to say cheerio and wish 'em good luck but I didn't know where to send it. I felt bad 'cause Mum wouldn't like 'em to go off wivout all of us sayin' goodbye. When I told 'er, Miss

Frances went straight to the telephone an' rang this person an' that person, even though Lady Marchmont was lookin' at 'er like thunder, till she turned up their address in the Navy. Men send her flowers an' chocolates – she gives 'em to me sometimes.'

For a minute Elsie was silent. Then she went on, 'There's ever such a lot of things in that 'ouse want polishin' or dustin' or puttin' away or gettin' out, an' it's scrub this and wash that an' sweep the other an' make the fires or black the grates, everythin' all proper. I never do things right an' the 'ousekeeper boxes me ears.' Elsie rubbed her cheek again.

Uncle didn't hold with hitting women, and Bernie felt a flash of anger with the housekeeper. 'Can't you go back 'ome?'

Tears welled again in Elsie's eyes. 'They ain't at 'ome now, are they? All evacuated, that's what. Somewhere called Yorkshire. The people they're billeted wiv were cross because Agnes and the boys didn't bring none of the things they was supposed to, except their gas masks. First thing, they cut off all Agnes's 'air an' shaved the twins' 'eads. Lice, they said. Agnes looked in the mirror at 'erself an' nearly died of coughin' brought on by cryin'. Mum wrote to me about it, wasn't 'alf cross they didn't tell 'er first, bein' as 'ow she's only in the next town with Vi'let an' Baby Jem. Agnes 'ates it where she is but they say she 'as to make do for the time bein'. The people Mum's billeted with don't like 'er usin' the kitchen an' their pots an' pans, an' she an' the woman argue about who's to tidy up until Vi'let 'owls. The man 'as asked them to move Mum somewhere else.'

Bernie was at sea with such a litany of domestic difficulties but he wanted to comfort her. 'You and me got to stick togevver and be friends. 'Ere, you said you like chocolate. I got a bit of Cadbury's.' Elsie's face brightened. He took a penny bar from his pocket, broke it in two and gave her the bigger half.

'Ta very much,' she said. She closed her eyes as the sweetness melted thickly across her tongue. She smiled in spite of herself.

She looked very pretty, smiling like that, Bernie thought. 'That's better,' he said, watching a rim of chocolate form round her top lip. He watched as her tongue crept out to lick it off. He wondered what it would be like to lick it off for her, then kiss her like he'd seen some of the men kissing the dance-hall hostesses. The thought of it sent a jolt through him. He drew in his breath so sharply that he startled her.

Her eyes flew open. 'Chocolate's one of my favourite fings,' she said. 'It's on my list.'

'Your what?'

'I got a list of fings I like to fink about when I go to sleep. Nice fings. Lace 'andkerchiefs. Penny buns. Silk stockin's.'

'Oh.' He thought about this for a minute. 'Are people on it?'

'Of course! Mum and Vi'let always was, but lately the boys are too, and yesterday I decided even Agnes is.'

'You'd be on my list, if I 'ad one.' He leaned closer, unable to resist touching the chocolate shadow on her lower lip with his forefinger.

Suddenly Elsie realized the lad was breathing funny.

There was a strange look on his face and it was now very close to hers. Quickly she jumped off the tomb. 'Blimey! Nearly gone tea-time. I 'ave to run – got to lay the tea things or Mrs Gifford'll box me ears again for bein' late. I'll wash your 'andkerchief an' give it back.'

He wanted to tell her to keep it but, just in time, realized it would be a way to see her again. 'Ta. Shall I see you 'ere, then? Tomorrow?'

'I don't mind.' She ran for the big house across the green, her little dark-clad figure merging with the dusk. The apron flapped white until she disappeared through a door in the garden wall.

9. Crowmarsh Priors, Late November 1939

It was a grey morning, rain beating dismally against the windows, and the morning room was cold. As usual, Elsie had neglected to lay and light the fire. Muriel Marchmont sat glumly at her desk, marvelling that she, who had never had children, now had three girls on her hands – three girls at a Very Awkward Stage Indeed. Girls, these days, didn't do as they were told, and she was exhausted with trying to do her duty by the thankless creatures.

First, there was poor, jilted Alice, whose mother refused to stir off her sofa all day and ordered Alice about until the girl was as limp as a tea-towel. All the useful tips Muriel had given her about how to make more of herself had been ignored – no wonder the young vicar took little notice of her. Mrs Osbourne, dreadful, selfish woman, was too busy complaining about her health to spare a thought for her daughter. Like far too many men, in Muriel's opinion, the late vicar had married beneath him for the sake of a pretty face.

Her goddaughter was even more vexing. Frances had been sent to stay at Glebe House because, lacking a mother, she needed female supervision and, her father had stressed, a firm hand: she had been running wild in London with a fast set of unsuitable young men. However, Tudor Falconleigh had failed to explain how Muriel was supposed to chaperone Frances, who now spent most of her time with Hugo de Balfort and his friends at Gracecourt Hall, or, she suspected, gadding about to nightclubs in Brighton. She had tried to put her foot down but Frances did much as she pleased.

This trouble with Elsie was the last straw!

Pen in hand and a fresh sheet of monogrammed cream writing-paper before her, Muriel struggled to master her irritation and compose her note to Penelope Fairfax.

My dear Penelope,

I regret to inform you that despite our best efforts for the past three months, Elsie Pigeon falls far short of what is desired in a housemaid. So much so, in fact, that I fear the arrangement must end at once. At first there was the matter of Elsie's intestinal worms and lice – though naturally Gifford coped, with her customary efficiency. Despite her efforts to train Elsie, though, things have gone from bad to worse.

The girl cannot learn to dust, polish, clean the grates, make a bed, or sweep a carpet properly. She cannot even wash a teacup without breaking it. She eats nothing but bread and jam, sometimes until she is ill, and cries in the night for 'Mum' and 'Vilet', who, I am told, is the youngest of her sisters. However, since we are at war, Gifford and I felt it our duty to make the best of things.

Little did we imagine there could be worse to come. Elsie has acquired a follower. She has been keeping company with a most undesirable young man, billeted in the village with Constable Barrows, in lieu, I understand, of being sent to prison. Elsie insists he is a friend from the dreadful part of London she calls home, but all Gifford has been able to discover is that he is an orphan brought up among criminals. The young man seems to

come and go at will, disappearing for days at a time, and if we
are all murdered in our beds I suppose we can thank the
authorities instead of the Germans.

So, I regret to say that, unless you can make other arrange-
ments for her, Elsie will be on the London train tomorrow.

Yours ever,

Muriel Marchmont

As she sealed the envelope there was a clatter of high heels on the stairs, then Frances breezed into the morning room in a cloud of Vol de Nuit, cosy in a ribbon-trimmed tweed coat and skirt, her fur draped round her shoulders. She was holding a hat trimmed with blue velvet flowers that matched her eyes. Rather *soignée* for a rainy Thursday in Crowmarsh Priors, thought her godmother, sourly.

'I say, Aunt Muriel, I went looking for a biscuit just now and found Elsie crying her eyes out in the scullery. She says she's being sent home. Whatever for, poor little mouse?' Frances stood before the mirror above the empty fireplace and adjusted her hat to an angle over one eye.

'If you got up in time for breakfast you'd have no need of biscuits, my dear. "Poor little mouse" indeed! Elsie, I'm sorry to say, is on the verge of ruin with some boy who would be in an approved school if the police had any idea of their duty. The housekeeper made a shocking discovery in her room.'

'Gracious! What?'

'Silk stockings, if you must know, chocolates. Scent!'

Frances turned her head this way and that, checking the effect of the hat. It would never do for Elsie to leave. She and Elsie were partners in crime: Elsie crept bravely

140

past the snoring Mrs Gifford to unlock the front door on the nights Frances went to Brighton and sneaked in before dawn. She returned the favour by helping Elsie to escape on errands to the village when they spotted her young man lurking near the laurel bush. She had given Elsie a becoming cardigan, two lace handkerchiefs, a bottle of lavender water far too insipid for herself and some face powder. Then, prompted by a new glow in Elsie's face, she had advised her not to let the lad she was keeping company with take liberties. Elsie had winked and said, 'Course not! I'd never! But I lets 'im fink he might, next time!'

'Very clever, Elsie darling, but do be careful . . .'

'Oh! I gave the stockings and things to Elsie,' Frances said quickly. 'She's been doing extra things for me, errands, laundering and mending, you know.'

'I must say, my dear, I had no idea Elsie was capable of anything so useful.'

Frances tweaked the little veil. 'Well, she's so good with my washing. And I gave her the stockings because she admired them. I've loads, you know, and one of Hugo's friends gave me an absolutely monstrous box of chocolates. Naturally I can't eat them, if I'm to keep my figure, and you mustn't eat them with your blood pressure, Aunt Muriel. And I don't think the boy can be as bad as all that. Elsie knew him in London. He was brought up by his uncle.'

'That's not the half of it, according to Mrs Gifford,' said her godmother, darkly.

Frances snapped open her handbag and rummaged for her lipstick. 'In fact I think he must be a good sort, really.

He's doing war work. Although it must be rather hush-hush, because –'

'War work? Preposterous! Whatever gave you such an idea?'

'Elsie said he goes off from time to time with what she calls toffs. Then when I was out for a walk last Sunday I passed Constable Barrows's cottage and was surprised to see a motor-car pull up, rather like the one from the Admiralty that calls for Father. I even recognized the driver, though it seemed odd he wasn't in uniform and pretended not to see me when I waved. I assumed they must want Constable Barrows for something, although why they would send an official car for a country constable I can't imagine. Anyway, the boy came out, got in and was driven away. There was another man in the back seat with him. Curious, isn't it?'

'From what I hear that boy's the dregs of the criminal classes and the girl's a useless baggage. The sooner she's sent packing the better.'

'Oh, please, Aunt Muriel! Elsie's a pet, and it would be too dreadful to send her back to the slum they live in. You mustn't! Her mother, younger brothers and sisters were evacuated up north, her older brothers have enlisted in the Navy, so she would be alone at home with her father. Elsie says he drinks and disappears for days at a time. Surely it's your duty to – to Penelope Fairfax to keep her here for a bit longer.'

Muriel Marchmont frowned. Poor Penelope was saddled with that dreadful daughter-in-law.

Frances rushed on: 'When we had drinks at the Fairfaxes' last time Richard was home on leave, his wife told me Elsie's made friends with the foreign girl billeted there.' Frances rooted in her handbag again. 'And Elsie says she's applied to become a land girl now that Hugo and Leander have agreed to take them on at the home farm – the men have joined up or been conscripted. They turned her down at first, because Elsie's so young, but she begged them to ask Penelope about it, and they did. Penelope's promised to see to it when she has time. Sending Elsie back to London now will only add to the WVS's problems. Penelope said she had a frightful time persuading people like the Pigeons to evacuate their children in the first place and now they're tearing their hair out because so many are coming back. People don't believe there'll be any poison-gas attacks.'

Muriel threw up her hands. On top of everything else, war was so unsettling for everyone. Normal life had been turned upside-down. Girls doing men's work, driving tractors and mucking out stables, and now there was a foreign child bride who didn't speak English, with a baby in tow, living in the village. So many people had poured into England and no one was bothering to find out if they were Bolsheviks or Jews or anything else dangerous. When Sir Humphrey Marchmont had been alive, he and his wife had seen a great deal of Archibald Ramsay MP, and had sympathized with the stand his Nordic League had taken on the need to resist the Jewish stranglehold on northern Europe. It was ridiculous of the authorities to discourage the League, she believed.

Now, of course, with the war on, she felt a twinge of pity for the women with their ragged headscarves and big-eyed children she saw on newsreels, driven out of their homes by the Nazis with only the clothes they stood up in, but they had undoubtedly brought it on themselves. And she didn't see why foreigners should be allowed to disrupt the domestic lives of people who lived quietly in the country. Particularly when she had shouldered the burden of responsibility for girls whose mothers had manifestly shirked theirs.

She thought of Alice with approval. At least one girl understood duty. If only Frances would stop gadding about and follow Alice's good example. She could learn such a lot from her.

'I'm just off to Gracecourt, Aunt Muriel.' Frances yawned, then looked at her little watch. 'Bridge, luncheon. Hugo's friends have mostly gone but we can make up two tables. Leander says it amuses him to have young people around.' She pulled a lipstick out of her bag and applied it carefully in the mirror. The prospect of the day before her was not very exciting. In fact, it was exactly like a great many other days, but she couldn't think of any other way of passing the time.

Muriel Marchmont watched disapprovingly as her goddaughter tucked the pretty leather bag under her arm and drew on her pale kid gloves as if she hadn't a care in the world. It came from a foreign education. She had been expelled from a series of sound boarding-schools in Devon and Wiltshire, chosen personally by her godmother. Finally, and against her advice, Tudor Falconleigh had sent Frances to a French finishing-school for three years. Frances had stuck it out because he had promised her a shopping spree in Paris if she did. She had returned to England in time for her début with a near-perfect command of French and equipped with an extravagant supply of day frocks, ballgowns, shoes and fetching hats that had cost her father a fortune.

Soon, however, she was showing signs that she had inherited from her French mother the dangerous something that turned men's heads, the same unfortunate something that had bewitched stolid Tudor Falconleigh into his too-brief marriage. It had got Frances into scrapes in London with all the wrong sort of men, and now it was having a similar effect on the men in the village, from the vicar to Leander de Balfort. Muriel intended to tell Tudor bluntly that their only hope was to get Frances married off before she was utterly disgraced and no one would have her.

She couldn't help noticing that, compared to Frances in her fetching outfits, Alice looked dowdier than ever, in her jumpers, pinnies and too-tight headscarves. She sighed, thinking of the luncheon party at Gracecourt to which she had taken Alice. It had not been a success. Alice had been seated between Hugo and a drawling fellow with a title and a monocle. She had been wearing too much rouge and a drab frock so awful that Muriel had suspected it had once belonged to Mrs Osbourne. After three nervously downed glasses of sherry, Alice had been red in the face and had talked a little too loudly about her late father's interest in Sussex history, then told a long, rambling story about a gang of smugglers and their underground tunnels.

The titled man had soon grown bored with the impromptu history lesson and turned to the vivacious girl on his left, leaving Hugo to struggle on with Alice. Bless him, he had pretended to be interested, which encouraged Alice to talk steadily until they left. Muriel had been silent with despair all the way home.

Alice, she had to admit, lacked sparkle. Frances, on the other hand, had far too much. How unfair life was. It occurred to her that Frances was just the person to take Alice in hand. Surely she could work a little change in Alice's appearance. Nothing too drastic – just enough to open Oliver's eyes.

'You should stop gadding about and take on some war work, Frances. Perhaps give dear Alice Osbourne a hand. She hardly stops to draw breath, though one wonders why she has quite so much thrust upon her, poor thing. Teaching, clothing drives, knitting circles, first aid, not to mention nursing that tiresome mother. She ought to be married. That nice young Oliver Hammet should marry too. So suitable, really, a vicar's daughter becoming a vicar's wife. But he . . . If only Alice looked a little more . . . A lily in need of gilding, so to speak. Perhaps you could smarten her up, my dear. Oliver would be bound to come to his senses.'

To Frances's relief, Hugo's roadster pulled into the drive at Glebe House. 'Oh, I know you wanted me to be friends with Alice and I tried but, truly, she's too, too tedious. Can't stick her. Must dash, Aunt Muriel.' Frances blew her a kiss and disappeared. A few moments later, the car pulled out of the drive, gravel crunching.

That Hugo was paying Frances what in Muriel Marchmont's day had been called 'marked attentions' cheered her and took her mind off Alice. Such attentions indicated that a proposal was in the offing, she thought, and marriage would steady them both. Hugo would buckle down to his responsibilities on the estate and Frances would soon be occupied with their children. She ought to write Tudor at once to let him know which way the wind was blowing. To avoid delays after Hugo had popped the question, his lawyers might as well look at the question of marriage settlements now. Leander was far too impractical to take the initiative there but Hugo needed money and Muriel thought how fortunate it was that Frances would inherit a considerable fortune on her marriage. Leander had never lived up to the responsibilities of the estate, which had been impoverished when he inherited, thanks to his grandfather's gambling and a lifetime's devotion to a series of actresses.

Leander had married well, but instead of ploughing his late wife's considerable fortune back into the estate, he had chosen to indulge his aesthetic instincts instead. He had squandered endless sums on his flamboyant projects at Gracecourt – hence the Chinese pagoda, the deer park stocked with small Japanese deer that had soon died, the tennis courts, and the latest dramatic scheme to redesign a Capability Brown lake as a series of shallow, modern rectangular pools to the specifications of a flamboyant, self-styled 'horticultural artist' with a velvet waistcoat and a foreign accent. Before the shooting luncheon Leander had taken his guests to see them. 'Too thrillingly exotic! So modern!' they had gushed, and gave the 'artist' a little round of applause. One of the illustrated papers had even taken photographs for a feature article.

To Muriel Marchmont they were big, flat and strange. 'So unnecessary!' she had muttered, under her breath. She had noticed, with surprise, that the house was in a shocking state. She had spotted broken panes in the leaded windows, woodworm in the Tudor linen-fold panelling, and the long gallery ceiling sagged under patches of damp. The drawing-room curtains were decidedly moth-eaten and there were pale rectangles on the walls where paintings had hung – sold, she imagined, to pay for Leander's ill-conceived schemes and Hugo's fees at Eton and Oxford, then his travels.

All most unwise, in Muriel Marchmont's opinion. The de Balforts had been at Crowmarsh Priors for centuries and the business of Leander's life, or perhaps Hugo's now, was to ensure they remained there. It was Hugo's plain duty to marry without wasting any more time, and to take an English wife with money and breeding, produce a son at once and pull the estate together before taxes ate everything up.

Frances would inherit her mother's money when she married and the Falconleigh money when her father died. As for breeding, although her mother had been French, the Falconleighs were not to be sneezed at. Muriel Marchmont hated to think that poor Hugo might be forced to look for an American heiress, like Winston's mother. Or that parvenu Nancy Astor. And one American in Crowmarsh Priors was quite enough.

She considered how best she could prod the young people along the paths she had chosen for them. Not for the first time she reflected on her will. She had no children and, other than Oliver Hammet, no relatives. She had always intended to leave her money, the house and her shares to Oliver. Then he could marry Alice. Of course, he already had the vicarage to offer Alice as a home, but Glebe House was far grander. Besides, Muriel liked to imagine Alice sitting in this room each morning, beneath the portrait of herself as a young married woman wearing pearls and court dress, and remembering her fondly. In the fullness of time Alice and Oliver would probably name a daughter Muriel . . .

As for Frances, Muriel decided it was incumbent on her to leave her jewellery to the future Lady de Balfort, with the contents of Glebe House, except for the morning-room furniture, and her portrait, of course. At Gracecourt, heaven knew, they could use her things – even the furniture was falling to pieces. And there was no point in leaving jewellery to Alice, who would look like a donkey in her pearls.

She shoved aside the letter to Penelope Fairfax and took a fresh sheet of cream writing-paper. She would dispatch a letter to Tudor at once. And another to her solicitor, instructing him to call on her as soon as convenient as she wished to discuss a few new alterations to her will.

She had drawn up an inventory of her jewellery before her solicitor's last visit. Where *had* she put it? She rifled through a mass of papers on the desk without finding it. Where, for that matter, had she put her jewel chest in which she kept all but the few items she wore every day? The key wasn't here either. She vaguely recalled hiding it somewhere as a precaution, in case Elsie's follower tried to burgle Glebe House. Perhaps her memory wasn't what it had been. But what was?

10. Crowmarsh Priors, Autumn 1940

Evangeline had come to dread the long nights. She tossed and turned, awake until the early hours before she was sucked into an undertow of nightmares until it grew light. In all her dreams she was back in Louisiana. Sometimes she was at her old home in New Orleans. It was silent and dim, the furniture was gone, and each door she opened led to another empty room while she felt something stalking her through the silent house, something horrible, getting closer as she tried to run but couldn't. Sometimes she was at school, looking out at the world through the convent's barred windows. But often she was in the country at her grandmother's, leaving Laurent in the grey half-light before dawn. Mist lay heavy over the cane fields and smelt of pond lilies. She was late, had to hurry and dress, Grandmère and the old ladies who never seemed to go home would soon be up, saying the rosary in the parlour, the servants would be awake – hurry, hurry, before anyone saw.

The house was just beyond the hanging moss on the next swamp oak, then the next, and the next. She began to run, faster and faster, but she couldn't find the way back in the mist, although she knew it was close because she could hear Inez clattering pots and pans and smell coffee brewing. A mule brayed and a bell rang, but she couldn't see anything. 'Too late! Someone knows,' said

Laurent, behind her. She whirled round to see who was there. They were coming closer through the mist and she saw that the human figures had Loup Garou faces. She turned to run again but Laurent's body swung in the hanging moss, blocking her way . . .

Evangeline would wake with her heart pounding and remind herself once more that she was no longer in New Orleans. Johnny was crying for his breakfast in Tanni's room. The birds were twittering in the old pear tree. She would thump her pillows, prop herself up in the four-poster bed, with its pink silk coverlet, and steel herself to wash hastily in the cold bathroom down the landing.

Twenty minutes later, still damp, she would put on yesterday's clothes, picking up the ancient grey jumper that had belonged to Richard's father from the floor where she had dropped it next to her boots and trousers. Once Evangeline had been fastidious in her dress, taking pains to match frocks, shoes and jewellery, but now she hardly cared what she wore.

She went to the kitchen and put the kettle on for tea. She hated tea but drank it for warmth, and waited for Tanni to come down before she made toast. Then she tried to think how to fill the day while she waited for Laurent to call and tell her to leave at once: this was the day. Her small suitcase was ready, packed with the few good things she owned.

At first Evangeline had thought she would go mad in England. She had meant to contact Laurent at once and tell him about the baby, but when she had arrived, it had proved harder than she'd expected. Richard had whisked her down to his mother's house in Crowmarsh Priors, and the telephone was in the echoing hall. A barely polite Penelope had come to stay, ostensibly to 'help Evangeline settle in', which meant watching her like a hawk. It was impossible to get in touch with Laurent, let alone make a plan to leave, with Penelope there.

After a few weeks, with Richard increasingly away on duty and her own war work demanding so much of her time, Penelope had gone back to her flat near Harrods. Evangeline had breathed a little easier. She had rung Laurent at the Marseille office and told him where she was. They agreed she would join him in France as soon as he found a place to live. 'Everything in Provence smells good in the heat, and from up in the hills you can see the sea,' he said. 'I got my eye on a pretty white house with blue shutters for us, trying to save some money for it.'

'Us? But how can we have the same house?' asked Evangeline, wistfully. She hadn't thought that part of the plan through.

Easy, said Laurent. There were many North Africans in France, with dark skin like *gens de couleur*. They mixed with the white population, intermarried, had children, everything. 'Long as you keep clear of the Fontaine employees in Marseille, we'll be fine.' It sounded impossible, but Evangeline tried to imagine their new life, their children running about, Laurent coming home each evening. She had patted her stomach. She had to tell him soon.

Then she had miscarried at five months, and was ill for weeks. When she was up and about again, pale and listless, she had an excuse to go to London – she needed to see a doctor, she said. There, she managed to contact Laurent in Marseille. Something new in his voice warned her that it was not the right time to tell him about the baby. He sounded drowsy. She wasn't sure if he was tired or – could she be imagining it? – wary. She decided to wait and tell him in person.

Evangeline had been surprised by how much she grieved for the baby, who would have made them a family. As long as no one knew that Laurent was coloured and she was white, she could not imagine a future for them that did not include children.

'How much longer, Laurent? I miss you so much.'

'Not long, darlin'. I miss you too.'

Week after week, Laurent promised they would be together soon. Then summer had ended, and a curt telegram had come from Penelope: she was to prepare a room for an evacuated mother and child. Two days later a tall, dark-haired girl, who looked very young but was holding a baby, stepped off the train at Crowmarsh Priors. The guard handed down to her a huge carpetbag. She looked around wildly, as if she didn't know what to do next, and the baby began to cry. Albert Hawthorne, the station-master, went to help her. When he learned who she was and where she was going, he chucked the baby under the chin and carried Tanni's carpetbag all the way from the station. 'She wants looking after,' he had told Evangeline firmly, as he put the bag down in the hall.

'Good morning,' Tanni had said carefully, in English, looking around the wide hall with the light flooding in, the curving staircase and the Turkey runner on the polished floor. She sniffed. Thankfully, there was no horrible smell of boiled cabbage and drains. At the door she had automatically checked for any signs saying that Jews were forbidden. Now she spied a small medallion of the Madonna and Child that Evangeline had scandalized Penelope by hanging in the hall, and thought she had better make sure. 'Jews are being permitted here?' she asked, shifting Johnny in her arms.

'What?' said the girl who had opened the door. 'Why on earth wouldn't they be?' She looked surprised by the question – and Tanni was puzzled by her: she was wearing trousers and a grey knitted thing with holes in the elbows. Tanni wondered if she was the servant, although surely a maid would wear a uniform. It was very odd. 'Come on, I'll show you where your room is. Here, give me the baby. Come to Aunt Evangeline, darlin',' she cooed, 'What's his name? I got some of Richard's old nursery furniture down from the attic.'

Having Tanni and Johnny around distracted Evangeline a little. As she waited for Laurent's phone calls she moved restlessly between the house and the garden, always busy but never out of earshot of the shrill ring of the telephone in the entrance hall. She filled the long days weeding the garden, playing with Johnny, cooking food she barely touched, writing to Richard. She refused invitations to tea with Lady Marchmont or for drinks and tennis at Gracecourt Hall, and made stilted conversation with whey-faced Alice Osbourne, who obviously did not like her but who called to see how Tanni was getting on. Evangeline could see Alice hadn't approved of the Madonna any more than Penelope had, but she didn't care what Alice thought. Alice was just another irritant in the purgatory that was England.

As soon as Laurent told her to come to him, Evangeline planned to put her wedding band with the sapphire and diamond ring, which had been Penelope's and which Richard had given her as an engagement ring – even though they hadn't had time to be engaged – into an envelope, with the letter she had written saying she was sorry and that he should divorce her. Poor Richard. He had rescued her and he seemed to be in love with her, but it never occurred to her to stay with him. All she could do was look for the gold baby – maybe there was a way to undo the *gris-gris* – but it was lost. All she could think of was Laurent.

Then war was declared, and winter set in. Laurent's rare telephone calls usually came late at night, after Tanni had gone to sleep. Evangeline could hear music and laughter in the background. He had made friends with a group of North African musicians who played in a water-front bar. He often joined them at night after work, he told her, filling in for the saxophonist or the pianist. It reminded him of New Orleans. North Africans looked coloured, although they lived among the white French people, and no one took any notice. 'Not much longer, darlin', just a little harder travelling with the war on. You mustn't come by yourself. I'll come get you soon.'

'When, Laurent? I miss you so!'

'Soon, darlin', soon. I miss you too.'

Just before Christmas Laurent rang to say that he was now living in Paris, and mumbled about lodging with a musician friend. He was looking for a place for himself and Evangeline to live in the city. 'Be patient, darlin'.

Findin' an apartment here's not easy, might take me a little longer.' The call ended abruptly.

Evangeline tried not to be alarmed as the dark days succeeded each other and still she waited. She ignored the war rumbling in Europe: each day she hoped it would be the one on which Laurent came to get her.

One morning in May she had been woken from her usual nightmare-ridden sleep by the clanging of the church bell. She was disoriented. She must still be dreaming, she thought, and pinched herself hard.

She was definitely awake, in a strange, rather dirty room, dimly lit by a bar of sunlight falling across a worn but garish carpet. Nearby a church bell was indeed pealing, probably at the old church she remembered having seen on the corner. The window glass had been stuck over with rice paper to prevent it breaking if a bomb fell nearby. A man and a woman were arguing drunkenly outside. A milk van rattled past. There were footsteps in the corridor and someone was talking in a low voice behind the thin partition wall. She was not in New Orleans or in Sussex, but in London, and now she was blissfully awake. Laurent was beside her, his warm naked thigh against hers, a little taller and more solid than she remembered, but sleeping soundly as he always did.

Joy surged through her as she remembered the telephone shrilling in the hall – it had been early afternoon and Tanni had nearly answered it. Laurent was in London! Evangeline grabbed her suitcase and rushed for the train, in such a hurry that she forgot to tear off her rings and leave the letter for Richard.

Last night had been their first night together in more than a year, but this time she didn't have to sneak home in the dark. Laurent said no one knew here who she and he were, or that he was coloured and she was white, or that they weren't married. They didn't have to sneak anywhere. Thank you, God, and please, please, let the church bell be ringing because it's a church bell and not because it's signalling a poison-gas attack or the invasion.

In the dark she and Laurent had fallen hungrily on each other without pausing to draw the blackout curtains. Their hurriedly discarded clothes lay in a heap on the floor, his hat and their gas masks on the dressing-table. His saxophone case was propped in a corner, and her running-away suitcase, beside it, was still packed. She stretched out a hand to replace the cork in the bottle of Cognac Laurent had brought from Paris. Then she snuggled back into the crook of his arm, and buried her head in his chest. Now at last they would have a chance to talk about everything, about the baby and how frightened she had been in New Orleans, how miserable after her miscarriage, what had happened when Laurent had reached Marseille. But instinct told her that, first, they had to get used to being together again. It had been a long time. Of course Laurent still loved her as much as she loved him, last night had proved that, but now they could make their plans and the past would be a bad dream. She realized she was still wearing her engagement and wedding rings. She would send them to Richard with the letter today.

But now . . . She sniffed and sat up again. Coffee.

Laurent's arm tightened. He nuzzled her neck.

'Laurent! Can you smell it?'

'Mmm – Schiaparelli?'

'Even better. Coffee! Oh, Laurent, I bet it's that Italian café down the street. Remember how, back home, the first thing you smelt every morning was coffee roasting? The tea they drink here tastes like dishwater. Sometimes I'd give anything to taste Creole coffee again. With a *beignet* to dip in it. I was just dreaming –'

'About breakfast?' He yawned.

'Um, sort of. In my dream Inez was making it.'

He rolled on to his back, laughing, and patted her flat tummy. 'You always were a greedy chile.'

She stretched luxuriously under his touch. 'Mmm, so were you. Remember how we'd eat *beignets* until we were sick? You ate nineteen once. Way greedier than me.'

Laurent folded his hands behind his head and considered. 'Inez sure could cook. Waffles. And *pain perdu*. With *boudin* sausage and grits on the side.'

'*Talmousses*, with cream cheese.'

He put an arm round her and settled into the pillow. 'Beaten biscuits with country ham. I really liked those.'

'And those lumpy rolls they called "bullfrogs".'

'*Grenouilles?*'

'Yes, those. Philippe said we had to poke holes in the side because they had live frogs in them that would hop down our throats unless we made a hole in the bottom to get them out. We both believed him. It made Inez so mad. "What's the matter with y'all, pokin' your fingers in my rolls like that?" Evangeline's smile faded. 'The food's awful in England. I miss Inez's cooking. Do you?'

'I eat pretty good in France.' Laurent laced his fingers through Evangeline's pale ones. The family resemblance was strong in the faces on the pillow, their build, and even their hands with the long index finger. Evangeline's hair was dark, spilling over her shoulders, while Laurent's was light copper, close-cropped and curly. His hand was strong and sensitive, a musician's. A lover's.

He played thoughtfully with Evangeline's big sapphire and diamond ring, turning it round her finger. 'You sound homesick, as well as hungry. Maybe they're the same thing. Me too, sometimes, when it rains and Paris is nothing but wet stones and strange faces, and I think about how everything used to be warm and folks sayin' hi and – But it's different for you. You're a married woman, got other things to think about. Looks like your husband's takin' good care of you.' He gave the ring a last twirl.

'I wasn't really married. Marriage by a ship's captain doesn't count in the eyes of the Church, so I can get an annulment and then we can get married when we –'

'*Us?* Get married?' He stared, looking surprised.

'Well . . . we can't just *live* together, Laurent.' Evangeline thought about the house in Provence – no, Paris – full of children and Laurent coming home to her every night. How could they do that if they weren't married? She blurted out, 'But, er, we have to. I almost had a baby, you know – meant to tell you – but I had a miscarriage . . .'

'When?'

'Last summer, while you were in Marseille. But I guess it was for the best I lost it. Richard might have made a fuss about it and that would have complicated things, now we're going to be together.'

He let go of her, turned away and reached for his cigarettes.

Evangeline watched him out of the corner of her eye. Something in his attitude made her uncomfortable. Was he upset, thinking she meant she had been pregnant with Richard's baby? That must be it. 'I wonder what would happen if I had your baby?' she asked, testing the waters.

Laurent smiled grimly and struck a match. 'If we were back home you wouldn't wonder about it. And in Europe the Germans would say it was impossible. They have this theory that mulattoes are like mules – sterile.'

'They've never been to New Orleans, then. In Sussex they think I come up to London to see a doctor about why I haven't had a child.'

'Thank heaven you haven't. Back home the girls used to get an old coloured woman named Mama La Bas to fix it so's they didn't have a baby.'

Evangeline took a deep breath. 'Let's not talk about it. Tell me what it's like in Paris now. The French must be relieved that the British Army's there to protect the border.'

Laurent plumped their pillows, settled back and pulled Evangeline to him. He rested his chin on top of her head and she didn't see the shadow pass over his face. 'Paris? You never saw so many desperate folks with nowhere to go. The Germans are coming fast – only thing travelling faster are rumours about what they've done in Poland and other places. Maginot Line never meant a damn thing. Invasion's almost official. People expect Pétain will nego-tiate an armistice. Everyone's so scared you can smell it. Men who aren't in the army have disappeared into the countryside. But for the moment,' he shrugged, 'there's coffee to drink, and the women still dress up, wear pretty hats and smell good. The clubs, casinos and the Folies are full every night. Folks drink champagne and dance, and try to act like what's comin' ain't comin'.'

'Can't you leave, come to England?'

'It's OK for me. America's not at war with Germany. Because I'm not afraid to stay in Paris I get work most nights, even with the Germans coming. Josephine Baker and the Revue Nègre were a smash. The French love jazz, blues and swing and what they call "exotic dancing", all that stuff from the Treme. I've played on records and people buy a lot of them so I make enough to live on. Like I told you, the Fontaine business is practically finished down in Marseille, and I heard André and Philippe are struggling to hold things together in New Orleans since your father died. They write every now and then, asking how I am. Do they ever say anything to you about that night?'

'Nobody can understand why I ran off with Richard. André's the only one who keeps in touch. He says no one's ever going to forget the scandal I caused. No girl from a decent family is allowed to dance with him now. He told me Daddy wanted to have my marriage annulled immediately but Mama persuaded him that that would disgrace the family even more, especially if I had a baby. If I ever set foot in Louisiana again I'll be arrested for shooting Maurice. But it doesn't matter. I don't want to go back, ever.' Evangeline ran her hand down the livid scars on Laurent's back.

He winced, slid down until he was lying flat, then pulled her on top of him. 'You're a dangerous woman, sugar. Come on, now . . .'

Afterwards they shared a cigarette in their old companionable way. Reassured, she tried another tack. 'Why can't you stay here? Not go back to Paris. It's dangerous. Or maybe we could run away someplace else, not England or France. At least we'd be together.'

Laurent drew deep on the cigarette and passed it to her. 'Dangerous everywhere – back home, France, here, with the Germans coming, unless the English can hold them off. Which they won't. I can't afford to leave Paris right now, but between the records I'm making and playing at the club, I can live. I just have to be careful, don't want to get on the wrong side of the Germans. They don't like coloured people. Or, come to that, anybody who isn't German. In Paris I mostly say I'm North African but I've got two passports for when the Germans come.'

'How do you get back and forth to France at a time like this?'

'I'm pals with some Frenchmen who used to come to the club in Paris. They've set up a headquarters in London, at the top of a pub – the Free French, they call themselves. As a musician and an American I can go back and forth pretty easily, so I have a job as their courier. Pays well.'

'Oh, Laurent, couldn't they let me do that too? I'm American and –'

'No!'

Evangeline's face crumpled.

'But I'll come back to England whenever I can. You know I will,' Laurent said.

'It seems so unfair. We've both come all this way to be

162

together and now we can't because of the damn Germans.'

After a moment Laurent put his arms round her again. 'I know, darlin', I know,' he said, nuzzling her ear. 'Let's not talk about it any more.'

The patch of sunshine crept across the carpet and disappeared as the day passed, while they made love and avoided any talk of their old home or their future one.

When they had dressed, late in the afternoon, Evangeline noticed Laurent's socks had holes and his shirt was frayed at the collar and cuffs. At dusk they went out and walked side by side through the streets. They drank coffee at the Italian café, self-conscious and nervous to be sitting side by side but no one glanced at them. They wandered through the blacked-out streets, then saw a poster for the new American film *Gone With the Wind* and joined the queue. Afterwards they walked back to the hotel through the balmy night, holding hands. 'I'm glad we're not in Atlanta,' said Laurent, 'with the siege and all.'

'Me too,' said Evangeline, and burst into tears.

They made love again, then sat tangled in the sheets afterwards. Evangeline's slender leg was draped over Laurent's as they shared a toothmug of Cognac and a bar of chocolate Laurent had brought. Laurent had rolled some cigarettes he said the musicians all smoked in Paris, made from Indian hemp. Feeling mellow, they dozed and this time Evangeline, wrapped in Laurent's arms, dreamed of nothing.

From below in the darkness of blacked-out Soho the sound of late revellers and a clatter of dishes in a restaurant floated up to wake them in the early hours. 'Time to get to the pub,' Laurent said, yawning. 'French boys are expecting me. I got work to do. But first, I brought you some presents.' Without drawing the blackout curtains he got up, his spare body silhouetted against the window. He handed a flat parcel and two bags to Evangeline.

She opened the bags first. 'What is it?' She felt inside. Sniffed. Tasted. Something stung her tongue. 'Oh, Laurent, dried hot peppers! How wonderful! English food is so bland I can hardly swallow it.' She plunged a hand into the other bag and exclaimed, 'Rice!' She hadn't had rice in ages. 'Where did you get this stuff?'

'Algerian friend in Paris. She's, uh, married to one of the fellows in the band, cooks for us all. They use hot peppers in Algeria like we do back home, make a sauce they put on everything. Now, before you open the big one, I've got something new I want to play you.'

'Oh, good!' Evangeline tossed back her hair, propped herself up, and hugged the sheet round her.

He winked at her. '"Evangeline's Blues", I call it.'

Sitting naked on the side of the bed, Laurent ran through some scales, then slid into a slow rhythm, the saxophone soft at first, just touching the notes, enjoying each one before letting it go and sliding into the next, bolder now, the power and the sadness and the sweet-ness of the music taking hold until the sound filled the room, and the scattered clothes, the curtains, the dirty window, the faded armchair, the stained wallpaper, the day of lovemaking were all part of it. Evangeline smiled sadly when the last notes faded in the darkness. She wished she and Laurent could stay for ever in this room where no one knew or cared about them.

Laurent drew the blackout curtains and switched on the cheap bedside lamp. 'Open the other present.'

She tore off layers of brown paper. 'Oh, Laurent! Your records! Thank goodness Penelope didn't take the gramophone when she moved into the flat! Now I can listen to your music every night and imagine you're there. You're better than Glenn Miller,' she said.

'Wish he thought so too,' he said, pleased. 'I'd give anything to play in his band. Back home, people buy his records, see my name on the cover, they'd know I hadn't vanished without trace.'

Evangeline threw caution to the winds. 'Oh, Laurent, *please* take me with you! The French don't care who we are. Or we can go to some other country – Sweden or . . . or . . . I don't care, there must be someplace. I don't feel alive without you and I just wait and wait. I'm so *tired* of waiting!'

He sighed impatiently. 'You're safer here, like I told you. It's not just about us, it's about the Germans and the war. It's getting worse and worse everywhere. When the war is over we can worry about it. Right now, I've got all I can do to stay in one piece, play some music, make a livin'. You've got to be patient. Wait for me where you are, darlin'. Stay with your husband for the time bein'.'

11. Crowmarsh Priors, October 1940

With France under Nazi control, and the British Expeditionary Force evacuated from Dunkirk in bloody disarray, the Germans settled in across the Channel and launched the Blitz in preparation for the invasion of England.

A month later the bombing seemed to have been going on for ever. Every day wave after wave of German planes and their escorts thundered across the Channel, darkening the sky over Sussex, then heading north. On their tails black swastikas flashed insolently in the last rays of autumn sunshine.

Sheep grazing on the downs ran in panic, their bleating drowned by the drone of engines. A moment later RAF Spitfires appeared but the endless German column banked and continued relentlessly towards its targets. Ack-ack fire erupted in the distance. Over Croydon a Spitfire spiralled down from the sky, black smoke billowing behind it.

Albert Hawthorne, hoeing cabbages behind his cottage, looked up, shook his fist and cursed.

Nell hurried their eight-year-old daughter, Margaret Rose, into the Anderson shelter at the end of the garden and shouted for him to join them. Instead Albert dropped the hoe and wheeled out his bicycle: he was in the Home Guard. Apron fluttering, she ran after him with his gas mask, muttering that it was all very well for the government, with their Home Guard posters, but were the unarmed Home Guard supposed to hoe the Germans to death when they parachuted into the village? She hoped he'd remember he had a wife and daughter in the shelter and that she'd queued for hours in Hurst Green to get sausages for tea, so mind he got home safe to eat them. He pedalled off, marvelling at women's priorities.

He almost collided with Alice Osbourne, now the local air-raid warden, who came running out of the church gate still in her flowered pinny. Tucking up her skirt, she leaped on to her bicycle, blowing an air-raid whistle. Her gas mask swung from the handlebars as she rode off, shouting, 'Air raid!' sternly at five little boys kicking a football about on the green. They scattered and ran for home.

Alice pedalled hard through the village, making sure no other children were out. There had been so many alarms since the Blitz began that they no longer took them seriously. When the bombing had started she and Oliver had devised an air-raid signal – 'Ring three times, pause, ring three times, pause' – using the St Gabriel's bell because they didn't have a siren. Now the War Office had ordered that church bells were only to be rung to signal that the invasion had begun. Oliver said it was a sad turn of events. The government had installed a siren in the parish hall, but it was temperamental and didn't always go off.

The knowledge that the Germans were only twenty-five miles away across the Channel terrified Alice. It was rumoured that bodies in Nazi uniforms had washed up on the coast and that *agents provocateurs* were everywhere.

People were to stay alert and report anyone who behaved suspiciously to the authorities. Alice had taken to calling in at Glebe House to hear the BBC news on Lady Marchmont's wireless each evening – it worked better than the little one at the Osbournes' cottage, and as a warden she needed to keep up with what was happening. Also, it was an excuse to put off going home to her mother. Frances Falconleigh, who had surprised everyone by joining the Land Army with the young housemaid Elsie, usually returned home on her bicycle at dusk. Then she and Mrs Gifford drew the blackout curtains, and all five women huddled round the wireless in the morning room.

They had listened to Churchill's ringing speech that England would 'fight them on the beaches but never, *never* surrender'. Weeks later, Frances had confided that her father had said Churchill ended the speech with an aside that they'd be fighting on the beaches with empty bottles because that was all they'd got. It sounded, she added, as if Britain couldn't hold out much longer: the French Army had been much larger than ours but it hadn't stopped the Germans overrunning Paris or the French government surrendering.

At this, Alice had closed her eyes in prayer.

Frances had regarded her with disgust. 'I wish I had a gun!' she said fiercely. 'If they invade I'd be sure to take a couple of Germans with me.'

Alice stopped praying and stared at her. She had never heard a girl talk like that.

And how could one person fight the Germans? She wondered if she would be afraid to die when the time came, and if she would be brave enough to 'take a couple with her', as everyone said you must. Perhaps Frances was right, and they did need guns. 'Sufficient unto the day is the evil thereof,' she muttered, which took her mind off shooting Germans and helped her concentrate instead on the people for whom she was responsible.

The new party of Land Army recruits were digging potatoes and picking the last of the apples at the de Balforts' home farm. They worked until dusk when they caught a bus back to their hostel, but Elsie Pigeon would get them into the home-farm shelter with their gas masks. Although she was the youngest of her group Elsie was good at bossing people about and Alice knew she could count on her. Frances had a day's leave and had gone up to London to see her father.

The air-raid siren kept up its piercing wail. It wasn't much comfort to know that it had also summoned the Home Guard, which consisted of Oliver, Albert Hawthorne, Hugo de Balfort, the publican's elderly father and uncle, Ted and George Smith, and several farmers' sons who were due to enlist. They had drilled with broomsticks until Hugo had donated Gracecourt's stock of old hunting rifles. Alice wouldn't give a twopence for the Home Guard's chances when the Germans came. The enemy had managed to spread the word that anyone resisting the invasion would be regarded as a traitor and executed immediately.

Puffing now, Alice halted to peer into Lady Marchmont's garden. Except for the lavender bushes and the flagstone walk, it had been turned into a 'Dig for Victory' garden. Mrs Gifford, in her white apron and cap, was following the old lady down the walk to their

Anderson shelter, laden with their gas masks, rugs and a Thermos of tea. Lady Marchmont couldn't move very fast with her cane but she was nearly there. Alice waved to her and sped by Penelope Fairfax's house.

Evangeline would have Tanni, Johnny and the three bombed-out evacuee children, who had recently been billeted with her, down in the musty wine vault where Richard's father had stored his claret and port – Alice and Richard had played Dungeons there on rainy days. It made a splendid bomb shelter, though – unless the house took a direct hit and buried Evangeline once and for all, which would serve her right. She stifled that thought at once, on account of Tanni and the children, but she couldn't help thinking of Richard.

He and his convoy were in danger somewhere out on the grey Atlantic. In the village hall she had hung a lurid poster – IT ALL DEPENDS ON YOU – to drive home the message that everyone needed to grow food, make do and mend, and help the war effort by being as self-sufficient as possible so the country didn't have to depend on supplies that had to be protected by convoys. The poster showed HMS *Glow-worm* sinking in flames after a battle with a German destroyer in April. Every day Alice prayed for all British ships at sea and those who sailed in them – she tried not to be too specific about Richard.

Now she was panting on up the hill, towards home and her mother, who got into a frightful state each time the Germans flew over, even though, so far, they had saved their bombs for the cities.

It was twilight by the time she reached the ugly Edwardian cottage, another ominously clear evening, good for bombing. The moon was rising over the horizon. To the north, the sky over London was full of silver barrage balloons. Ominously it glowed orange, and flashed with searchlights and explosions. Alice parked her bicycle, and scanned the countryside with her binoculars, looking for any signs of light that might help the German pilots navigate – a carelessly drawn blackout curtain, a forgotten autumnal bonfire still smouldering, an absent-minded torch-user or some idiot who had turned on his car's headlamps. Even Sister Tucker was allowed only a pinprick of a light on her bicycle, and she preferred to do without it, maintaining that her eyes were better in the dark.

She peered into the ground-floor windows behind the overgrown hydrangea bushes and saw, with irritation, that the blackout curtains had not been drawn. She had warned her mother several times that if she forgot and put the light on they'd be fined for signalling to the Germans. She hurried inside, hoping her mother had already gone to the cellar and lit the lantern they kept there. They used the old coal store down there as their shelter.

Inside, the passage smelt of boiled turnips. 'Mummy?'

'Alice? Where have you been? You know how anxious I get when you're off gallivanting. I heard the aeroplanes, then the siren. I didn't know what to think! They keep talking on the wireless about gas.' In the dark the sofa rustled as Mrs Osbourne sat up, querulous, hands clutching the plaid rug with which she covered herself when she had a nap. She was only fifty-five but, thanks to ill-health, real and imagined, she seemed much older. 'When your father was alive . . .' she began.

'No gas tonight, Mummy. If there was, it didn't get me and I'm the miners' canary,' said Alice, loudly, to forestall her mother's litany of complaints. She knew she should wear her gas mask, but she could hardly pedal round the village, then up the hill to the cottage with it on. As for her mother, she flatly refused to wear hers. She said it brought on her attacks.

Alice pulled her mother to her feet. 'The village are all in their shelters, snug and sound, and we must go straight down to ours.'

'It's so damp down there! I don't know what your father would have said about all this, I'm sure.' Mrs Osbourne shuffled her feet into her slippers and took her daughter's arm. With her free hand, Alice felt for her mother's crocheted shawl on its hook in the hall, which was stacked with boxes. 'I'll be glad when this war's over,' quavered Mrs Osbourne, 'and you can put your father's books and papers into the coal store. This house is so much smaller than the vicarage, and as for storing things in the hall . . .'

Germans or no Germans, her mother would not be hurried. In fact, she seemed to go as slowly as possible. Alice ground her teeth.

Somehow they made it down the stairs, one at a time. In the cellar Alice lit the lantern and settled her mother in her father's old armchair. Then she perched on a frayed ottoman and took up some mending from the workbasket she kept there. The coal store was not large and their knees almost touched.

'What does the new vicar do for a shelter?' Mrs Osbourne asked, arranging her shawl round her shoulders. She made a point of not referring to him by name: he had had no business taking her husband's place.

'The Reverend Oliver Hammet has one of those new Anderson shelters at the bottom of his garden. Some volunteers came from the bishop's office to put it up for him. Funny-looking things – they're barrel-shaped, with a metal roof and sides, and there's room for two bunk beds, perhaps four if people squeeze up a bit. Several people in the village have them – the Hawthornes and even Lady Marchmont. The rest use their cellars like we do.'

Alice didn't mention that the vicar's Anderson shelter was now almost impossible to reach beneath the brambles that had also smothered his short-lived victory garden. Taking the War Office advice to help the war effort with food production, he was talking about keeping chickens or rabbits instead of growing vegetables. Alice had told him that a goat would be a better choice, and they had both laughed.

Oliver Hammet was no longer a source of discomfort to Alice. Since the war began, the need for civil-defence procedures meant they had been thrown together frequently and she had realized that although Oliver Hammet was a thoroughly kind and good man she would never feel the slightest romantic interest in him. She sensed he felt the same about her. She knew Nell Hawthorne still cherished hopes of their marrying in the end, but Alice didn't care: now she could carry on her activities at the church without feeling awkward. That, at least, was a relief. But there was no point in trying to explain all that to her mother.

'What other news is there?' Mrs Osbourne inquired.

'Hmm . . . Constable Barrows told me that a shop-keeper in Lewes was caught selling eggs to customers without coupons and nearly sent to prison. Then, let's see, the Mothers' Union is sewing a new banner for the Sunday School corner, and the Dorcas Society were donated some oiled wool so they'll hold knitting sessions in the vicarage parlour three mornings a week to make socks for the troops. Shame you can't go that far, Mummy, because I know they can use every pair of hands. You're good at knitting and crochet. You'd be doing something useful for the troops and you'd have a bit of company.'

Mrs Osbourne had pursed her lips at the mention of the vicarage parlour. She remained pointedly silent. Alice looked up from the mending and changed tack quickly. 'The three children evacuated from London settled in well on their first day at school, considering what a dreadful time they've had. Their names are Maude, Tommy and Kipper Johnson. They were bombed out, lost everything they had, and Penelope Fairfax said it was a matter of urgency to find them a place at once so she felt she had to –'

'Billet them at her own house,' Mrs Osbourne finished for her. 'With only that American strumpet to look after them. What can Penelope be thinking of?'

'Mummy, please!' Alice snipped her thread ferociously. 'Penelope is too busy to worry about things in Crowmarsh Priors. The WVS are at it night and day, with so many people bombed out of their homes now and using the Underground stations for shelter. It sounds chaotic trying to keep order – all those people are scared, hungry, worried about what they'll find when the all-clear sounds. Mothers lose their children and panic, men get into fistfights when they've been drinking, and Penelope said the lavatory is usually just a bucket behind a sheet – sometimes not even that. One night a woman even gave birth during a raid. But Penelope, of course, simply gets on with things and *doesn't complain!*' Alice bit her lip. When she spoke next she tried to sound cheerful, but it was hard work. 'So, here we are, all safe and sound, Mummy. No fires, no gas attacks and, so far, no bombs. Mustn't grumble.'

There was silence for a blessed few minutes as Alice sewed. She felt exhausted.

Finally her mother cleared her throat. 'It's past tea-time. We should have brought a Thermos down with us. Why must you always forget, Alice? I'm the last person to complain but –'

'Have a boiled sweet, Mummy.' Alice hoarded them for such emergencies.

The ground under the cellar vibrated. The coast was taking it tonight, as well as London, thought Alice. What about 'those in peril on the sea'? No safe shelter in the cellar or an Underground station for them, just heaving, icy waters. Was Richard ever afraid?

'I will never, never understand why Richard jilted you, Alice. I simply don't know what your father would say if he were alive. If Richard had married you as he ought, we would have been living at the Fairfaxes' house now, instead of that dreadful American and the shiftless gypsy girl with her brat,' said her mother.

'As I've told you and told you, Mummy, Tanni's not a

gypsy, she's Jewish. Not at all the same thing. She's married to a young professor who volunteered as a translator at the War Office so she and her baby need somewhere to live. Sometimes you're worse than Lady Marchmont. It's our Christian duty to welcome her and her child, who, I must say, is very well looked after.' Alice stabbed her needle into her cotton reel with such force that it snapped. 'Here you are. Your nightdress is mended, good as new,' she said, through clenched teeth. '"Make do and mend", you know!'

'I suppose I have no choice *but* to make do in this horrid little cottage, have I, with your father in his grave and Richard disappointing us so?'

Alice closed her eyes, and prayed silently, Please, God, either let the all-clear come or send a bomb to fall on this house now and put us out of our misery. Amen.

12. London, February 1941

Admiral Tudor Falconleigh put down the latest intelligence report and pushed his chair away from his overflowing desk at the War Office. He rubbed his eyes. Beyond the grimy glass of the window behind him, London lay in ruins. Intelligence reports often contradicted each other, but the pile on his desk contained no good news, only different scenarios for the expected invasion. The RAF lads were throwing themselves as hard as they could against the Luftwaffe, but the latest report had warned that the Germans were developing a pilotless plane.

If so, it was the end. The Admiral and most of his colleagues believed a coastal invasion by sea-borne German troops was coming any day, and they wished the Prime Minister would concentrate on remobilizing and re-equipping the regular army to repel it before it was too late. But Churchill had become fixated with guerrillas and resistance movements, first in Europe and now at home.

He had already diverted resources so that Colin Gubbins could set up the Special Operations Executive, to parachute British agents behind enemy lines to support the resistance in occupied countries. It was pointless. The French Resistance was chaotic: the Communists clashed with the Maquis, who were at odds with local organizations, who disagreed among themselves. It was the same in Poland and Holland. Now Churchill had ordered Gubbins to organize an English resistance, with Auxiliary Units as its backbone, who would go to ground and sabotage the Germans after the invasion.

The Admiral and the Prime Minister had clashed bitterly at yesterday's War Office meeting over these units – 'Auxis', as Churchill called them. They would be trained in the same skills as the SOE: radio telegraphy, laying mines, using explosives, and killing in hand-to-hand combat. The Admiral knew it would never work. For a start, they would have to draw on anyone not already called up – call-up evaders, schoolboys, criminals and the like. There were the reserved occupations, of course, miners, farmers and so on, but there was a limit to how many could be diverted from work that was essential to keep people fed and the country running. Once trained, Auxis would have to be armed and, in the end, they would be given what amounted to a suicide mission. The Admiral decided he would have to try again to change Churchill's mind.

And, as if that weren't enough, he had to deal with Frances.

The Admiral loved his daughter, but he was a man's man, and didn't pretend to understand women. Least of all Frances. Girls were a mother's department. Unfortunately his pretty half-French wife, whom he had never understood either, had died three years into their marriage, leaving him in charge of their only child, who was just beginning to walk.

He had known nothing about children and, until her mother died, Frances had lived out of his sight in the top-floor nursery. He was only occasionally reminded of her presence when he saw her in her pram, with Nanny at the helm, on the way to the park. After his wife died, though, he had felt it his duty to take a closer interest in her. When he visited the nursery for the first time, he was taken aback when the angelic two-year-old, in a smocked dress and tiny pearl-buttoned kid shoes, had a fearsome tantrum because he had brought her no sweets. He had soon learned that she was headstrong and fearless for such a dainty creature. Indoors, Frances climbed fire-guards and bookcases, fell down a heating vent, and threw whatever she could reach into the lavatory. In the park she was snapped at by strange dogs, whose tails she grabbed, and frequently escaped from Nanny. Once she had tottered into the Serpentine among the ducks – a policeman had rescued her in the nick of time from a watery grave.

Soaking wet, chilled to the bone, scratched by the cook's cat, or bruised after a tumble, Frances never cried, but when thwarted she threw herself into a fury until the Admiral roared at her to behave. Frances roared back. A succession of nannies came and went until, in despair, the Admiral had turned to his old friend, and Frances's godmother, Muriel Marchmont. She advised a governess. When this, too, proved a failure, Frances was sent to a series of boarding-schools, selected by Muriel. Letters from headmistresses became a regular feature in the Admiral's morning post. Each woman regretted that her establishment was not right for Frances, and would the Admiral please remove her. All agreed on two things: first, that Frances was remarkably clever when she could be persuaded to work, and second, that she was easily bored, undisciplined, a troublemaker, who broke rules flagrantly and encouraged others to follow suit.

Tudor Falconleigh had dispatched her to the French finishing-school as a gesture of respect to her late mother, and because nowhere else would take her.

Muriel Marchmont's most recent letter had sat reproachfully on a corner of his desk for some time. He often put off reading her missives, because he felt unequal to dealing with another catalogue of Frances's misdoings, and also because Lady Marchmont tended to over-dramatize. However, in recent months, she had evidently felt that Frances was beyond her, and suggested that she should get married. Then she would be her husband's responsibility.

Now the Admiral slit open the latest envelope. He was relieved to find that his old friend considered there was Light at the End of the Tunnel. Frances was being courted by a suitable man. In fact, although the girl had not confided in her, Muriel had felt she should let dear Tudor know without delay that she was as good as engaged to Hugo de Balfort. In the circumstances, she wrote, it was imperative for him to summon Frances to London: 'At a time like this, it is a father's duty to have a serious talk.'

His heart sank. A 'serious talk' with his daughter always ended in a row and sulks, with the Admiral threatening to reduce or withhold Frances's allowance. Still, if Muriel thought it possible that a conversation with her might hasten her marriage to a suitable man, he would have a word. He agreed with Muriel that a woman's proper estate was marriage, and if there was any prospect that his talking to her would hasten Frances's, the Admiral would talk to her. However, he mustn't stir up her rebellious streak because if he did she would do the opposite of whatever he recommended. He would discuss a financial settlement and leave the wedding arrangements to Muriel, who would know what ought to be done.

If he understood Muriel correctly, Frances's inheritance was important to the de Balforts, who, like many aristocrats, were land rich and cash poor. But, in return, his daughter would marry into one of England's oldest families and gain a title.

Before he could ring Frances, she had phoned him to say she would be coming up to Town that week and would like to see him. He would like to see her too, he said – 'Give you lunch, m'dear.' He had said goodbye and put the phone down. At least where his troublesome daughter was concerned, he had thought, everything would be fine.

When the moment came for the chat, he was less certain. At the War Office he stared at Frances, sitting across from him on an uncomfortable NAAFI chair, ankles crossed demurely, looking frivolous and out of place with the uniformed Wrens bent over their typing. She wore one of her expensive hats with a wispy veil, a smart suit, a fur and soft gloves. Seeing his expression she said, 'Well, Father, I could hardly wear my land-girl breeches up to Town. They're covered with muck. In any case I wanted to make a good impression on you because I have something important to ask you.'

The Admiral had smiled indulgently and raised his eyebrows.

'I've had an official letter from someone named Gubbins, who apparently knows you and has heard of me. Not sure why but that doesn't matter. He asks if I'd be interested in working for a new organization . . .'

There was silence in the office, the kind of silence that presages a storm. He looks like a volcano about to erupt, thought Frances. She smoothed the gloves on her lap. She had suspected it might be a mistake to ask him, but at her interview in Baker Street they said that, given his position and that she was under age, she had to have his permission to join them. It came hard to her to ask him, but she was determined to keep calm.

Admiral Falconleigh stared at his daughter in stunned disbelief. Who the hell had put her name forward? And why would Gubbins want to recruit Frances? There could hardly be a less likely candidate in England for Winston's crazy organization.

Perhaps she had volunteered – or perhaps not: he couldn't imagine how she would have heard about the SOE or the Auxiliary Units, both of which were supposed to be secret. It wasn't clear which one they wanted her for but, either way, it wasn't as if they were advertising in *The Times*. He knew that candidates' names were put forward by personal contacts. Which of his acquaintances had suggested Frances? He was sure, however, that whoever it was had done so to make him drop his opposition to Churchill's plan.

'No, Frances. I forbid it. I will speak to them personally, if necessary. No daughter of mine –'

'Oh, yes, do speak to them, Father – perhaps they can convince you, if I can't, of how frightfully useful secret agents will be in supporting the Free French and the Resistance.'

'My dear girl, you haven't the foggiest notion about the Free French or any Resistance or Gubbins's organization, but the whole lot are perfectly useless. De Gaulle is holed up issuing proclamations from a Soho pub – no good to anyone militarily.' The Admiral stopped. Frances would have no idea what he was talking about.

Frances was on the verge of retorting, 'I know all about the Free French and the pub because Evangeline Fairfax told me,' but for once in her life she held her tongue. Until she was twenty-one, her father had to give his permission before they would take her. This was not the moment to upset him.

'The Special Operations Executive isn't a more amusing way to help the war effort than working as a land girl. It's a cock-eyed cowboys-and-Indians scheme that will only get in the way of those who are fighting for England.'

'Actually, Father, a great many people will soon be fighting in a different way, and it sounds much more interesting and useful than herding cows. They need wireless operators and couriers and –'

'Aside from being ill-conceived, it's dangerous, it's behind enemy lines and it's for men only. I disapprove of saboteurs and resistance groups. The SOE are no better than mercenaries! Thugs! Trained assassins! Not quite the thing! It's underhand. As I've told Winston many times, no gentleman would have anything to do with it, but of course he didn't listen to me. Never listens to anybody. It's risky enough for the men and it's no place for girls. Most unfeminine. Anyway, girls are far too emotional, likely to go to pieces and compromise everyone.'

Frances took a deep breath and tried again. 'Quite. But,

Father, girls are extremely useful in providing back-up for the men, organizing passports and ration cards, decoding messages and suchlike, you know. And I can translate. They said they need people who can speak French like natives and I can and –'

'How do they know your French is perfect? Have you already been speaking to these people behind my back? I tell you again, no daughter of mine will join the SOE or those half-baked Auxi whatnots!'

'But, Father, they're the only organizations that have any work where I could – Do be reasonable! Please – just listen! They know my French is perfect because, yes, I went to see them today and this darling man asked me questions in French the whole morning. He said he was frightfully impressed.'

'It's out of the question! And as you're still under age you cannot go without my consent.'

'Oh, bother!' If Frances hadn't been sitting down she would have stamped her foot. 'I'm twenty! If I'd been a boy I would've had a real war job, flying Spitfires or Hurricanes or something. Being a land girl is all very well for some, and I thought it would be a lark when I joined up with Elsie – she's Aunt Muriel's housemaid – but looking after pigs and digging potatoes and milking cows and getting all muddy in the fields and wrestling with hay that doesn't want to be baled is so tedious. I can do more – I know I can. I feel wasted. I loathe milking. The cows simply hate me and they kick. If I'm to do my bit fighting the Germans I want to do more than hold a milking pail steady.'

The Admiral's patience was evaporating. He was a very busy man and Frances – as usual when her heart was set on something – was digging in her heels. But it was out of the question. Frances would remain in the Land Army at Crowmarsh Priors, no matter how many strings he had to pull to keep her there. Muriel Marchmont was right: the sooner his daughter was married the better.

'I didn't want you to come up to London to discuss your latest madcap idea but for an entirely different reason,' he began. Frances had opened her mouth and her eyes had the steely glint that presaged an argument or tantrum, but she said nothing. The Admiral continued: 'As your father, and as a member of the War Cabinet, I insist you oblige the country and me by doing your bit with the Land Army. We'll have no more talk about Gubbins's nonsense. Now, to change the subject, your godmother tells me you're seeing a good deal of a certain young man – Hugo de Balfort. A bit of a bright young thing, according to Muriel, and –'

'Father, calling someone a "bright young thing" is too old-fashioned for words! But I can't imagine why Aunt Muriel mentioned him to you. He's just a pal.'

'Indeed? She says he's all but proposed.'

'She's a meddling old buffalo!'

'But,' he held up a hand, 'it's a very sound family. Leander married Venetia what's-her-name, an earl's niece. Hope of the nation, the landed gentry, especially now. Your godmother's quite right about that. Understand Hugo's health or something kept him out of the forces but there's nothing, er, to prevent him marrying and, er, having children and so forth.'

'What?'

The Admiral saw he had floundered into deep waters.

'I gather she felt it her duty to confront Leander. She asked him point-blank about the, er, state of Hugo's, um, health. Naturally you, well, babies, children and, er, all that sort of thing . . . Muriel has, er, no doubt . . . Apparently Leander told her. Sons, naturally, keep the estate in the family.'

Frances was too aghast to speak.

Her father had gone red in the face and was gazing out of the window. 'Ahem. Title and all that – keep it in the family. Marriage, very serious step . . . leads to all sorts of responsibilities. Er,' he stuttered, 'children, of course, we've covered that, and there's the question of money. Your money. To be precise, your mother's money.'

The Admiral felt the ship steady beneath him as he steered away from the rocks. 'A good deal of it. We've never spoken of it before but marriage settlements have to be dealt with by someone when young people are too busy being in love. For their own good, future happiness and all that.'

The Admiral stopped. The expression on Frances's face did not resemble that of a girl in love. Neither did it encourage him to continue. Heaven help her husband, he thought. Then there was a knock and the door opened to the sound of typewriters clicking briskly. 'Excuse me, Admiral.' The Wren was holding out a sheaf of telegrams. 'Urgent, sir.' She frowned at Frances, as if to say, 'Why are you sitting there, all dressed up, when some of us have a war to fight?'

He turned with relief to the telegrams and the war.

While her father busied himself with dispatches and barked orders into the telephone, Frances tapped her toe and stared out of the window at grey London skies and rubble. Damn! Damn! Damn! Why did bloody Aunt Muriel have to interfere in everyone's lives? The way she pushed Alice Osbourne at Oliver Hammet was bad enough, but writing to Father about Hugo and discussing everyone's . . . reproductive faculties? How *dare* she?

Frances was irritated to think that her own behaviour had led her godmother to believe Hugo was courting her. Hugo's father, dear old boy, had always been nice to her, and he was a long-standing friend of Aunt Muriel's so perhaps the two old people had encouraged each other. Frances understood that a man in Hugo's position would be under pressure to marry and produce an heir, but although she had seen a good deal of him, she had always been more interested in his glamorous friends. Hugo was rather dull.

Frances had fallen in easily with the set staying at Gracecourt for shooting, tennis and bridge, then cocktails, dinner and dancing in Brighton. That gay crowd, mostly consisting of minor Continental aristocrats and artistic types whom Hugo had befriended on his travels, had disappeared since the war began. Hugo was still a pal, of course, but he was busy with crops and livestock and she, not to put too fine a point on it, was one of his farmhands. There had never been any of what Elsie called 'that kind of thing' between them.

Although, now she thought about it, she ran into Hugo quite often in the course of her work – in fact, she saw him every day. He always stopped to talk to her – just being friendly, she'd imagined.

Frances didn't think Hugo was in love with her or that

he wanted to marry her, but if his father was pushing him towards her she didn't want to encourage it. Anyway, since Colin Gubbins's letter and her interview she had been able to think of nothing but that. It had all been most interesting. They had asked how she thought women might best fit into the organization.

Frances had said that in many ways they would be more useful than men, because it was so easy to change their appearance with their clothes and hair. A girl could look anything between fifteen and fifty, pregnant, fat, thin, ugly, pretty or sick, while men were harder to disguise. Also, in her experience, men assumed that women weren't doing anything particularly important, so they were less likely to be conspicuous and get caught. And, of course, they could get round men without them noticing.

In fact, she had said disingenuously, eyes wide, she found nothing easier, unless it was her father. The little man interviewing her had laughed at that, and said it was true and that he quite saw she would be particularly good at it. However, for the time being women weren't being recruited to go behind enemy lines, although things might change . . .

They'd noticed her outfit – made in Paris? Could she tell them what details marked the difference between French and English clothing? What would a French peasant woman wear? An ordinary housewife going about her business in town? Frances had given them a lengthy lecture about the finer points of French tailoring as compared to English, and the way Frenchwomen walked, wore hats, talked to their families, what they ate and even thought.

'Observant,' the little man said approvingly, and made a note. Had she any serious medical conditions? Could she ride a bicycle? Did she think she could learn to survive on her own in the countryside?

Of course she could ride a bicycle! She was never ill. As for the last . . . After a moment's thought Frances had grinned and said she could. A friend often went poaching when rations ran out and was good at snaring rabbits and pigeons, even pheasant.

'Have you been poaching, Miss Falconleigh?'

Frances leaned across his desk. 'Not yet, but I intend to learn how. If I poach a brace of pheasants for you, will you take me?'

The little man had roared with laughter. 'You *are* determined! If we can't get the Admiral's consent for the SOE or the Auxiliary Unit, well, we can find you something to do.'

'It's a bargain,' Frances had said, and held out her hand.

He shook it. 'Bargain sealed,' he said, 'provided I get those pheasants.'

Frances had told him she would be twenty-one in November when she would no longer need her father's permission. Perhaps by then they would be letting women agents join the men behind enemy lines. Now, that *would* be thrilling.

The Admiral was still busy. Frances glanced at her watch. She thought how useful it was to have a friend like Evangeline who could do all sorts of surprising things. At first Evangeline, with her slow voice and languid ways, had seemed odd but, then, Frances had never known an American, and the fact that Aunt Muriel disapproved of her so vigorously had driven Frances to make friends with her. Sometimes Evangeline borrowed one of the Home Guard's old rifles, which Leander had donated, and went hunting in Richard's waxed jacket. She brought home pigeons – she called them doves – and even pheasants for the whole village. When Frances had explained about poaching, Evangeline had shrugged, clearly unconcerned. Game wasn't rationed and everyone in the village was hungry for meat.

Frances had been flabbergasted to find that her friend could do more than hunt: she was frightfully clever at making a lovely meal out of what she shot or trapped. She knew how to grill pigeons or rabbit on a spit over a handful of damp applewood chips. Also, she grew vegetables and had acquired a couple of hens: since eggs from your own birds weren't rationed, there was mayonnaise for the artichokes and tomatoes she produced. She baked apples and pears in honey . . . Evangeline said where she had grown up all girls learned to cook before they got married so they could make sure their own cooks did it properly. Frances's stomach rumbled. There hadn't been time for breakfast before the train and the biscuit tin had been empty for ages. Father had promised to give her lunch and she hoped he would remember.

The Admiral finished with the telegrams and the Wren took them away. Frances was fidgeting again. He'd give her lunch, then put her on the train, he thought. Before the war they would have gone to the Savoy or possibly the Ritz. A glass of sherry. Oysters. Roast chicken. Stilton. Trifle. Burgundy. Now, thanks to rationing, the food was dreadful everywhere so they might as well nip into one of the new British Restaurants. He knew it would be brown soup, bubble and squeak, then some sort of sweet in a puddle of custard that tasted of dried egg, but they would be in and out in a jiffy and he could get back to the war. Girls! The sooner they got married and stopped wasting their fathers' time the better.

13. Crowmarsh Priors, March 1941

Johnny's fretting usually woke Tanni early, but this morning it was a pair of jays squawking in the pear tree outside her window. She got up sleepily and put on the dressing-gown she had made from some old towels that Evangeline had discarded for rags. They had been frayed at the edges but a pretty faded blue and, using her coat to trace a pattern on to newspaper, Tanni had fashioned a soft, serviceable garment, with deep, turned-back cuffs, pockets and a sash. She had only white thread, but her stitches, tiny and neat as Frau Zayman had taught her, hardly showed.

'Wherever did you learn to do that?' exclaimed Evangeline. 'It's lovely! I've never had the patience to sew anything. The nuns used to rip out my stitches and make me do it over and over.'

Flushed with pride, Tanni offered to make her one too, pleased to have a way to thank her for taking them in. A few days later, Evangeline was putting on a becoming pink dressing-gown made from an old bedspread. She was so thrilled with it that Tanni asked if she could rummage through the boxes of old clothes and bedding in the Fairfaxes' attic for more things to alter. 'Help yourself. They're not doing anybody any good up there,' said Evangeline.

The government was urging everyone not to waste

material and everything related to clothing was in short supply, from needles to buttons, patterns and zips. There was a rumour that clothes would soon be rationed, as well as food. Using whatever odd pieces of material she could find, Tanni made underwear for herself and outfits for Johnny, who was outgrowing everything fast. Word spread round Crowmarsh Priors and the surrounding farms that Tanni could do wonders with old clothes, and before long she was never without the old gardener's basket filled with sewing commissions and a little notebook for recording people's measurements. Albert Hawthorne brought her the newspapers when he and Nell had finished reading them so that she could make patterns. Women brought worn frocks for restyling, taking in or freshening up with a new collar and cuffs, their men's trousers for new pockets or patching where the seat had worn through, their children's things to be lengthened and let out. Tanni even made two christening robes, finished with beautiful smocking. The women paid what they could afford, or with jam, pies, fruit and vegetables. In the autumn Constable Barrows's pregnant wife had paid for three maternity smocks and some baby clothes with a precious pair of laying hens donated by her mother. Evangeline's flock had increased to four.

Evangeline was grateful for the food that Tanni contributed to the household in this way. Only a few years ago Aunt Celeste's instructions in household management had bored her to tears. Now she struggled to recall everything she had been taught – after all, until Laurent came up with a plan, she was stuck in the village and they had to eat. Maude, Tommy and Kipper were always starving, and resourceful though Evangeline became at stretching the rations, feeding four children and two adults – four if Frances and Elsie were with them – was a daily struggle.

Tanni saw how hard they all worked, Evangeline in the garden and at foraging to put food on the table, Elsie and Frances on the farm, and Alice Osbourne with her clothing drives for refugees, knitting for the troops, first-aid classes and teaching at the school, and was glad she could be useful too. Colour came back into her cheeks and she faced each day confidently, reminding herself that she was a wife and mother, a grown woman with work to do, no longer a frightened schoolgirl.

Now she poked up the embers in the fireplace and put on a log, changed Johnny and glanced out of the window into the long, narrow garden behind the house. Just before Jimmy, the butcher's boy, had joined up the previous autumn, he had helped Evangeline dig up the flowers and shrubs to plant neat rows of winter cabbages, Brussels sprouts and leeks. They had missed some bulbs, though, and between the vegetables, crocuses and daffodils blossomed now, bright as stars. She had not noticed them until today. She pointed them out to Johnny, then took him into her bed, pulled the covers over them both and sang into Johnny's soft hair. Johnny played peek-a-boo, squirmed and chuckled.

She was so happy. Yesterday she had had a surprise telegram from Bruno. He had an unexpected few days' leave for Passover and was coming today to take her and Johnny to London for a *seder* with the Cohens in Bethnal Green. She had only seen Bruno twice since she left London. Both times she had gone by train with Johnny to Cambridge, but had had only a few hours with Bruno before he was called away unexpectedly. She had come home feeling lonelier than ever. Please, she thought, don't let Bruno's leave be cancelled this time. Although he telephoned whenever he could, she had not seen him for so long.

She was also anxious to see the Cohens. They had been interned for months in a camp on the Isle of Wight but had finally been allowed to leave after a tribunal had decided that an elderly rabbi and his wife were not dangerous enemy aliens or German spies. The Cohens were relieved to be home, but shaken by the experience. Tante Berthe couldn't understand how the authorities would believe that Jews were Nazi agents. They had been cheered when Tanni wrote to tell them that people were very kind in Sussex and everyone loved Johnny.

Evangeline had taken to the little boy straight away, and Alice had been friendly in her bossy way, calling to see if Tanni needed anything, bringing pamphlets about orange juice and cod-liver oil, and an English grammar book. Tanni noticed, though, that Alice disliked Evangeline and barely spoke to her. In the weeks after her arrival Tanni had worn herself out in trying not to upset anyone, and the sadness that had descended after Johnny's birth often gripped her. The English books and pamphlets gathered dust on her bedside table and it was all she could do to give Johnny his orange juice. Sister Tucker looked in as often as her busy schedule allowed, to reassure her that new mothers often felt like that, but Tanni was convinced that the dark feelings must be her own fault.

Then, little by little, she had begun to adjust, so that in the last few months she had felt better, more like her old self, and Johnny was thriving. Evangeline and Alice were her friends, even if they weren't friends with each other. She had found a way to make herself useful. She kissed the photo of her family, which was propped against the mirror. Now that Bruno was taking her to London she would be able to ask Rachel if they had found them yet.

The growing bubble of excitement inside her at the prospect of seeing Bruno meant she could hardly swallow her tea and toast. After breakfast Evangeline took Johnny when she walked with the older children to school so that Tanni could get ready. As soon as they were gone, the doorbell rang. It was Alice, on her way to school. She handed Tanni a parcel wrapped in brown paper. Inside, Tanni found a pullover and cap she had knitted for Johnny in heavy oiled wool she had purloined from the Dorcas Society's stock. Tanni thanked her profusely and gave her a hug.

As soon as Alice had gone, she bathed, careful not to fill the tub above the four-inch mark painted inside it. Then, wrapped in her blue dressing-gown, she washed her hair and rinsed it with vinegar to make it shine.

When Evangeline and Johnny reappeared, she was drying her hair in front of the stove. The doorbell rang again. This time it was Frances, in her land-girl uniform. She held out an elegant dressmaker's box with a French name on it in gold lettering.

'For me?' asked Tanni in disbelief. Frances was so glamorous that Tanni had always been too shy to say much more than 'good morning' to her. Frances nodded, smiling, so Tanni thanked her, opened the box and gave a cry of delight. Inside, beneath the tissue paper, she had found a delectable silk nightdress and peignoir, with lace and wide satin ribbons. 'It'll help keep his, um, morale up, darling,' Frances said wickedly. 'Take off that dressing-gown and try on the peignoir – yes, just as I thought! That cream is perfect with your dark hair. And, lucky you, you've more bosom than I have.' Tanni blushed – the négligée would show a great deal of it.

'I've got just the thing to go with that,' Evangeline exclaimed, and ran upstairs. She returned with a bottle of French scent. 'Schiaparelli,' she said.

Tanni remembered a similar bottle on her mother's dressing-table, and the dark feelings hovered, but she decided resolutely that they were not going to ruin the day. She dabbed a little on her wrist. 'Bruno will hardly know me!' She giggled.

In her best frock, feeling clean and new, Tanni was in the sun-filled morning room, humming while she put her new things into the carpetbag with Johnny's clothes, nappies and toys. 'What a fine house!' a voice said behind her.

Johnny, who had been about to crawl under the sofa after the cat, paused to stare at the stranger. Then he scrambled to his mother and hid behind her legs.

Tanni was gazing at the solid form of a short, vaguely familiar man with glasses, who was taking off his over-coat and pulling funny faces at her son. Suddenly flustered and shy, she felt like hiding too. Then Bruno bent down to sweep a startled Johnny into the crook of his right arm and hugged her tightly with his left. He kissed her cheek. 'So,' he said.

'Oh, Bruno!' They had spent so little time together as husband and wife, that Tanni was more accustomed to thinking of herself as a mother than as a wife. Now she would have to get used to being married all over again. She remembered how much she liked the solid feel of him under his rough tweed jacket.

Johnny squirmed, the cat fled, and Bruno swung his son over his head. Soon Johnny was shrieking with laughter and kicking. Tanni protested that Bruno would make him sick, so Bruno produced a boiled sweet, unwrapped it and popped it into Johnny's open mouth. There was silence as Johnny sucked, so Tanni, uncertain what to talk about, took a pile of Johnny's clothes out of the carpetbag, unfolded and recounted them. Several times.

'What a lot of things,' said Bruno, eyeing the pile on the sofa.

'Everyone's been so kind. My friend Alice, who teaches the children at school, made this.' She held up the jumper Alice had brought, one arm longer than the other. Bruno raised his eyebrows and she giggled. 'Constable Barrows carved him these animals when he was making some for his own baby, and Evangeline made a quilt with the alphabet on it, and got down her husband's old nursery furniture from the attic. It has rabbits painted on it and –'

'Tanni!' Bruno said, and swept her into his arms.

A few moments later they were talking softly, absorbed in each other, when Tanni saw, from the corner of her eye, that Johnny had pulled himself up on a side-table and his sticky fist had grasped a Limoges shepherdess he had had an eye on for weeks. His mouth was wide open and he was about to test his new front teeth on the frothy china skirt when Tanni swooped.

Just then the motor that had dropped Bruno half an hour earlier pulled up, with two figures in the front seats. Tanni fetched a basket that contained a few of the household's precious eggs and a pot of honey, and another with hyacinths from the garden. She kissed Evangeline goodbye, then pinned on her hat. The driver put the carpetbag and the hyacinths in the boot while Tanni and Bruno got into the back seat, with Johnny between them, and the basket of eggs on Tanni's lap. The car drove away.

The young man billeted with Constable Barrows was in the front with the driver but the glass partition was up so Tanni could not hear what they were saying to each other. His profile reminded her of a little English animal that Alice called a ferret. Several times he looked back and winked at Johnny, so Tanni smiled at him. She knew his name was Bernie. Elsie talked about him when she brought potatoes and sometimes illicit tins of beef or fish that she traded for one of Evangeline's game pies.

Tanni had so much to tell Bruno about her life in Crowmarsh Priors when they were alone. Alone! She felt a thrill of anticipation. The sun-drenched spring landscape rolled by and she and Bruno took turns to point out the cows and horses in the fields to Johnny. She glanced at her husband, wondering if he felt the same excitement as they approached London.

But the sight of the devastation the enemy had wrought

since she left dented Tanni's high spirits. By the time the
car reached Bethnal Green, picking its way through the
rubble and yawning spaces where buildings had been, the
sky was overcast. Rabbi Cohen, looking older, came out
to welcome them with Tante Berthe, who gave Tanni a
long hug and made much of Johnny. She exclaimed with
joy over the eggs, the honey and the flowers.

Inside, the house smelt deliciously of soup, baking and
something familiar. Tanni sniffed. Cinnamon. She closed
her eyes, seeing the Passover table in her own home, set
a day in advance with a damask cloth, the best dishes and
newly polished silver; the kitchen had been a hive of
activity, with her mother at the centre of it. Frau Anna
and the maids would have been sent home, exhausted
after a thorough spring-clean of the entire house, while
Frau Joseph, enveloped in a white apron, chopped and
roasted, showing Tanni how to add a pinch of this or
that, demonstrating how finely apples should be sliced or
horseradish grated, and letting the twins pick over a bowl
of dried fruit.

Tanni opened her eyes. Tante Berthe was holding out
a plate of sugared matzoh and almond biscuits. She took
one, and broke off a bit for Johnny. 'Everything smells
delicious,' she said. 'Thank you so much for inviting us.'
A long table had been wedged into the sitting room, at
an angle to accommodate as many people as possible,
and was covered with an embroidered white cloth,
gleaming china and glasses. Beneath the smell of cooking
Tanni detected bleach and fresh ironing. The rabbi had
disappeared into his study with Bruno. Tanni felt herself
relax. Thoughts of what would happen when she and

Bruno were together and she was wearing her négligée filled her mind. In fact, it was hard to think of anything else.

Tante Berthe thought Tanni looked blooming. The WVS woman had been right to send her to the country. The last time she had seen the girl she had been a spectre with dark circles under her eyes, distraught at having signed a paper that meant she had to go away or be put in a camp. That had been eighteen months ago.

'Come, my dear, I'll show you where you're to sleep.' She led the way up the stairs to a tiny room under the eaves. A good-natured impulse had inspired her to put her best embroidered linen sheets, often borrowed for bridal nights, on the two narrow beds she had pushed together, and to tuck Johnny's cot round a corner on the landing. Tanni stroked the sheets. 'What lovely work. It reminds me of . . . Oh, Tante Berthe, don't make me wait. What news is there of Lili and Klara?'

'You must be patient. Rachel is the only one who can answer your questions. She and her family are coming for the *seder*, and you can speak to her.'

When Tanni opened her carpetbag to give her aunt their ration books, the silk négligée spilled out and Tante Berthe smiled to herself. It cheered her to think of young people under her roof – and who knew? Maybe they would begin another baby here. She pinched Tanni's cheek affectionately. She must fatten her up a little, in case . . .

So many of the Cohens' friends arrived later to squeeze round the table for the *seder* that the sitting room was packed. Rachel, with her mother, husband and four-year-old son, arrived last. She was pregnant and so large that everyone had to move sideways again to make room for her. The candles were lit and after the Kiddush everyone shifted a little, pretending to recline to drink the first cup of wine. The glasses were refilled and the rabbi continued with the Hagadah, and the ritual foods, the lamb bone, the matzohs, the parsley sprigs, the slivers of horseradish root. They ate the last with Tante Berthe's special *haroseth*, a recipe passed down on her mother's side of the family for generations, which combined dried apples and dates, raisins, spices and wine. The rabbi's voice quavered as he answered the ritual questions put to him by Rachel's little boy, because Johnny was too young. When they came to the hard-boiled egg dipped in salt water, people at the table were weeping for loved ones in Europe.

Eventually Tante Berthe wiped her eyes and got up to serve the rest of the dinner, which she had spent days preparing. Most of those present had lent her their ration books on the day she had scoured Whitechapel, begging, cajoling and bullying greengrocers and kosher butchers to get what she needed. Tanni rose to help her.

Soon the table was crowded with dishes and Tanni marvelled that Tante Berthe had managed to make such a delicious meal despite the rationing. There was beet-root soup with egg drops, gefiltefish with horseradish, chopped liver, sweet and sour chicken, *tzimmis* with short ribs, a potato *kugel*, a vegetable *kugel* and aubergine salad. Then came a dish of baked apples stuffed with dried fruit and a honey-soaked sponge cake made from matzoh flour. Finally Tante Berthe produced plates of tiny macaroons.

Afterwards everyone joined in reciting grace, then drank the third glass of wine. Unused to alcohol, Tanni felt light-headed as they sang the closing prayers and songs. She emptied her fourth glass of wine, hardly tasting it, her cheeks pink, then got up unsteadily to help Tante Berthe clear the table. 'I'm going to talk to Rachel in a minute,' she whispered in Bruno's ear.

'No, you help Tante Berthe, and I'll speak to Rachel,' said Bruno, firmly, 'while you put Johnny to bed. I'll be up soon.'

Rachel followed Bruno into the rabbi's study. She had been dreading this moment.

'Tanni has been very ill,' Bruno began, 'and we must take care that she is not made ill again. She feels responsible for her sisters – she hopes and believes they are in England. She is anxious for your committee to find them. She intends speaking to you herself, but if you know anything, please tell me now. If it is bad news I will break it to her gently. Also, you may have information about which, officially, I must know nothing. You will understand that I must not compromise my position with the authorities, but on the other hand I must help my wife and our families. In return for what you can tell me, I will do what I can to assist your committee's work without jeopardizing mine. For example, if you have information that needs to be confirmed, there may be ways I can help.'

Rachel rubbed the small of her aching back and considered. Bruno did not have to say any more about the need for discretion. She didn't know what he did but, with his languages and his sharp mind, she was sure he was working for Military Intelligence at a high level. Her committee, on the other hand, operated out of desperation and on a shoestring, far outside the scope of officialdom, so the authorities had paid it little attention, but the War Office had found that its network of informants could occasionally provide useful information about RAF pilots missing in enemy territory. They were unconcerned about Jewish civilians behind enemy lines.

'As far as the Joseph twins are concerned, there is bad news. They are definitely not in England – if they were, we would have found them by now. With some difficulty we traced them to the last *Kindertransport*, which did not leave Austria until June. There were problems when the border guards demanded bigger bribes than had been agreed to let the train pass. By the time the negotiations were complete, the train had been diverted to France where the children were taken off. They were kept at a transit camp for most of August, then put on trains for Le Havre and the ferry to England. They were due to sail on the day England declared war. That meant they became enemy aliens and were not allowed entry. We think the children were put back on the train at Le Havre, and it went south. They could be anywhere, but are probably in a displaced persons' camp.'

Bruno grimaced. He knew that those camps were hell-holes, overcrowded with Republican refugees from Spain who dared not return now that the Nationalists had triumphed. Food and medicine were in short supply; crime and disease were rife. It was no place for two unprotected little girls.

'I know that the Quakers and the Jehovah's Witnesses

are allowed into the camps to help with relief operations, and the American consul in Marseille is sympathetic and helps unofficially as much as he can. Is there information through those channels?' he asked.

Rachel nodded. 'The Quakers try to keep track of unaccompanied children, so that they can be reunited with their families. So far there is no record of the Joseph girls in the camp but, of course, some children may have died or been removed from the train *en route*.'

'But you will keep looking?' Bruno asked, although he wondered what they could do even if the twins were found alive in a camp.

'Of course, but we're trying to help so many people that it is like emptying the sea with a thimble.'

'And Dr Joseph and his wife – my mother? I have made every possible inquiry through every possible channel. Other than that they are no longer in my mother's flat, I have met only dead ends.'

'Our contacts have been able to give us a little information. An elderly man, a relative of one of my colleagues, had been Dr Joseph's patient and confirmed they were living with your mother, but that the night Lili and Klara left with the *Kindertransport*, the Germans arrested all the Jews in their quarter. If Tanni's parents and your mother were among them, they were probably deported to a German labour camp to make munitions. They say people from the quarter your mother lived in have been seen in Oswiecim, also called Auschwitz. But until we know for sure, say nothing to Tanni.'

'We have American contacts in Marseille who pass funds to the Quakers for the transit camps. I will ask them to keep trying. But Auschwitz . . .' Bruno shuddered.

'We will do what we can,' promised Rachel, wearily. She repeated it many times each day. They were overwhelmed with people like Bruno and Tanni begging for information about their families.

When Bruno went upstairs, he found Tanni wrapped in a peignoir, brushing her hair. Johnny was asleep.

She turned to smile at him, laying a finger on her lips. 'Johnny was exhausted. His first proper *seder*! Now, Bruno, tell me what Rachel said. Don't keep me in suspense. I'm sure you have good news.'

Bruno's mother had once warned him that the Josephs would not consider a dressmaker's son a worthy husband for their beloved eldest daughter. But there she sat, his wife, the mother of their son, her hair tumbling over her shoulders, glowing with contentment. Bruno's heart tightened. He would protect her from unhappiness for as long as he could and tell her only that Rachel and her group still had no definite news. But even that could wait.

He took the hairbrush from her, sat on the bed and began to brush her hair slowly. How soft and shiny it was.

'Bruno! Tell me!' But Tanni shut her eyes and relaxed against him. Bruno put down the brush and buried his face in her neck. She turned and they put their arms round each other. 'What did Rachel say?' Tanni murmured.

Bruno pulled her down with him. 'Ssh, not now, my sweet one. Not tonight. We'll talk about it tomorrow.'

14. Sussex Downs, August 1941

There had been no air-raid warning, only the drone of an approaching aeroplane as the children went out to play after lunch on Saturday. Then a lone German Heinkel 111 roared low over Crowmarsh Priors. By the time anxious mothers had dropped the washing-up and rushed out in their aprons to drag their children to safety, the bomber was over the downs, twisting and rolling across the sky to escape the RAF Hurricanes now in pursuit.

Albert Hawthorne thought they were trying to force the German away from the village and out over the Channel before they shot him down but, to his surprise, the Heinkel turned back sharply and headed for cover in a bank of dark clouds rolling inland from the sea. Too late.

'Go to it! Get 'im, lads!' Albert shouted, as the RAF gunners opened up. Mesmerized, the village watched as the Heinkel veered off-course, belching black smoke. Half a minute later it was circling back towards land, wobbling in the sky, tipping sideways and falling out of the clouds, nose down. It disappeared out of sight and a loud explosion sounded somewhere on the downs.

The excited children whooped and waved at the departing Hurricanes. 'Three cheers for the RAF! Hip-hip . . . hooray!' The mothers wiped trembling hands, still wet, on their aprons, feeling faint at such a close shave.

*

In his study Oliver Hammet had heard the planes through the open window, but the crash jerked him to his feet. Abandoning the next day's sermon, he hurried to unlock the cabinet under the vicarage stairs where the Home Guard kept the de Balfort guns.

At Ashpole Cottages Albert handed Nell his hoe, and joined the publican, Harry Smith, who hobbled past, leaning on his walking-stick. The farmers' sons had enlisted and gone, so it was just the three who gathered at the village hall to wait for Hugo de Balfort. Ten minutes later he screeched to a halt outside in a battered shooting brake. The Home Guard was assembled.

The older children clamoured to help find the Heinkel, but their mothers wouldn't let them out of their sight.

In the muggy August heat, the Home Guard set off in shirtsleeves. Hugo and Oliver were armed with the de Balfort hunting rifles and a handful of ammunition. Albert Hawthorne carried a scythe he had honed to razor sharpness, and Harry Smith brandished his stout knobbed walking-stick, which he called a 'fool killer'.

When a German plane was shot down, it was the Home Guard's job to find the wreck and either verify that the occupants were dead or, if any German airmen were alive, to arrest them and wait for an ambulance or the military authorities to take them away. War Office directives repeatedly stressed the danger of allowing shot-down Germans to escape into the countryside where they would assist the invasion, and the Home Guard knew that British Nazi sympathizers would be prepared to shelter and assist them. The War Office's instructions were unequivocal: there must be no escapees. If a German refused to surrender or tried to escape, he must be shot.

Combing the downs was tiring at the best of times, and Hugo's shooting brake was too decrepit to be useful on the uneven terrain, so the men had to go on foot. The downs were bigger than they looked. What appeared to be a gentle rise and fall from a distance became a series of steep climbs but, mindful of their duty, the Home Guard went as fast as they could. From time to time they paused to catch their breath while Hugo scanned the countryside through his binoculars.

'First time one's been shot down so near,' puffed Albert. 'We're in luck, might actually catch the buggers. Good sport, I'd say.'

Soon Harry Smith gave up, unable to climb any further on his bad leg. 'Sorry, lads,' he gasped, red in the face, as he collapsed on to a rock bent over his walking-stick. 'If you find anyone, chase him past me. The fool killer'll give the murdering bastard something to remember England by!'

Hugo hurried on ahead of Oliver and Albert. Oliver knew he drove himself hard on Home Guard exercises because he had been rejected as unfit for active service. Albert had to fit his Home Guard duties round the train schedules and eventually he had to turn back to meet the three forty-seven from London. He wanted nothing so much as to find a German trying to escape, he grumbled. He'd give Fritz a taste of his scythe, see fear in the man's eyes.

With the exercise he got as a member of the Home Guard, Oliver had become tanned and was easily the fittest of the four, but as the youngest member, he normally let the other men set the pace. As a clergyman, he had not been obliged to join but with so few able-bodied men available he had felt it his duty. When Albert was gone he ran ahead to join Hugo, who looked done in. He was as white as a sheet and panting hoarsely as he swatted away swarms of midges. 'It's nothing, really, lung collapsed on me when I was a child. Do very well with just the one – army should have taken me.' He doubled over, gasping for breath.

'Have a rest.' Oliver shifted his gun, and put his free hand on Hugo's shoulder. 'Sit down. I'll go on ahead and you follow when you've got your breath back.'

Oliver hurried on up the steep path. He was enjoying the exercise until he reminded himself that he was supposed to be looking for Germans.

At the top he saw that the downs were deserted, except for a few anti-aircraft guns covered with camouflage nets. No one was manning them, and he realized he was on his own as he pinpointed the Heinkel's location by a rising column of smoke, barely visible against the grey sky. He scrambled over a rise towards it. Moments later he was looking down on a smouldering mass in a green fold of the hills. His hand tightened on his gun as he scanned the downs for anyone running from the wreckage. Could he kill a man – even a German? Oliver had taken it as a matter of faith that, for the present, God and the Prime Minister were on the same side and he was duty-bound to obey the government's orders. He also felt it would be hypocritical to pray for England's military success when he was too squeamish to confront the enemy. But . . .

The smell of burning hit his nostrils and he spotted what looked like two dolls in grey uniform on the ground. It was the first time he had seen a downed plane outside newsreels. He braced himself for Germans living or dead as he hurried towards it. He prayed that any who were alive would surrender and that he would not be put to the test by having to shoot them.

A fierce blast of heat hit him, but he kept on towards the wreck, gagging on the smoke and a horrible smell. He wadded his handkerchief against his nose, but the stench grew worse as he drew nearer — a mixture of burning petrol, burning rubber and what he knew instinctively was burning flesh. He thought airmen must be trapped inside — certainly the gunners at the back. The heat was too intense to allow him to get close enough to see inside so he searched for the two figures he had seen from above. Finally he tripped over one and saw the other lying nearby. He guessed they had either been flung from the cockpit, which hung open, or had crawled away from the flames. Oliver bent over, shielding his face and eyes with his arm.

The man he had stumbled over was clearly dead. He lay face down, singed boots awkwardly pigeon-toed. His head was at an impossible angle. The leather cap was split and something oozed round the edges on to the ground. Oliver was no stranger to death in cottage bedrooms or at the local hospital, but he had never been confronted with it in so violent and deliberate a form. What terror the airmen must have endured as the plane went down. He struggled into the scorching heat towards the other figure.

It moved. The man lay twisted on his back. He had pulled off his helmet, but his hair was gone, burned away from his oozing scalp. As he inched through the blistering heat and the fumes, Oliver could see the man's chest heaving as he gasped for breath. Blood covered the raw head. It had been more than two hours since the plane had gone down. The man turned his face towards Oliver. There was a hole where his nose had been. Oliver wondered if he had been conscious all that time.

As he looked at the man lying on the ground, any desire Oliver had felt for revenge on the enemy melted into despair and anger that human beings should make such suffering for each other. He wished he had thought to bring some water. He dropped his gun and fell to his knees beside the man.

In the distance the three forty-seven whistled as it left the station in what was, at that moment, another world. Then there was no sound but the crackle of flames.

The German stirred. He opened a blue eye. His eyebrows and lashes had been burned away too. '*Wasser*,' he moaned. Oliver groped helplessly for the German he remembered from university – he had read Goethe... The German croaked something else. Oliver caught '*Frau*'. The man pawed helplessly at his breast pocket. '*Bitte*', he whispered. Oliver took his hand gently. It felt as if the bones inside were broken. For lack of anything else to do, he began to recite the prayer for the dying.

'*Bitte*,' whispered the man again, staring intently at him with one blue eye. '*Fotograf*.' He touched his pocket with their clasped hands. At last Oliver understood. *Frau*. Wife. He interrupted the prayer, reached into the man's pocket and withdrew a snapshot of a pretty young woman with fair hair in plaits round her head, sitting on a rug and holding a child. It looked as if they were in a garden or a park, having a picnic. The little girl was laughing and the woman was smiling down at her. He tried to close the man's fingers round the photograph but they wouldn't work, so Oliver slipped the photograph between them and held it there.

'Kristina,' the man whispered raggedly, '*liebe Frau.*' Blood trickled from the corner of his mouth. Then he gave a shudder and died.

Oliver felt unbearably tired. He had conducted too many funerals lately, the latest for two brothers crushed when an airfield mechanics' hut had taken a direct hit. The family had been wild-eyed with grief, and a local farmer's daughter at the back of the church had sobbed uncontrollably on her mother's shoulder. She had been engaged to one of the boys, who had left her expecting a baby. The villagers had condemned her as no better than she should be and cold-shouldered her and her family.

He wanted to rage at God. What is it You expect me to do in the face of all this killing and human despair? I have buried local lads killed by other young men like these two and laid them in the graveyard next to the men from their families who died in the Great War and whose names are on a memorial plaque in the church. Now we will bury these men, and somewhere in Germany their families will weep and there will be more names on other memorials. All across Europe people are killing each other, girls cry over unborn fatherless babies and God-fearing people blindly reject the gift of a new life. Eventually all that's left of civilization will be names on gravestones. Why?

As he thought of the scene before him being replayed day in, day out, the slaughter at Dunkirk, in Poland, Belgium and everywhere else, Oliver felt an overwhelming urge to lie down beside the dead man and sleep.

A clap of thunder roused him. He glanced up and saw Albert and Hugo coming towards him. Lightning flashed over the coast and the wind blew harder. Time to get off the downs.

'Tonight for once they'll sleep in Hythe – the Civil Defence in London too, while this storm lasts,' said Albert. Everyone followed the weather anxiously now, dreading clear spells. Bombing was at its worst then, because the enemy could navigate easily, especially when there was a moon.

'Pray the storm keeps up along the coast,' said Oliver, forcing himself to stand as the first drops of rain sizzled on the hot metal. Over the sea he saw more flashes and heard another threatening rumble of thunder.

'Come on. No use standing about up here to get struck by lightning,' said Hugo. 'I'll contact the police to collect the bodies before any children find them – I'll phone from the vicarage, if I may. I suppose we'll get stuck with burying them.'

'Amazin' how Jerry always picks clear nights to cross the Channel,' Albert muttered.

Hugo was looking sick. 'He got it wrong today. Have you ever thought what we'd do if we actually captured a German and he tried to escape? Could you shoot him?'

'If he tried to run away,' Albert fingered his scythe, 'yes.'

Suddenly Oliver knew with absolute conviction that, having watched the German die, he could not. Whatever happened, even if it were to cost him his own life, he would not kill another human being. He squared his shoulders. His duty was clear. He would continue to pray for the armed forces, but as far as he was concerned, whatever the government's orders, his first duty was to God and the preservation of life. To be certain of something, he thought, even in the most horrible circumstances, was strangely comforting. Like being in quicksand and suddenly finding a rock under your feet. He offered up a silent prayer of thanks.

15. Crowmarsh Priors,
September 1941

War, thought Muriel Marchmont, crossly, was a noisy, inconvenient business. Planes chasing each other overhead, shattering the peace of the afternoon, the dreadful air-raid siren, whose shrill summons they all had to obey, no matter when it sounded. And this rationing, with coupons and points, was so confusing. First it had been sugar, butter and meat, and then, before one knew where one was, one needed coupons to buy cheese and eggs, bacon and even clothing.

The cook, Mrs Barkins, had given notice at Christmas and gone to work in a shipyard, of all places. Mrs Gifford had been obliged to fill in but cooking was not her forte. Now indigestion kept Muriel awake all night. And while Mrs Gifford struggled in the kitchen, the house became more and more untidy. Housemaids were not to be thought of: they had all gone to work in munitions factories or as bus conductresses.

Muriel could sympathize with those friends of her late husband who laid the blame for this misconceived war with 'foreigners', especially the French and the Poles, who had influenced Churchill. Surely things had reached a point where it was in England's best interests to make peace with Germany. She would have liked to shake politicians until they saw sense. And all the intractable young people for whom she had made such suitable plans. Were any of them prepared to be guided by their elders? Were they the slightest bit grateful? Age made Muriel easily vexed. She hardly knew whether she was more irritated by the war, by Frances's refusal to help Alice make herself attractive to Oliver or by Alice's cowed look and pale face. Hugo, she knew from Leander, had not yet proposed, and Frances had gone up to London twice without telling her. As for Oliver . . .

He had buried two dead Germans in the furthest corner of the churchyard. She had rung the bishop to protest that they had probably been Lutheran and, as such, had no business in an Anglican graveyard. The bishop, who had dealt with Muriel Marchmont before, temporized, hummed and hawed, said it was wartime and the deed was done, and the Church authorities were not keen on exhumation. Finally he had sent her into a lather of fury by suggesting she pray for her enemies. She had slammed down the telephone, which brought on a dizzy spell.

She had been sadly mistaken in extending her patronage to Oliver. He had forgotten what he owed her and was behaving in far too independent a manner for her liking. Mild-mannered as he was, he had become a figure of authority in the village. The war had matured him. The boyish look had disappeared and he now juggled services, christenings, the Mothers' Union, the parish accounts, visiting the sick and the Sunday-school rotas more or less efficiently with his Home Guard duties. A naturally shy man when he had first come to Crowmarsh Priors, he had wrestled for days to perfect a sermon. Now, with less and less time to spend at his desk, his sermons were much more affecting because he spoke from the heart, another source of irritation to Muriel, who disliked the low-church evangelical streak that had lately been in evidence. Oliver had developed a knack of making a connection between daily and biblical events, which had proved comforting in these difficult times to everyone but herself. Although Evangeline Fairfax was a Roman Catholic, she had dragged Tommy, Maude and Kipper to a special children's service, at which she had confided to Frances that Oliver reminded her of the coloured preachers in New Orleans: 'In a minute he'll shout, "*Amen*, brothers and sisters!"'

Worst of all, Oliver had shown a disgraceful laxity in upholding the village's moral standards. Several babies had been born to unmarried mothers, the fathers away fighting, killed or missing in action. Oliver had visited them all and, with some difficulty because the girls were so ashamed, persuaded them to let him baptize their children. Muriel Marchmont had been shocked when she learned that he planned to do so in full view of the congregation at the next Sunday service, just as he did the children of lawfully wedded parents. She wrote a furious note ordering him to do nothing of the kind and assumed that that would be the end of the matter.

On the Sunday Oliver had designated for the baptisms, in lieu of the usual private ceremonies, she was astonished to see several unmarried girls with babies at the back of the church. Oliver had preached a most persuasive sermon about new life being a gift from God that should be cherished in the midst of war and death. It had had people looking shamefacedly at each other. Several middle-aged women who had lost their sons and were longing to acknowledge their grandchildren burst into tears. Such was Oliver's authority that afterwards most of the congregation went to admire the babies. There were offers of outgrown prams and cots, and Constable Barrows promised to carve each child a set of building blocks.

Muriel had been outraged almost, but not quite, to the point of speechlessness. She paused at the door, in front of fellow parishioners waiting behind her to shake Oliver's hand. 'It won't do! Babies out of wedlock won't do, I tell you. Send them away – lock them up! I won't stand for it, young man!' she spluttered. She ordered him to promise he would never do it again.

Oliver listened patiently. Then he imprisoned her gloved hand in both of his and replied, for all to hear, that he would baptize every child in the parish as long he was vicar. 'Have a peaceful Sunday,' he added.

For once she had been silenced. He had told her publicly that she was wrong! No one had ever spoken to her like that. Behind her, people grinned at their feet. Lady Marchmont and her tirades were wearing and they were pleased someone had stood up to her. Aside from the matter of the fatherless babies, she had been particularly nasty to Tanni Zayman recently because she was 'foreign', and everyone in the village was fond of the young woman and her sweet-natured little boy.

The next afternoon Alice and Oliver were in the vestry, discussing arrangements for the annual Harvest Fayre.

'Every house in the village, except the vicarage, has a victory garden and competition is keen over the vegetables,' said Alice. 'Nell Hawthorne has a new way of making dried-apple pies for the home-produce table, and we've lots of prizes for the tombola – Tanni has embroidered a baby's cap, the pub has donated a bottle of whisky, Constable Barrows has carved a wooden Noah's Ark and animals, his wife Edith has sewn fifty lavender bags and even Mummy has crocheted a table-runner. And there's Shirley Temple, of course.'

In the spring the village had clubbed together to buy a piglet. It was fed on table scraps and vegetable peel-ings, and was to be butchered and shared out at Christmas, but in the meantime the children had named it Shirley Temple, and it had become a pet. 'They want Shirley Temple to have a pen at the Harvest Fayre. Margaret Rose Hawthorne has made a ribbon for her substantial neck,' Alice went on. 'Oh, and Nell said that if you don't mind she'll come and pick the blackberries in the churchyard for jam. It's terribly overgrown since Jimmy signed up, but looking on the bright side there's a good crop and she can sell the jam with her pies. Goodness, is Mrs Gifford *running?*'

Lady Marchmont's housekeeper came breathlessly through the church gate, her apron crooked. 'Vicar, come quick! It's her ladyship! I've sent for the doctor, but she wants you, Vicar,' Mrs Gifford panted. 'She was gardening this morning in the heat, then after lunch she felt faint. I was washing up when I heard her fall. I helped her to bed and sent to the home farm for Miss Frances and the doctor, but she's gone all peculiar in the face, and –'

Oliver grabbed the items he needed to administer Holy Communion and hurried off to Glebe House.

An hour later the doctor arrived and pronounced Lady Marchmont dead of a massive stroke.

Three days later two solemn men in black, one old and one young, with bowler hats and large briefcases, stepped off the morning train from London. Albert recognized Lady Marchmont's London solicitor with his clerk. Over the years she had summoned them frequently. 'Last time you'll be needed, I dare say.' They frowned at him and marched off.

At Glebe House Mrs Gifford served weak coffee to the two men, Frances and Oliver, who had been summoned from the vicarage. She started to withdraw but the solicitor asked her to stay while the will was read. He had advised the Marchmont family for many years, and had come to dread her ladyship's periodic summonses to Sussex to amend her will. She had always ignored his advice, and now it was full of the tortuous and incomprehensible provisos upon which she had insisted. He settled his spectacles on his nose, cleared his throat and hoped that he could make sense of the bewildering document.

He began with the least complicated provision, a small legacy for Mrs Gifford and the right to stay on for life in her two rooms behind the kitchen. The solicitor paused. The housekeeper sniffed and said she was glad of the money but that after thirty years she fancied a change, thank you very much. She planned to take on war work at a munitions factory near Reading.

The solicitor continued. Lady Marchmont had not had time to alter her will before she died and Glebe House was still left to Oliver, her only living relative. However, he had just received notification that the War Office was requisitioning it for the duration: it would be used as a recuperation home for wounded servicemen. The clerk interrupted to explain that, as land girls, Frances and Elsie would be allowed to remain in the house since the land-girl hostel near Brighton was full and no other billet was available in the vicinity. There was something about shares and money for Oliver, while the contents of the house and Lady Marchmont's jewellery went to Frances. 'Though as far as we know,' the solicitor said, shaking his head, 'there's nothing of great value. Surprising, really. There was a great deal of jewellery once. Now there are only her everyday items – her watch, a few rings, some antique brooches. A few items of paste. There should be an inventory but she was somewhat vague about it last time I asked.'

During the reading Frances watched Oliver on the sofa. She wasn't particularly interested in jewellery or furniture. His eyes were closed and she wondered if he was following what the solicitor was saying. If so, he didn't look particularly happy to know that he was now a rich man, the owner of a grand house, even if he couldn't live in it yet. Now he opened his eyes and rubbed them. He seemed to be thinking of something else. It struck Frances how much he had aged since she arrived. He often looked sad and worn with the extra demands the war placed on him. Of course, Aunt Muriel had bullied him relentlessly, and he had just had word of the death of a local girl who had volunteered to drive an ambulance in London. It had taken a direct hit. Frances knew he had spent hours the night before with the bereaved family.

All of a sudden Frances thought that Oliver was lonely. He was a tower of strength for other people in their hour of need, but did anyone care for him? God, naturally: Oliver seemed firm in his faith . . . But on a more human level . . . Frances felt a surge of sympathy and an impulse to put her arms round him. As the solicitor's voice droned on, it occurred to her that he was taller than she was, and if she stood on tiptoe and he bent down a little . . . Her mouth opened as the scenario turned into a kiss and . . .

The solicitor was staring at her, one eyebrow raised quizzically. Frances dropped her eyes and stared at her knees until at last they reached the end of the will. The solicitor asked if there were any questions, then solemnly accepted sherry and biscuits from Mrs Gifford. Afterwards he and the clerk packed up their papers to return to London.

When they had gone Frances moved to sit beside Oliver and said, 'Since the house now belongs to you, Elsie and I can try to squeeze into the hostel, but perhaps I may store some things in the cellar for the time being?'

'Of course. But Cousin Muriel told me it would be only a matter of time before you needed them for your new home.' Oliver took off his glasses again and polished them with his handkerchief.

Frances noticed that his white clerical collar set off the tan he had acquired from walking on the downs, and that his eyes, with little lines round them now, were a deep brown. They held hers steadily. 'Mmm,' she said. 'She meant me to marry Hugo.'

He nodded. 'I think most people here shared her expectation.'

Frances shrugged. 'Then they're doomed to disappointment. For a start Hugo has never asked me. And speaking of matches she planned . . .' She grinned.

'I know – oh, I know!' Oliver groaned. He pushed his hair off his forehead and put his glasses back on. 'She made it so obvious, and it was frightfully embarrassing at first. Then one day Alice let slip that she'd once hurled an entire basket of apples through the vestry window and used every bad word she knew because Nell Hawthorne had tried to wheedle her into making apple tarts for me. We both laughed and it's been a joke between us ever since. But *only* a joke,' Oliver added, in his new firm voice. 'Alice is a brick, but marrying her would be like marrying my sister.'

'You don't think Aunt Muriel will come back and badger us from beyond the grave? She always wanted to have the last word. Jolly awkward of her, leaving things here and there. Much simpler if she had wanted you and me to make a match of it – that way her house, money, furniture and jewellery could have stayed together,' Frances babbled, suddenly feeling that she had gone much too far. 'Daft, really,' she finished feebly, and blushed.

Oliver looked taken aback and Frances cursed herself. Then he smiled at her – in a way that plainly he hadn't for a long time, because the little lines round his eyes deepened. 'Vicars are warned about elderly female parishioners, and I felt I was just getting the hang of dealing with her when she died. If she comes back as a ghost, I shall get the bishop's permission to hold an exorcism. He had a run-in or two with her himself.' Oliver patted Frances's hand in a vicarly way, then gave it a little squeeze.

Frances was just thinking how pleasantly warm and strong it was when he removed it and stood up. 'Of course you mustn't think of leaving the house. Nice to think of you living here. Elsie too, of course.' He glanced at his watch. 'Mothers' Union meeting at two. Must press on.'

Frances sat on in the morning room, absurdly happy that Oliver wasn't going to marry Alice. She felt a sudden surge of sympathy for her. Imagine spending one's days in the infants' school and going home to that dreadful mother afterwards. No wonder Alice was so bedraggled. She would try to be nicer to her.

16. Crowmarsh Priors, November 1941

The Wednesday three days before Frances's twenty-first birthday began badly. At the farm the land-girl team leader assigned her her least favourite job. Grumpily Frances banged the pail on to the ground and sat on the milking stool. She fumbled for the cow's teats and the animal mooed and tossed her head. 'Do shut up and stand still, Queenie,' she muttered. The cow shifted, knocking her sideways into the straw. Frances picked herself up and slapped Queenie's rump. Irritated, Queenie kicked her hard with a mucky foot.

Lugging milk pails back to the dairy she decided to take a shortcut through the bull's pen since its occupant wasn't in sight. Then, out of nowhere, the bull was charging towards her from the far end of the field, head lowered. In her hurry to get away Frances didn't shut the gate properly and he got out. He ran off down the lane, tossing his head and bellowing. Fortunately two farmers were passing and went after him with a prod and a large forked stick. 'Damn!' muttered Frances, sloshing milk into the tops of her boots.

At midday the team leader ticked her off in front of everyone. Frances yawned ostentatiously. 'Now, for the rest of you, we'll have a jolly good singsong over our sandwiches,' said the team leader.

Frances snapped, 'Not another! It's like a bloody

nursery! "Back to the land / We must all lend a hand!" is too stupid for words, and I'll be damned if I sing it again, war or no war.'

Uncertain how to cope with mutiny in the ranks and trying to hang on to her authority, the team leader said, 'I shall report you for insubordination!'

'Do. I'm going to the pub for lunch.'

Elsie put down her spade. 'An' me! I bloody 'ate singin'.'

'Elsie Pigeon, I'm reporting you too!'

Elsie made a rude gesture with two fingers and muttered, 'Bugger off!' She and Frances cycled off for some cider, leaving several land girls snickering and the team leader in a temper.

An hour later, somewhat the worse for wear, they wove back to the farm on the bicycles. Elsie stopped. 'I don't fancy goin' back. I'm fed up wiv farmin'.'

'Me too, darling. So tedious! Whoops!' Frances wobbled as she turned a corner, then tumbled off. 'Oops!'

'You 'ungry?'

'Always, darling!' Frances rubbed a bruised leg, light-headed from drinking cider on an empty stomach.

''Ere. I was savin' this.' Elsie grinned. From beneath the pullover in her bicycle basket she produced a packet of ham sandwiches on thickly buttered bread, slabs of chocolate and American cigarettes. The two girls fell on the food.

'Ham! Oh, lovely, lovely ham! Where on earth – with rations and all?' said Frances, when she was licking choco-late off her fingers. She helped herself to a cigarette and lit it.

'Bernie,' said Elsie.

'Of course,' said Frances, guiltily. Elsie always had treats in spite of rationing – a pressed-powder compact, perfumed soap, lipstick, stockings, chocolate, talcum powder, silk underwear, tinned salmon . . .

'Bernie's dealing in black-market stuff, isn't he? Darling, he'll get caught! The papers are full of dire stories about people who break the rationing laws. Shopkeepers get fined and go to prison just for selling the tiniest bit of butter without a coupon. Penal servitude. Months and months of it.'

'Bernie? Naaoow, they never,' drawled Elsie, exhaling American tobacco smoke luxuriously. ''E's too good at it, knows 'ow to go about it wivout callin' attention to 'imself. Butter. Sugar. Petrol. Whisky, even. You name it, there's a lot of it floatin' about, an' a lot of people ready to pay for it. 'E knows where to get it, so 'e does a bit of tradin' 'ere and there, this an' that. Lot of it goin' on, Frances. Government can't get their 'ands on everyfink. And anyway they turn a blind eye to what Bernie gets up to.'

'Whatever does Bernie do, darling, to get away with it? I suppose it's the most terrific secret.'

'Oh, exactly what he done before the war,' said Elsie, coolly. ''E's not s'posed to talk about it but 'e can't 'elp tellin' me. Forgin' and burglin', well, scavenging after the bombin's mostly.'

'What?'

'Before the war, the coppers was always tryin' to nick Bernie an' send 'im away. Now 'e 'as a motor to pick 'im up and bring 'im back and they gives 'im room and board with Constable Barrows to keep an eye on 'im. They even pay 'im. You got to ask, what can the government want wiv Bernie Carpenter? Not like they need 'im to fix a dog race or for protection work or to fence a dodgy lorry-load of cigarettes or jam, is it? The forgin's one fing. 'E told me 'imself. It's like 'e's got a gift for it. 'Nother is, I fink, 'e goes scavengin'. Bomb 'its a jeweller's or a bank, or a big 'ouse where they might keep jewellery, Bernie goes in quick. 'E's supposed to find diamonds, crack a safe to get 'em if need be. 'E gets a police guard, even, to warn people away while 'e's doin' it. I fink the War Office needs diamonds. Dunno for what, but Bernie says some fings they get up to you'd never believe. But that's on the quiet, mind. Bernie says it's all right for the people who owned the diamonds, they got insurance and all.'

'Elsie, be careful. Even if he gets away with all this stuff now he's bound to end up in prison eventually. He'll leave you high and dry.'

Elsie smoked and thought for a minute. If Mum had been there she would have agreed with Frances. But Elsie was on her own now, and for the time being she was following her heart. She would take care, though. 'See, Frances, you don't know 'ow folk like me and Bernie 'ave to live. You only know 'igh-ups, and 'ow *they* live. Lady Marchmont and Sir Leander and that 'Ugo – even Alice and 'er mum, who fink they 'aven't much, but they'll always 'ave more'n most.

'You don't know nuffink about what it's like round Norf Street, wiv the men out of work and not many jobs anyway, the glue factory smellin' enough to make your 'ead ache, me mum skimpin' every day just to feed us our dinner and keep a roof over our 'eads. Always 'ungry we was, but Mum tried her 'ardest. She sold almost everyfink we owned, even her weddin' ring, so's she could pay the rent man. She 'ated sellin' 'er ring worse than anyfink. Always said no matter 'ow bad things got, at least people could tell she were a respectable married woman. One fing I learned, you get a chance, any chance at all, not to live that way, you got to grab it quick, Frances. Ain't many chances for folk like Bernie and me. Bernie, 'e grabbed 'is chance to put somefink by for when the 'igh-ups are finished wiv 'im and toss 'im back to Norf Street. An' anyway, what wiv what 'e knows about them givin' 'im orders to do the forgin' an' safe-crackin' and all, if they make trouble for Bernie, 'e'll make trouble for them.'

'Ah. Blackmail. Good luck to you both, then. And thanks for the sandwiches. They were delicious,' said Frances, deciding she didn't care a hoot if they were black-market or not.

They were terribly late back and the team leader was in a frightful sulk. She sent Frances to join the potato diggers in a boggy field where the heavy mud clung to her boots like cement, and Elsie to oil the tractor. She ordered the others not to speak to them for the rest of the day. Elsie, feeling the effects of the cider, stalled the tractor when testing it, then drove it into the ha-ha. She emerged swearing, leaving the tractor on its side. The rest of the team glowered, and Frances was glad that she and Elsie didn't have to go back to the hostel with them. For the time being they still enjoyed the relative comfort at Glebe House. As usual when Bernie was around, Elsie disappeared the minute work was finished.

It started to drizzle, and by the end of the day Frances was chilled to the bone. Her shoulders ached and there were black half-moons of dirt under her fingernails. Scrubbing her hands with hard yellow soap in the cold scullery in the November twilight, she thought wistfully of rose-geranium bath salts, fresh white towels, manicures, nicely dressed hair, pretty dancing frocks ... nightclubs, music and laughter. Now it was all mud, baggy trousers, dreary weather, bad news, grey skies, worry, nasty Woolton pie and potatoes.

She gazed down at her grubby jumper and baggy green corduroy breeches and wondered what idiot at the War Office had thought that describing land girls as 'strong, sturdy and weather-beaten', then giving them outfits to match would raise their morale. And now clothes rationing had been introduced, not that Frances could see it would make a lot of difference in the countryside because there was nowhere to go, except the parish hall to watch a film once in a while, or a dismal dance at the land-girls' hostel. Soon they would all resemble Alice, in the ghastly outfits her mother had discarded, with the tatty headscarf she tied on so tightly that her head looked shrunken, or give up altogether, like Evangeline who was slim and would have been beautiful if she had made any effort. She didn't seem to care what she looked like, with Richard away.

Cleaning her nails with the point of a vegetable knife, Frances reminded herself that the minute she came of age she could escape from the cows and potatoes. Evangeline had shown her how to set snares and Frances had taken the little man his brace of pheasants. He had said they would see her after her birthday.

Absently she washed her hands and dried them on the

evil-smelling scullery towel that neither she nor Elsie had thought to wash since Mrs Gifford left. With a war on, who bothered about housework?

No, what Frances minded, and wouldn't have admitted to a soul, was that she would turn twenty-one on Saturday without any celebration. It was frivolous to think of a birthday party with a war on, but it was too depressing for words to have nothing to mark her coming-of-age. Frances was a stranger to self-pity but tears welled. She brushed them away. She jolly well *would* celebrate, she decided. Why not have a little supper party on her birthday? It would give her and the other girls an excuse to be cheerful and dress up a bit.

But how did one give a party? She had no cook and no one to serve the food. But Frances was resourceful. If Evangeline could conjure up something special for them to eat, Frances would offer to look after Tommy, Maude and Kipper when next Evangeline had to go up to London to see her doctor – the evacuees ran rings round Tanni. She would invite Elsie, of course, Evangeline and Tanni – Alice too. For men, there were Hugo and Oliver and, even though he was so young and cheeky, Bernie. He made it no secret that he found Frances 'a bit of all right' and Frances, amused, thought he was rather a pet – although Alice considered him 'not quite the thing'. Johnny, and consequently Tanni, adored him, and Elsie, of course, was smitten.

And there was one thing she did have for her party: drink.

When she had been clearing her godmother's silver and china into the furthest reaches of the cellar to store it before the workmen arrived to turn Glebe House into a convalescent home, Frances had made two discoveries. The first was a stock of dust-covered claret, half a dozen bottles of brandy and a stone flask of something labelled 'Genever'. She brought it all upstairs and cleaned off the dust. The wine and brandy had French labels. She wasn't sure about the genever but she didn't care. These days, drink was drink – and a rare treat.

Frances's second discovery had been even more surprising. When she had found the wine, she had stubbed her toe on something wedged under the rack that held the brandy. She shone her torch down, and saw brass hinges gleaming dully on a lacquered Chinese chest. She tugged it out of its hiding place and blew off the dust. There was a key in the lock. She turned it and opened the lid to reveal several jeweller's boxes of different shapes and sizes. She opened the largest one and gasped. It contained a triple string of perfectly matched pearls with a large emerald and diamond clasp. It was the necklace that Aunt Muriel was wearing in the portrait over her desk. Then she found a set of bracelets to match, a pair of old-fashioned diamond clips, rings, brooches, and a man's gold watch with a beautifully worked filigree case and chain, the Marchmont arms on the back. The missing jewellery! Her godmother must have hidden the box there and forgotten it.

Frances adored clothes, but had never been fond of jewellery. However, she could see that the contents of the chest were worth a great deal of money. Especially the pearls. Hmm . . . For her party Frances decided to fish out a favourite dress she had not worn for ages, an amber velvet tea-gown that enhanced her colouring most becomingly and had little silk slippers to match. What fun to look her best for a change. Oliver had never seen her dressed up. She would even wear the pearls, just this once, in honour of the occasion. Then perhaps Bernie would know where she could sell them discreetly.

Her conscience had pricked. She should tell the solicitors she had found the jewellery, she thought. She suspected there might be tax to pay. She could ask Oliver what he thought. Then she decided not to. Oliver was so good that he would advise her to tell the solicitors at once.

Next morning, cycling to the farm half an hour late, Frances stopped at the Fairfaxes' to invite Evangeline and Tanni, who was hugely pregnant with her second baby and darning children's jumpers on the sofa. Evangeline agreed to see what she could do in the way of food, and said she would ask Margaret Rose Hawthorne to come over and keep Johnny and the evacuees out of trouble so that she and Tanni could enjoy the evening.

Then Frances called at the infants' school, where Alice was busy putting up new posters in the classroom. 'Coughs and sneezes/spread diseases/use your handkerchief!' warned one. 'Is your journey REALLY necessary?' admonished another.

'I wanted to put that one up at the station where Evangeline Fairfax would see it next time she goes gadding off to London, but Albert Hawthorne says no. He's already covered the walls with posters,' said Alice. 'Really, Evangeline is so thoughtless.' She sniffed.

Still, when Frances issued her invitation, even Alice

cheered up and said she would bring Woolton fudge, the latest invention of the Ministry of Food. 'Delicious! You'd never guess it's made from carrots.'

'Fancy!' said Frances. All of the ministry's wartime recipes seemed to involve carrots, which Frances detested. How they could be turned into fudge didn't bear thinking about. She suppressed a shudder and cycled away.

On their way to and from the farm, that day and the next, Frances and Elsie scoured the damp fields for the last walnuts and chestnuts. All five girls had pooled their cheese rations so that Evangeline could make one of her cheese puddings. She would use real eggs in it instead of the powdered ones that left a peculiar aftertaste. Bliss!

Eggs from a household's own hens were still not rationed and, thanks to Tanni's sewing, Evangeline and she now had an elderly cockerel as well as the hens and a handful of pullets that pecked about in the back garden where the onions, cabbages and artichokes grew. The eggs were a godsend: Tanni refused adamantly to eat the odd-tasting corned beef, wouldn't consider bits of ham or bacon on the rare occasions that it was available, or the dubious 'mince', often the only meat available on rations. Neither would she feed any of it to Johnny. Sister Tucker clucked and remonstrated but Tanni was firm, so Sister saw that they both received their full allocations, with a bit extra, of cod-liver oil, orange juice or rosehip syrup, and milk.

The evening before the party, Frances threw herself into the preparations. She retrieved some of her godmother's pretty china and silver from where she had stored them in the cellar. 'At finishing-school we had to learn table setting and placements,' she began, hovering round the table with a basket of cutlery and mono-grammed linen napkins, 'but I can't remember exactly what to do. I never paid much attention.'

'Why'd you learn it? So's you could train the servants?' asked Elsie, with sarcasm that was lost on Frances.

'Well, actually, yes, darling. They said it was frightfully important to be able to train servants when a girl married. What if she went abroad somewhere and the servants weren't used to doing things correctly? They would get the forks the wrong way round, or serve dinner in the wrong order, not to mention the horrors of getting the seating wrong if someone important came to dine, and –'

'La-di-da!' said Elsie, rolling her eyes. She'd had no idea Frances was so daft. Anyway, thanks to her brief house-maid's training, she considered herself an expert on that sort of thing and enjoyed sitting on the sofa instructing Frances on the best way to lay fires in the morning room and dining room, how to polish glasses and iron damask table cloths. Later she got up to help her hide the worst of the mess they had made since the old lady's death, shoving things into cupboards and behind furniture until the house was almost tidy.

'Too exhausting,' pronounced Frances, finally, 'but it looks rather nice, don't you think? No need to dust, is there, darling? If we just have candles and the fire for light, it won't really show . . .'

17. Crowmarsh Priors, Frances's Birthday

When Frances finished at the farm on Saturday she cycled home as fast as she could. She was alone because after work, through gritted teeth, the team leader had demanded 'a quiet word' with Elsie, who had been driving the tractor too fast and nearly run her over. Steeling herself against the cold, Frances took a hasty bath in the tepid four inches the War Office allowed. As she watched the filthy water gurgle down the drain, she had a short battle with her conscience, then had another bath. This time the water was more or less clean when she let it out. Shivering, she washed her hair and rinsed it with some flat beer that she and Elsie kept for that purpose.

By the time Elsie came home and clattered into the kitchen to make sandwiches, her one culinary accomplishment, Frances was wrapped in a dressing-gown, with a towel round her head, smelling of hops. She drew the blackout curtains, lit the fires, tipped the last bottle of her godmother's sherry into a decanter, then opened several bottles of claret and left them on the hearth to breathe and warm a little. For good measure she opened the genever and drew the cork on a bottle of brandy. Frances had a swig of the genever for warmth while she huddled close to the morning-room fire to dry her hair. The pungent herbal smell and strange taste made her shudder but it was nicely warming.

The blaze crackled merrily and she had another sip. Then another. She poured some into a glass and drank that too. Her cheeks tingled and she felt much warmer, quite cheerful, really. Would Oliver think she looked pretty tonight? she wondered, as she tripped up the stairs. She slipped into the tea-gown, which was cut on the bias and swirled gracefully round her hips, making her small waist look even slimmer, then the matching slippers. She peered critically into the wavy old mirror in her bedroom to pin up her hair and fasten the pearls round her neck. She finished with scent and lipstick, thinking how delightful it was to be wearing a pretty dress. Her reflection in the mirror reassured her that she looked like her old self, at least in the dim light. She gave a little twirl and the skirt swished round her ankles.

Someone knocked on the door.

Oliver!

Hurrying downstairs she felt a little dizzy. She clutched the door for support as she swung it open. It wasn't Oliver but Hugo, in evening dress and a white silk scarf, with a bouquet of roses and a bottle of champagne. 'Happy birthday, Frances! How lovely you look! Somehow one forgets land girls are, well, girls.'

Embarrassed, Frances exclaimed at the size of the bouquet and buried her nose in the fragrant blooms. 'Oh, Hugo. Roses! They're my favourites. Wherever did you get them in November?' She kissed his cheek rather more warmly than she might have done, had she not had the genever, then led him into the morning room, gaily explaining that she and Elsie had planned to use the drawing room, then decided everyone would freeze. The morning room was easier to warm with a small fire. 'With Alice coming, we daren't light one big enough to thaw the drawing room – you can imagine the scolding she'd give us for wasting fuel. You know what she's like.'

Hugo gave her a conspiratorial smile and Frances went off to the larder for a vase.

When she came back with the tallest crystal one she could find, Hugo was standing with his back to the fire and his hands in his pockets. She began to arrange the roses, thinking how lovely they smelt, when Hugo cleared his throat and said, 'Frances, I've come early because I've something particular to say.'

She looked up from the flowers. In her slightly inebriated state, his profile seemed handsome in the firelight, and it was like old times to see a man in a dinner jacket. Hugo was the sort of man she was used to.

'Frances, I want to ask you . . . will you marry me? You must have seen how I feel about you – I haven't made much of a secret of it, hanging about wherever you're working. Even the other land girls have noticed. I intended to ask you sooner, but then your godmother died and I felt it wasn't quite the thing. But now that you're of age . . .'

'Oh, Hugo!'

'Darling Frances, if you say yes you'd make me the happiest man alive. And we suit each other so well – surely you've seen that? I believe we should be very happy together. I'm to tell you from Father that he would be almost as pleased as I, if you did me the honour. It's high time Gracecourt had a new Lady de Balfort and a young family growing up to carry things on. And with the war there doesn't seem to be much point waiting. If you'll have me, that is.'

'Oh, Hugo!' said Frances again. She was surprised and flattered. Fancy being proposed to − with the prospect of becoming Lady de Balfort! Ermine and coronation robes! 'You've taken me by surprise!'

'You needn't answer at once,' said Hugo, leaving the fire and coming to put his arms round her. He had never tried to kiss her before.

Instinctively she pulled away. 'I don't know what to say.' She moved towards the fire and pretended to warm her hands. 'I'm sorry, I wasn't expecting . . . I must think.'

'It's a lady's prerogative to take her time, I believe,' Hugo said smoothly. He didn't seen too distressed by her reaction. In fact, he smiled complacently and glanced at his watch. 'I found another old hunting piece for the Home Guard, promised to deliver it to Ted Smith. I'll come back later with Oliver. I hope you'll say you'll make me a happy man so that everyone can drink to our engagement. Father said I was to give you special love from him and ask if you can come to lunch on your next free Sunday.'

'Delighted,' murmured Frances. Her engagement!

The front door shut. Marry Hugo? Do exactly as Aunt Muriel had wished? Her father would be thrilled.

Frances stood up, took the vase of roses into the dining room and put them on the table. They made an arresting centrepiece. A new thought reached her addled brain. What if Hugo decided to confide in Oliver? 'Congratulate me, old boy. Finally popped the question to Frances, waiting for an answer, you know how girls are, but I'm rather optimistic. Hope you'll marry us when the time comes – quite soon, I expect. Trust you'll be called upon to baptize an heir too, before long.'

'Oliver! Whatever will he think? Oh, hell!' Frances whispered, suddenly sober.

She heard the knocker again, and rushed into the hall.

This time it was Evangeline with food and Tanni with Johnny, whom Tanni had refused to leave behind with Margaret Rose and the other children. Tanni, Frances thought, with a start, looked awful, white and drawn, despite her bulk. She handed Frances a thin round apple cake that smelt of cinnamon and admired her dress. Then she settled on the sofa with her feet up, while Evangeline laid a sleepy Johnny beside her and covered him with his ABC quilt.

As usual Frances was starving. She followed Evangeline into the kitchen, hovering and admiring the food her friend unpacked and set on the range to keep warm. 'In honour of your birthday I sacrificed one of the fowls,' Evangeline drawled, unwrapping a clean tea towel to reveal a handsome pie. It gave off the fragrance of chicken, herbs and field mushrooms and had a pastry rose on top. Frances sniffed appreciatively. Next to it was the golden cheese pudding. Tanni had made her special dish, red cabbage with onions and apples, sharpened with vinegar, cloves and garlic, and sweetened with a little honey. It was nothing like its horrible boiled green cousin, which cropped up everywhere. For pudding, besides Tanni's apple cake, there was a special treat: two tins of raspberries, discovered in the depths of Penelope's larder.

Frances poured them into a glass bowl, the closest she had come to cooking anything. 'And what's that?' she asked, peering under the cover of the last steaming dish.

Evangeline grinned. 'Dirty rice.'

'Oh, darling, how very . . . thrilling and clever and . . . um, exotic!' Frances recognized bits of onion and celery, but 'What are those little black bits?'

'Chicken gizzard. It's a New Orleans dish,' Evangeline said.

'Gizzard?' repeated Frances, faintly, wondering what unmentionable bit of the chicken that might be.

'We used to eat it in New Orleans every Saturday night. Inez, my grandmother's cook, taught me how to make it. My cousin Laurent and I used to hang around the kitchen and Inez would let us help her.' There was a sudden catch in her voice.

'Evangeline, you must be so homesick. Here you are in England in the middle of a war, and who knows whether the Germans will invade or what will happen to us if they do? You could be safely at home in America, with a nice American husband and automobiles and chocolate, and no rationing or evacuees who wet their beds –'

'But then I wouldn't be married to Richard, would I? And, no, I don't wish I was back in New Orleans. Not at all. Never.'

She was very definite about it. It made Frances wonder if she could love Hugo as much as Evangeline loved Richard, putting up with a war and everything for his sake. 'Shame Richard doesn't get leave more often. You've only seen him three or four times.'

'Three, and only because his ship was in port for repairs,' said Evangeline, shortly. 'It wasn't for long, either.'

'And I know how much you want a baby . . . That doctor you see in London . . .' Frances tailed off. It had struck her that if she married Hugo he would want a baby at once, then another. Usually people with titles needed 'an heir and a spare'. Fond as she was of Johnny, she couldn't imagine having a baby of her own any time soon.

'You never know what might happen when the war's over,' said Evangeline. 'I must tell you, Tanni got another letter today from those people she knows in London. It's upset her and she's trying not to say anything about it tonight because she doesn't want to spoil your evening. She says you've been so kind to her.'

Frances was conscience-stricken. All she had done was give her a spare négligée.

In the morning room, Tanni had got up to stretch. 'Genever!' she cried, recognizing the bottle on the sideboard. 'Wherever did you get it? My father used to make his patients take it after meals. It tastes horrible.'

'I know. I tried it while I was dressing,' said Frances, making a face. 'Warming, though. Like some?'

Tanni nodded. 'It's practically medicine so it'll be good for the baby.' However vile it tasted, genever was a reminder of home. She turned away so that Frances would not see her smile fade.

After the Passover *seder* Tante Berthe, still upset by her internment, had warned Tanni never to speak German, not even in private, because you never knew who might overhear and report you as a spy. Tanni must be especially careful, she had added, not to offend any of the people in the village where she was living.

According to Tante Berthe, nowhere was really safe for Jews. 'Internment,' she said, in a frightened whisper, was what the Germans were doing in Europe to them. Who knew what else was going on? The British might even decide to follow the Germans' example – Rachel said that, because of the labour shortage, conscription for women was coming and some people, especially the upper classes, were saying there should be peace with Germany. Tanni knew that was true – she had heard Lady Marchmont say it. It was just as well that Tante Berthe had never met her.

Bruno had reassured Tanni over and over again that his job as a military translator meant that he, Tanni and Johnny would not be locked up in a camp, but after the Cohens' experience, Tanni knew that nothing was certain, no matter how kind Evangeline, Alice, Frances and Elsie were.

Tante Berthe had also warned her that with the baby coming it was not good to worry, but Tanni had found that trying not to worry was even more of a strain. Although she kept everything to herself, her mind was as swollen with worries about what she must and must not do or say as her stomach was with the new baby.

Frances poured glasses of sherry from the decanter on the writing desk, then handed Tanni a generous quantity of genever. Tanni closed her eyes. It smelt worse than she remembered, but she gulped it down. In no time she felt light-headed and more relaxed.

A little later Alice arrived, her hair arranged inexpertly in the new 'victory roll'. She had with her a plate of grey slabs. 'Carrot fudge!' she announced proudly.

'Too delicious!' exclaimed Frances, trying to look delighted but surreptitiously parking the plate behind Tanni's apple cake.

Alice had discovered an ancient lipstick while she was tidying her mother's room and now applied it in the mirror over the fireplace. Then she craned her neck to check the effect with her new hairstyle in the candlelight.

Evangeline had brought records for the gramophone, lively new music that she said was called 'swing', and slower, moody sounds she referred to as 'jazz'. She told the others they had been recorded by a friend in Paris. In a change from her usual slapdash attire, she had raided the trunks in the attic and found a beaded dress that dated from Penelope's youth. She had also dug into the jewel box Richard had given her for some amethysts that had once belonged to his grandmother, unaware that he had once promised to have them reset for Alice. The overall effect was perfect, and for once her beauty was apparent.

When she saw the jewellery on Evangeline, Alice took a sharp breath and tossed down her sherry in one gulp.

Elsie came in with a red silk scarf draped dramatically over her shoulders, then flounced out again. She returned, brandishing an ebony cigarette holder, with two platters of inexpertly trimmed sandwiches covered with damp tea-towels. 'I made these meself. Surprise! Tinned salmon!' she announced triumphantly. 'And . . . fish paste,' she said, less certainly. Bernie had sworn Frances would like it. The toffs where he worked had made a carry-on when a consignment of it turned up at their offices. They'd assured him it was 'quite the thing'. He told Elsie it cost the earth, that he'd tried it and it was disgusting. Toffs didn't 'alf 'ave strange tastes. Elsie had licked it off her fingers in the kitchen and gagged as the nasty little black things popped fishily in her mouth. Bernie was right. It tasted like the fish Mum bought cheap on a Monday, past its prime. She whipped off the tea-towel.

'Bloater?' asked Alice, wrinkling her nose at the smell and squinting. 'Hasn't it gone a bit black?'

'Elsie darling! Caviar!' gasped Frances.

Elsie told her it was a present from Bernie, who had sent his apologies. She mouthed, ''E's been sent for, urgent.'

Dressed up, bathed, and looking forward to a special dinner, the five young women relaxed. They felt glamorous and worldly as they sipped their drinks, listening to jazz and waiting for the men. They stopped thinking about responsibilities and rationing, shortages and aching backs, drawing out the moment as long as they could. They finished the sherry, and Frances said they might as well have some of the wine.

Tanni drank more genever. Now that she was used to the taste it wasn't so bad.

A cosy, cheerful glow settled over them. 'Whatever can be keeping Oliver and Hugo?' they asked each other from time to time, but they hardly cared.

All at once they had their answer. The air-raid siren shrilled, and they heard planes approaching in the distance. Alice, whose cheeks were flushed with unaccustomed alcohol, muttered, 'Damn! They must have been warned to stand by for Home Guard duty. Shelter, everyone! I have to run.' She threw on her coat and left.

'Bloody Jerry!' muttered Frances. 'Come on, we ought to go to the shelter – or down to the cellar, at least,' she said. 'Otherwise Alice will –'

'To 'ell wiv Alice! We shan't all fit in the shelter, anyway, not wiv Tanni so big. I'm stayin' put for once,' said Elsie, defiantly, lighting another cigarette. 'To 'ell wiv Alice and to 'ell wiv the Jerries!'

'Let's have another drink, then,' said Evangeline, in no hurry to get up either. Now that she had a chance to sit down, she realized how exhausted she was after all the cooking, then wrestling a screaming Maude, Tommy and Kipper into the bath before they went to bed, something they loathed, mistrusted and resisted. Their family had taught them that baths in winter were unhealthy. Margaret Rose Hawthorne was sensible for her age and would get them down to the wine cellar.

If only Laurent had taken her to France straight after she had come to England. She tried not to think about what she had overheard the drunken little Frenchman in the Soho pub say to him. Not realizing that Evangeline spoke French and could understand every word, he had nudged Laurent knowingly and referred to the North African girl with two children who depended on Laurent, so much so that he could never stay long on his rare trips to England.

'Just a joke, darlin',' Laurent had muttered later. 'You know I love you . . .'

Evangeline closed her eyes, waiting for drink to blot everything out. She knew in her bones that the North

African girl had been more than a drunken Frenchman's joke. Laurent was what they called at home a 'hot-blooded man', and she had had no word from him for months.

'So, it's unanimous!' said Frances, brandishing the wine and genever bottles, then refilling everyone's glass. For the next hour the four stayed put, daring Jerry to make them move, getting hungrier.

Very late, Alice returned to giggles and drunken bravado. She was chilled to the bone in her thin coat and huddled by the fire with a sandwich and a large brandy, since they had finished the sherry. There was a full moon and the ARP had rung to say there had been heavy raids over London, Birmingham and Exeter. Though the all-clear had sounded in the village, the Home Guard had been ordered to stay on duty.

At last Evangeline said they had better eat or the food would be ruined. They went into the dining room and filled their plates, admiring Frances's carefully laid table with Hugo's roses in the centre, opening a little in the warmth. Frances poured more wine, and they lifted their glasses to each other.

The evening wore on. They moved back to the morning room, feeling warm and pleasantly full. They had eaten most of the food, drunk all of the wine, smoked all of Elsie's cigarettes and finished an entire bottle of brandy. Frances pulled the cork from another and they all laughed. Chestnuts roasted on the hearth. The fire crackled, and from time to time they took turns to crank the gramophone. In the background the jazz was lovely, if somewhat melancholy.

'No reashon to leave this to go shtale,' said Frances, tipping more brandy into everyone's glass. They were all rather drunk, especially Tanni, who had got through most of the genever by herself.

'Poor Oliver and Hugo, shtill on duty,' Alice said dreamily from the depths of her armchair. She supposed she was tiddly. It felt nice.

The clock struck eleven, then midnight. No one moved. Frances was glad that Hugo hadn't come back, and it was just as well that Oliver hadn't either. She was now finding it too much effort to get out of her chair. The bottle was being passed round.

'Blimey, Tanni, you've bloody finished the gen-wossit!' exclaimed Elsie, suddenly spotting the empty bottle rolling on the floor. The tip of Tanni's nose was red and she had gone quiet, staring into the fire.

'Lordy,' said Evangeline and hiccuped. 'You shouldn't have done that . . .'

'Don't care,' muttered Tanni, propped in a nest of cushions. She was eating the carrot fudge.

'Me neither,' said Evangeline.

Alice hiccuped too and raised her glass. 'To . . . end to the war. God shave the King. The Prime Minister, and – and – abshent friendsh, thoshe in peril on the sea.' They drank.

'You next, Frances. 'S your birthday.'

'To . . . Evangeline . . . lovely shupper, Tanni'sh new baby . . . Johnny, Elsie and Bernie and Oliver . . . To the war's end, of course. And to . . . the end of the black-out and clothing coupons and no more whalemeat *ever*

... Dancing at the Shavoy ... gardenia corsages ... Madame Vionnet ... Parish!'

'Hear hear!'

'Amen,' said Evangeline, brooding on the Algerian woman and not in a mood to toast anything.

'Elsie?'

Elsie stood up unsteadily. 'To me promotion! Leader said. Appointed. Me!'

'The leader promoted you?' Frances was incredulous. The woman had recently accused Elsie of being a German saboteur, because she was so hopeless with farm machinery and animals.

'I'm 'ead rat-catcher now, ain't I?' Elsie said proudly.

This was greeted with shrieks of laughter. 'Head *rat*-catcher?'

'Well – there's only one for the time bein' – me – but when there's more I'm to be rat-catchin' team leader. Fancy! Me own personal supply of poison and all. Arsenic! Cyanide! Talent for destruction, she said I 'ave, might as well use it on rats because I'd used it on every-thing else. Wait till Agnes and Mam and Vi'let and Jem and the twins 'ear.'

'Congratulations!'

'Well done, Elsie!'

Tanni began to cry. The others stopped laughing. Bewildered, they looked at each other, then at Tanni. Then, one by one, they got up unsteadily and gathered round her. Alice asked, 'Is it the baby? Oh, Tanni, you aren't due for ... weeks!'

'Maybe we ... ought to – um – ring Sister Tucker?' asked Frances.

But Sister Tucker would be scandalized to find them all, especially the expectant mother, drunk as lords.

The genever had sapped Tanni's usual restraint. 'Not the baby.' Her face crumpled and she burst into tears. 'It's the others . . . the twins!'

18. Crowmarsh Priors, Frances's Birthday

'What . . . is . . . she . . . talking about?' asked Frances, struggling to sit upright.

'Must have been something Elsie said. She should have known better, sho thoughtlesh of her!' said Alice accusingly.

'Do shut up, Alice!' said Frances, who was trying to think clearly.

Elsie perched on the arm of Tanni's sofa, patting Tanni's shoulder and glowering at Alice. Alice didn't know nuffink about people, she thought. Tanni was the only person Elsie knew who seemed to understand when she talked about missing Mum and the others. Bernie and Frances meant well, but neither had much family to miss. Evangeline clammed up if you mentioned hers, and as for Alice – the less said about Mrs Osbourne the better. It occurred to Elsie for the first time that, besides Bruno and Johnny, Tanni might have a family somewhere too, even though she'd never talked about them. And now she was crying . . .

"Ere, Alice, you're the sort as always 'as 'ankerchief. Tanni needs one.' Sullenly Alice groped for it and passed it to Elsie.

'There, there,' said Elsie, bending over Tanni. 'Blow yer nose, and tell us what's the matter. Was it somefink I said?'

Curled up in an armchair, Evangeline was finishing her brandy. 'Elsie, you weren't to know but Tanni pinned a photo over her bed. Two women, a man and two little girls who look alike. Family, I think. She won't talk about them. Asked her. Her aunt Berthe warned her not to – said she might be arrested if she did.'

'Who'd arrest Tanni?' demanded Elsie, indignantly. 'And where are her family?'

'Tanni, try to calm down – not good for the baby, you know. Tell us about it. Won't let . . . anyone . . . 'rest you,' said Frances.

The look of concern on everyone's faces was too much for Tanni. She blurted out, 'Evangeline's right. I mustn't . . . Oh, all right, I will tell you.' She reached into her pocket for an envelope and unfolded Rachel's letter. 'From London. Some friends there are trying to find out what has become of everyone.' She wiped her eyes. 'They can't find my parents or Bruno's mother. They've disappeared, probably arrested and sent to a work camp in Poland with all the Jews in their neighbourhood.' Tanni gave a sob. 'But Lili and Klara are probably in France, in a displaced-persons' camp . . . if . . . they're not dead!' She started to cry again.

'Why aren't they in England?'

'Elsie, *hush up* and let Tanni tell us!' ordered Evangeline.

'Tanni, stop crying,' Frances said sharply. 'Do you know where in France?'

Tanni found the place in the letter with her finger. 'It's called Gurs.'

'Wait. Let me see if Aunt Muriel had a map. My geography's a bit fuzzy.' Frances went into the room that had been Sir Humphrey Marchmont's study – which had been kept as he had left it – and returned with an ancient Baedeker. She turned the pages clumsily, hunting for a map of France, thinking what a bit of luck it was that the Home Guard were still on duty and it was just the five of them. Tanni would never have said anything with the men around. She found the page and put the book on Tanni's lap.

Evangeline and Alice came across to lean over Elsie's shoulder. Tanni peered at the map. 'Here.' She pointed to a place not far from the Spanish border. 'My friends learned that when Lili and Klara's *Kindertransport* was turned away from England it went here, to Gurs, where there is a big displaced-persons' camp. It was set up a few years ago for refugees from the Spanish civil war. Many Spanish people stayed, but the camp is now full of people fleeing the Nazis who thought they would be safe. When the children arrived in Gurs the Germans had not occupied France.'

'How on earth did you find them?' asked Evangeline.

'Some Americans, Quakers, I think, keep records of the names and ages of all the children who are without their parents. My friends sent them money and told them that the Joseph family in England were hunting for twin girls who should have been on the train. The Quakers finally sent word that there was no record of Klara and Lili Joseph in Gurs, alive or dead. They always noticed twins because the Germans had several times sent the police, the Milice, to the camp to find any and they always took them away. Then the Quakers heard that a priest had taken some children as they got off the train to live with local people, and tried to find out if Lili and Klara had been with him. But they had to be careful and it took a long time. Finally they heard that twin girls might be living with an elderly couple in a village some distance from the camp. The priest admitted he had placed them with his sister and her husband. One had been slower than the other and he thought their name badges had said "Klara" and "Lili". The Quakers are willing to help, although they're not supposed to because the Germans have ordered that Jews, even children, who are not French must be turned over to them. Informers are everywhere and the priest, the Quakers and those hiding Jewish children are at risk of being arrested and even shot.'

'I didn't think the Germans controlled that part of France yet,' said Frances.

'The Vichy police – the Milice – are like the SS. They do what the Germans want. They take people from Gurs and send them to another camp at Drancy, near Paris. From there they are taken to a prison in Poland, at Auschwitz.'

Her voice faltered. Rachel had not minced words in her letter. They would keep looking for her family but Tanni must be prepared for bad news. 'My friends say Auschwitz is very bad, that terrible things happen there, more than anyone knows . . . The Germans say they will eliminate all Jews from Europe, from the face of the earth, even. If my parents and Bruno's mother are there, God protect them. But it sounds as if Klara and Lili are not. Yet.'

Evangeline twisted a strand of hair. The Free French she knew in London talked about Auschwitz and the other

German camps with horror. Some of their members had fallen into Nazi hands and two had escaped with stories almost too terrible to believe. Evangeline had been appalled by what she had heard. She had asked if the British government knew about the prisons. The men had snarled that the British were not interested in anyone's hides but their own. Now Evangeline nodded. 'I think the news is censored to avoid scaring folks any more. Everyone would just give up otherwise.'

'Is it true that no more foreign children can come here now?' demanded Alice.

Tanni nodded.

'It's outrageous. We mustn't stand for it.' It was unlike Alice to question authority. 'I bloody won't stand for it!'

The others were even more astonished to hear her swear.

'Perhaps I could ask Father if there's a way . . .' Frances mused. 'But knowing him –' She broke off.

'He'll prob'ly say rules is rules. What then?' Elsie knew that the Admiral came from the class who made rules to suit themselves. If they didn't fancy a law they changed it. People like Bernie and herself broke it and went to prison. Anyway, what came of the government's bleedin' rules? Bernie had shown her a newspaper story about a ship full of refugee children torpedoed *en route* to Canada because the law had stopped them coming into England. 'Good fing your Agnes and Vi'let and them others are in Yorkshire and not on that, innit?' Bernie had said, meaning to be comforting. The ship had been the *City of Benares*, Elsie remembered. Many children had drowned while their ship burned and sank. She felt a wave of such hatred for the Germans that she nearly choked. And she hated the British officials who had sent the children to sea. No difference between them, really.

Suddenly Elsie was grateful to Evangeline's bossy mother-in-law for persuading Mum to take her family out of London. Bernie had been right: even if they were all separated, the little ones were safe in Yorkshire, away from the bombs and the German fiends who torpedoed children. Even if Agnes had had her hair cut off, it wasn't the same as being taken away by the Germans or drowned. She shivered – Mum would have said someone had walked on her grave.

Evangeline tried to think of something to cheer Tanni. 'Maybe the girls will be all right. Lots of French hate the collaborators. The Free French in London send the Resistance supplies and guns, and Resistance people rescue our pilots if they're shot down and get them home before the Germans capture them.' Then she remembered something else she had overheard. 'Maybe the Quakers could get them out of France some other way. Isn't there an organization called something like Secours des Enfants, which smuggles Jewish children over the Swiss border? And there's the Chemin de Liberté, which goes over the Pyrenees into Spain. It sounds like a long walk over a mountain pass, but not impossible.'

Evangeline's familiarity with France was surprising. 'How do you know so much?' Alice demanded.

'Er, at the, um, clinic last time I was in London, one of – one of the nurses was married to a Free French officer and we chatted.'

'"Careless talk costs lives".' Alice quoted a War Office poster. 'And I can't see why this nurse would talk so much.' Then, with a dreamy smile, she imagined Evangeline being arrested as a spy.

'Even if the Quakers get them away before the Milice find them,' said Tanni, tracing the route with her finger, 'Klara might be able to walk through the mountains to Switzerland or Spain but Lili is weaker and slower. She depends on Klara for everything. And Klara would never leave her.' They must believe I have abandoned them, she thought sadly.

The clock in the hallway chimed one. Alice had taken up her knitting but her eyes weren't focusing and she kept dropping stitches. There was a silence while everyone tried to think what to say next. The small fire flickered in the grate, the shadows shifting on the walls.

'Isn't there anything we can do?' asked Evangeline. 'I mean, could the girls escape?' She thought of her own desperate flight from New Orleans.

'They need a way out of France. And then a way to get into England, which will be illegal.'

'What about unofficial, like?' asked Elsie. 'Could they get into England wivout anybody findin' out?'

Alice stabbed her knitting needles viciously into the tangled mess that would have to be unravelled in the morning. Too much brandy had given her a headache. She was fed up with the war. The War Cabinet didn't have to sit knee to knee in the coal cellar with her mother, night after night. Bother the War Cabinet! And bother Mummy, she thought, forever whining, 'What would your father have said?' The familiar refrain went round and round in her head. 'What would your father have said?' She wanted to sleep. She was tired of wondering what he would have said if he were there . . . 'Black Dickon's gang used that for forty years,' he would say, pointing to a spot where the mouth of an old smugglers' cave was tucked into the cliff. 'It's just visible at low tide, large enough for a boat to slip in unseen. Right under the excisemen's noses.'

Alice! Her father was beside her. *You can't have forgotten! Right under the excisemen's noses.*

'But . . . Defence Zone now,' Alice muttered.

We drew maps, said Alice's father firmly, and was gone.

'Yes, Father, maps,' Alice said.

Alice was as dotty as her mother, Frances decided.

Evangeline raised her eyebrows. 'Anybody want tea?' she asked, and disappeared into the kitchen. She came back with a tray and cups.

'Smugglers,' said Alice, taking hers, 'did it.'

'Alice, we've all drunk more than we're used to. Have your tea. Did what?'

'Pay attention,' said Alice. 'Another way out of France into England. Well, there is one. Smugglers' tunnels. Used to be a lot of smugglers along this coast. They brought in things from France, like lace and brandy and tobacco, so they didn't have to pay duty. If they were caught they were hanged. Anyway, my father had an old book about the parish and a famous smuggler named Black Dickon had a secret cave on the coast the excisemen never found. They could just get a boat into it at low tide but when the sea came in the entrance was blocked. The smugglers unloaded inside and used tunnels to carry the contraband away from the coast.'

'Alice, that was a long time ago –'

'No, listen! Father and I found it! We used to go for a walk together every Saturday afternoon and we found it at low tide. He made maps to work out where the tunnels might have led because the parish book said there was an entrance in our churchyard. He thought the de Balforts must have been in on the smuggling, because Gracecourt was such a fine house.'

Elsie's eyes narrowed. 'Could you smuggle fings in from France today, like people?'

'Dangerous. Although . . . it must have been dangerous all those years ago when the King's soldiers hanged the smugglers they caught. And the government must think it's possible, because there are loads of posters up, warning that Germans might get past the coastal defences and to be on the lookout,' Alice replied.

It was amazing what you learned when people assumed you didn't understand French, Evangeline thought. 'Hand me the map. Somewhere off Brittany the Resistance operate escape lines. They pick up RAF pilots right under the Germans' noses and take them across the Channel. It's an odd name.' She ran her finger along the Brittany coastline. 'Here! Plouha. It's got high cliffs. Could someone be persuaded to bring two children with rescued pilots, do you think?'

'Evangeline, the children are hundreds of miles from there,' said Frances, impatiently.

'The Resistance need money and a lot of other things, though, ammunition, guns, medicine and radio transmitters,' said Evangeline, thoughtfully. 'For enough money, they'd do anything.'

'How much? And where would we get it?' asked Alice.

'That's the problem.'

'Not necessarily,' said Frances. 'There's Aunt Muriel's jewellery. The solicitors thought she'd lost it or sold it but she'd hidden it. I found it in the cellar and it's mine now. She left it to me. Look at these – they're worth a fortune.' She unclasped the pearls and passed them round. 'And there's more – bracelets and diamond clips and things. They'd be worth thousands if they were sold. That should be enough.'

'But even if the Quakers agree to take the girls away from Gurs, how would they get to the coast? Would the Resistance take them all that way? And even if someone agreed to bring them across the Channel, how would they get them past the authorities into England? We couldn't ask RAF pilots to break the law by smuggling children in and, anyway, I daresay they'd be met by the authorities.'

'And once they got here, it would be impossible to hide foreign twins in Crowmarsh Priors,' said Frances, thinking ahead. 'Everyone knows everything. Where else could they go?'

'I know a place no one would notice – no one likely to tell the authorities, anyway!' exclaimed Tanni. She was remembering when she had visited Tante Berthe in Bethnal Green before the war and had seen the two well-dressed Englishwomen staring at a line of black-clad children following their father. Penelope Fairfax's friend had commented on how alike the family of Hassidic children looked and wondered how the family could tell them apart. But it was Penelope's casual comment, 'One quite sees why the Germans . . .' that had made Tanni's blood run cold. Now it gave her an idea. 'In London where my friends live, there are whole streets with only large Jewish families. Some are very old-fashioned and dress their children in long dark clothing. The English see only the clothes and think all the children look the same. Two more would fit in without the authorities noticing – as long as they could get identity cards and ration books.'

'Nuffink easier, Bernie says, not even worf forgin' those 'cause so many go missin' from the post office. You can buy 'em on the cheap.'

'But would any family take the risk? They'd be arrested if they were caught, Tanni,' said Frances.

'Well, what about the people hiding the twins in France now? They're at risk of being shot,' said Tanni. 'A rabbi I know always says that to save a life many things are permissible, and this would save two. So, I'm sure someone would be willing. I'll have to ask carefully and not mention any of this to Bruno yet,' she added. There was a new firmness in her voice. 'In fact, it is better that he doesn't know.' In case he forbids it, she thought.

'How would we get them from Crowmarsh Priors to London? I don't think the train would be safe. There's Albert Hawthorne for one thing. He knows everything that goes on.'

'Bernie's ever so good at getting things. 'E can get a car and petrol – and 'e will too if I tell 'im. Never mind restrictions. Oh, don't turn up your nose, Alice! 'E'll see the girls up to London safe and sound, if 'e knows what's good for 'im. See to their ration books too, 'e will.'

'If we could get them there before anyone saw them . . .' said Frances, slowly.

They looked at each other, then everyone stared at Alice. 'Do you think the smugglers' tunnels still exist?' asked Frances.

'Probably.'

'If they do,' said Evangeline, 'can people still get through them?'

'If they haven't collapsed. It was a long time ago.'

'Mustn't get ahead of ourselves,' said Frances. 'We don't know where the tunnels are, whether anyone would agree to bring the girls, whether –'

'When you're desperate, you find a way,' said Evangeline, with feeling. She whispered to Frances so that Alice couldn't hear, 'We could ask the French people I know in London whether they would take the jewellery in exchange for bringing the children.'

Frances nodded. Then she said, 'Alice, did you keep your father's maps?'

'I think so. We've boxes and boxes of his papers stacked in the hall at the cottage. Mummy's been after me to sort them and move them to the boxroom. We trip over them every time there's an air raid. But one thing at a time,' said Alice, primly, in her best schoolmistress voice. 'I'll find Father's maps, and try to work out where the cave is. And we need to find out if there really is an entrance to the tunnels from the churchyard. Even if it's there it may have collapsed.'

'At home I went caving with my brothers and Lau –

If we find the tunnels I'll go down on a rope and see what they're like,' Evangeline volunteered. 'I don't mind. I've done it lots of times.'

'Do we tell anyone else?'

'No! If Tanni's not going to tell Bruno, we shouldn't say anything to anyone. Not even Bernie yet. One step at a time.'

'Shouldn't we mention it to Oliver? If we're prowling in the churchyard he's bound to wonder what we're up to.'

'No,' said Frances. 'Better not. He'd want to save the children, of course, but he's awfully conscientious. He might disapprove if it's illegal. And it must be. Let's not tell him until we have to. We've got to be very, very careful or we'll all end up in prison, and then there'll be no one to help Lili and Klara.'

Suddenly Tanni felt guilty: Tante Berthe would be aghast if she knew what they were planning. But she *had* to do something. The baby kicked, and she squirmed on the sofa. Then she realized that something else was happening . . .

'Tanni! What's the matter! Oh! Oh dear!' exclaimed Frances.

Tanni's face was screwed up and she gripped the armrests hard as a fierce contraction took hold. She let out a deep groan: 'Oooh!' A stain spread on the sofa as her waters broke.

'Now we *must* send for Sister Tucker,' said Frances.

'That'll be the baby comin', all right,' exclaimed Elsie. ''Took Mum the same way – 'er waters broke all over the place, and next minute Vi'let were there, 'owlin' 'er 'ead off! Alice, ring Sister Tucker – quick!'

19. London, November 1941

The night that Frances celebrated her birthday and Tanni went into labour, the German bombers that had disturbed the birthday party in Crowmarsh Priors flew on to hit London hard. The sirens screamed across the city, and in the streets firewatchers and air-raid wardens hurried to their posts, while ordinary people rushed from their homes or the pub into the nearest Underground station, clutching children, bedding and gas masks. The rattle of ack-ack fire opened up on the approaching planes, followed by the first pounding explosions on the outskirts. As the bombers came closer people pushed harder to make their way into the shelters. The air-raid wardens blew their whistles in a bid to prevent panic.

Arc-lights sliced up through the night sky between the silver barrage balloons as the bombers flew over and building after building disintegrated in an avalanche of masonry and broken glass. Flames erupted and devoured whatever was left inside, seeking a whiff of gas from a damaged main or a store of paraffin.

From the east, over the docks, there came a roar so loud it drowned everything else. London shook. A warehouse where rum had been stored in barrels had taken a direct hit, and a river of flaming liquor spilled into the street. A gasometer was damaged and a lone repairman went up swiftly, silhouetted in the searchlights as he fought to stop it exploding.

Even deep underground they felt the reverberations. At her WVS canteen post on a platform Penelope Fairfax tried to smile calmly as she poured tea and doled out buns or cigarettes. She hoped the two lads who had come in drunk and arguing wouldn't overturn the lavatory cubicle again. It smelt terrible already, a fug of unwashed bodies and urine, with cigarette smoke and dust shaken loose by the bombing. It got in one's hair and nostrils and made everything gritty. Wearily, Penelope wiped her hands again on the damp tea-towel they used to mop up spills. She felt sticky and badly in need of a bath.

The hurricane lamp in a far corner went out. Children whimpered in panic. 'Miss, oh, Miss, the lamp,' called a woman, panic in her voice too. They were all afraid of the dark – anything could happen: people were robbed, girls raped and the rats came out, searching for crumbs, scurrying over the sleepers.

'Just coming! Soon have it lit, don't worry,' she called, as she picked her way past bunks filled with people lucky enough to get a ticket for them, then over whole families who had camped on the filthy floor, playing cards, gossiping, or asleep, rolled in blankets. She attended to the lamp and the children calmed down. How could so many children still be in London? she wondered, as she went back to the canteen. They had tried so hard to get every one to safety. Some of the mothers recognized her and wouldn't meet her eye: they had had enough of the billeting and brought their children home.

Back at the canteen Penelope nudged her co-worker

and nodded in the direction of a pimply boy standing at the entrance. 'That Communist lad Ted's got in again tonight.' He was holding a pile of printed sheets and arguing with a man who eventually told him to shut up because people were trying to sleep. Ted ignored him and began his whiny singsong chant: '*Show* your solidarity wiv the working class, *support* our Russian brothers-in-arms on the second front against Fascist Nazi imperialism. *Buy* your copy of the *Mornin' Star*, the voice of the workin' class, the ones what's really fightin' this war. *Support* our Russian comrades . . .'

There was a chorus of 'Shut up! Worse'n bleedin' 'Itler 'e is!'

'Let the workin' class get a bleedin' bit o' sleep!'

'*Show* your solidarity wiv the workin' class!'

'I'll give 'im solidarity!'

There was a scuffle, then a loud 'Ow! Bloody 'ell!', the sound of paper ripping, and silence.

They didn't sound the all-clear until long after the bombing was over, to keep people off the streets while the worst of the rubble was cleared and the emergency services hunted for survivors. The siren went off just after dawn on Sunday morning. People asked each other if they were all right, then climbed warily up the stairs, anxious to get home but fearing that home might not be there.

'What the Jerries don't bomb the bloody looters'll 'ave while your back's turned,' muttered a weary woman, pulling her three grubby children up the stairs. 'They nicked my sister's sewin'-machine – it were brand new. She saved three years for it to start a little business makin' curtains and cushions.'

The woman next to her shook her head and tutted in sympathy, 'Looters is as bad as the Germans, I say, stealin' from their own.'

Squaring their shoulders to prepare for the worst, both women came round the corner and saw their street. Their jaws dropped. Everything was gone.

Until last night the area had been a rabbit warren of small terraced houses, home to hundreds of people. Now it was a landscape of destruction, a few walls with blown-out windows still standing in a wasteland of smashed bricks, bits of window-frame, chunks of roof and chimney, blown-apart stoves, shreds of carpet, split cushions, the odd table leg, a pram with the wheels torn off, a hairbrush, toys, a man's boot with the laces ripped out, shattered chamber-pots and a cat, dead, its teeth bared in a grin. The cloud of smoke and dust still rising from the bombed houses was so thick that it hid the broken glass that crunched underfoot. A smell of gas hung in the air. 'Put out that cigarette,' barked the ARP warden, at a dazed man in pyjamas. 'You'll send us all sky high!'

The shovels and pickaxes that had chipped at the rubble since daybreak continued as the day wore on. Somewhere a child cried intermittently, though not as loudly as it had cried that morning or even an hour ago. There were still faint cries of 'Get me out! Oh, please, get me out!' and 'Over here!' A grey blanket of fog descended as the diggers struggled to pinpoint where the voices were coming from, but they carried on with superhuman will, hauling up the dead and the nearly dead. The triumphant shouts of 'Ambulance, over here!' grew fewer as the day wore on.

Now furtive figures darted through the gloom, stooping and digging, well away from the emergency workers. They paused from time to time to lift something from the rubble, anything from household goods to jewellery – not likely in this street – to broken light fittings and pieces of electrical flex, which was in short supply and particularly valuable now. When the warden saw them, he chased them away. 'Looters!' he muttered. 'At a time like this! They'd steal the knicker elastic from a corpse and sell it.'

'How many do you suppose are still down there?' asked one of the rescue team, who had been digging since daylight. His arms were shaking uncontrollably.

A time bomb detonated in the distance.

'There was more earlier,' said another rescuer shortly, lifting his tin hat to wipe his brow. The afternoon was drawing on and the dull, smoky light would soon go. He was listening for a child he had heard below, focused on getting it out. He had four of his own at home and kept thinking what if . . .

Their shift was over, but the rescuers carried on. A girl from the mobile canteen handed them steaming mugs of cocoa. 'Just let us know when you can get water and milk down to anyone trapped below,' she said quietly. Not 'if' but 'when'. 'Have it for you in a flash. A drink helps them hold on a little longer.'

'They wanted to come back,' said the warden, angrily, to no one in particular, and swung a pick with all his might at a slab of brick wall that had fallen across two houses that lay in ruins. 'Evacuated with the children, they were, to the countryside and all, but when nothing happened they got fed up, wanted to come home. Had to look after the old man, missed their homes, missed the neighbours. They and the kiddies were safe, but oh, no, *that* wasn't good enough! They had to come *home*! So they packed up, came home and brought the kiddies. And then Jerry turned up.'

'Ssh!' snapped the digger.

The child cried again, feebly and briefly, and a woman groaned something that sounded like 'Help the kiddies. Get us out. Please get us out,' somewhere below the brick slab the warden had just split.

'It's all right, dear,' shouted the warden. 'Just another few minutes and we'll have you out. Nearly there now.' He was hoarse from shouting to mounds of bombed building. 'You'll be 'avin' a nice 'ot cup o' tea before you know it. Brewin' up now, they are. Come on, lads,' he shouted, so that she could hear him. 'Mustn't keep the lady from 'er tea. Nearly there, my love. How many of you, do you know?' Keep her talking.

'My baby! Where's my baby? Please find my baby!' another woman cried, shrilly, somewhere down the street.

'My baby! My baby! My baby!' echoed down the street.

The tired diggers were joined by the ambulance driver, a strapping young woman from Yorkshire, who silently took the shovel from the man whose arms could no longer lift it and began to dig. 'It's all right. You rest a bit. Me family's all miners. Diggin's in me blood,' she said stoutly, when he protested. 'Can you tell where the child was crying from?' she whispered to the warden, shifting a smashed wardrobe. Clothes fluttered inside.

'Just hereabouts,' he muttered, gesturing at the side of the mountain.

'Baby! Baby! Baby!' The shrill voice was cracking. An older woman came from somewhere and put her arms round the distraught mother, who collapsed, sobbing and unable to walk. Another woman hurried forward to help and they half supported, half carried the limp figure towards the mobile canteen at the end of North Street. The canteen girl wrapped her in a blanket and put a strong cup of tea with two extra spoonfuls of precious sugar into her hands. The woman clutched it, spilling tea as she rocked back and forth.

It was the word 'tea' that had brought Mrs Pigeon round again. She had been talking to someone just now about tea. What had she said? The last thing she remembered, she had been getting the tea . . . It was terribly dark. Was it because of the blackout? A buzzing noise came and went. Sometimes it sounded like people talking and she had heard them say, 'tea'. She tried to turn her head but it hurt . . . Darkness and pain, everywhere, inside of her, pressing on top of her . . . everywhere. She heard the buzzing and wanted to shout again, but she was too cold and sleepy. She whispered, 'Sausages.' A treat for tea, sausages.

'Did you hear that? Somebody moaned near my foot. Lend us a hand and we can shift this slab now. Hello, can you hear us? We're coming for you, nearly there now. Don't give up – call out if you can.'

Mrs Pigeon looked into the darkness for the voices. She couldn't tell whether they were above or below her. She tried her best to call again but something kept filling her mouth. She choked.

'Hello,' came the voice again. 'Let us know where you are. How many?'

But she was drifting, thinking of how the butcher on the corner had waved them in, said he'd kept a few back, and seeing as how Mrs Pigeon and the kiddies had come home . . . He'd wrapped them in a piece of newspaper with a wink, adding an extra one at the last minute 'for the little girl' . . . What little girl? Violet.

Jem and Violet – where were they? They ought to be sitting at the table where she'd left them, plates ready . . . waiting for her to cook their tea. Then they'd had to get to the shelter because the siren had gone . . . but . . . The room had heaved sideways and the ceiling had come down . . . She spat to clear her mouth and gathered the last of her strength to shout, 'Three!'

'Listen, was that someone saying, "Three?" Calling Jem, asking if he can hear her? Good, found her now, just here . . . We're coming, love. We're coming. Kiddies, yes. Yes, we've got your kiddies safe here. Names? Vi'let, yes indeed.'

The warden looked at the other diggers in a way that dared someone to contradict him. No one did. They had to keep her hopes up if there was any chance of getting her out alive.

The ambulance girl saw small fingers reaching through the rubble. Relieved, she reached down to grasp them. 'Hold on,' she urged. She gave them a squeeze and a small severed hand came easily out of the rubble. She reminded herself fiercely that the people trapped down there were counting on her to help them. She wasn't going to be sick now. Keep digging. Be sick later. She choked down rising bile with a mighty force of will and concentrated on lifting the debris, piece by piece. Then she uncovered something with a bow in its hair – a little girl. She dug out the rest and found a smaller child. A boy. She laid what was left of the children to one side, covered them quickly and helped to heave away a broken beam. The little boy was still warm. Debris rattled over their feet and they could see the woman now, the gleam of her eyes, in the faint light. She seemed to be conscious. They had to keep her awake, they knew, keep her talking.

'Come on, lads,' said the warden, 'nearly got her now. Easy, missus, this lass from the ambulance has a stretcher. You're safe now. Can you talk to us, tell us your name?'

The ambulance girl and the driver dug as hard as they could to free the woman's legs.

'The kiddies – Vi'let and Jem. Did you find the kiddies? They was with me . . . on the train all day, comin' 'ome . . . nuffink to eat all the way from Yorkshire. 'Ungry after the train . . . I stopped at the butcher on the off-chance – sausages . . . No sausages in ever so long . . . Siren went but I only stopped for a minute to get their bit of tea. Thought we 'ad time . . . never 'ad the sirens in Yorkshire . . . Vi'let!' she wailed. 'Where's Vi'let? Where's Jem? 'Ave they finished their tea yet?'

'Easy, dear. They're fine. You'll soon see them.' Slowly they eased the woman from beneath a broken beam and on to a stretcher. 'Soon, love.'

She was soaked through. Looking back into the hole where she had been the warden saw water. 'Mains burst,' he muttered. Sometimes people survived the bombing only to drown in the rubble.

The ambulance girl tucked a blanket round the woman. 'The children are dead,' she mouthed over her shoulder.

'They mustn't 'ave a cold tea again. First sausages we'd seen in months. I only stopped a minute . . .'

'That's right, dear.' The warden was waving the ambulance back to where they stood. Where the hell was the man with the morphine?

'Where we was billeted, such a carry-on when I used 'er kitchen, called us dirty. Most nights, the kiddies and me, we made do with bread and marge, instead of a cooked tea. Ooh . . . can't feel me legs, nor me arms neither. Why's that? Oh. Oh! That 'urt! I'll be all right long as I know the kiddies is safe . . . Let me tell them . . .' Suddenly Mrs Pigeon felt sleepy again. The fog made it hard to see and it was getting dark. Long past teatime. Jem and Vi'let were hungry . . . The girl in the tin hat was leaning over her, saying something to her, shouting, but from a distance. Bossyboots . . . No older than Elsie, ordering her to do something or other. It sounded like 'Keep talking to me' but she was fed up with being shouted at . . . The woman with her la-di-da house in Yorkshire had shouted, 'Filthy! Like filthy gypsies!' The kiddies were so happy when she'd said enough was enough and they'd go home today . . . Sausages! Bit of luck. Their favourite. Sausages . . .

A minute later the ambulance girl extricated her hand from the woman's and felt for a pulse. 'She's gone.' She covered the grey face with the blanket and helped to lift the stretcher into the back of the ambulance with the two dead children. No need to hurry. She sat down in the rubble and rested her head in her hands. The canteen girl brought her a mug of tea. 'Drink this, love. Plenty of sugar in it.'

'Like this every bloody night,' muttered the warden, looking off into the distance. His jaw clenched and he looked at the ambulance girl. She'll soon get used to it, he thought. It was getting dark again. He prayed the Germans wouldn't be back but mostly he begged God to help the anti-aircraft gunners to blow every last German plane out of the sky, and to help the RAF bomb every last city in Germany and every last German in it to smithereens.

''Allo, what's this?' muttered his mate. He was in the hole from which they had pulled the woman out. He'd found a newspaper parcel and opened it gingerly. 'Crikey! Sausages. Bit dusty, but no need to let them go to waste.' He slipped them into his pocket.

The ambulance girl watched him. Then she thanked the canteen worker politely and managed a glassy smile. 'I'm all right. Back to work.' She drank her tea, then tried to stand up, doubled over on to her knees and vomited.

20. Crowmarsh Priors, December 1941

It was a sober, frightened congregation who attended morning service in Crowmarsh Priors. The previous Monday Japan had bombed the American base at Pearl Harbor, and two days later Germany had declared war on the United States.

The church was packed. Oliver was grey and sharp-featured, as if he had not slept for a week. There had been more German planes during the night and heavier bombing over London and Birmingham, with many more civilian casualties. Rumours abounded that German airmen had parachuted into the countryside and were hiding, waiting for the invasion. Anything seemed possible. It felt as if the end of the world had come.

Ever since the telegram with the news of the death of her mother, Jem and Violet, Elsie had been fierce, uncommunicative and red-eyed with grief. She had howled like an animal, cursed the Germans and refused to be comforted, even by Bernie. Oliver had had the sense not to offer religious platitudes. Now she sat in church, face set, with Frances on one side and Evangeline on the other, each gripping one of her hands. Maude, Tommy and Kipper sat on Evangeline's other side. Maude and Tommy had said their parents was chapel so they weren't going to no church, but Evangeline had insisted and, for the first time ever, threatened to box their ears if they made a fuss. Tanni was still in bed, recovering after giving birth and feverish with an infection.

Now Maude and Tommy squirmed and kicked each other but Kipper, feeling anxiety in the air, laid his head quietly against Evangeline's arm. A deathly pale Alice frogmarched her mother down the aisle. It was the first time that Mrs Osbourne had been seen in church since her husband's death, but today Alice made no allowance for her ailments or nerves. Land girls from the hostel had crowded into a pew at the back. They had chapped red hands and anxious faces. In frocks and hats they seemed vulnerable and young. Even the team leader came.

Hugo de Balfort read the lesson gravely.

When it was time for Oliver to step into the pulpit, he said that today he would not preach: they would just pray. As well as the usual prayers for the King and Queen, the government, the armed forces, the bishop and the country, Oliver said special ones for local people serving in the forces or volunteer services – Richard Fairfax on his destroyer escorting supply ships across the north Atlantic, those nursing at the North African front, Penelope Fairfax in the WVS in London, all of the men and women serving far from home, working in factories or driving ambulances.

There were a few smothered sobs.

Lastly he told his congregation to keep faith with each other, with all those for whom they prayed and, above all, with their Creator.

As she looked about her at all of the heads bent in prayer, Frances felt furious that the Germans could terrorize the world like this. At war, are we? she thought.

Very well. She intended to fight the bloody Nazis. She bent her head, but not in prayer. She swore an oath to seize her opportunity to train as an agent, for the Special Operations Executive or the Auxis, whichever would do the most damage to the Germans. And as for Tanni's family . . . Now Frances grasped that, for people like Tanni's family the war wasn't about inconvenient rationing, ugly blackout curtains and unpleasant land-girl jobs.

After the service everyone was subdued, but kept a stiff upper lip for the sake of the rest. Alice nudged her mother firmly into the queue to shake Oliver's hand.

Frances walked out of the church, then paused to wait for Hugo. She was meant to have lunch with him and Leander at Gracecourt. She had accepted the invitation the day of her party, then had been too distracted by the birth of Tanni's baby and a racking hangover to make an excuse. Now she realized that to both men it might appear that she would be there to celebrate her and Hugo's engagement.

Hugo had a word with Oliver, then came over and took her arm possessively.

'Hugo, I must speak to you at once.'

'Frances darling, could it possibly wait? I've been summoned to a meeting of all the Home Guard units in the area, and I shall have to join you and Father later. Then we can –'

'Hugo!' Frances turned to face him. 'This can't wait. I have to tell you that I can't marry you. I'm terribly, terribly sorry. I'm fond of you but I'm not sure I feel quite – oh, I don't know – in love enough to be very good wife material. And with the war on, well, I just don't . . .'

'I see.'

She was uncertain whether he was angry or offended. 'In the circumstances I oughtn't to lunch with you and your father. I'm so sorry if you're disappointed but it's for the best.'

'Frances, do, please, have lunch with Father. I shan't be there and he's been looking forward to it. I can drive you – I must go home to pick up a few things for the meeting,' he said stiffly.

'I'll go on my bicycle,' said Frances. 'I must change first anyway. Oh, Hugo, I wish we might stay friends.'

'Do you?' He looked at her intently. 'Then so do I. And perhaps I might change your mind one day. I shan't lose hope.'

Oliver called him, and Hugo shouted, 'Coming!' then turned away before Frances could say anything else.

It would be horribly awkward alone with Leander today. And the promise they had made to help Tanni's sisters weighed increasingly heavily on Frances's mind. In the cold light of day she realized what a far-fetched plan they had devised, but the worst of it was that Tanni was depending on them now – Oliver's words about keeping faith with one another had hit home. To complicate everything, she had been told to attend a second interview with the little man in London at Christmas and that if they accepted her she would go immediately for the first stage of her training: her absence from the farm would be less noticeable when all of the land girls had Christmas leave. Well, if they accepted her she would find a way to keep her promise to Tanni. She'd cross that bridge when she came to it, she decided.

At Glebe House Frances changed her hat for a head-scarf, donned her godmother's old mac and cycled off in the drizzle. She was in a bad mood by the time the towers of Gracecourt loomed into sight, in the middle of the vast sweep of park.

She found Sir Leander alone. As she hung her wet mac on the fireguard, he said, 'Kind of you to keep an old man company, my dear,' and poured them a glass of sherry.

The small sitting room off the long gallery that he used as his study was cosy. Two logs blazed on vast Tudor firedogs and the panelling glowed. Beyond the curtains the park was grey and wet. Looking out of the window, Frances saw that the tennis courts were overgrown and abandoned, and the box bushes along the brick path needed trimming. The rectangular pools of which Sir Leander had been so proud were only half full. It was hard to remember Gracecourt before the war, when it had been the scene of such gay times, tennis, lunch on the lawns, summer cocktails in gardens strung with paper lanterns, weekend house-parties, when Hugo's cosmo-politan friends had come to shoot pheasant.

There was an awkward silence. Sir Leander, now confined to his wheelchair, looked terrible. He turned to face Frances, who was perched on the sofa. 'Not often I get to lunch alone with a pretty girl, these days.' He raised his glass. 'Here's to the good health of you energetic land girls. In my day no one would have worked women so hard. Doesn't seem right, you having to clear ditches, do all that rough work, war or no war.'

'The cows are the worst,' said Frances, lightly,

wondering how to tell him tactfully that she had refused Hugo.

He saved her the trouble. 'Now, my dear, I'm going to come to the point. Hugo was here for a few minutes a little while before you arrived, and I understand you've turned him down.' He raised his eyebrows.

Frances nodded.

'But I hope and trust that you will change your mind.'

'I'm very fond of Hugo, of course, but with the war on, everything's so unsettled . . .'

Sir Leander shook his head. 'He told me what you'd said, and I encouraged his belief – his hope – that you would come round. You know, young women often believe a lot of twaddle about romance and being swept off one's feet, that sort of thing, but it's really not sound, my dear, not sound at all. Of course Hugo's terribly fond of you, but in these troubled times young people, especially in a family as old as ours, need to take a longer view. When it's a question of a certain position in society, continuation of an ancient, distinguished family . . .'

Sir Leander had always been kind to Frances, taking an almost fatherly interest in her, marking her out for special attention and small courtesies even in the days when more prominent women guests had been present. Frances had become genuinely fond of him, and now she stared at her lap, wishing she hadn't made an old man unhappy. When she looked up, though, she saw that, despite his frailty, Sir Leander's demeanour was haughty and aggrieved. He looked at her keenly. Oh dear.

'I speak for your own good, my dear, *in loco parentis*, as it were. I realize that your father may have been too busy to . . . ahem. But let me remind you that in marrying Hugo you would become mistress of a fine estate, and after my death, you would be Lady de Balfort, secure in the state that is what all women are meant for, marriage and motherhood, in the highest station of our society. Your father approves. His solicitors and mine have already discussed marriage settlements. Forgive my bluntness, but if you felt you could be tolerably happy with Hugo I should like to see the two of you married before I die, and I should like even more to know that an heir was on the way to ensure the future of the estate.'

This was too much! Frances stared stonily into her glass, feeling she could cheerfully have strangled the solicitors with her bare hands.

Sir Leander continued: 'The Admiral's no time for beating about the bush, and he rather feared you'd hatched some madcap scheme for doing *intelligence* work or some such thing.' He chuckled as if the idea was preposterous. 'Surely not. He and I agree it's hardly a job for girls.'

Frances seethed.

'Think it over, my dear. Now, if you've finished your sherry, my cook has left us something on the sideboard in a chafing dish – probably quite dreadful, with all this rationing and whatnot. We'd better go and eat it, though. I can manage, thanks very much.'

He led the way in his wheelchair.

In the long, dark dining room, with its rows of family portraits, the polished table was laid for two with ancient Limoges china and crested, if tarnished, silver. Something was steaming over a spirit lamp. It did indeed smell dreadful. Frances took the plates and spooned on to them brownish lumps in a thin grey gravy. There was a dish of limp boiled cabbage and another of carrots. 'Corned-beef rissoles, I think,' muttered Sir Leander. 'Promise me that when you become mistress of this house the first thing you will do is engage a housekeeper who understands plain cooking.'

In despair, Frances helped herself to mustard.

'Fortunately,' her host said, with a smile, as he lifted a dusty bottle left open to breathe at his place, 'there are still a few bottles of burgundy in the cellar – laid down long before the war. Thought we'd have one today to celebrate your engagement, but if that's not to be the case, at least it will help this travesty of a meal go down.'

The wine was lovely. Frances managed to cut her rissoles into tiny pieces and hide them under the cabbage. Later she fetched the pudding from the sideboard – spotted dick and custard – and gamely ate a bit, trying not to notice how dried eggs made things taste of dried egg no matter what you did. Sir Leander poured her the last of the wine.

There was a small fire in the grate and the French clock on the mantelpiece ticked musically. The small dining room was one of the oldest rooms in the house and still had leaded windows. Frances made them a jug of ersatz coffee, then excused herself.

'You know where it is, of course?'

'Yes, thank you.'

She headed for the downstairs cloakroom, which was next to the gun and boot room at the far end of the panelled passage with more de Balfort portraits on the walls. She peeped into the little gold and white salon on the way. It had been Hugo's mother's sitting room and Frances had spent many delightful evenings in it before the war. It had always been her favourite room in the house, with its full-length Venetian mirrors, painted ceiling and view of the park beyond.

Now, like the rest of the house, it was somewhat the worse for wear. A pane of glass in the french window was broken and patched with cardboard, and the parquet floor was warped. The ceiling had a dark patch of mildew. The de Balforts must be short of money. Aunt Muriel had been highly critical of Sir Leander's extravagant schemes and now Frances thought that perhaps she had been right. Why had he not spent his money on keeping the house in order? It was in a dreadful state.

She continued down the passage to the cloakroom, opened the door and squealed. Something large and black was blocking the lavatory. She peered cautiously. It was a dead bat. She shut the door and went back down the passage towards the grand staircase. There was a bathroom on the landing. A whiff of tobacco smoke told her that Sir Leander was having his after-lunch cigarette. She wouldn't disturb him by mentioning the bat. She tiptoed past the half closed door and up the wide staircase with its worn Turkey runner. Half-way up, a noise from somewhere higher in the house stopped her in her tracks.

The housemaids' rooms were in the attic, but they had all left for factory jobs. Now there was only the cook, who was too old for the factory and always had Sundays off to visit her sister in Brighton. Hugo was at the Home Guard meeting and Sir Leander, unable to climb the stairs to his bedroom on the first floor, now lived on the ground floor in the butler's old quarters. She listened harder and tiptoed up to the landing. Something was moving about on the second floor where Hugo had told her the day and night nurseries were.

'Hello?' she called. There was no reply. It must have been a rat, she thought, or had squirrels got in? Frances listened for another minute but heard no more. She went on to the bathroom. It was covered with cobwebs and full of old books and broken chairs, but at least the Victorian plumbing contained no bats. And it flushed. She washed her hands with a scrap of desiccated soap and looked for something to dry them, then remembered that airing cupboards were often positioned next to hot-water pipes. A heavy gilt picture frame was leaning against the stretch of wall behind the bath but she could just make out the outline of a cupboard door. She nudged aside the frame and opened it, but there were no towels, just a broken radiogram, a rusty oil tin and a large torch.

Frances wiped her damp hands on her skirt. She picked up the torch, wondering if Sir Leander had forgotten where it was and might need it, but put it back, not wanting to explain how she had found it.

When she went to join Sir Leander, the warm glow that the wine imparted had worn off and she was cold. The old man was sitting with a tartan rug over his knees, looking pinched and done in. The wireless was on in the corner and she could hear Beethoven. Outside it was getting dark.

'Sublime music,' said Sir Leander. 'This war is a sad business. Should never have happened, you know.'

'It's getting late and I should be off,' Frances said. 'I'll draw the blackout curtains for you first. I hate leaving you on your own, though, Sir Leander. It's the cook's day off, isn't it? Is no one else here?'

'No. I always hope Mrs Jones won't go off leaving something to burn or catch fire in the kitchen. Not as young as she was. Never know how she manages the journey to Brighton. The buses are so unreliable – can't use their lights to see where they're going, just creep along. Shame Hugo isn't here. Perhaps you'll see him on his way home. Will you remember what I said, my dear?'

'Of course. Thank you for lunch.' Frances pulled the black drapes across the windows. 'Getting married is such a serious decision, isn't it?'

'Very', said the old man, staring into the fire. 'Everything depends on it, my dear. Everything.'

21. Crowmarsh Priors and Norfolk, December 1941

At the end of the third week in December Bruno had a week's leave for Christmas and hurried down to Sussex anxious to see his new baby daughter, who was now almost a month old. He had been worried when he had received the telegram that told him Tanni had given birth at Glebe House after a party. He had rung at once and spoken to Evangeline, who had said there had been a problem with the birth and Tanni had been ill afterwards, but the baby was fine.

When Bruno arrived he rushed upstairs to find Tanni better but still tucked up in bed, pale but pretty in a faded pink bed-jacket, her dark hair tumbling over her shoulders. Her face was thinner but her eyes lit up when he came into the room, kissed her and told her how much he loved her. She insisted on sitting up with her sewing basket to hand, and stitched away at things she had promised villagers, feeding the baby and reading to Johnny. They had named the little girl Anna.

Bruno made himself useful, carrying meals on trays to Tanni and seeing that she ate them, helping an overworked Evangeline, playing with Johnny and the evacuees, and, whenever he had a free minute, scooping up Anna, sleeping or not, to sit with her in the rocking chair Evangeline had found in the attic. He was entranced by his small daughter, who stared at him solemnly from the crook of his arm. 'She has your eyes and my nose,' he said to Tanni, stroking Anna's downy little head. 'Are all baby girls so beautiful?'

He was amazed at how people from the village called to admire Anna, bringing outgrown baby clothes, nappies, and toys. Margaret Rose Hawthorne begged to hold her, and he let her, but hovered nervously. 'She's so little,' cooed Margaret Rose. Even the vicar came. Bruno was taken aback to see him in his clerical collar, bending over the cot, but when Oliver smiled and held out his finger, Anna curled her tiny fingers round it. Babies seemed to like Oliver – even the fussiest ones at the baptismal font calmed when he held them. 'This dear child is cheering up the whole village in a very dark hour indeed,' he said. 'Am I imagining things or does she have her mother's eyes?' Bruno warmed to him at once.

Too soon the happy interlude was over. Ten days after his arrival, Bruno kissed Tanni, Johnny and Anna while they were still asleep and left Crowmarsh Priors in the dark. On the way the driver stopped for him to buy a packet of Player's cigarettes from a shop that had opened early, then motored on to Norfolk. The car stopped at a windswept airstrip where they waited until a military vehicle pulled up and a man in handcuffs, accompanied by an armed guard, got out. He and the others were given breakfast in a hut – powdered eggs scrambled into a watery mess, sausages, heavy grey buns and lukewarm tea. Bruno usually made a sandwich of the sausage and the bun. He was never hungry so early but he ate those breakfasts, awful as they were, because he knew it would be a long time before he got another meal.

Afterwards the three passengers boarded the waiting Norseman aircraft with two pilots on board. No one spoke as the propellers roared and the small plane taxied down the runway, creaking and rattling. The light flickered on and off as the plane lifted and climbed sharply, bouncing through air pockets. Bruno hoped they wouldn't run into a snowstorm, although he knew the plane could land on ice or water if it had to. He wanted more than anything to be back in the warm bed with Tanni, Johnny and Anna but forced himself to focus on the job ahead.

The weather grew worse as they flew north, and Bruno sat back, bracing himself. The plane was not made for comfort and the passengers – Bruno, the man in handcuffs beside him and the military guard – were all bundled against the piercing cold in heavy coats and scarves.

The man beside him looked steadily away from him through the window. He had a thin, haughty profile, stern eyebrows and an unblinking, fixed expression. He had not touched breakfast.

Hours later he turned to Bruno. 'Sweden. We are headed for Sweden judging by the time we've been flying.' It was a statement, not a question.

'Near Sweden,' corrected Bruno.

'Ah, so I thought. The coast. The island where your government and mine exchange prisoners-of-war. Secretly, of course. One spy for another. *Quid pro quo*, as you English say. Though you are not English yourself, but Jewish.' The haughty face smiled mirthlessly. 'One can always tell. Something . . . inferior in the face. They send my Jewish interrogator to escort me to the exchange

289

as one of their subtle insults. The English understand the nuance of insult better than any other race.'

Bruno regarded him impassively. The man was an Anglo-German with important connections in aristocratic circles. He had had a job in Military Intelligence, where he had been spying for the Germans for years, eluding detection. He had even had access to Churchill and passed confidential information to his superiors that had resulted in the loss of untold numbers of lives, before he had been traced and arrested.

'The British spy for whom I am being exchanged – I must assume he is someone important?'

Bruno said nothing.

'You will not tell me his name, naturally. Perhaps it's one of your girls. Your Special Operations Executives. Not one of their little wireless operators, I expect, or a decoder. They are expendable and, in any case, we normally shoot them ourselves after extracting all the information they can give us. A few are remarkably brave, of course. But for me there will be someone important. Ah, well, whoever it is, I shall be in Berlin soon. We'll meet again when the Führer decides the time has come for the invasion. There are many more like me in England, waiting for the final victory. And we shall be victorious.'

The man fell silent and Bruno waited, silent too. Finally his ears popped, a sign that they were descending. The plane banked and circled over a small island in the midst of an endless expanse of water. The ground was dusted with snow. The man looked out of the window, smiling, craning his neck for sight of the plane bringing the person to be exchanged for him and take him back to Germany.

He was vain and longed to know how the British gauged his importance. A crudely marked landing-strip ran the length of the island, but otherwise it was bare and deserted, save for rocks, a few pine trees and a hut. No other aircraft.

'So, we're first, and they're late,' he muttered, 'which is discourteous, but the bad weather explains it, no doubt.'

Still Bruno said nothing.

The Norseman bumped hard as it hit the ground and taxied down the runway to a stop. The prisoner peered again at the bare, empty island and then at the sky. The pilot and co-pilot got up and stretched, then opened the door. A blast of freezing air swept in. 'Come on. This way.'

The man looked at Bruno, the pilots and the guard. 'But the other plane isn't here. Where is it?' he demanded. No one said anything. He looked from one to the other. Slowly, realization dawned. His face crumpled in disbelief and his lips formed 'No!' but he didn't say it.

Instead he turned to Bruno again. 'May I have a cigarette?' It sounded like an order.

Bruno, who didn't smoke, took the packet of Player's from his breast pocket, opened it and tapped one out. The man raised manacled hands to take it. They shook only slightly as Bruno struck a match.

They all waited in silence as the man smoked. He finished the cigarette and ground the butt under his heel. 'I am ready,' he said, standing up straight. The military guard led him down the steps of the plane, and the pilots walked on either side of him, heading for the clump of pine trees next to the water.

Bruno followed them down the steps, stretched and stamped his feet in the cold. He had been present at the prisoner's interrogation and knew that he deserved what was about to happen. He thought of his mother and the Josephs, the hell they must be enduring. If they were alive. Of Lili and Klara, just a few years older than Johnny, wherever they were. What if Johnny and Anna . . . He could not bear to think of his children in Lili and Klara's situation.

That was why he could do his job. He had escorted a dozen enemy agents to this bleak island for the same purpose. The next time he came here, he hoped it would be with whoever was sending those clear-weather reports to the Germans.

A volley of shots echoed in the cold silence. The military guard and the pilots returned without the prisoner. They nodded to Bruno. 'It's done.' Briskly they refuelled the plane from the supply in the hut and, with the propellers whirring, turned it to face down the narrow runway. The little aircraft gathered speed and, at the last possible moment, lifted up and over the bare rocks, climbing slowly. Bruno thought of his mother and the Josephs in some German work camp, wishing he could believe that today's act of justice would help them.

22. A Training Camp, January 1942

From below no one could see the two men standing in the rain on the castle battlements. They were looking through field-glasses, observing the new recruits, who had spent the morning practising with explosives and were now being put through commando training. They were taking it in turns to recover heavy containers, the kind that would be dropped behind enemy lines with ammunition and equipment, from the icy waters of the lake that had once supplied the castle with fish.

Both men's glasses paused on the same recruit. 'Ah, Miss Falconleigh!' exclaimed one. 'Tudor will be furious, of course, when he finds out. Where does he think she is? And how is her training coming on?'

'He thinks she's in Reading on a land-girl welfare committee. Her reports are excellent, and the training's going well,' said one, watching a slim figure slithering beneath a muddy hedge. 'Surprising aptitude for it, though you wouldn't think it to look at her, pretty little thing like that. If they send her behind enemy lines they'll make her plainer with dowdy clothes and a country girl's shoes. She convinced us of how useful that might be.'

'The most unlikely people have a talent for this sort of work. You'd never think it to meet her in the street, but she's not afraid to handle weapons and runs well. Quick mind too. Observant and keen to do something active.'

'Fortunately she's matured since the first interview, but we're still concerned that she's young. And she struck us as a bit . . . a bit . . .'

The other man smiled. The first speaker had been the 'little man' of Frances's first interview. That he had committed himself to her for a brace of pheasants was a standing joke in the organization.

'Tudor had quite a time with her. Ringleader, trouble-maker, expelled from every school he sent her to. Scandalous photographs in the papers as a débutante. Unsuitable escorts, arrested for madcap pranks . . .'

The first man nodded complacently. 'Her type is out for adventure. But she has intelligence, determination and speaks perfect French. Just needs to learn a bit more self-discipline, how to take orders, that kind of thing. She wants a posting to France but we've decided not to send her yet. She's our youngest recruit, a bit of a firecracker, might get over-enthusiastic, endanger other agents on the circuit. The Old Man decided she needs a longer proba-tionary period, so we'll assign her to the southern Auxi mission after her mock-exercise, see how she gets on. She went to Wiltshire for Auxiliary Unit training. Booby traps, sabotage. She's got a cool head, kept her nerves steady.'

'She'll need steady hands too. Auxi units use those sticky-bombs, God help them. Enough nitro-glycerine to stop a tank but hard to detonate through the metal cover. Regulars won't touch 'em.' He thought for a minute and added, 'Ought to suit Miss Falconleigh, though.'

'She'll go to Beaulieu for the final leg of wireless training, then home for her mock-exercise. Jerry has plenty of help from this side of the Channel, and the

Old Man's worried about whoever is helping the German pilots with their navigating. Not sure how. Perhaps lights in the blackout. Another bugger sending weather reports to the Luftwaffe on the French coast, signalling the all-clear for a raid. Haven't found him – or her – yet. When I think what he's responsible for, I'd gladly shoot him myself. We call him Manfred. The Auxis down there are looking, but Manfred could be a whole cell of fifth-columnists, or just one German agent who's slipped in.'

'So, you plan to send her back to Sussex to help look for Manfred?'

'Wouldn't go as far as that. Doubt there's anything suspicious in Crowmarsh Priors. It's too small ... but it's in a sensitive location, close to the Coastal Defence Zone. They say Lord Haw-Haw has a nephew in Brighton, and the Nordic League always had a lot of sympathizers among the county families down there – before the war the country-house set had German friends. Nazi connections. We're keeping a close watch on them. Even if they aren't personally involved, Intelligence is worried about what mischief their German friends might have had time to make before the war. "Off for an afternoon walk, old chap. Just take my camera, amateur photographer, so jolly."'

'We're assigning Miss Falconleigh to practise her surveillance skills at the de Balfort place, Gracecourt Hall, for her mock-exercise.'

'She been told yet?'

'No. As I said, she expects to be posted to Europe. But the Old Man says she should carry on as normal for the next six months or so, possibly longer, keep her eyes open and report anything that seems a bit off. We know something's fishy down there and, you never know, she might turn up something.'

The first man exhaled. 'If the Auxis *do* find Manfred, he ought to be taken alive for questioning, of course, but it may not be possible. Anyway, he's likely to be a nasty piece of work, and he'll know what the stakes are. So, lessons in silent killing tomorrow. A few tricks from the Shanghai Police.'

'Jolly good. From what I've seen so far she'll like that almost as much as the sticky-bombs. What about parachute training?'

'In a few months, just in case we have to drop her in France when . . .' He didn't finish the sentence. The other nodded. And neither mentioned what they both knew: when a female SOE operative behind enemy lines was betrayed, arrested or killed, they had to be ready with her replacement. A trained Auxi like Miss Falconleigh could be held in reserve against just such an eventuality.

23. Auschwitz, March 1942

On good days after work, the guards did not set the dogs on anyone for sport: instead they drove the inmates back into the compound and tossed in a few loaves of stale bread for them to fight over. Icy winds blew through the cracks in the walls, and the prisoners lay hungry and shivering in their bunks, trying to hang on to life and the last vestiges of their humanity. For some a happy memory provided them with respite from hell, but for more it intensified the horrors of their existence.

Dr Joseph sought escape in the thought that all of his children were safe in England. He told the story over and over again. His eldest daughter was married to a good man, a professor, who had taken her to Britain and safety. He had put his younger children, twin girls, on the *Kindertransport* and sent them to Britain too, where they lived with that sister, who had always been a little mother to them. The twins had missed their train in January 1939 through illness but, thank God, they had recovered and by a miracle he had managed the impossible by getting another place on a train that left in the summer of that year. His children were together and safe.

He dwelt on that to stop himself thinking of his wife in the women's block. He caught a glimpse of her now and then, her shaved head and gaunt cheeks ... He remembered how she had looked on the day he proposed, then on their wedding night, and later as a pretty young matron in a coat with a fur collar and muff made by Frau Zayman, smiling down at five-year-old Tanni.

Poor Frau Zayman had been ill with pleurisy, coughing and feverish in the sealed railway car *en route* to the camp. There had been nothing to eat or drink, and she had not been able to lie down. She had breathed her last crushed in a corner.

A man who had failed to get places on the *Kindertransport* for his own children wept. A new prisoner inquired politely if the married daughter had children yet.

'We heard that my Tanni was expecting,' said Dr Joseph, dreamily, 'just before we were taken away. The baby will be three this summer. We do not know whether it is a boy or a girl.'

'Congratulations,' several men whispered, in the darkness, from the crowded bunks. 'May the mother and the baby be well and the baby have a long and distinguished life.'

'Ah, to know your children are together in England, safe, with enough to eat, learning, even playing, perhaps. Milk. Sunlight. It must be a great comfort,' another man murmured. It was unimaginable here.

Not all of the camp prisoners were lying in their bunks, despite the late hour. A work detail was awake in another building, this one brightly lit, where the Doctor was still at work. His arch-rival, Ernst Schafer, had failed in his expedition to Tibet to find a lost Aryan race. Now the Doctor's eugenics programme had finally been given the go-ahead. It was a great coup for him. He had always thought that Schafer's theory was rubbish but, for as long as Himmler had taken an interest, it had got the man out from under the Doctor's feet. When Himmler had finally lost patience with Schafer, he had looked to the Doctor's experiments as the best means of assuring the supremacy of the Aryan race.

But the programme was not producing results as quickly as he had promised, Himmler was increasingly impatient, and the Doctor was increasingly worried that he was no closer to satisfying Himmler's demands. For the time being he procrastinated, hiding behind 'procedures' and 'evaluations', recording every detail of the experiments in his old-fashioned handwriting, then drawing up specific, lengthy criteria for the next. He insisted that patience and precision would pay off, and it was now a matter of selection of specimens. But the answer had eluded the Doctor – so far.

Meanwhile he kept assuring Himmler that, given a little more time, his proper scientific methods, not madcap adventuring schemes, would achieve the desired result. His aim was beautifully simple: to establish scientifically the pre-conditions for giving birth to twins, which would enable German women to produce twice the number of babies. Aryan reproduction would double at the same time as inferior non-Aryans were eliminated. The Doctor hinted to Himmler of the vast breeding camps he envisaged, stocked with carefully selected Nordic women, mothers of the pure master race who would fulfil Germany's destiny, all bearing two perfect children at a time. So efficient!

The Führer himself was taking a keen personal interest in the project.

But hints and promises had to be fulfilled. The pressure was mounting and the anxious Doctor had considered expanding the research to triplets and even larger multiple births, before concluding reluctantly that the undoubted efficiency of such births was outweighed by the risk of weakening the Aryan genes by spreading them too thinly between several babies. Twins were the safest bet. In any case there was a shortage of triplets and other multiple births in the camp on which to conduct satisfactory experiments.

Tonight the Doctor was just finishing. The teenage Gypsy boys, fine, healthy specimens and identical twins, lay dismembered on the bloody operating table. The Doctor pondered the number of differential tests he had made, comparing how the systems of identical twins deal with toxic substances, whether one had superior resistance and so on. He would write up the results in his usual meticulous way once he had examined the organs, but he felt a faint anxiety as to whether he had been able to establish any important new criteria before the specimens had died. Perhaps if he had used anaesthetics they would have lived a little longer, which would have allowed him to conduct a wider range of tests.

He needed to examine what 'identical' meant from a different angle. He frowned, thinking, while he scrubbed his hands and changed his bloodstained white coat, leaving the inmate doctors to dispose of the mess. Four thin prisoners in lab coats shuffled forward. When the trains of deportees had arrived, doctors were ordered to step forward. They always did so voluntarily, expecting to be assigned medical care of the prisoners. Instead they were put at the Doctor's disposal. They were less trouble and more efficient than ordinary prisoners when they cleaned his laboratories, but more than one had responded badly to his refusal to waste anaesthetics on experiments. One had even killed the specimens. The guards had dealt promptly with him as an example to the others. The Doctor sighed over the wasted experiment.

Perhaps a fresh approach to twin births . . . He had had a supply of twins made available to him, mostly Jews, culled from displaced-persons camps and ghettos, schools and hospitals, in every country Germany occupied. They were housed in a special children's wing of the camp. The supply of twins, however, had now dwindled to nothing, and the majority had been boys. He needed twin girls, to study the development of their reproductive organs.

Then he had a brainwave. It would be valuable to conduct experiments on the parents of the twin-child specimens. Though this presented him with another practical difficulty: the twins in the children's house had been separated from their parents before they arrived at the camp.

He felt squeamish about conducting experiments to benefit Aryans using Jewish specimens but even Jews, wily as they were, weren't clever enough to foil conclusions reached through proper scientific methods.

The Doctor turned to his assistant. 'We have reached the next stage in the research and for that I require twin female children *and* their parents. It is a matter of the highest priority. Extra bread for any prisoners who can identify parents of female twins.'

One of the inmates cleaning the experiment room raised his eyes. 'Bread,' he whispered to himself. He thought of his fellow prisoner Dr Joseph whose bunk was below his. Dr Joseph had not stepped forward when all the doctors had been ordered to do so.

The inmate had been arrested at the same time and almost on the same street as Dr Joseph and his wife. Out of kindness he had not told Dr Joseph that he knew the June train bearing Dr Joseph's twin daughters had not reached Britain before the Germans invaded Poland, and war was declared. His own son had been on it and, he had thought, safe in Britain, like Dr Joseph's daughters, until, to his horror, the son had appeared in the men's block at Auschwitz. At Gurs they had selected the men and boys for deportation first, sent them to Drancy, then finally on the cattle car to Auschwitz, the boy had told his anguished father. Two months later he had died of pneumonia, aged twelve.

In the unlikely event that Dr Joseph's twins had been so fortunate as to reach England, they were beyond the reach of the Germans until the invasion when their fate would be sealed. If they had not, they must still be in Gurs or at Drancy. There would be records, of course – the Germans were meticulous.

If the girls were in either place, they would eventually fall into German hands. It was only a matter of time before they died or were sent to one of the larger concentration camps as his son had been – and his younger children. So, he rationalized, it wouldn't matter if he informed the Doctor of their existence and that of their parents. All he could think of was bread.

He knew that Dr Joseph's wife had been taken to the women's camp. He had seen her there across the wire. She was emaciated and probably tubercular, but she was alive.

To ease his conscience, the inmate weighed up the advantages to the Josephs. If he told the Doctor about them and their daughters, the authorities would soon find the girls if they were in a French camp. They would be brought to Auschwitz without delay and the Josephs would be reunited in one of the cells in the medical-experiments block.

He knew that there was no hope for anyone in this place of horror, but for a little while the Joseph family would be together, and as subjects of medical experiments, they would be given soup and porridge, maybe even an onion or some boiled cabbage. And he himself would have extra bread . . .

So he would not be increasing the Josephs' suffering, if he exchanged the information for bread. Quite the opposite. For a time their lives would be better. Until the end. He did not think long about what always happened in the end.

He would do it.

As the prisoners shuffled out of the door to empty their buckets of dirty water, he paused in front of the Doctor's assistant and asked permission to speak. He had information that parents of twin girls were in the camp and that the children could be traced.

The Doctor listened and made notes in his precise

handwriting. He smiled. He would give the order for extra bread when he had all four of the subjects safely in his laboratory. But that would not take long. Given the Führer's interest in the project, he would soon have the Joseph children if they were at Drancy, at Gurs or even in the vicinity of the displaced-persons' camp. Meanwhile he ordered the Joseph parents brought to the experimental wing and given blankets and soup.

24. Crowmarsh Priors
January–May 1942

When Frances went away over Christmas and stayed away for weeks afterwards, Oliver missed her. When she returned his heart lifted. After morning service on that first Sunday, he kept hold of her hand while he asked if what he had heard was true, that she had been assigned to some committee in London.

'Yes. Land-girl welfare thing. Father's volunteered me.' Frances rolled her eyes. 'You can imagine it – are we doing enough to keep land girls' spirits up, keeping an eye on their moral welfare? They need help to stay on the straight and narrow apparently. Especially now the Americans have arrived with, um, all sorts of things like chocolate and Coca-Cola. Some of the girls might be – er – led astray.'

'If there's any pastoral assistance I can give, if I can be of any help at all,' he said earnestly, still holding her hand, 'please let me know.'

Frances dropped her eyes. 'Thank you. It's good to know I – we – can call on you.'

Frances had been told to use the Land Girl Welfare Committee as cover to explain her absences. It was part of an agent's work, but she hated lying to Oliver as she gazed into his clear brown eyes. Honesty was so deeply engrained in him that it would never occur to him to lie about anything. What would he think of her if he knew?

Her thoughts turned to the mock-exercise she had

been assigned. It was the final test for all recruits, and Frances had been hoping for something daring, such as blowing up a target under the noses of the authorities. However, she had been sent home to Crowmarsh Priors and ordered to carry on as a land girl but do surveillance on the de Balforts and report any sighting of their friends and acquaintances. It was very tedious indeed: there were no longer any visitors at Gracecourt. Also, it would be uncomfortable to keep Hugo and Sir Leander under surveillance, particularly as it involved seeing Hugo, whom she would much rather avoid. Worse, Oliver might get the idea that she was encouraging him – as, indeed, might Sir Leander and, of course, Hugo. Frances, who had always cut up rough at the slightest hint of discipline and having to do what she disliked, thought, Bloody hell! But she bit her lip and followed orders.

Meanwhile she, Evangeline, Elsie and Alice were determined not to let Tanni down. Evangeline said the plan was no more outlandish than others that had worked. No one thought to ask her what she was talking about. Elsie was still beside herself over the loss of her mother, and for her, fighting the Germans was personal now. She took out her fury on the rats but she had plenty to spare. Even Bernie was alarmed by the new steely glint in Elsie's eye.

Only cautious Alice held back: she said the plan had been conceived in a moment of drunken madness, and she was sorry but, really . . .

The other three gave her no peace, and finally Frances exercised her considerable powers of persuasion: 'Alice, darling, of course you're right, and it is rather daring, but what else can we do? If we do nothing we might be sentencing the children to death. Do we want that on our consciences? Anyway, we're friends – one for all and all for one, as we used to say at school.' She had used the motto freely in those days when she was inciting her friends to wild escapades that had invariably landed everyone in trouble. Alice, on the other hand, had been a model pupil. 'We can't possibly do it without you,' Frances urged. 'You're indispensable, Alice! You're the only one who can find the tunnel.'

'Oh, all right,' said Alice, against her better judgement but worn down by the flattery. She had never been included in any 'one for all' thing at school, never had friends and never felt in the thick of things. She hoped they wouldn't be arrested.

'Besides, we need your good sense, Alice, to keep us steady.'

Alice suppressed a little smile. She could quite see that. She felt important already.

Oliver was startled when Alice told him that she, Frances, Evangeline and Elsie had decided to tidy the appallingly overgrown churchyard. Faith manifested itself in the most unexpected ways, he thought.

From his study he watched in amazement as they tackled the area around the Great War memorial first, where it was just possible to see that a patch of ground was now bare near eight new graves, all with jam-jars of snowdrops propped against home-made markers. Elsewhere only a few weathered headstones were visible above the blanket of nettles, brambles, Virginia creeper and ivy that had taken hold, then climbed up the sides of the church and the squat bell tower.

Alice had unearthed a pair of rusty secateurs from a drawer in the vestry and, as a miserable January gave way to an even colder and wetter February, Oliver grew used to seeing one or other hacking away when they had an hour to spare and it wasn't too dark to see what they were doing. Alice came after school when she didn't have a knitting session, a first-aid course or air-raid-warden work, or on Saturday mornings after she had sat with her mother for a bit. Evangeline nipped in for a few moments snatched between the children, the garden, the chickens and her hunting expeditions. Even Elsie surprised him by stamping into the church in her workboots demanding, 'Where's them clipper things, then?' Frances came on Sunday afternoons, when the land girls were off duty. Oliver offered to help her once or twice but she had said no, firmly, she knew what she was doing.

Sitting at his desk now, trying to compose his thoughts for a Lenten sermon, his attention wandered again to Frances. He watched her slim figure bending, clipping and tugging. She paused occasionally to swear when she ran a thorn into her hand. She had a neat waist, he thought, and a pretty shape even in those trousers and that baggy jersey. The thought made him smile. He did not think of himself as a man who noticed women's figures . . .

Progress in the graveyard slowed when it snowed heavily for a week in early March. Then Elsie stomped in with her case of cyanide and poked about in the undergrowth. 'Huntin' rats,' she said to Oliver.

'Don't rats do most damage where food's stored, in pantries and barns?' asked Oliver, puzzled. 'Do you find many in churchyards?'

'Everywhere, rats are, you'd never credit it,' Elsie the expert assured him. 'Burrow around, rats do, graves and that. You want to get them in the spring, er, when they're nestin', you know. 'Scuse me, must get on. P'raps people ought to keep out of the churchyard on account of the danger.'

'Well, no one's ever been attacked by rats here,' said Oliver, mildly.

'But there's poison and 'orrible traps and suchlike all over, 'idden. Cyanide! Very dangerous. Don't want any of the kiddies gettin' 'urt. Or poisoned and dyin' an 'orrible deaf,' said Elsie, darkly.

'Oh dear! I'll put up a notice.'

By the end of March Tanni was anxious again. She hadn't seen Bruno since he had made a fleeting visit in early February, and Rachel had written to her that, if their information was correct, the Germans were sending large numbers of children to Auschwitz. Now that Germany and America were at war, the American Quakers trying to run their relief programme in south-west France were being arrested, and the helpful American consul in Marseille had left. Rachel was doing what she could to find someone in Gurs who could verify that the twins seen on a distant farm were Lili and Klara, but the weeks went by with no word.

*

One day Evangeline returned from London to tell Frances that a colonel in the Free French had agreed that, for a price, the Resistance would transport the children, if they could be found, along one of the rescue lines used for the RAF. However, they might not be willing to do it until harvest time when farm vehicles loaded with straw would make it easier to hide two children and move them across France to Brittany.

Then, out of the blue, Richard wrote to say that he had a fortnight's leave in early April. He and Evangeline would go to the coast and have a proper holiday.

The others were thrilled for her. 'This will stop you moping, darling!' exclaimed Frances.

But Evangeline found it hard to be enthusiastic at the prospect of seeing her husband, even though the others bustled round to help her get ready.

Frances took a critical look at her and said, 'Really, Evangeline, you have rather let yourself go.'

Evangeline was surprised when Tanni voiced her agreement. Her English had improved as her confidence had grown, and she sat Evangeline down in the kitchen and trimmed her unruly tumble of hair with the sewing scissors. 'Much better! I know you don't care how you look, Evangeline, but think of his morale!' she exclaimed, admiring her handiwork. 'Now for your nails!' She handed Evangeline the nailbrush. Later she cut up an old pillowcase to make a fresh collar and cuffs for Evangeline's least shabby frock.

Frances ransacked Glebe House for something suitable to give Evangeline and came up with two precious sets of lace-trimmed silk knickers. It was now against clothing regulations to sew either silk or lace on to underwear, but Frances said she didn't see how anyone could check. Evangeline protested that she had everything she needed, but Frances overrode her: 'Darling, it's practically your honeymoon. You had no time together after you got married because Richard went straight to sea. Women's underwear, these days, is too grey and dreary and dreadful for words. Sometimes I can't bring myself to wear it.'

'Frances!'

'Well, I can't – it scratches. And here's a hat! You're *not* to meet Richard in that disgraceful old trilby that belonged to his father.' Frances presented her with a hatbox. 'And gloves. They were Aunt Muriel's, and she'd had them since the Flood, but at least they're kid. Here's a pair of stockings – and a petticoat.' Then Tanni tucked the nightdress Frances had given her into Evangeline's case, with a bottle of whisky from Bernie, sent via Elsie, who was going to move into the Fairfax house to help Tanni with Maude, Tommy and Kipper while Evangeline was away.

Evangeline thanked them all, but said, 'I really shouldn't be leaving you with so much work . . .'

'You'd think she had honeymoon nerves,' said Frances to Alice. 'Don't people get over those?'

'How would *I* know?' snapped Alice.

Next morning, with Richard's train due at eight, everyone but Alice gathered in the Fairfax hall to make sure that Evangeline had not backslid when she was getting dressed. They were all surprised by how smart and trim she looked. She glanced at her reflection in the hall mirror – a sleek, dark-eyed stranger stared back, one she hadn't seen even when she was ready to meet Laurent in London, an Evangeline she had thought she had left behind her on the night she ran away. She blew them all a kiss, picked up her suitcase and set off for the station, leaving five-year-old Kipper in a howling tantrum because she was going away. Elsie had had him in a headlock to stop him running after her.

She walked slowly, but she was still too early for the train. She waited nervously on the platform, listening for it and trying to remember what Richard looked like.

When it pulled in a tall naval captain got off. Evangeline waved and walked slowly towards him. 'Richard?'

His weatherbeaten face broke into a smile. 'Darling! You're even more ravishing than I remembered!' He swept off his cap and kissed her hard, right in front of Albert, then swept her up and swung her round in a bear-hug until she was breathless. The hat Frances had lent her went flying. 'Richard, put me down!' she gasped, but she couldn't help laughing. He did so and took her case, then Evangeline repinned her hat and smiled nervously at him as they waited for the next train. He seemed older than she remembered, and exuded command.

He put an arm round her and looked down hungrily at her upturned face. 'I keep thinking you'll disappear like you do in my dreams.'

'Nonsense!'

They stepped into a carriage and Richard swung Evangeline's case into the overhead rack, then made sure she had the window-seat. He checked their tickets and put them into his pocket. He had made all the arrangements for their holiday. Evangeline sat back in her seat with a magazine he had brought her, unsure what to do with herself. It was such a novelty to be looked after.

'Every day I think how brave you are to be in England, my darling, when you might be safe in America with your family.'

'No,' she said quickly. 'I don't want to be there, I want to be here.'

'I'm a lucky man. Now,' he said, taking her hand, 'letters are all very well but lots don't get through, and then there's the censor. You can't imagine how I've longed to hear about everything you've been doing.'

Evangeline had dreaded being cooped up for two weeks with a man who was almost a stranger, and at first, with Richard watching her so intently, she could only smile stiffly and give brief answers. She mustn't think of Laurent – she mustn't! But it was evident that Richard really wanted to hear all about her and Crowmarsh Priors and, somehow, her reserve melted. When she was with Laurent she was always on edge, wrestling with jealousy or worried about what he was doing with the Free French. After their lovemaking, they talked about Paris or the band; he was preoccupied with his own precarious existence, less and less interested in Evangeline's life in an English village, with her garden and the evacuees.

By the time they arrived at the guesthouse, Evangeline felt that the fortnight would be manageable. It was clean and comfortable, and the grey-haired lady who ran it had a son in the Navy. She gave the Fairfaxes her best room, decorated in a faded toile print, with a sea view and a four-poster bed. She winked at Evangeline and said that most nights she could manage 'a nice bit of fish' for them, if they should fancy a quiet supper in.

The nice bit of fish often turned out to be a lobster or a boiled crab, which she served in the small parlour, on a table laid by the fire with the blackout curtains drawn. Every night Richard asked if Evangeline wouldn't prefer to go out to a restaurant or a nightclub, but she insisted she was most comfortable curled up next to him on the sofa, listening to the wireless and chatting. It was lovely not to go out to a smoky, noisy nightclub, she thought.

Richard didn't want to talk about life at sea. He wanted to know about everyday things in the village, and was entertained by Evangeline's tales of Tanni and Johnny, and of Anna being born in Lady Marchmont's morning room, and of how Evangeline went hunting on the de Balforts' land because it was so hard to manage on rations and there were still pheasants and rabbits to be had, even wild ducks occasionally. Fortunately the gamekeeper had died so she hadn't been caught.

'Poaching! You?' Richard roared with laughter.

She told him how Kipper trailed after her like a puppy, about Elsie and the rat-catching, and how Lady Marchmont had tried to marry off Alice to the vicar and Frances to Hugo.

A shadow crossed Richard's face at the mention of Alice. 'Darling, I have a confession to make. I'm afraid I was once terribly unkind to Alice. We were engaged, but when I met you, that was it for me. I was bewitched or something . . .'

Evangeline put a finger across his lips. 'Ssh. I know. I hadn't been in Crowmarsh Priors long before Lady

Marchmont was dropping hints, and I soon figured out why Alice hated me. But . . . nothing that happened to either of us before matters now,' she said, wishing it could be true.

They went for walks. After so long at sea, Richard noticed everything, was thrilled to see the first crocuses and daffodils. And every night they made love in the four-poster. Evangeline was shy at first, but to her surprise it was wonderful. Richard paid as much attention to her in bed as he did out of it, and night after night she lay by his side after he had fallen asleep, feeling content and secure. The nightmares disappeared. Suddenly she thought, I'm so happy! When she tried to conjure up Laurent's face she found she couldn't, so she curled up against Richard, laid her cheek on his shoulder and went to sleep.

One morning as she lay luxuriating in bed for a last few minutes before braving the chilly bathroom down the passage, Richard said, 'Darling, have you thought how nice it would be if there were another baby? I know you had a dreadful time of it before, but my mother says a miscarriage doesn't mean there won't be children later. Or perhaps, with all you have to do at the moment, you'd prefer to wait. It's just that, well, with the war, things are so uncertain, we may not meet again for some time . . .'

'Would you like a baby, Richard? Really and truly?'

'A whole nurseryful, my darling.'

'Let's try and see what happens,' Evangeline murmured eagerly.

Three days before Richard was due to return to his ship, there was a phone call at teatime. Grim-faced, he packed hastily. Evangeline watched, stunned, retreating behind her customary dreamy mask so that he wouldn't see her misery. She didn't want to send him off worrying and didn't want him to go. Ever.

But he had to. That evening they stood together on the railway platform. Evangeline, whose bright smile hurt her face, would take the morning train. As they waited she rummaged in her handbag for the handkerchief she promised herself she wouldn't need until Richard left. She felt something at the bottom and held it up. Her eyes widened. 'Oh, Richard, it's the gold baby! I kept it for luck. Take it for luck now.'

He slipped it into his pocket. Then he put his arms round her. She leaned against him and neither said anything as the train approached. As it pulled in, Richard took her face in his hands. 'I want to remember you exactly. When I got off the train in Crowmarsh Priors I had forgotten how beautiful you are. I can't think how I managed that.' He kissed her forehead, then got on to the train and was gone.

Evangeline returned to the guesthouse and went to her room, where she collapsed on to the four-poster, and cried.

While Evangeline was away, Alice had kept the thought of Richard at bay by keeping busy. The afternoons had lengthened and there was an hour of daylight between school and her mother's teatime. She found a pair of gumboots left in the cottage by a previous occupant and, when the weather allowed, went for long walks, tramping through the muddiest fields and coming home at twilight to a litany of complaints. She stayed up long after her mother had gone to bed, rummaging through her father's papers for the old parish records and his map. Eventually she found both and pored over them late at night. The records mentioned an entrance to an old smugglers' tunnel in St Gabriel's churchyard beneath a grave, but nothing specific. The next day Alice went to see if anything looked likely among the mounds and headstones that were emerging as the undergrowth was hacked away. It was clear that finding the right grave would be like looking for a needle in a haystack.

By early May they had made a path to the oldest side of the church under the bell tower, but that was all. Alice wanted to give up, but the others wouldn't let her. So she went over and over it in her mind – if you started at St Gabriel's and ended on the beach . . . But she had only a hazy recollection of where the opening was and, anyway, there were coastal defences, mines and barbed wire, so unless they could find the beginning of the tunnel, assuming the Army hadn't found it and blocked it off . . . Alice wished heartily that she hadn't mentioned the wretched tunnel at Frances's party, but Tanni had heard that Lili and Klara might have been found, Elsie remained determined, Frances wanted to keep her promise and Evangeline had come home from seeing Richard as keen as Alice was to keep busy.

'I'm a bloody fool,' Alice muttered, having tramped miles to get as close as she dared to the coast where signs warned, 'Danger: MINES. Keep Out'. There had been a slope and a narrow inlet, which she remembered had been invisible until she and her father were peering down into it. He had pointed to a dark place that looked like a submerged rock, but as the tide went out Alice had seen the opening at the waterline. She despaired of getting close enough to find it again but she felt sure it wasn't far away. She and her father had walked to the cave and back between lunch and teatime. She racked her brains. It had been an early lunch, she recalled, during the summer holidays.

One Saturday afternoon she passed the secateurs to Elsie just before two. She had a blister, and hoped her mother had managed lunch on her own. Now she had to polish the altar brasses, but first she unwrapped a sandwich she had brought with her and sat down beside the church gate to eat it. They weren't getting anywhere, she thought.

Elsie plunged into the undergrowth and she heard a thrashing sound, then Elsie's squawk followed by 'Bloody 'ell' and a scraping noise. ''Ere, you'd better look at this,' she called.

'What is it?' Alice got up and went to her.

'The tomb with the bloke lyin' on top is under these briars. Me and Bernie used to sit on it and talk when we first come 'ere, before I went to be a land girl. Think it's sunk a bit. Cor, what a thicket – like it's been wove round it. You'd not know it was 'ere.' There's a skull stickin' out on the end, on a neck like – a long one, like a snake. Creepy, if you ask me, but I s'pose that's what they liked in them days . . . Anyway, I was lookin' to see where it had gone and caught me foot on that bramble and fell. I grabbed the skull and summink shifted but I can't see what it was.'

Alice took the secateurs, clipped back some runners and edged through the tangle. Elsie showed her the stone panel with the skull, which grinned up at her. There was a large gap between the panel and the corner of the tomb. She tried to think what her father would have done. She took hold of the skull and noted how neatly it fitted her hand, how her fingers slid easily into the eye sockets, and her thumb through the grinning mouth. Peculiar, but . . . Alice pulled. Nothing happened.

'I think I pushed it when I tripped. Try pushin',' said Elsie.

Alice pushed. Nothing. ''Arder,' urged Elsie.

Alice leaned and pushed with all her might, twisting the skull as she did so. It rotated with a scraping noise. She twisted again and a panel swung open, releasing a blast of cold air and a rotten, fetid smell. 'Phew!' said Alice, stepping back.

'Blimey!' said Elsie. 'Do you think we finally found the tunnel or summink?'

'I bloody well hope so,' said Alice, and bit back the urge to add, 'Some*thing*, Elsie, not *summink*!' She was forever correcting the evacuee children, even though recently she herself had taken to swearing rather dreadfully. 'Let's come back tonight with a torch. Meanwhile we've got to hope nobody else finds it. We can pile the clippings round it . . .'

From his desk in the study window Oliver watched, puzzled, as the two women put back the briars they had just cut away. Why on earth would they do that? The door opened behind him. Nell Hawthorne, in her overall, her hair tied up under a knotted scarf, had come in, ready to attack the cleaning. 'Those two are certainly hard at it,' he remarked, nodding at Alice and Elsie who were dragging yet more cuttings back to the place they'd just cleared.

Then he noticed that Nell looked distracted and anxious. 'Come in.'

She wiped her eyes.

'Nell, whatever is it?'

'I thought you'd have heard, Vicar. Albert just came to tell me that Mrs Richard caught the eleven-thirty to London this morning in a dreadful state. He heard her calling and he held it up for two minutes, though it's against the rules. Said he'd never have done it but he could tell by her face it was an emergency. She told him that someone had telephoned her to tell her that Mr Richard's convoy was torpedoed by one of them wolf packs of German subs last week. It did for the ships and most of the men, but a few were rescued. Mr Richard's alive but Mrs Richard said he's burned bad. He and the others was out in all weathers half dead until an American ship spotted their lifeboat. He's been taken to a special hospital near London for burns.'

Oliver couldn't think of anything to say, so Nell went on, 'Seeing the other girls out there with their minds on gardening makes me think Tanni must be the only one besides Albert who knows, and she's got her hands full with those five children. I'd better tell Elsie and Miss Alice. Unless you'd be good enough, Vicar.'

Oliver nodded. 'Of course. At once.' He stood up.

'And to think,' said Nell, starting to cry, 'only last month Mr Richard was home on leave, and him and his wife went off on the train, happy as larks, according to Albert. That poor girl and his poor mother. Sometimes, Vicar, I get so angry about this war. I pray God will strike Hitler and all the Germans dead, though I don't suppose I ought to. Anyway, I suppose if He wanted to He'd have done it by now and saved a lot of misery.'

25. London and Crowmarsh Priors, May 1942

At the hospital a haggard doctor ushered Evangeline and Penelope into a side-room. He was kind but didn't mince his words. Richard had extensive burns and had nearly died from exposure before an American destroyer rescued him and the few other survivors. At first they hadn't been sure that he would live. For eleven days Evangeline and Penelope kept watch by his bed in a curtained-off area in the critical ward, full of bandaged, groaning men.

Once they were past the worst, the doctors still couldn't say how fully Richard would recover. He was unlikely to see again and, at the very least, once he was allowed up, he would need a wheelchair. Now he lay bandaged under a tent of sheets and blankets, sleeping or drowsy with morphine.

The nurses brought cups of tea and cut the insignia off his uniform, which they gave to Evangeline with the few things they had found in his pockets, including a little lump of gold. The nurse peered at it, thinking it looked almost like a baby. A charm. She had seen many talismans that men carried and although this one looked worthless she knew better than to throw it away. She put it with the officer's other possessions – a comb, his paybook and a damp wallet with a photo of Evangeline in it.

Evangeline and Penelope kept their voices bright and

steady in case he could hear. From time to time Penelope got up, went to the lavatory and cried. Then she bathed her eyes and returned to her chair. While she was away, Evangeline would lean close to Richard and whisper to him that he must try, that she believed he had survived for her and now that he was back on dry land she wasn't going to let him go. 'Please, Richard, get better. I love you.' When Penelope came back she would straighten up. Sometimes she silently prayed the rosary and occasionally she ran to the lavatory to throw up.

If Richard woke, asking for a drink, Evangeline held the straw to his lips and tried to smile, forgetting at first that he couldn't see. She stroked his cheek where there were no bandages.

Anxiety for her son had aged Penelope. Her hair had gone grey and she seemed to have shrunk inside her uniform. But she needed to be cross with someone, so she turned on Evangeline, who was as careless as ever about her appearance and who had arrived at the hospital breathless and perspiring in her gardening clothes, without having brought so much as a comb. 'I must say, Evangeline,' she had snapped, 'most wives with a husband in hospital would make some effort to look nice. Other women manage to keep tidy and smart, even with clothes rationing.' Evangeline had stared at her, aghast, and Penelope suddenly remembered that it didn't matter, that Richard wouldn't see how any woman looked – perhaps never again. She fled to her refuge in the lavatory.

After they had spent days sitting by Richard's bed, snatching a few hours' sleep in shifts, Matron told them that they should be getting on with their lives, now that he was out of immediate danger, and that it often helped – here she lowered her voice – injured men to know that the world went on and their sacrifice hadn't been for nothing. Also, of course, the country needed every pair of hands.

'Would you like to come down to the country for a while, Penelope? I'm sure the WVS will give you a few days more,' Evangeline urged. But Penelope declined, remembering the chaos that had greeted her on her last visit to Crowmarsh Priors, with five children living in her home. She preferred to keep busy in London and go home at night to her orderly flat, exhausted enough to sleep deeply, sometimes undisturbed even by air-raid sirens.

Now Evangeline bent over Richard and whispered that she had to go home but would be back as soon as she could. Meanwhile, he must get better: she was going to take him home as soon as she was allowed to. Would he promise to do whatever the nurses told him? 'Richard, I know you can hear me, and I shan't go until you promise,' she murmured. Finally he nodded. Evangeline cast a look of despair at the nurses, one of whom said at once, loudly and brightly so that Richard could hear, that Evangeline wasn't to worry and her husband was mending as well as could be expected. They would see her again soon.

When her train pulled into Crowmarsh Priors, Albert hurried to open the door and helped her on to the platform. 'There there,' he said helplessly. Evangeline, who had managed so far without breaking down, clung to his arm and lost her rigidly maintained self-control. 'When the nurses . . . the critical ward is so . . . so . . . and they're

trying so hard with Richard . . . So brave . . . Oh, Albert!'
He led her to a bench where she sat until the flood of
tears subsided.

When she got home Kipper threw himself at her and
clung to her like a limpet.

Frances, Elsie and Alice arrived after work.

'Oh, darling,' said Frances, and gave her a long hug.

'Bastards!' hissed Elsie.

Tanni shooed the children into the garden with a
promise that she had hidden sweets for them to find, then
made tea.

'I have to go back next week,' said Evangeline, 'but all
I want now is to think about something else, anything
but lines of beds with injured men in them. How are we
getting on?'

Tanni got up and picked up something that lay on the
sofa. 'Look what I made while you were gone,' she said.
Now pregnant with her third child, Tanni had stitched
together a kind of tent from blackout material to drape
over the growing pile of brambles they were stacking
around the de Balfort tomb. They needed their torches
to see what they were doing at the entrance, but in the
blackout the faintest glimmer of light at night would
give them away. She had heard from Rachel that the
Germans had stepped up deportations of non-French
Jews and was anxious over the delay. Work had kept
panic at bay.

They had also needed rope but it was impossible to
get hold of any, even at the farm. Before Richard had
been injured, Evangeline had suggested they could tear
up sheets, plait them into long strips, then sew them into

a rope. But where on earth would they get sheets now that everything was rationed?

Elsie had come up with the answer. A huge pile of bed linen had been delivered for use when Glebe House became a convalescent home, and was stored in the scullery. They could jolly well help themselves to some of that.

Tanni had balked. It was theft of government property, she said, but Elsie had hauled it all over to the Fairfaxes' one evening in a wheelbarrow. Thereafter, as soon as the five children were in bed, Tanni had cut guiltily into the purloined sheets and, for the next week, plaited and sewed late into the night. She had prayed that Bruno wouldn't find out.

Alice looked at the rope and also thought about stealing government property but decided she didn't care: she wasn't the bloody government's watchdog. 'I think I've found where the cave is,' she said, 'but I can't get past the barbed wire to see from the cliff above. The signs say it's mined anyway.'

'Well done, Alice,' they said, perking up.

Alice described how she had set out for her evening walk, altering her course a little each day, looking for a slope and a narrow inlet. 'But we won't know for sure unless we go down the tunnel,' she finished.

They waited for a night when stormclouds brought early darkness and heavy rain kept everyone indoors. Wearing oilskins, Evangeline and Frances crossed the green with the rope Tanni had made. Alice left her mother a flask of cocoa and a cold supper of potato pie, then cycled off with complaints about the state of her mother's digestion and her own unladylike behaviour ringing in her ears.

Evangeline was wearing one of Richard's oldest pullovers under her oilskin. When Alice recognized it, she burst into tears.

Frances patted her shoulder. 'Do shut up, darling, and concentrate.'

Elsie was the smallest and, to her horror, had been assigned the task of going with Evangeline. She was terrified of being underground. She watched Evangeline knotting one end of the rope round her waist. 'I 'ope you know what you're doing,' she quavered.

'I've done it lots of times,' said Evangeline, confidently. 'I always enjoyed it. Come on.'

Elsie peered into the black hole. 'It's dark down there and it stinks to 'igh 'eaven! An' anyfink could be down there, lurkin'.'

'Elsie, don't be a coward. I need you in case I can't get through a narrow bit.'

'Bloody *'ell*!'

'What do we do if anyone comes to investigate?' asked Alice. 'We're bound to be arrested. Practically everything's against the law or helping the enemy, these days, so this probably is too. What if someone's watching?'

'It's midnight and it's pouring. Who could possibly be watching?'

'Come *on*, Elsie,' said Evangeline. She shone her torch down and they saw worn steps carved into one wall, with a series of niches occupied by ancient coffins in the other. They averted their eyes and concentrated on the steps.

'Those look a bit narrow. Men's feet must have been smaller two hundred years ago,' said Alice, peering over her shoulder.

'I'll go first,' said Evangeline.

Elsie followed her down the first few steps. 'It's freezin'.'

'It's too late to go back now,' said Evangeline. 'Remember, watch out for steep drop-offs, and if you see a puddle or a pool of water, don't put your foot in it. It might be deep. Just keep close behind me.'

Alice and Frances watched as the pinprick of light from Evangeline's torch disappeared into the dark passage. She and Elsie were to go for as long as the first torch lasted, then come back using the second. If there were forks, Evangeline had said they would retrace their steps to the entrance and find a way to mark their route – if they got lost they might never find their way out . . .

Evangeline and Elsie inched along the narrow, twisting passage. "Ow d'you suppose they managed to get their smuggled goods up them steps?' asked Elsie, and shrieked as something flapped over their heads.

'Only a bat,' said Evangeline, waving her torch about. 'They hate the light.'

'You didn't say nuffink about bats.' Elsie kept looking back over her shoulder, thinking how horrible it was to have all that black behind them. The walls were closing in and something brushed her hair as it flitted overhead in the dark. 'Ow! This is like 'avin' a nightmare!'

'No, it's not,' said Evangeline. 'Come on, you're not scared of rats – think of all the girls who'd throw up their hands and scream at the thought of one. You're head rat-catcher! Anyway, bats are a good sign. Means there's a way out – they need to fly out at night to find food.'

'They bite people!'

'No, they don't.'

''Ow do you know?'

'Because at home I spent my summers in the country on my grandmother's plantation. We had everything out there, bats, alligators, bears, cottonmouths. I only had my older brothers to play with, and I wanted them to take me with them when they went hunting and fishing. They'd have left me behind if I'd made a fuss about a little thing like a bat.'

'What's that big dark thing there?'

Evangeline's beam swept over a black gap in the wall. There was a swoosh as more bats flew out of it. 'A cave, with something on the wall.' The torch beam picked up something circular, then glanced off something pale. Both girls screamed.

Skulls grinned up at them and other bones were scattered about with something that looked like rags. Chains set into the rings in the walls had rusted.

Evangeline took a few deep breaths and crossed herself. She said shakily, 'Alice told me the smugglers kidnapped excise men who couldn't be bribed. They must have chained them up down here. No one could hear them above ground and no one knew where they were.' She shuddered.

'Knowin' what I know about rats, they must have eaten the . . . Bugger this! Let's go back, Evangeline! Please!'

'You can if you like.'

'Not by meself! Bloody 'ell! Prob'ly the excisemen's ghosts are just waitin' to get even.'

'The Germans are worse than ghosts. And, unlike ghosts, they're real. Now, hush! Other people got through here and nothing can have changed much since they did. We've promised to help Tanni because no one else will. What if it was your sisters?'

'I'd like to catch them German pilots when their planes crash an' all, an' drag 'em down 'ere, chain 'em up and leave 'em to be the rats' dinner,' Elsie whimpered, as they went on step by careful step. ''Ow long we been down 'ere?'

'About an hour and a half.'

'Can't we go back now?'

'No.'

'Bugger!'

The floor was slippery with bat droppings, but the ceiling of the tunnel was higher now, and they could feel air moving.

Recently Elsie had been going through a moody patch. A few days earlier she had had a frightful row with Bernie, who had slammed the door of the official motor-car and disappeared in a huff. Now, to distract her from her fears, Evangeline said, 'I saw Bernie was back. He looked quite the gent in a suit with an overcoat round his shoulders. He even tipped his hat when he saw me. Looked like he'd had a haircut. Did the two of you make it up?'

'No.'

'Why not?'

''E wants us to get married.'

Evangeline halted in her tracks. 'Married? Elsie, you're way too young – and Bernie can't be much older.'

'Nineteen, 'e is. He finks 'e's nineteen, anyway. Though it's possible, 'e says, 'e's a little older. 'E don't know for sure. 'E's got the War Office finkin' he's older. 'E says you got to make 'em fink you're old enough to know what's what.'

'But that's too young to get married.'

''Ow old were you when you married Richard?'

'Well, eighteen but . . .'

'And you said you 'adn't known 'im long – a few days, by the sound of it. I've known Bernie three years. Near as dammit.'

'Are you, um, having a baby?'

'No.' Elsie giggled. 'Bit of luck I'm not, really, but just at the – you know – moment when – Anyway, Mum comes into me 'ead, talkin' about respectable, and I says, "No." Drives Bernie wild it does. Me too. Don't know 'ow much more of that either of us can stand. No, reason I were cross wiv Bernie was 'e's asked me to marry 'im on account of a wife can't testify in court against her 'usband, which would be an 'andy fing, from 'is point of view. 'Is words exactly.'

'That's no reason to get married! Even if they turn a blind eye now, sooner or later all that black-market stuff will land him in prison. What will he do when the war's over and they treat him like a common criminal?'

'Well, that's what I fought. Wife testifyin', I says! 'Ow much of 'is proposin' was 'im wantin' to get married to me and 'ow much was it 'im not wantin' to go to prison? Bernie looks all confused and starts mumblin' about will you or won't you. So I says, "Bernard Carpenter," I says, "if I says yes, there's conditions. There's to be no more of the burglin' an' scavengin' when the jewellers and the toffs are bombed – I don't care 'ow bad the War Office needs them diamonds. Lootin' bombsites is disgraceful. No goin' back after the war to the safe-blowin' an' muckin' about with them gangs, especially them Italians in Clerkenwell. Mum always wanted us to be respectable. She said then people can't look down on you, no matter what class you are. I says, "I owe it to Mum." Course, Bernie cut up rough at that, said, "'Ow's a leopard to change 'is spots?" and, more to the point, 'ow's 'e to make a livin' and take care of a wife an' all? But I looked 'im in the eye and told 'im straight. "Bernie Carpenter, it's all or nuffink wiv me. All or nuffink. Eiver you turn over a new leaf or I wouldn't marry you if you was the last man on earth." So 'e went off cross, like. Couldn't let 'im see I was worried sick 'e wouldn't come back, could I?'

'Are you in love with him?' Evangeline had a catch in her voice. 'It's just that sometimes you think you're so in love you'll die unless you can be with the person and later you find out you were dead wrong. You have to be careful when you're in love, because you never know where it will take you.'

'Don't I know! Mum was in love wiv me dad once. Look where that got 'er, into a right dickerment, she used to say, so I'm not rushin' into nuffink.'

'Good,' said Evangeline, who was in a predicament herself. Once again, she counted the weeks since her last period. She had last seen Laurent five – no four – weeks before Richard had come home on leave. He had been rushed, even more so than usual, and they had had only a few hours in the afternoon before they had hurried to the Soho pub. He had had a furtive, distant air, which made Evangeline feel she must have done something wrong. He smoked a lot of the sickly cigarettes he said all the musicians used. They gave Evangeline a headache and made her dizzy, but Laurent had been cross when she said she didn't like them.

At the pub Frenchmen had swarmed everywhere and Laurent was summoned to de Gaulle's room. The president of the French government in exile, he had just returned from North Africa, and Evangeline had gathered there was an important meeting about German successes there. Before it began, she had cornered the Colonel about bringing Lili and Klara. Laurent had remained closeted with the others and she had taken a late train back to Crowmarsh Priors.

Then Richard had come back ... Please let it not be Laurent's baby.

Behind her Elsie was rattling on about Bernie: 'An' anuvver fing. 'E says 'e wants to look after me but I fink it's 'im what needs lookin' after. So it 'as to be me decides a few fings straight off. If 'e's goin' to be my 'usband, I says, I want 'im wiv me, not off down the pub like me dad, or wiv them gangs and specially not in prison . . .'

There was a definite sound, a low, rhythmic roar.

'Oh, Elsie, it's the sea – come on!'

The torch dimmed and flickered.

'Uh-oh, this one's going out.' Evangeline sighed. 'Time to go back. Mustn't take any chances. But . . .' she sniffed '. . . I think I can smell fresh air and the sea. Alice said she thought that when the tide comes in,' she pointed the dying beam at the walls, 'the water level rises in here. We don't want to be caught when that happens.'

'Evangeline!' exclaimed Elsie, forgetting the cold, the bats and her love life. 'We done it!'

26. Auschwitz, Late Spring 1942

The Doctor was furious. Imbeciles! It was four months since he had ordered that the Joseph parents should be brought to the medical wing, fed and treated for tuberculosis, but in all that time the fools had failed to locate their twins. Instead they had brought him two forty-year-old women, twins to be sure, Austrian and from the camp at Gurs, but how had such an idiotic mistake occurred? It had been a specific, direct order to find two seven-year-old girls named Lili and Klara Joseph.

He had been told some nonsense about the records not showing any Joseph twins in the camp. The Doctor had raged and pointed out their names – Lili Joseph and Klara Joseph – written plainly on the *Kindertransport* manifest. And now the Führer was demanding every day to know when the breeding programme would begin. If the Doctor did not produce a result soon . . .

He threatened to have every tenth man in the unit shot unless the Joseph twins were found wherever they might be in south-west France. It was clear that Frau Joseph would not live much longer, and he would have to begin searching all over again for parents of twin girls.

Meanwhile the forty-year-old sisters were sent to a secondary breeding programme, an experiment the Doctor wrote up with as much obfuscation as possible, buying himself a little more time. Both women had died, and he had begun what he called 'preliminary work' on the Joseph parents . . .

27. Bethnal Green, East London, June 1942

It was late on Sunday morning but the blackout curtains were still pulled tight across the windows of the narrow terraced house, whose address Tanni had written down. Two young women in siren suits stopped and squinted at the number.

'This is it. Oh, Evangeline, my head hurts like the devil!' moaned Frances. They had spent the previous evening in the Free French headquarters in Soho, at the Coach and Horses pub, where Evangeline seemed to know a great many men who all asked after someone called Laurent. She had introduced Frances to a short French colonel with soulful dark eyes and a large black moustache. Evangeline had smartened herself up a bit, and Frances was looking particularly fetching: she had done her nails and hair, and worn one of the pretty pre-war frocks from Paris, which Tanni had shortened to show off her legs. The Frenchman had recognized couture and was greatly taken with her. He had sat with the two women at a corner table for hours, ordering brandy and more brandy, and becoming quite emotional towards the end of the evening when Frances disengaged his hand from her knee and insisted they had to go.

'A hangover's a small price to pay, Frances. Look, you got heaps of information out of him. Plus, if I remember his parting words correctly, he adores you, his heart is eternally yours and he's going to show you Paris when the war's over. And he'll be waiting for you this afternoon in the pub, as you arranged . . .'

'And I'll have to fight him off by myself this time. If only Tanni knew what we've been through! Come on.'

Evangeline knocked on the door and the curtains parted briefly. Someone had been waiting for them. Then an elderly woman in a kerchief and an apron opened the door a crack. 'Quickly, come in.'

'How do you do? We're Tanni's friends. I'm Frances Falconleigh, this is Evangeline Fairfax, and you must be Mrs Cohen,' said Frances, trying to see in the dark hall after the brightness outdoors.

'Ach!' groaned the woman, rubbing her forehead. 'Come.' She led the way to the kitchen at the back of the house. 'Please sit down. Rachel will be here in a minute. It is she who knows everything.' The kitchen faced into a cramped back garden and was a little brighter. Mrs Cohen bustled about, moving a *Make Do and Mend* pamphlet and a pile of jumpers with holes, then busied herself with a kettle, muttering to herself in a language they did not understand. Finally she handed them tea in little glass tumblers. 'I am sorry. I am so worried I forget my manners. You are welcome.'

Evangeline put down the roll of papers she was carrying under her arm, and Frances stood Tanni's carpetbag on the floor.

'A little something to eat?' asked Mrs Cohen.

Both girls shook their heads and said, 'No,' with feeling. 'But thank you.'

'The rabbi and I heard your husband was badly hurt,'

said Mrs Cohen to Evangeline. 'I am so sorry. Will he get any better?'

Evangeline gazed at her tea. 'The doctors aren't sure yet. I'll see him later – it's my day to visit him at the hospital. We all hope he's improving, but it's a slow process. I expect Tanni told you that the house Frances lives in has been requisitioned for the wounded. It's close to where I live now with Tanni, her children and some evacuees. The doctors say Richard can be transferred to the convalescent home as soon as it's ready and it'll be better for him than living in our house because it's being specially fitted out for patients and it's quiet. He can't stand noise now – his nerves are still mending.'

Mrs Cohen shook her head sympathetically. Then, hearing footsteps outside, she scurried into the hall to open the door. She came back with a younger woman in a headscarf, whom she introduced as Rachel.

'The rabbi is away,' Mrs Cohen whispered. 'I didn't tell him, Rachel – you told me to say nothing but it's so hard keeping a secret from him.'

'You're right not to tell him, Berthe. He needs more worries? Let's get on. I should be at the office and can't stay long.' Rachel put down her gas mask, yawned and accepted a glass of tea. 'I'm sorry. I'm so tired. Give me a moment to remember what we found out about the Joseph twins . . . There was something new . . . I have to remember so much and our records are in a muddle.' She smiled apologetically at Frances and Evangeline.

'Tanni Zayman's family?' Frances prompted. 'Her parents, Dr Joseph and his wife? Her husband's mother, Mrs Zayman? Lili and Klara, who should have arrived in

England three years ago but didn't? If you only knew how desperate Tanni is . . .'

'Yes, the Joseph sisters. We believe they have been found. We had made contact with the American Quakers at the Gurs camp before Germany declared war on the US. Technically the Quakers are non-partisan but the Germans are suspicious of pacifists and only tolerate them because they can use them for propaganda purposes – to say that the Quakers run relief operations in the camps. It is one of the lies the British government chooses to believe.'

Mrs Cohen wound and unwound a spool of thread, muttering prayers under her breath.

'We told Bruno months ago that either the girls had died on the train or that they didn't reach the camp for some other reason. Then we learned that a priest had hidden some children with local families. For a long time we could not find out where, until one of our contacts cycled out to an isolated farm where he had heard an elderly couple had twins. He reported seeing the girls, aged six or seven. The old couple insisted they were their granddaughters. Our friend was worried because they would be arrested or shot if they were hiding Jewish children, and the children would be shot too, or deported. We had passed on the information that the girls' family in England were looking for them and, in any case, our friend knew that if word had reached him of the children's whereabouts it wouldn't be long before the Germans came. He urged them to let him take the girls and hide them elsewhere, but at first the couple refused. It turned out that the priest was the old lady's brother. Finally they gave in.'

Rachel drank some tea.

'The area is under Vichy control now but the Germans are expected to extend the demarcation line south at any minute. The Nazis are rounding up all French Jews, and are looking for foreign Jews who have taken refuge in France. They are already combing the area around Gurs for children from the *Kindertransport* manifest who are not in the camp, but we are hearing rumours of something else too. A doctor at Auschwitz may be conducting medical experiments in human reproduction on prisoners. We heard there is a special order to seek out twins, and rewards offered for any found. Our friend was right – it is only a matter of time before the Joseph girls are discovered or betrayed.'

'God forbid!' Mrs Cohen put her head in her hands.

'May God forbid,' echoed Rachel.

'So we need to act before the Nazis find the children or those helping them. Can the Quakers hide them a little longer,' Frances asked, 'until we can make arrangements to get them out of France?'

Rachel considered. 'They have to be careful to act only as neutral humanitarians. Any more will jeopardize the small amount of good they are permitted to do. Nevertheless, some are less neutral than they were and they are a link through which we have sent money to the Resistance for medicine, guns, ammunition, wireless sets,' she said. 'It buys us information and favours in exchange. They can sometimes help someone escape if he or she is important enough to justify the risks involved and, like the airmen shot down over occupied territory, they can be smuggled along escape routes, with the help of local

Resistance networks, to pick-up points on the French coast, then taken to England. But do not forget, the price is not just money. The Germans execute civilians in reprisal for Resistance activities. But the Quakers would probably agree to do what they could to help get the girls to the coast, if there was some prospect of reuniting them with their family. The Resistance, however . . . I'm less sure that they'd be willing to use their escape routes for children – but for enough money, who knows? And assuming the children reached England, then what?'

Frances said, 'We think we have a way to . . .'

Rachel stopped her and looked at Mrs Cohen. 'Berthe, I am sorry but it would be best if you would please leave us by ourselves now. It is for your own protection that you should not know what is said. Then, if the authorities ask you, you can truly say you know nothing.'

'But, Rachel!'

'For the rabbi's protection, too, you must be able to say you know nothing.'

Mrs Cohen sighed and left the room.

'First, we can pay the Resistance to bring the girls along the escape route to the coast and then across the Channel,' said Frances, steadily.

'The authorities would only send them back!'

'Undoubtedly, but we have a way to get them into the country without them knowing.'

'But the Coastal Defence Zone is impenetrable.'

Evangeline spoke up: 'No, it isn't, which is why the government are so worried about Nazis slipping through. We've found a way into the country that people used hundreds of years ago – an old smugglers' cave on the coast and a tunnel going inland. We believe the authorities don't know it's there. Look at this.' From the roll of papers she pulled out Alice's tracing of her father's map and spread it on the kitchen table. 'This was drawn twenty years ago by a vicar in our village, an amateur local historian who died a few years ago without showing it to anyone but his daughter.'

'So?' said Rachel, bending over to look.

Frances pointed to a spot on the Sussex coast. 'The smugglers went back and forth to France from here.'

Evangeline explained how they had discovered and explored the tunnel, then pointed out how it ran to St Gabriel's, and was still usable if the children could be brought to the coast.

'It seems a bit far-fetched,' Rachel muttered, 'although . . . in some cities Jews are escaping through the sewers. Once, that would have seemed far-fetched too.' She bent over for a closer look at the map. 'Did this ever work?' she asked dubiously.

'Very well. The government never stamped out the smuggling gangs – the industrial revolution came along and men stopped making a living by sea. This is probably the only map in existence. And it was just as dangerous when the smugglers used it – the coast was crawling with troops and excise men ready to hang any smugglers they caught. The smugglers still got through.'

'So, here is the cave on our side, but what about the French coast? The Germans are everywhere.'

The time that Frances and Evangeline had invested in charming the Free French colonel had paid off. Frances said, 'We know that sea rescues of the RAF take place

343

from Plouha where the cliffs are steep, as they are at Dover. Right under the Germans' noses.'

Rachel was wavering, they could see, but she said, 'Crossing the Channel in a small boat is dangerous – there are mines and submarines. The captain, probably a French or Spanish fisherman, would have to weigh the risks and decide what he can and cannot do. There is no guarantee he will not turn back. And you say the children will come out at night from this tomb here?'

'That's right.'

'And then what? I suppose there will be a car waiting, full of petrol obtained despite the regulations, waiting to pick them up . . .'

'Actually, yes, and it's better if you don't know.' Lord love Bernie and the black-market, thought Frances.

Rachel gave a small, wry smile. 'I understand. And then?'

Evangeline took a deep breath and explained how Tanni had suggested the children might be hidden. Ration books would be provided.

Rachel stared at her, dumbfounded. Then she said, 'Tanni may be right. My sister, perhaps. Let me think . . . We'd have to make sure no one knew where the girls had come from, so no one could give them away . . .' She thought for a minute. 'My sister Judith and her husband Dovid have a large family of ten children. Berthe does not know Judith and rarely leaves Bethnal Green now, so she is unlikely to hear of the girls being in Tottenham. I will ask Judith if she and Dovid would be willing to take in two children, mentioning no names or where they come from. Only Tanni and we will know who they are. My sister and her husband will do anything to help Jewish children. Dovid's cousins in the Lodz ghetto have been taken by the Nazis. It helps that they do not know who Tanni is. If either is arrested they will say they took in two children whose parents went missing after a bombing raid. I think Tanni is right. For once the authorities' lack of interest in Jews will help. Now, you say you have money. How much?'

'No money, but we plan to trade these.' Frances lifted the carpetbag on to the table and pulled out a towel-wrapped bundle. Inside were three old-fashioned black velvet jeweller's cases. She undid the brass clasps and Rachel gasped at the sight of Lady Marchmont's splendid triple string of pearls with the emerald and diamond clasp. Then Frances opened the two smaller cases to reveal the matching bracelets. The pearls glowed against the black satin of their case, while the emeralds and diamonds winked and sparkled.

Rachel, whose family had a shop in Hatton Garden, knew immediately that they were worth a fortune. She hadn't expected anything like this. 'They aren't stolen? If we're caught there will be enough trouble without that. They must be worth thousands.'

'I inherited them. And there's more in the bag. I'm on my way to show them – or a few of them – to a man I met last night, a colonel in the . . . Well, it's better that you don't know. We'll offer them part now, the rest when the girls are here.'

'It's a risky and dangerous plan, but I cannot imagine there will be another way to rescue the children. It is worse to abandon them if there is a chance. All right, we'll help. Tell Tanni to be brave,' said Rachel.

'You know she's pregnant again? The midwife says it's too soon – Anna was only born last November. Bruno had leave in February and now this baby's due in November too. She hasn't been very well and we can't let her down. Now we must go,' said Frances. She closed the jeweller's boxes and returned them to the carpetbag.

Rachel stood up. 'We'll be in touch as soon as we have some answers. And one more thing. Tanni can see her sisters briefly when they arrive in your village but then they must leave at once. After that Tanni must not know their whereabouts in London or the name of my sister and her family. It will be sad for the girls and for Tanni but you must make her understand the risks for them – and for Bruno – if she or he knows anything. She must be satisfied that they are safe.'

Frances and Evangeline promised they would make her understand. 'Good luck, Rachel.'

'Good luck to you, too.'

As the front door closed behind them they heard Rachel exclaim, 'Two lives. Two out of hundreds of thousands . . .'

Evangeline went to the Underground while Frances walked down the street, which was bustling now with everyday activity. She was more worried than she would admit about the part of the plan that involved hiding Lili and Klara so openly.

Now she tried to see the busy street through the eyes of the authorities. She caught snatches of conversation in what she assumed was Yiddish. There were women in headscarves tied like Rachel's, with shopping baskets and children. In fact, children were everywhere, mostly dressed in black and carrying satchels. The boys wore little caps on the backs of their heads and sidelocks. The girls had on the thick stockings their mothers wore, and skirts that came nearly to their ankles. Now Frances saw what Tanni had meant about Lili and Klara blending in. Among the close-knit Jewish community in Tottenham they would be newcomers but, as Rachel had said, it would close ranks. To outsiders, two more little girls in thick stockings and black dresses would be lost in the background. It was a plan that even the SOE controllers couldn't have bettered. Good for Tanni.

Frances found a tube station and bought a ticket. She had to find a place to change out of her siren suit into her pretty frock, fluff out her hair.

Two hours later, glamorous once more, she tightened her grip on the carpetbag and entered the smoky gloom of the Coach and Horses. She paused dramatically and tossed back her hair. Every male head swivelled and the Colonel strutted forward importantly before any other man could waylay her. 'Ah, my dear Mees Falconlee!' He put an arm round her waist to lead her to a table.

Frances reassured herself that, if the worst came to the worst, the lessons of the Shanghai Police were fresh in her memory, though she hoped it would not be necessary to put them into effect.

At the same time, Evangeline emerged five Underground stops to the north, near the hospital. A one-armed man was selling punnets of strawberries at the entrance and she bought one for Richard: he couldn't see flowers but he could taste strawberries. He had been moved to a side-ward, and on her weekly visit Evangeline spent the day at his side, reading to him, smoothing his sheets, giving him sips of water and telling him the latest bits of news from Crowmarsh Priors. But, no matter what she did, Richard remained passive and unresponsive.

'Shock,' the nurses had assured her. Most of the time he slept, and then Evangeline sat quietly, wondering what she was going to do. This afternoon a doctor at the hospital had confirmed that her nausea and dizziness were due to pregnancy. When she asked how far along she was, the doctor was exasperated. 'Two months from your last period,' he exclaimed. 'All you need to do is count backwards.'

Evangeline had chewed her lip. She still couldn't remember whether her period had come before or after she had last seen Laurent. Unaware of her dilemma, the doctor advised her not to tell Richard yet, but wait till he was stronger.

She had persuaded Frances to wait till tomorrow to go home because Laurent was coming to London tonight and, hard as it would be, Evangeline knew she had to face him, possibly for the last time. He was her cousin, and while the realization that she no longer loved him had come as a surprise – and a liberation – she worried for his safety, going back and forth to France. And she wasn't sure whether to say anything about the baby. He would be furious, but if the child was obviously coloured . . .

At six she walked slowly out of the hospital towards the tube, still not certain what she was going to say.

Later, in a dim café in Soho, Evangeline and Laurent

drank beer and ate the day's special, Mock Duck. 'This tastes like a duck would taste if it was made out of potatoes and old turnips,' said Laurent. 'Awful. Less to eat in Paris, though.' He looked different – thinner and older, no longer a boy. He had wolfed his 'duck' and its puddle of gravy, then finished Evangeline's. For pudding they had stodgy jam roly-poly. 'That's awful,' muttered Laurent, making a face and drinking more beer. 'When are they moving Richard home?'

'Soon. When Lady Marchmont's house is finished there'll be a place for him there – too many stairs at Penelope's, and we're crammed already with three evacuees, Tanni and her children. But we should talk about –'

Laurent interrupted curtly: 'I've got a job to do, honey. They keep me busy, can't tell you about it exactly, got to live. Don't keep askin' to talk about it!' He jiggled one leg under the table, a nervous tic he'd developed. 'One day to the next is all I can manage. They've given me French identification papers but the Nazis are good at detecting fakes, especially in Paris, and I had a bad minute last time I was there. Gestapo stopped us – me – but they decided the papers were in order and I got back all right. When they heard about that close shave, de Gaulle called a pal, and had him get me a new set. There's some young fellow at the War Office here – they say he's the best and so far no one's spotted his fakes. But you know . . .' He shrugged.

'Laurent, I have to tell you –'

A drum roll and a clash of cymbals on stage drowned the rest of what she said.

Laurent perked up and changed the subject: 'You worry too much. Wait till you hear this band. They use me sometimes if one of the musicians can't play. One has a brother with Glenn Miller, says he can get me a job when they come over to play for the troops. How about that?'

He took out cigarettes for them both and lit Frances's, then his own. They smoked through the first numbers, Laurent keeping time with his knee, never taking his eyes off the stage. Evangeline stared down at her empty glass, trying to decide when to get up and leave. When Laurent slapped the table she jumped. The tempo had picked up. 'Come on, sugar! Let's dance and forget about the damn war.' He yanked her out of her chair, swung her on to the floor and spun her away.

Three American GIs in Ike jackets, named after General Eisenhower, sat in the corner watching the dancers. When their beer came they tasted it and grimaced. It was their first night in London. As their eyes got used to the gloom one drawled in a flat Georgia accent, 'Son-of-a-bitch, y'all look at *that*!' He nudged the soldier next to him. 'That's a *white* girl for sure. And she's dancin' with a *coloured fellow*!'

'Where?' said his friend from Nebraska, who had been sizing up two single girls at the bar. He squinted at Laurent. 'Him? Looks white to me.'

'A high yellow, we call 'em. Some white blood but you can always tell a nigger! Back home he wouldn't be dancin' with her long, I promise you that.'

Evangeline felt dizzy as Laurent spun her away, spun her back and hugged her tight. 'Just follow me, honey,' he said, into her neck, and kissed her ear. 'It's like old times again, and your train isn't till tomorrow.'

No, it wasn't like old times, she wanted to scream. It never had been like old times ever since she'd followed him to Europe. She would never regret saving his life, but she didn't want to be here with him. She wanted to be at the hospital where Richard lay. She wanted to turn back the clock and be in a seaside guest house, curled up on the sofa with him. She wanted to see him striding towards her on the railway platform, holding out his arms to scoop her up, not caring that Albert Hawthorne was watching. She wanted to talk about the baby they were going to have . . . She wanted to run. When the dance was finished, Evangeline snatched her handbag from the table and did exactly that, without looking back. Laurent was clapping and shouting for an encore, and the musician whose brother played with Glenn Miller was pulling him up on to the stage. She knew it would be some time before he noticed that she had gone.

28. Crowmarsh Priors, July 1942

The wedding about to take place that sunny afternoon was a distraction and a relief from the horrors of war. With most of the young people called up, with handsome Richard Fairfax lying half dead in his bandages in hospital, with the Germans on their way, and the mute testimony of the bare earth over new graves in the churchyard, Crowmarsh Priors heard the dogs of war howling at its gates.

Now, though, everyone was in church, in their best clothes, and there was the usual air of anticipation as they waited for the bride to arrive. No one minded that she was late: they could luxuriate in a rare sense of normality. They said the things to their neighbours that they always said on these occasions. Not necessarily important or profound things, just normal things. It was a luxury to indulge in banal, timeworn sentiments.

'What I say,' whispered Nell Hawthorne, to the butcher's wife beside her, 'is that a wedding is a wedding and young people will be young people, war or no war. You have to wish them the best, and she'll be the making of him.'

The butcher's wife nodded in agreement. 'Takes you back to your own wedding, doesn't it?' she whispered back.

There was a buzz of similar conversation and a bobbing of ladies' hats as they admired the decorations. Alice,

Frances and Evangeline had arrived at dawn with armloads of flowers and greenery to decorate the church. Now a handsome pair of tall Limoges vases that had belonged to Lady Marchmont stood on the altar, spilling over with sprays of jasmine, roses and ivy, while pretty smaller vases filled the window alcoves, turning the little church into a sweet-smelling bower of green and white. Tanni had made strips of a worn-out sheet into white bows for the end of each pew and tucked a bit of baby's breath into each.

To everyone's surprise Mrs Osbourne, who had once played the harmonium at weddings conducted by her late husband, had been cajoled and flattered by Nell Hawthorne into resuming her place at the instrument. She was wearing a feathered picture hat that had not seen the light of day for years and watched for the signal from Oliver to begin the Bridal March. Meanwhile she was playing 'Jesu Joy of Man's Desiring', her particular favourite, over and over again. They had played it at her own wedding. The dusty feathers on her hat quivered tremulously as she threw herself into the music, trying different keys.

Margaret Rose Hawthorne, sitting beside her mother, shivered with anticipation. Weddings were so exciting! Some day, her mother had said, it would be her turn.

At the altar in his vestments, Oliver craned his neck to see if Elsie and her bridesmaids had arrived on the porch yet. Bernie was fidgeting in front of him, hoping he hadn't done something to make Elsie change her mind. He had come back from London after their row two months ago, miserable without Elsie and determined to ask her to marry him properly. He could see now that he had gone about proposing the wrong way – fancy pointing out that a wife couldn't testify against her husband! Anxious to get it right the second time, he had shamefacedly made inquiries among his colleagues about how you did it. The toffs had explained, and Bernie had returned to Crowmarsh Priors with a speech he had practised over and over: would Elsie do him the honour of becoming Mrs Bernard Carpenter? He had brought a beautiful antique sapphire and diamond engagement ring in case she accepted him.

He had spoken his piece and held out the ring. Elsie had stared at him open-mouthed. To his horror, she had stamped her foot and said, 'Bernie Carpenter, I wouldn't marry you if you was the last man on earth! Mum would turn in 'er grave, she would!' Then she had walked away, muttering darkly about lootin' and safe-crackin' and prison, and Mum bein' right and, inexplicably, something about ferrets. She never wanted to see him again and good riddance.

It had been the worst moment of Bernie's life. Bewildered and frightened, he had run after her and said all right, he could see she didn't want an 'usband what was always in prison but 'e wasn't a reformed man until she married him so she'd better marry 'im quick. Meanwhile he planned to have just the one engagement ever in his life and the toffs he worked for said to do it proper you needed a ring and – It dawned on him that Elsie might think he'd stolen it. Honest, he hadn't done no lootin' to get it, no dodgy deals: he'd traded some Polish airmen 'a bit of paperwork' for it. All legal and above board. It was the same work he did for the War Office, and since the Poles and the War Office were on the same side fightin' the Germans, that ought to be all right, oughtn't it? No gangs! Bernie emphasized, no safes, no lootin', no burglary involved. Specially, he added, no lootin', out of respect for how her mum, Jem and Violet had died. Besides, he said, as something else occurred to him, he loved her. So would she marry him? Please?

Mollified, Elsie reconsidered. For once she wished she knew what Mum would have advised. On the one hand she had no intention of leading Mum's life, or worse, and whatever he promised now, something told her that Bernie and the law would never be friends. But Mum was dead. It would be up to Elsie to keep Bernie on the straight and narrow, she reasoned. Well, she had learned a thing or two from her mother about keeping men in line. For a moment she wondered whether she was up to it for the rest of her life. But as she gazed into Bernie's anxious face, she decided she was. Finally she gave him a smile, said, 'All right, then, Bernie, I don't mind if I do,' kissed him, slipped on the ring and sighed. 'Fancy! Me engaged!'

Elsie seized every opportunity thereafter to call Bernie 'me fiançay', and Bernie felt proud, although he didn't know what the word meant exactly.

Now fiançay or not, he wondered if someone could stop the old woman playing the same tune over and over and over. Hot and self-conscious, he ran a finger round the inside of his collar, which felt too tight. He wasn't sure what you were supposed to do standin' up front like this with everybody starin' at you. Probably laughin' be'ind their 'ands, too. He didn't know why they had to make you so nervous. It was all very well having Constable Barrows as his best man – something else the toffs said you needed – but he wished Uncle was there.

Bernie hadn't known much about getting married and vaguely assumed you just ran off to Gretna Green and did it. But, oh, no!

Constable Barrows said you were supposed to see the girl's father first and ask permission to marry her. Then you had to speak to the vicar, and get a licence, and there were the banns . . . Bernie scratched his head and said the first was a mite difficult as no one knew where Elsie's dad was. He hadn't been seen for years and he was probably dead in the bombing or of drink. Constable Barrows had considered and said, 'In that case, better speak to the vicar,' so he and Elsie had done that. Next thing he knew Elsie didn't have any spare time for him: the women were busy chasing a dress for her to be married in and Tanni was sewing like blazes. Something called a trousseau.

He nudged Constable Barrows. ''Ere! A bit awkward, innit, standin' in front of everybody, waitin'? Shouldn't Elsie be walkin' down the aisle by now?' What if she'd changed her mind at the last minute?

'They all do this, lad,' said Constable Barrows, with calm authority. His wife Edith had assured him men had no idea, *no idea at all*, of the last-minute crises with hairpins and veils, garters and bouquets on the most important day of a girl's life. Now he smiled at her in her best hat, holding the baby, looking sweet and plump and unconcerned in the front row on the groom's side of the church. She was chatting happily to Nell Hawthorne and the butcher's wife.

'Feels like we've been standin' 'ere ages. What if she isn't comin'?'

'She'll be here, lad, don't you worry.'

'That tune's gettin' on me nerves,' said Bernie, as Mrs Osbourne began to hum along. 'Must 'ave played it a thousand times already.'

Oliver looked down at his vestments and tried not to smile. Bernie and Elsie had turned up on the vicarage doorstep and abruptly demanded he marry them. Bernie had been so nervous he had blundered into his joke that if Elsie married him she couldn't testify against him in court. Elsie had flashed him a stern warning look and, to Oliver's surprise, cocky Bernie went as quiet as a lamb. Oliver had asked about baptism and confirmation and other things they had never heard of until their eager eyes glazed over. Finally Bernie leaned forward, desperate to get the upper hand of this wedding thing in Elsie's eyes, and said, 'That's all very well, but oughtn't vicars to stop immorality in the parish? Unless you marry me and Elsie there'll be immorality every chance we get.'

Elsie had blushed but nodded defiantly.

Trying to keep a straight face, Oliver thought, Oh, why not? Elsie was the only thing likely to keep the boy from a criminal career, and if he didn't marry them there would be another illegitimate birth in the parish before long. The old saw 'Strike while the iron's hot' crossed his mind. He bent church rules all the time, these days. When the bishop finally heard of it there would be trouble, but he had his hands full of more urgent matters at the moment and Oliver was beginning to think that too many church rules got in the way of Christianity.

The other girls had pitched in to help Elsie. Wedding

dresses couldn't be had on clothing coupons. 'Even the War Office hasn't suggested a Utility wedding dress, darling!' said Frances. Alice, so active in clothing drives, recollected that a lady welfare officer named Barbara Cartland had collected a supply of wedding dresses from her society friends that could be borrowed by service brides. Alice tracked then down and sent off Elsie's measurements. The frosty reply came that the dresses were only available to girls in the military service, not the Land Army. Furious, Frances made a phone call to her father and threatened to ring every half-hour of the day and night unless he did something. The Admiral muttered that he would see what he could do.

The day before the wedding a large cardboard box that had obviously been posted many times before arrived by special post. Tanni spread a sheet on the floor and she and Evangeline carefully cut the string, saving it for use later. They gasped as they unpacked an elegant white *peau de soie* dress and veil, done up in layers of tissue paper. 'Worth,' whispered Frances, reverently, reading the label.

Tanni made Elsie try it on at once. 'It's perfect except you're so short that this hem must come up,' she said. 'Hold still while I pin it.' She had already done the same with the négligée and peignoir Frances had given her, which she had lent to Evangeline when Richard was on leave. They were now pressed and folded with a sprig of lavender in a smart overnight case lent by Frances, waiting for the weekend's honeymoon in Eastbourne.

On the afternoon of the wedding Albert Hawthorne, who was to give Elsie away, was waiting for the girls in the shade of the laurels at Glebe House. 'You can do with the practice,' Nell had said briskly. 'Some day Margaret Rose will be wanting you to do the same for her.' She brushed his best black suit, then polished his shoes until they shone like patent leather. Albert took out the gold pocket watch his grandfather had received for fifty years' service as station-master at Crowmarsh Priors and, with a sense of ceremony, draped the chain across his waistcoat. Might as well do the thing properly.

He had arrived well on time beside the laurel hedge, and now began to shift from foot to foot. What the blazes could the girls be doing? If the trains ran as late as weddings the whole country would grind to a halt.

Inside, Tanni, Alice and Frances, who had afternoon leave from the farm, fussed around Elsie, removing pins from her hair and draping a towel round her shoulders while they powdered her face. Elsie was almost shivering with excitement and her eyes sparkled. Evangeline, looking lovely in a drop-waisted 1920s frock she had found in the attic, was chasing the four older children to give their hair a final brush. At five months pregnant, in maternity smocks, Tanni had tried to beg off being a bridesmaid, but Elsie wasn't having it: she had insisted she needed all of her best friends to stand up with her so Tanni wore an everyday pink cotton smock, freshly laundered, with a lace collar made from an antimacassar tacked on to it. She had warned Elsie that she would probably have to carry Anna, so that she wouldn't scream, and Elsie had responded, 'The more bridesmaids the merrier,' so Tanni had dressed Anna in a pink smocked frock with her little bit of dark hair brushed up and tied with a large pink bow on top of her head. She was resplendent in Richard's old pram, which was decorated with a spray of honeysuckle and white ribbon. She nibbled her bare toes, watching the proceedings solemnly.

'Stand up and let us slip the dress over your head. Slowly does it.' There was a rustle of material and a swishing as the folds were patted into place. 'Hold still! There! That's the buttons done. Now the veil. No, pin it here. And here.' They fussed and turned Elsie this way and that.

'You can look now,' said Alice, finally, leading Elsie to the full-length mirror in the hall.

Elsie caught her breath. Agnes and the twins would have been startled into silent amazement, and as for Mum – whatever would she have said? Born on North Street – now look at her! Grand as grand could be – all silk and lace, a train behind like she was a queen, four bridesmaids and even Johnny dressed up as a little pageboy to hold the ring on a pillow until it was time for Bernie to put it on Elsie's finger. The page-boy had been Alice's idea. And all this grandeur went hand in hand with being a lawfully wedded wife! And she was about to be married properly in a church! Given away! She didn't quite understand what would happen, even though the others had explained it all, as if they went to weddings every day of the week. Her stomach fluttered. Like Bernie, Elsie had never been to a wedding, only seen pictures in the papers.

There was even a wedding cake for after. It had surprised Elsie to learn you needed a cake on top of a dress and everything else. The girls had pooled their month's sugar and butter rations and Evangeline had made a small wedding cake and decorated it with real roses she had brushed with egg white and sprinkled with sugar. Bernie had some bottles of champagne that the toffs had given him. Perhaps. Today Elsie wasn't going to ask.

Her engagement ring winked encouragingly on her finger.

'We ought to go before this lot get dirty again,' said Evangeline, marshalling the overexcited children who were chasing each other round the garden. She pulled up Johnny's page-boy socks again. 'Don't want Bernie to think you've changed your mind.'

The bridesmaids put on straw hats trimmed with fresh flowers and ribbon. They had bare legs, but had carefully painted a seam up their calves with burned cork. They gave each other a last-minute inspection to make sure the 'seams' were straight.

'Ready?'

'The bouquets!' exclaimed Frances, running back to the scullery for five posies of Queen Anne's lace and roses.

'Here,' said Alice, wistfully, to Elsie, 'loop the train over your arm, like this, while you walk to the church.'

They went outside and Albert offered his arm to the bride. Elsie took it and looked up at him. Suddenly her smile wobbled and tears brimmed in her eyes. 'Thinkin' about me mum, wish she could see me.' She sniffed. 'She wouldn't 'alf be proud.'

Albert blessed Nell for the extra clean handkerchief she'd known he would need. He handed it to Elsie, who dabbed her eyes, blew her nose and returned it. 'Fanks. Don't want me intended to see me wiv red eyes, do I? There, I'm ready.'

Afterwards everyone agreed it was a shame there was a ban on ringing the bell at St Gabriel's when the happy couple came out of the church, but it had been a lovely wedding. Bernie said, 'I will,' several times more than he needed to, and in the wrong places, but very earnestly. Oliver preached a wedding sermon about being in the midst of life at a time for rejoicing and, to impress the seriousness of the occasion on the bride and groom, who were whispering endearments, emphasized that the Church regarded marriage as an indissoluble union. When he pronounced them man and wife and told Bernie he could kiss the bride, Elsie threw herself into Bernie's arms.

They all trooped over to the Gentlemen's Arms for the wedding breakfast. A grinning, relieved Bernie's hand was wrung by the men. Constable Barrows slapped him on the back and said, 'Well done, lad!' and Harry Smith, in his role as publican rather than Home Guard, stood him a couple of brandies. Besides the bottles of champagne, there were jugs of beer and shandy, lemon barley water for the children, and plates of sausage rolls, thin cucumber sandwiches with the crusts off, tinned salmon with salad and a raised pie Evangeline had contributed that was filled mostly with vegetables but enough hard-boiled egg for each slice to have a pretty yellow and white round in the middle. Nell Hawthorne and Edith Barrows had supplied fairy cakes. Everyone cheered as Elsie, flushed with happiness, and Bernie cut the wedding cake and a tiny piece was handed round to each person with a glass of champagne.

Nell Hawthorne nudged Edith Barrows and looked significantly at Evangeline in her drop-waisted dress. Both women smiled. 'You can always tell,' said Nell. 'A baby's the best thing that could have happened. It'll take Mr Richard's mind off things when he comes home. And she's so good with all those children that aren't even hers!'

When the time came Elsie didn't want to throw her bouquet, but Nell Hawthorne said firmly that now she was married it was only fair to give another girl a turn. 'Like Alice Osbourne,' she whispered purposefully. There must be *someone* for poor Alice. Nell turned Elsie and her train round until Elsie's back was to the guests. Just in time she spotted Margaret Rose preparing to spring forward and catch. Nell shook her head mouthing, '*Don't you dare!*'

'Aww?' wheedled Margaret Rose.

'No,' said Nell, firmly, and Margaret Rose sulked away. 'One, two three, *throw!*'

Elsie pitched the flowers high over her head, then pivoted to see who the lucky girl was. 'Oi, Frances, you caught it! You're next, then!' she shouted gleefully. Frances looked quite startled.

'Know who that'll be, don't we?' she heard Albert Hawthorne say, winking at Nell and nodding in Hugo's direction.

Frances considered throwing the flowers back to Elsie.

'Better think of getting changed, you're off on the train soon,' said Frances, after the last toasts had been made.

'I hate to take the dress off – it's been the best day of me life!'

'Tanni's got your going-away outfit all ready in the saloon bar. Harry says you can change there, because everybody's outside in the sunshine. Come along, Mrs Carpenter.'

Elsie beamed.

Albert Hawthorne confided to Nell that he was looking forward to getting home to a cup of tea and taking off his shoes. They pinched.

There was a little procession to the station to see Elsie and Bernie off. Albert led the way with the bride and groom, and the other girls followed clutching small paper parcels, the skirts of their summer frocks blowing in the breeze. The children scampered about, playing tag. When the train pulled in, it was crammed full of servicemen who leaned out of the windows and cheered when Albert said, 'Just married! Let the bride and groom on, lads!'

Tanni and Evangeline, Frances and Alice undid their parcels and threw flower petals over Elsie and Bernie as they got on to the train, and everyone was waving as it departed. Then Albert went on ahead, anxious for tea and his armchair, leaving the others to wander home slowly, enjoying the warm evening, the sunset and the glow left by the wedding.

Behind the others Alice ran back to the station platform, stooped and gathered up a handful of petals. She wrapped them in her handkerchief and stuffed it into her pocket. 'For luck,' she whispered. 'Mine.'

29. Crowmarsh Priors, August 1942

After their three-day honeymoon, Elsie and Bernie came back to Crowmarsh Priors to live at Glebe House. Bernie was thrilled by the idea of living anywhere so grand, and housing was in such short supply, with so many people bombed out, that a young couple had to take what they could get. Neither of them fancied being squeezed in with another family, and with Bernie away so often, Elsie thought it would be nice to have Frances's company.

One day workmen appeared to turn Glebe House into the long-promised convalescent home, and from then on the place rang with hammering, sawing and welding. 'Soon have it done,' the foreman told Evangeline, knowing she was calculating how long it would be before she could get her invalid husband back to the village. Frances, Elsie and Bernie had been turfed out of their bedrooms, but told they could stay on in the huge attic, so Frances and Elsie began to clear space up there for their possessions and bedroom furniture.

In the middle of the commotion, Frances had been summoned away. 'Bloody welfare committee!' she had groaned, putting down the telephone on a coded message. 'Land girls' morals are in tatters, thanks to American GIs with their nylons and Hershey bars. The committee head-quarters have been flooded with complaints from furious parents wanting us to chaperone the girls more closely. Too tiresome!'

So, Evangeline and Elsie were left to sort out the attic to accommodate a married couple and a single land girl. They piled Lady Marchmont's trunks and boxes to one side and arranged two makeshift bedrooms at opposite ends under the eaves. 'Still, it beats the hostel,' said Evangeline, trying to shove a wardrobe into place as a kind of barrier. 'If you and Bernie take that end you'll have privacy behind this thing, a big window and a nice view of the downs. He'll be surprised to find it all ready when he gets back – even if Frances is at the other end. I'm sure she'll put a pillow over her ears.'

'Will you stop messin' about wiv that wardrobe, Evangeline, in your condition?' Elsie grabbed her friend's arms and sat her on a mattress.

Evangeline was wearing a smock now, which Tanni had made for her. She patted her swelling belly. 'It's starting to kick like mad. Richard felt it when I was at the hospital last week. I'm so glad I told him. The doctors were wrong to say I mustn't. It's made such a difference to how he feels ... Is it beginning to cloud over, do you think? It's supposed to rain.' Evangeline was torn between happiness and anxiety. Was it Richard's baby?

Elsie leaned out of the window. 'Maybe. A bit. I 'ate all this waitin' about – months it's been, and two false alarms. Goin' all the way down that bleedin' tunnel and nobody there. If only we'd some idea where the kiddies are. Thank God they got away before the Germans came lookin' and shot the old people wot looked after 'em. Murderin' buggers. Wish we'd 'ear summink.'

'I wish we could think of somewhere better to keep them than a cold passage full of bat droppings while we wait for Bernie to bring a car.' *And I wish I knew who my baby's father is.*

'Evangeline, that's nuffink compared to the rest of it!'

'I suppose not. It wouldn't be so bad if Tanni could see them, but Sister Tucker says she has to stay in bed now until the baby comes. It seems cruel those poor children won't understand what's happened, probably scared to death. Then up to London under a blanket and more strangers, but we can't risk anyone seeing them.'

'At least Tanni'll know they're safe.'

'Are you up there?' Alice called, from the bottom of the stairs. She sounded breathless.

Evangeline and Elsie looked down into the stairwell. 'We're moving things. Any news?'

Alice ran up to them. 'The workmen are having their tea.' She lowered her voice anyway. 'Rachel just phoned. She's had another message that the twins might be on their way.'

'Really? She's said that twice before and the messages were wrong.'

'It's certain this time. The local Maquis took them from wherever they've been hidden all summer.'

'The thing is,' fretted Evangeline, 'they're right under the Germans' noses. We have to trust some pretty rough characters. The Resistance colonel Frances and I met in London was furious that we wanted them to bring two children across the Channel. Asked did we take them for nursemaids? He refused point-blank until Frances showed him some of her jewellery and said she'd hand over more when the twins arrived. He changed his tune then, but he said that the men he knew would abandon them at the slightest difficulty. He plied her with brandy he'd bought under the counter, hoping she'd go upstairs with him, so she let him think that was part of the bargain, provided they brought the children.'

'Bet that worked. Did he tell her how they planned to get the girls to the coast?'

'He wouldn't say anything except it would be done, and he didn't like it, called some of his friends over and his friends didn't like it either. Said they'd drug the children to keep them quiet, if they had to. Frances didn't like the sound of that but they were adamant that no one would risk being shot for the sake of two unimportant *enfants*, no matter what Frances was paying.'

'Maybe it isn't such a wonderful plan, after all,' said Alice, who had had cold feet from the start.

'It's the only possibility if the alternative is leaving them to the Germans and one of those camps.'

Alice had remained sceptical. 'Do you think the camps really exist? You never hear about them on the news. If they're as bad as Rachel says, you'd think someone would have noticed. Oh, I know, I know, Evangeline, we don't hear everything on the news, so we stand by and wait. Again! I don't know why we let Frances talk us into this.'

'Of all times for her to be away!' grumbled Elsie. 'What's she do on all them committees anyway? Land-girl welfare! I ask you!'

'She expects to be home next week. Hope she's in time but we'll have to manage. We're ready as we'll ever be, aren't we?' said Evangeline, stretching her back, which ached. Her mind returned to the baby, calculating. If it was Laurent's, there was a chance it would be quite fair-skinned – he was half white or more, even, because his mother had white blood too . . .

'Blankets, dry clothes, handkerchiefs, first-aid kit, brandy for the boatmen, sandwiches and flasks of cocoa.' Alice went over the list again, although they knew it by heart.

'I fink we got everything except the sandwiches and cocoa, and there's no sense in makin' them ahead. 'Ow's Tanni today?'

'Not too well. Sister Tucker didn't care for her colour and is worried that her ankles are so swollen. Worry is bad for her and naturally she's worried sick. Upset, too, that she can't see the twins.' Evangeline chewed a fingernail. What if the baby looked white but had that tell-tale coppery hair?

'She'll be fine as soon as this is over.'

'Evangeline, are you feelin' all right?' asked Elsie. One minute her friend was glowing, the next she looked like she was in another world and didn't hear when you spoke to her. 'Evangeline! Are you listenin'?'

'Fine. Why?' She had been trying to calculate for the millionth time when her last period had been.

Below, in the hall, a door slammed and someone ran up the stairs. 'Hello – anyone up there?'

'Frances! You're back early.'

'Just in time! Rachel phoned, wait till you hear . . .' They all began to talk at once.

Frances knew she looked remarkably fit and deeply tanned for someone who had been stuck in a London office with

369

the old biddies of the Land Girl Welfare Committee. When Alice commented, she said, 'My land-girl glow,' and hoped it sounded plausible. In fact, she had been summoned to Manchester for parachute training at a nearby airfield. Her practice jumps had been too thrilling for words and she hoped that now she would be sent to France. But, to her dismay and annoyance, she had been dispatched back to Crowmarsh Priors.

But her mock-exercise had become real: there had been a briefing at the training camp. Military Intelligence were redoubling their efforts to find Manfred on the south coast, and Auxi agents in southern England were on red alert after a panicky report that two German airmen had escaped when their plane was shot down over Kent. One was believed to be a senior member of the SS, with orders to assassinate Churchill and the King.

Military Intelligence had quickly drawn up a list of possible fifth-columnists, with real or suspected German connections or sympathies, and anyone with whom an enemy agent or spy might hide. Its accuracy was doubtful because it did not discriminate between those people known to have had pro-German, if not pro-Nazi, sympathies before the war, or to have attended Oswald Mosley's rallies, and those, like Alice Osbourne's father, on the grounds that he had twice travelled to Germany as a student and had drunk beer with German students who had included several now-prominent Nazis.

The little man who had interviewed Frances thought she should step up surveillance in her area. 'We know that, before the war, all those great families had a mixed crowd at their weekend house-parties, including

Continental friends. There were inevitably some Nazis among the guests, so they had an excellent opportunity to photograph the area where the coastal defences are. You know the sort of thing, "Walk before tea? Splendid scenery along the coast – I think I'll take a few photographs." You can keep your eyes open for anything suspicious, and if there's nothing, eliminating unlikely suspects will save our time.'

Frances's superiors had learned that Hugo de Balfort had proposed to her and she had turned him down. At first they had made a joke of it. 'She'll probably marry him eventually – she complains he's been damned persistent, won't take no for an answer. May as well keep her watching Gracecourt. We'll be able to eliminate the de Balforts from the list right away, stop her pestering us to go to France.'

Since the Auxis were stretched thin in the south, Frances could extend her surveillance over a wider area, and the Land Girl Welfare Committee was the perfect cover. 'Manfred's down there somewhere,' the little man reminded them. 'We need to comb the countryside.'

Then, to Frances's alarm, they had stopped joking about Hugo. The Old Man had suggested that marrying him would provide her with the best possible cover. She could always divorce him later, they said placatingly. Frances's eyes took on the steely look her father knew so well. She would stay in Sussex but she would *not* marry Hugo.

Training as an Auxi had been as thrilling as she had hoped, and given her a chance to use her intelligence. It had also increased her determination to fight the

Germans. But on the other hand, the possibility of being ordered to marry Hugo had forced her to recognize something else: she was in love with Oliver Hammet.

Frances knew that no matter how much Oliver liked her – and he did like her, she knew, very much indeed – and for all his breaking of minor rules of the Church, he was a clergyman. She remembered the sermon he had preached at Elsie and Bernie's wedding. If she married Hugo it would put her beyond Oliver's reach for ever. He would never accept that those whom God had joined together could be put asunder, except by death. He would feel bound to follow the Church's position on divorce, even if it broke his heart and hers.

She wouldn't let the damned Germans ruin her life in that way. The minute she was finished she grabbed her things and left the training centre before the Old Man ordered her to marry Hugo. Now, in the attic of Glebe House, when she should have been paying attention to Alice, Elsie and Evangeline, who were all talking at once, she was listening fearfully for the telephone. She knew that, when he learned she had gone, the Old Man was likely to roar an order at her down the line. How could she refuse a direct order?

'Frances! Are you listening?' Alice demanded. 'Oliver wants to . . .'

Oliver!

Below in the hall the telephone shrilled. What could she do? She felt trapped until an idea occurred to her, but she knew that if she hesitated she would never act on it. She must go now, before she lost her nerve.

Alice had started for the stairs and the phone. 'Don't

bother, I'll get it,' said Frances, racing past Alice. 'Then I'm going out for a walk to clear my head.'

'A walk? Now? But, Frances, you've only just come in and we have to tell you –'

But she wasn't listening. She threw a cardigan round her shoulders, ignored the telephone and walked as fast as she could to the vicarage. Her knees felt weak and Frances, who was never normally at a loss for words, had no idea what she was going to say. She was terrified.

If she paused to knock she might reconsider, so she didn't. 'Oliver?' she called, opening the door. 'Oh, Oliver, please be at home. I so need to talk to you.'

'Up here,' he called, from the study. 'Be down in a jiffy.'

But Frances was already running up the stairs. 'I need you to do me the greatest favour in the world! You're the only one I can trust to help me.'

She dashed into his study as he stood up behind his desk. 'What can I do for you?' he asked.

For a minute as she looked into his steady brown eyes she couldn't say it. Then she thought about Hugo and the wedding night. 'What if a person needed to get married very, very quickly? At once, even. Is there a special licence?'

'Yes, the bishop can sort it out immediately, if necessary.'

A look of dismay crossed Oliver's face and Frances rushed on: 'I want to ask you something . . . A girl doesn't normally do this . . . but you might want to and if you did want to it would have to be now, right away. Unless you do it soon it may be too late. It will save me from a great deal of misery and allow me to keep . . . doing something important, without losing . . . And . . . and . . . if you think for a moment you don't want to, you're too honest to . . .' Tears sprang to her eyes. 'The thing is, can you trust me even if I couldn't tell you everything?'

Oliver wondered what on earth was upsetting her so. She was making no sense and she was almost crying. 'Frances, as long as it's legal I'd do anything you wanted.' He came round the desk and stopped himself putting his arms round her. Vicars mustn't do that with upset parishioners. Even if the vicar loves the parishioner more than life itself.

Frances gulped. She gazed up at him, her sapphire eyes wide, and blurted out, 'Oh, it is legal, but it has to be kept secret.'

'Very well. You know vicars are bound to keep the secrets with which they're entrusted, and I promise to keep any mysterious secret of yours, whatever it is.'

'And you would have to trust me . . .'

'I'll trust you till my last breath, and I'll do anything you ask of me.'

'No, don't promise till you know what it is.' She gathered her courage and blurted out her request. Immediately she wanted to take it back. She held her breath, and watched as Oliver's face was transformed by disbelief, and then delight.

'Do you want this? Truly?'

She nodded. 'Yes. So much!'

'Oh, Frances,' he said, reaching out for her. 'It's like being offered a miracle. If you only knew. Yes, a thousand times, yes.'

*

374

Late the next day there was a knock on the Old Man's door. 'Come in,' he said. 'And while you're at it, where in hell has Miss Falconleigh got to? Get her on the telephone at once. Been trying her all night.'

The man who had entered was fidgeting. 'Out with it!' barked the Old Man.

'It's Miss Falconleigh, sir.'

'Well, what about her? Gone to keep an eye on the de Balforts, has she?'

'Yes, sir. Actually there's something else –'

'What is it, man? There's a war on in case you hadn't noticed and we've not got all day!'

'She's eloped, sir.'

'Ha! Married that Hugo fellow, has she? Excellent! Knew we could count on her!'

'Actually, no. It seems she's married the local parson. Ahem! Our Miss Falconleigh is now Mrs Oliver Hammet. Most awkward, sir. Makes it impossible for her to marry Hugo de Balfort.'

The Old Man expressed himself with fury and a great many expletives for the next fifteen minutes. He was not used to being thwarted, and when he was told that Mrs Hammet had said the vicar agreed that their marriage should remain secret for the time being, he was not placated. There was no reason, though, why she should not carry on as before while she awaited her posting to France.

30. Crowmarsh Priors, September 1942 and After

'Blimey, wot you doin' 'ere?' demanded Elsie. She had returned to her and Bernie's area of the attic to find her sister unpacking a shabby suitcase. Agnes's things were strewn everywhere. 'You're supposed to be in Yorkshire! Billeted.'

Agnes looked up sulkily. She was taller and her skirt and cardigan were several sizes too small. 'Aren't you glad to see me?'

'Course I am,' said Elsie. 'You're my sister. Look at you, taller than me!'

'Well, I'm fifteen now so I'm not billeted no more, am I? Them people in Yorkshire, they was caught, wasn't they? They just 'ad me and the twins, but they was sendin' in billetin' forms to get the allowance for six evacuees. So the magistrates sent 'em to prison. Serves 'em right, too.'

'But –'

'Me and the twins was sent to another billet, but they was full to burstin' already and it was 'orrible. They told me where you was and that you was married an' all. "No more billets for me," I says. Twins aren't 'appy either. Can I stay wiv you? This 'ouse must be bigger'n Buckin'am Palace, so there ought to be room for me and the boys.'

'Well, I'll 'ave to see about the boys but . . . course you can stay.'

'Won't be for long. I'm thinkin' to take a factory job to keep meself. I met a lad at the station, when I changed trains in London, givin' out leaflets about the Russians and the eastern front. We got talkin' an' 'e showed me where to get me ticket an' I 'elped 'im wiv the leaflet fings for a bit, waitin' for me train. 'E says it's easy to get a factory job in London, and if I've been up in Yorkshire it'll do me good to be wiv workers and comrades in London, where that urban prole . . . prole . . . oh, urban wossname is.'

'Agnes, you got to be more careful! You mustn't go takin' up with every strange Tom, Dick an' 'Arry in the station!'

''Is name's Ted.' Agnes scowled defiantly.

All of a sudden Elsie felt much older, more like Mum than she would have thought possible. She sighed. 'We'll make you a bed on the floor 'ere in our room for the time bein'. Rest of the 'ouse is requisitioned. They're turnin' us into a convalescent 'ome for the wounded. Can't 'ear yourself think for the poundin',' she said, as the workmen resumed hammering somewhere in the house. She gathered up Agnes's things. ''Spect you'll be wantin' a barf.'

'But it's only Tuesday!' exclaimed Agnes, who bathed only on Saturday night.

'That's all right,' said Elsie, grandly.

'La-di-da!' muttered Agnes, under her breath. 'A barf on Tuesday! Don't mind if I do.'

Next morning Agnes looked a bit brighter for a good night's sleep and some clothes of Elsie's that were much nicer than her own, if a bit short still. She insisted on accompanying Elsie when she went off to her rat-catching, and stuck close by until, exasperated, Elsie said that she was going to get poisoned too unless she gave her a bit of room.

That night Agnes was in the room when Bernie returned. He was not best pleased. 'Can't you put 'er somewhere else?' he muttered. 'Uvverwise it's a bit difficult to, you know . . .'

The next day Elsie went round the village knocking on doors to see if anyone had a space for Agnes. The Barrowses offered their boxroom, but not for long as Edith was expecting again. Agnes collected her things and went off grumpily, muttering, 'A copper! You're jokin'!'

As October approached the workmen completed a fire escape outside Frances's window in the attic. As Elsie and Bernie were wrapped up in each other they never noticed that she slipped out most nights or that a visitor climbed up to her room when she was in. She spent a fair amount of time with Oliver – someone, she said, had to distract him from what was going on in the churchyard.

Hugo had become tiresome, hanging around her during the day, inviting her to go for a drink at the pub, offering lifts whenever he had one of the farm vehicles. One day when she refused he cornered her in a barn, and begged her again to marry him. He did not take her rejection kindly. A few days later he burst unexpectedly into Oliver's study and found her flushed and Oliver distracted. Thereafter he found excuses frequently to pop in on Home Guard business.

He suspects something, thought Frances, so next time Hugo invited her to have a drink with him she agreed, and even flirted a little to throw him off the scent. Hugo took this as encouragement to propose again. This time he was furious when she turned him down. He stared at her coldly and told her it was plain who his rival was.

'Rival? What on earth do you mean?' bluffed Frances.

'Oliver Hammet, of course.'

'Really, Hugo, how likely am I to become a vicar's wife?' said Frances, and stalked away.

Tanni was a bundle of nerves, hollow-eyed and jittery. Sister Tucker told her not to think of getting out of bed and not to pick up Johnny or Anna. Evangeline, who was getting bigger too, had her hands full trying to cope with all of the children. When Alice came round one day with Woolton pies and turnip jam, she burst into tears. 'What would we do without you, Alice?'

Alice patted her on the back. She had never quite got over her dislike of Evangeline but it was her Christian duty to forgive.

Evangeline was too pregnant now to go hunting, but hungry as they were, no one could face whalemeat or the 'poison mince', which was often all that was available at the butcher's. Eventually Frances surprised them all by snaring some pigeons, fat on harvest grain; Evangeline stuffed them with windfall apples and roasted them.

In fact, hunting expeditions became part of Frances's cover. Military Intelligence had pinpointed a radius in southern England from which they believed Manfred's signals were being sent, and she was under orders to search country houses whose location near the coast made them a convenient hiding-place for any Germans who slipped into the country. She had even been issued with an official firearm. 'He's there somewhere. Keep looking,' she was told.

She thought it was pointless to include Gracecourt and said so, but her superiors had insisted, so whenever Hugo was on Home Guard duty with Oliver, she broke in and made a methodical check of all the rooms and outbuildings, but found nothing. Afterwards she hurried back to Glebe House, yawned ostentatiously for the benefit of Elsie and the sharp-eyed Agnes, then slipped off to the vicarage or waited for Oliver to creep up the fire escape. Their time together was so precious that they never wasted it in sleeping. They were blissfully happy, if very tired.

'Darling, I look forward to the day when we can behave like a respectable old married couple,' said Frances, one night. 'It'll be so lovely to get up and have breakfast together.'

'Won't it? Vicars don't normally climb into their wives' bedrooms like thieves. Rather fun, although the bishop would be horrified.'

'Bother the bishop!'

Twice she nearly had an awkward confrontation. One night in early October Hugo came back to Gracecourt unexpectedly and nearly caught her climbing out of the cellar. He called, 'Hullo? Anyone there?' several times. She flattened herself in the shrubbery, held her breath and prayed he didn't have a torch . . . which made her remember the upstairs bathroom and the airing cupboard in which she had found one. Perhaps she should check it next time.

A week later she was back. She had seen Hugo cycle off, so she climbed in through a back window and slipped upstairs. In the bathroom the gilt frame was gone and the airing-cupboard door hung open. She crept closer and felt inside to see if the torch was still there. It had gone. Instead there was a wireless. Frances frowned. Then she jumped as she heard the front door bang and Hugo call to his father that the meeting had been postponed. She slipped down the back stairs and out through the window she had left open, and was creeping outside under Sir Leander's study window when a heated argument broke out.

'I tell you she is!' The old man was pounding the floor with his cane. 'There's too much at stake. It's your job – persuade her! I've been in touch . . . They'll deal with Hammet.'

Frances forgot about the wireless. It sounded as though she and Oliver were in serious trouble. 'They'll deal with Hammet' could only mean the bishop and the Church authorities. Someone must have noticed the amount of time she and Oliver spent together, and had complained to the bishop that they suspected the vicar was having an affair with a parishioner. There would be almost as big a fuss about why they were keeping the marriage a secret, and Frances would have to think of a way to avoid revealing her Auxi status. Bloody hell! She strained to hear Hugo's response, which was something like 'Hold on, I've . . . something else they'll pay for.' Frances wondered how she could warn Oliver about the bishop, without explaining how she knew.

*

381

Rachel rang and said she'd heard that Tanni was expecting twins. Definitely, she said. She felt it in her bones. They ran in Tanni's family.

It was the signal they had been waiting for: it meant 'tonight'.

Alice took the message. She rushed her mother through tea and hurried back to the others. She found that Frances had gone off on one of her rambles, Agnes was hovering around Elsie as usual and Evangeline was lying down. The latter got up and helped Alice to cope with the children. They could have a bath holiday just this once, she said, as long as they went to bed early.

'Not unless we have a washin' holiday too!' demanded Tommy and Maude.

'Washing too,' Evangeline agreed, far too tired to chase them with a soapy cloth.

'An' no brushin' teef!'

To make matters worse, the previous night's Home Guard meeting at the village hall with two other nearby Home Guard units had been postponed to tonight. They would be coming and going just across from the churchyard. The girls would have to be very careful that they weren't seen.

'Bloody 'ell! What'll I do about Agnes? She never goes back to the Barrowses' before bedtime,' muttered Elsie to Bernie. At least he was at home and could bring the car he had hidden in a disused barn straight away. That meant the twins could be driven straight to London while it was dark. By morning they would be safe.

First, though, they had to deal with Agnes. Elsie was desperate to give her the slip so that she could collect blankets and make flasks of cocoa.

"Ere,' said Bernie. 'Give 'er these.' He produced two little tablets.

'I can't poison me own sister!'

'It's not poison, it's sleepin' pills.' Bernie looked sheepish. 'I got some from . . . a man I know when Agnes was sleepin' in our room . . .'

Elsie kissed him, and when Agnes came in a few moments later, she gave her a large mug of cocoa, with the pills dissolved in it.

By nine o'clock Agnes was snoring, her head on the kitchen table. 'Best get her upstairs,' said Elsie. 'You take 'er shoulders, I'll get 'er feet.'

'Not our room again!' said Bernie.

'Look, if she's comfortable she'll sleep better. Stands to reason. Put 'er in our bed. We're not likely to need it tonight. And we can 'ardly carry 'er to the Barrowses', can we?'

By nine thirty Agnes was tucked up in Elsie's attic bedroom, dead to the world. Bernie told Constable Barrows that she hadn't been feeling well and Elsie wanted to look after her.

Then Elsie, Bernie, Alice, Evangeline and Frances gathered in the churchyard. Bernie had hidden the car a mile down the lane behind a hedgerow. The Home Guard meeting had ended and Hugo de Balfort had been the last to leave, looking around him as he walked away. Then the village was quiet, tucked up behind its blackout curtains. It began to rain – a blessing.

Alice checked her watch. 'Low tide in two hours. Frances, it's time you and Elsie started down.'

'Right.'

'Blankets an' sandwiches 'ere in this bundle.'

'We don't know how long it'll take to get them back from the entrance. If anything delays us . . .'

They tried not to think about what might be happening to the children. Alice had told them what the parish record said about how the smugglers had towed contraband in barrels under the water. The idea of the twins lying drugged in the bottom of a boat dodging mines in the Channel was bad enough, but if they had to be submerged, they might suffocate or drown, like unwanted kittens, if anything went wrong.

When it stopped raining, a nearly full moon was emerging from behind the heavy clouds as they unwound the ropes and checked the torches, emergency candles and matches. 'Oh, no!' The rope was tangled and had to be unwound. 'I wonder if anyone can see us, now the moon's out,' Alice said.

'Everyone's probably asleep.'

When Elsie operated the skull lever, the tomb slid open smoothly. 'Glad this 'as got easier to shift. First time we tried it, it wouldn't 'ardly budge.'

'Concentrate and keep calm,' muttered Frances. 'Damn this bloody rope!' She had told Oliver she couldn't see him tonight – it was one of those times when he had to trust her. In that case, he had said, he would get some sleep: he was exhausted. Frances hated to think of him sleeping alone.

Then, unbelievably, they heard the drone of planes coming towards them from the Channel.

'Oh, no! Oh, bloody hell!' said Frances. 'They're coming straight over us.'

They all looked up, then flattened themselves in the shadow of the church, waiting for the planes to pass overhead and hearing distant anti-aircraft fire from Brighton.

Closer and closer the planes came. A bomb fell on the downs, then another and another. The Germans had never before bombed Crowmarsh Priors.

'Why are they dropping bombs on the downs? They normally fly on north!' The earth shuddered.

'I'll have to go back. Tanni and the children need to get down to the cellar and she'll never manage on her own.' Evangeline ran off as fast as she could.

'Bernie, you get home with Elsie,' Alice ordered. 'Agnes will be terrified if she wakes up. They'll be gone soon.' Elsie and Bernie needed no urging, and ran for Glebe House where Agnes was sleeping in the attic, the most dangerous place.

Alice watched them go. She knew she had to get home to her mother, so she didn't pause to think of the danger. With the ground shuddering beneath her feet and flashes all round her she sprinted for her bicycle, hidden in the bushes, and leaped on to it. She could be home and back within an hour.

Frances raced for the vicarage as the planes roared closer. 'Oliver!' she screamed. 'The shelter! Hurry!' But Oliver was already at the door, shouting, 'Frances!' as the first plane flew low overhead. He grabbed her and pulled her inside, then under the staircase as an explosion knocked them off their feet and shattered the vicarage windows. 'The church,' said Oliver, in disbelief, his arms tight round his wife. 'Why are they bombing the church?'

On the floor Frances clung to him, burying her head

in his shoulder. He held her tight, bracing her against another explosion. The ground shook violently as another bomb hit the churchyard. They heard glass shatter and the bell pealed incongruously as the tower crashed down. Masonry and gravestones were flung into the air and thudded back to earth.

The planes went as quickly as they had come. Frances and Oliver touched each other gingerly as they pulled themselves to their feet. 'Close,' Frances breathed. Both were shaking and stunned. The vicarage door was off its hinges.

Outside, they clutched each other as they gazed at the devastation. The church was on fire. 'The tower!' gasped Oliver.

'Oh, no,' said Frances, peering at the place where the knight's tomb had been. 'Dear God, no!'

Oliver held her shoulders. 'I hate to leave you, I know how shaken you are, but I must make sure no one in the village is injured or dying and needs me.'

'Of course,' said Frances faintly, sick at the thought that the old tunnel might not have been strong enough to withstand the bombs. 'Go, darling. As a vicar's wife, I understand.' As an Auxi with demolition training she understood all too well. But she had to be sure.

'Oh, Frances . . .'

'Go on!'

Oliver hugged her quickly and hurried off.

She made her way towards the flames. The knight's tomb was covered with rubble although most of the tower had collapsed on to the other side of the church, where a Victorian stone angel now lay on its face. Frances gritted her teeth and began to tug at chunks of masonry. She had to try to get to the children. Finally she managed to heave the last of the heavy pieces off the tomb. The handle with the skull was still intact and the tomb was still open.

She found the rope, which they had untangled before the bombers went over. Then a torch. She tied the rope round herself and fixed the other end to the tomb. She tested it to make sure it would hold, then lowered herself down the narrow steps. She moved quickly, flashing the torch ahead, up and down the walls, checking for damage. There were intermittent showers of dust and earth, which she knew meant the tunnel was unstable, but she hurried on.

When she reached the area where the smugglers had left excisemen to die the torch beam picked up the small metal trunk from Evangeline's attic in which they had packed a supply of blankets, chocolate, candles and matches. The light flickered and her torch went out.

She groped her way to the trunk, rummaged in it and found a candle and the matches. Something scurried past her in the dark and she imagined she could hear breathing. 'Bloody hell,' she muttered, but the thought that the children might be stuck further along left her no choice but to keep going.

The path sloped down now, but Frances realized something was wrong: Evangeline had said she had been able to hear the sea and had felt a breeze . . . Sure enough, she soon saw that a pile of rocks blocked her way. It nearly filled the passage but she dug a bit near the top, shouting, 'Lili! Klara!' There was an ominous trickle of dust and small stones from overhead. She dared not risk a landslide. There was nothing she could do now but go back.

By the time she reached the stone steps she had to drag herself up. What could they say to Tanni? Clutching at straws, Frances decided to contact Rachel. There was a slim chance that tonight had been another false alarm. Half-way up, she heard Elsie call her name.

Bernie leaned over to haul her up the last few steps and Frances collapsed on to the ground. Far below in the tunnel they heard a rumble. She started to cry. When she had pulled herself together and blown her nose, she went home and dialled the special number she had been given.

'There's something odd here, not sure what's going on exactly but it might be to do with Manfred. I'll be there in the morning,' was all she said. Next day, before anyone else was up, Frances had left for another land-girl welfare meeting.

31. Crowmarsh Priors, November–December 1942

The ugly little Edwardian cottage at the top of the hill where Alice and her mother had lived was nearly empty. On a dismal afternoon Alice was alone in the bare front bedroom where the blackout curtains hung limply, packing up the last of her mother's things. On the night that the Germans had bombed St Gabriel's, she had got home as fast as she could but it had been too late. She had rushed into the dark, silent cottage and found her mother in bed, the covers pulled up to her chin. She had died alone and in terror. What, indeed, would her father have said? Alice knew she would never forgive herself.

In shock, she had stumbled back to the front door and seen St Gabriel's burning. The vestry, she mused, must have been a tinderbox of dry wood and vestments. The bomb had narrowly missed the vicarage and Oliver... Then the full horror had struck her. She knew at once that the tunnel had collapsed.

For some time afterwards Alice had been numb. She continued teaching, and with her war work, but she had lost all sense of purpose. Now she emptied her mother's cupboard and drawers automatically, her progress slow. She kept having to stop because she was crying. Poor Mummy. Poor children.

But she had nearly finished. Into the last box she put a few mended nightdresses and two dressing-gowns with frayed sateen cuffs, some seashells her parents had collected on their honeymoon, a half-empty tin of talcum powder, a collection of prayer books, a set of lace doilies. The feathered picture hat. As she tied up the box Alice thought that she, too, was fated to die alone in some dismal bedroom with a few faded mementoes of a life even less momentous than her mother's had been.

She sat down on the bare mattress. She had hated leaving the vicarage because it had been her home, but now, in the bleak little room, she felt nothing. As soon as Christmas was over she would be gone to London. Every time she passed poor shattered St Gabriel's she remembered the happy hours she had spent there. Now it was gone, and Richard lay injured in a London hospital. It was time to leave Crowmarsh Priors.

Penelope, with her endless list of contacts, had been a brick, getting Alice work with the WVS, and finding her lodging with two elderly sisters who had a spare room at the top of their house in Connaught Square. She had even come up with a replacement teacher for the infants' school, a middle-aged woman who had taught before her marriage. She had been widowed in an air raid – on the same night that Alice's mother had died, and many others, Alice had learned. Penelope, who never complained, had been shaken enough to tell Alice that she had had a narrow escape. The sirens had blared and there had been a horrible accident at the East End Underground station where she was on duty. The police had tried to force too many people in. A great many people had been killed in the crush, though Alice wouldn't see anything about it in the papers: the authorities didn't want the incident reported lest it stop people going to the shelters.

Alice wondered how the world could hold so much sadness.

As Tanni had lain in bed worrying about Lili and Klara, she had been frantic when the first bombs dropped on the downs. But as the planes came closer she had forgotten everything but the need to get five sleepy children down to the cellar. In her panic she had picked up both Anna and Johnny. By the time Evangeline had got back, Tanni was in labour. Sister Tucker had come as soon as she could, but it was too late. Tanni had given birth to another little girl, who had cried once and died. She did not seem to take in the sad news. She neither cried nor showed any emotion. Sister Tucker said shock could do that to a person, that sometimes people blotted terrible things out of their memory altogether.

Next morning Evangeline tried frantically to contact Rachel and the Cohens in London to tell them about Tanni, the baby and the bombs, but the telephone operator said there had been heavy bombing in the East End again, and many exchanges were out of order. She also wanted to contact Bruno, but only Tanni knew his whereabouts and she was drifting in and out of a stupefied sleep and didn't seem to understand any questions. An overworked Sister Tucker had been called away on other emergencies, and Frances was gone, leaving Alice, Elsie and Evangeline helpless and frightened.

Ashen-faced, they tried to decide what ought to be done about the baby, whose tiny body lay wrapped in a linen napkin in the cold dining room. 'We have to do something.'

Finally, at dusk, they gathered by Tanni's bed and Evangeline said gently, 'Tanni, darling, we're all so sorry but we have to bury the poor little baby. I know this is hard but you must tell us, if you can, how we should do it. Does she have a name? Constable Barrows offered to make a coffin and a little marker for her grave.'

'What baby?' Tanni had whispered. Then she stared at the ceiling, her lips moving silently. She refused to eat or say anything else, either to them or to Sister Tucker, who had called, grey with fatigue, to check on her. There was no question of Tanni getting up for the burial, Sister Tucker said. She gulped a cup of tea and told them they would have to manage as best they could.

The next day passed, and there was still no response from the Cohens. Finally Evangeline went to the vicarage and told Oliver that the baby had to be buried even if they couldn't get in touch with Bruno. Did he know of anything special that should be done for a Jewish child?

Oliver rang the bishop, who said that as far as he knew the child should be buried within twenty-four hours of its death, and promised to try to contact a rabbi. He found one in Portsmouth, which had been bombed, so his hands were full. He would try to come to Crowmarsh Priors, he said, but with petrol rationing and the uncertain bus service it might be some time. The bishop told Oliver he was sorry but that as it wasn't the child of Christian parents he didn't think there was anything Oliver could do. Angry for once, Oliver slammed down the telephone.

'What should we do?' the girls asked each other wearily,

as the afternoon waned. They trooped back to Tanni's bedside. 'Tanni, we thought we'd bury her in the far corner of the garden, where there are still some rosebushes and that funny old sundial. Darling, can you just say if you agree?'

Tanni remained silent.

There was still no word from Bruno, Rachel or the Cohens.

'How much longer can we wait?' they wondered, as it grew dark. 'It's more than twenty-four hours now since the baby died.'

'We must give the poor child a name,' said Alice. 'We can't bury her without one.'

'What about "Rebecca"?' suggested Evangeline.

The next morning, in the cold dawn light, just a little more than forty-eight hours after Rebecca Zayman had been born, Alice, Evangeline, Elsie, Bernie, Oliver, Agnes, the Barrowses and the Hawthornes stood round her small grave as it was filled in. Constable Barrows stepped forward, bent down and placed on it a smooth stone with the painted inscription 'Rebecca Zayman, 28 September 1942'. Oliver recited the Twenty-third Psalm and asked them all to pray silently for Tanni and Bruno. Tears rolled down the women's faces.

Oliver had tried desperately to track down Bruno through a stone wall of bureaucracy. All anyone would say was that he was 'unavailable'. Five days later, when he finally reached him, Bruno said he would come at once and arrived within hours. He hurried to Tanni's room, then spent more than an hour at the end of the garden. He came back with red-rimmed eyes and said that, in the circumstances, he had no choice but to take Tanni to a sanatorium until she was better. There was a place close to where he was based, so he could visit her often.

Evangeline helped him dress her. She had packed some of Tanni's things into the old carpetbag and was about to ask if Anna and Johnny might go to the Cohens for a few weeks when her own baby was born, but Bruno pulled her out of Tanni's room and told her some grim news. The Cohens, with Rachel, her husband and two children had been killed in an accident at an air-raid shelter: the police had herded too many people too quickly down the stairs, the crowd had panicked and some had been crushed to death. 'Oh, Bruno, how awful!' said Evangeline – it sounded like the incident Penelope had witnessed. She promised she would look after Johnny and Anna, although she wondered how on earth she would manage five children and a newborn baby. She couldn't add to Bruno's problems by telling him what she thought had happened to Lili and Klara.

The girls hugged an unresponsive Tanni goodbye. 'Get better, darling,' whispered Evangeline. Then Bruno put his arm round his wife and steered her into the car.

At long last the doctors told Evangeline that Richard could be moved to Glebe House now that it was ready. His condition had improved a little: most of the bandages had come off, and he had regained sight in one eye. When he arrived, Hugo de Balfort came to see him. Richard was in a wheelchair and when Evangeline wheeled him into the visiting area, he reached forward to shake hands. Hugo seemed taken aback by his old friend's scars.

'I say, old chap . . . lost for words, really.' They chatted awkwardly for a quarter of an hour, then Hugo muttered something about the Home Guard and left. Next day he sent word that he and his father were in bed with chills and unable to visit anyone for the moment.

Richard had made an effort for his visitor but talking tired him. The only person he responded to was Evangeline, and he loved to feel the baby move inside her. The doctors told her it was a stroke of luck that Crowmarsh Priors had its own convalescent home. Richard's nerves were mending but he was in no state to cope with a noisy houseful of children, perhaps in time . . . Well, they would have to wait and see.

Elsie looked after the children while Evangeline was with Richard, but much of the time Evangeline managed on her own. She was busier than ever with her baby to prepare for and no Tanni. It was due during the first week in January, and she hoped that, after the birth, she and Richard could make a fresh start.

Before she knew it, it was nearly Christmas and she was late getting the winter cabbage in. She dug ferociously in the garden, wearing an ancient pair of trousers that, in happier days, Tanni had altered, with laces on the sides, to make room for Evangeline's expanding belly. She swung her spade, and felt a warm trickle down her legs as her waters broke.

That afternoon Sister Tucker arrived, and sent Tommy and Maude to fetch Alice after school. Someone had to let Richard know, she said, but Alice told her that Elsie would.

Evangeline was in labour for two days, and fought the

contractions, terrified by what might happen if the baby were born with African features or colouring. Eventually, however, she gave birth to a son. She lay still, pale, exhausted and frightened, while Sister Tucker bustled about efficiently, then handed her a tightly wrapped bundle. 'We're a few weeks early, Mummy, but we're very well all the same,' she chirruped.

Evangeline hardly dared look, but when she did, the baby's eyes were blue and his hair, of which there was a great deal, was straight and brown. A tiny pink mouth opened in a yawn, which turned into a howl. Evangeline, too, began to cry – with joy and relief. He wasn't Laurent's. 'There, there,' said Sister Tucker. 'All over now and he's lovely. Have you thought what to name him?'

'Please . . . will you tell Richard he's arrived?' she whispered. 'And I think we'll call him Andrew. I have a brother named André.'

When Frances returned to the village, she, Elsie and Alice took turns to sit with Evangeline. Nell Hawthorne brought some broth, plumped her pillows and cooed over the baby, while Edith Barrows made custard and jelly from her own mother's recipe to 'keep Evangeline's strength up'. 'It's like we're repopulating the village!' Edith said, patting her own large bump.

While Evangeline was recovering, Elsie made Agnes help with the scrubbing, the laundry and minding the children, while a resentful Agnes complained bitterly that Elsie had turned into a right bossy-boots.

With so many crises, the one thing they avoided mentioning was Lili and Klara Joseph, but they had a permanent reminder of what must have happened to them in the shell of the church: the remains of the tower stood open to the sky, surrounded by masonry, broken glass, smashed wooden pews and slates. The impact had wrecked many graves, so headstones and marble slabs mingled with the other debris. The knight's tomb was still in its place, but had sunk almost out of sight. There was no way now to reach the entrance. Their only hope was that the boat bringing the twins had not reached the cave, but if that was so, where were they now?

Frances said that she and Evangeline could ask the Free French: someone in their network of contacts might know whether or not the girls had been brought to England. But at the moment neither she nor Evangeline could go up to London.

Christmas brought two visitors, of whom one was Penelope: she wanted to spend time with Richard, and admire her grandson. The other was a gangly lad with acne who slouched off the train. 'It's Ted!' exclaimed Agnes, joyfully. 'I wrote to 'im, didn't I? Told 'im where I was,' she informed Elsie. She was living with Elsie and Bernie again because the Barrowses' baby was due at any minute. As Frances was often away, she slept on her side of the attic.

When Ted arrived he established himself in the garden shed at Glebe House, almost before anyone realized he had done so. In return for a camp-bed and a spirit-lamp, he helped Evangeline with the gardening and odd jobs. He wanted them all to become socialists, and the longer he stayed, the more convinced Elsie was that Ted had driven his family mad with his political views and they had thrown him out. He lectured and hectored everyone: Oliver about religion being the opium of the masses, Albert about the working class, Frances and Evangeline about suppressing the workers and imperialism, and Alice about social revolution and why the Church was a bourgeois tool of oppression. When he harangued Bernie about the inherent flaws in the capitalist system, Bernie snapped, ''E's drivin' me round the bleedin' twist! Woss 'appened to me peace and quiet, eh? Like a bleedin' circus round 'ere. We get married so's we can be togevver, then Agnes is 'angin' around in the room wiv us, an' now we got bleedin' Ted! Either 'e goes or I break 'is jaw to shut 'im up.'

'Bernie, I got to keep an eye on Agnes 'cause I'm afraid she'll go off wiv 'im. Ted's always goin' on at 'er about free love – I 'eard 'im. Next fing you know, she'll be in trouble an' 'e's not the marryin' kind. Where'll she be then? Family's family, and there's such a thing as responsibility. I owe it to Mum to look after 'er. Blood's ficker than water.'

'Glad I never 'ad no bleedin' family!'

'Bernard Carpenter! You 'ave got a family! You got me, 'aven't you?' Elsie put her arms round Bernie's neck. 'Always will, too, if you know what's good for you.' He relented and gave her a kiss. It was hardly the perfect moment for her to tell him that she had had a letter from the people who had taken in her brothers: they had had a fire, so they and seven children were now living on top of each other in a neighbouring family's tiny two-up, two-down cottage, the only accommodation available. Since Elsie was now a married woman they were sending the boys to her. She put off telling Bernie for as long as she could, which wasn't long because she discovered the boys were due to arrive on the weekend train. 'At least you'll be together for Christmas,' wrote the woman whose house had burned down. Elsie groaned.

'Wot we need,' she told Bernie, when she confessed that the boys were on their way, 'is an 'ouse of our own. And for once I don't care 'ow you get it so long's we can all be togevver.'

'Only on condition Ted don't come too,' said Bernie, firmly.

And he did find them a house, which was a miracle with housing in such short supply. It was at the end of a once-genteel terrace in Eastbourne. Shabby and near-derelict, it had five bedrooms, a double drawing room, and bells everywhere for summoning a now non-existent maid. It was filled with an odd assortment of furniture, left behind by the previous owners who had had an over-whelming fondness for red velvet, chandeliers, mirrors and brightly patterned carpets. 'Blimey, it's a palace, innit? Velvet curtains an' all!' exclaimed Elsie, gazing at Bernie in wonder. 'However did you find it? No, don't tell me!'

Bernie didn't want to tell Elsie it had been a brothel that Uncle had owned. On his shady solicitor's advice, Uncle had registered the property in the name of Bernard Carpenter, who, unknown to the Land Registry, had been a child at the time. Shortly before Uncle went to prison, he had told Bernie what he had done, in the knowledge that the boy was too much in awe of him to attempt to deprive him of his property. Now, though, Uncle had died, and the former inhabitants had gone on to greener pastures in London. Bernie guessed the house hadn't been requisitioned because the authorities didn't like requisitioning brothels, so it must be his to move into.

Agnes balked at going to Eastbourne, insisting that she would stay on in Elsie and Bernie's room at the top of Glebe House. But Elsie wasn't going to leave her alone with Ted. She asked to transfer to rat-catching in Eastbourne with Agnes as her assistant.

'I'll miss you,' said Evangeline, sadly, 'especially with Alice leaving too, and Frances away so much.'

'I 'ate to fink of goin', but what else can we do?'

After Christmas Evangeline and Alice waved Elsie, Bernie, Agnes, Dick and Willie off to their new home. Before long, much to Bernie's annoyance, Ted appeared at the house, and stayed.

The day after the planes had bombed Crowmarsh Priors, and feeling guilty that she had been so preoccupied with the twins that she had neglected to mention it earlier, Frances had hurried to London, sought out the little man and asked his advice. She wasn't sure whether it meant anything but she had found a wireless in the airing cupboard at Gracecourt, which might or might not be odd, and Hugo was increasingly persistent with his marriage proposals. She had begun to think him deranged. Also, no sooner had he accused Oliver of being his rival than the church was bombed. It had been an odd target. What was the point in bombing an isolated church and a few hills?

The little man said they mustn't jump to conclusions, but she should watch Gracecourt and the de Balforts as closely as she could. If Frances was right it wouldn't be only the de Balforts who were involved. She mustn't give the game away before they could spread a net to catch everyone. 'And, Frances,' he warned, as they parted, 'never forget for a minute how dangerous these collaborators are.'

Frances stayed in the village for Christmas instead of going to her father. She disappeared on long rambles into the country and came back with pheasants, rabbits and even a small roe deer. She had decided that poaching to help Evangeline provided her best alibi. In training they were told that when they had to lie, they should stick to the truth as far as possible.

Alice had been ordered to report for duty in London early in January. On New Year's Eve, after the children were asleep, she came to say goodbye to Evangeline. She was wearing her new WVS uniform for the first time. She had lost weight and the skimpy skirt showed off her slim figure and long legs. Its tailored style suited her. She had made an effort for the first time in months, manicuring and buffing her nails, applying lipstick – a going-away present from Elsie – and under the jaunty cap, her hair was arranged in the neat victory roll she had finally perfected. She looked like a different person: efficient and capable, but rather glamorous, too, like a forces' pin-up in uniform.

Over the last bottle of wine from Lady Marchmont's store, she, Frances and Evangeline chatted. Frances had been devoting her few spare moments to helping Oliver with the makeshift chapel he had arranged in the vicarage dining room so that the village had a place to worship. 'So good of you, Frances,' Alice remarked.

Frances made a face. 'You were always the mainstay of St Gabriel's, and someone's got to help Oliver keep the parish together when you've gone,' she told Alice.

Evangeline thought Frances an unlikely candidate to fill Alice's shoes, but she and Oliver seemed always to be together now, and when they weren't, each was looking for the other. Odd.

'Anyway, darling, since you're leaving us, I've a little present for you.' Frances changed the subject. 'You never know what might happen or who you'll meet in London. If the right man comes along, I daresay you'll need this.' She handed Alice the crocodile dressing-case Albert had seen her with on the station platform the day she arrived in Crowmarsh Priors.

'Oh, *Frances*,' breathed Alice. She stroked it, then opened the catch. It was the most exquisite thing she had ever seen, let alone owned. Inside it was beautifully fitted in silver and mother-of-pearl, with a brush and comb, a manicure set, a sewing kit, a crystal powder bowl with its own large puff, holders for three lipsticks, and two Lalique scent bottles, each half filled with Vol de Nuit. There was a mother-of-pearl-handled toothbrush, a little box for tooth powder, a padded drawer for jewellery and a clean handkerchief edged with lace. In the back a mirror swivelled out on a clever little hinge. 'Oh, Frances, I've never owned anything so pretty!' she said. 'When I die they'll find it and say I – that I . . . a friend . . .'

'Let's not be morbid, darling. No tears! Something in my bones tells me you're going to meet a wonderful man soon. Promise to write and tell us all about it when it happens.'

After she had gone, Evangeline and Frances finished the wine and gazed into the fire. 'You and Oliver,' said Evangeline, after a while, 'you're in love with him, aren't you?'

When you have to lie, stick as close to the truth as you can. 'Yes,' Frances said, 'but, Evangeline . . .'

'I can keep a secret,' said Evangeline. 'You've no idea.'

'If you're my friend keep it and, please, don't ask me anything else. But if anything ever happens to me – a bomb falls on me or something – promise you'll look after him.'

'Promise.'

'Feels like the war's gone on for ever, doesn't it?'

32. West London, August 1944

Alice had struggled all day to get a grip on herself but that morning she had got out of the wrong side of her bed. She hadn't been able to concentrate properly all day. She felt irritable and longed to be somewhere that wasn't cold, dark, dirty and dangerous. Somewhere she could have a proper bath instead of a hasty wash from a tap in a bathroom with a broken window.

Now she concentrated on arranging biscuits in neat circles on a cracked platter. She straightened the teacups, waited for the urn to bubble, and wondered why she had volunteered to play hostess at another church social when she hated them – especially when she was exhausted and would rather be in bed. Never again, she promised herself.

Suddenly one of the dreaded V2 rockets whooped over the church. The ominous sound drowned the gramophone, the chatter stopped and everyone in the hall froze. There had been no warning siren and no time to run for the air-raid shelter. You were all right as long as you could hear the noise. It was when you couldn't that it was dangerous, because that meant you were directly beneath it.

'Under the tables, everyone!' Alice shouted, just as they heard it hit. Another followed and fell close by, probably intended for Paddington station. The third whoop stopped suddenly, and the rocket brought down half of the ceiling and put out the lights. Alice crouched, eyes tight shut, seeing again the little boy lying dead in the street yesterday after a direct hit. She had picked him up and asked the neighbours, dazed survivors, who he was. Nobody knew. She had kept a stiff upper lip, of course: she had tucked the little corpse into an ambulance, then got on with directing stunned people who no longer had homes to temporary shelters and hot food.

When the raid ended the church hall was full of fragmented plaster, broken glass and people asking each other if they were all right. Someone produced a torch. The urn lay in a puddle on its side, surrounded by broken cups. The blackout curtain rails were askew across the broken windows and they could see searchlight beams across the sky. 'Extinguish that torch!' someone ordered, and the tiny gleam of light disappeared.

Alice felt limp and was gasping for breath, her throat gritty with dust. Somehow the tall American airman who had been talking to the vicar had an arm round her shoulders and was trying to help her up. But Alice wasn't sure she could stand. She felt so weak she wanted to collapse in a heap. Tears pricked her eyes. Mustn't cry, she told herself sternly. It would never do for the WVS to give way. They had to set an example and carry on. She was just tired, she muttered to the airman. They were all tired – Ellen, Judy and the vicar. Suddenly she realized how comforting it was to have a man's arm round her in the dark.

'You're the first girl I met over here could quote the scriptures,' he said in her ear.

From the number of very white teeth Alice could see

in the gloom, she grasped that he was smiling. He had an odd way of talking, as if he was in no particular hurry to say what he had to say. 'I beg your pardon?' she said.

'You just said, "Sufficient unto the day is the evil thereof."'

'Did I?' Her colleague Ellen had warned her that she had been talking to herself. I'm turning into an eccentric and bitter woman like Mummy, she thought. The knowledge weighed her down like another wartime burden. 'Well, those were rather close. Still, we must count ourselves lucky, remember that others are worse off.' She had tried for a brisk tone – why had her voice wobbled? Deep breaths, my girl. You've lasted this long, she reminded herself.

'If those bombs had fallen any closer we're the ones that would've been worse off, ma'am,' he said, in that slow voice. The 'ma'am' was respectful but he had managed to keep his arm round her shoulders. It felt nice and strong. Weakly, Alice decided she would let it stay there for a minute, just until she had stopped shaking and collected her thoughts. But she continued to shake. The man put his other arm round her and held her tightly to him. 'It's all right,' he said. 'You English are somethin' else. That rocket scared the daylights out of me and I'm in the Air Force. You're just a gal and gals've got a right to be scared. I bet you been through this lots of times since the war started, and you're still tryin' to act like everything's normal. It isn't, but it's all right now.'

After a short time the shaking wore off and Alice began to enjoy the solid feel of the man close to her. Then she reminded herself that Americans had a shocking reputation, so she shouldn't encourage advances. He was probably married, anyway. First Richard, now this fellow . . . They were all married. Alice sighed, fought back self-pity and began to pick glass out of her hair. She sniffed and something splattered on to her jacket.

'You're bleeding,' said the airman. 'Hold still.' He took out his handkerchief and held it to her nose.

'It's only a nosebleed – I'm hardly a war casualty,' she wanted to say, but instead she quavered, 'Thank you. Oh, no! I've bled all over the front of your uniform!' She wished the earth would open and swallow her, bloody nose and all. First the rockets, now this – on the first occasion she'd talked to an attractive man in ages.

He was grinning now. 'That's all right. Have a good cry if you want. Go ahead, I'm used to it. Women always feel better after a good cry – least, that's what my sisters tell me. And I have five. Somebody's always crying, getting something out of her system. I'm Joe Lightfoot, US Air Force.' He wetted his handkerchief in some of the spilled water from the urn and gave it to her. 'And you?'

'Oh. Yes.' Sniff. 'How do you do?' Sniff. Alice mopped her face and eyes, then dabbed her nose again. 'I'm Alice Osbourne. Women's Voluntary Service. How long have you been in England?'

'Six months. Flew some missions over Germany, helped back up the invasion on D Day. Pretty busy. Had a weekend leave so I decided I'd better see London. Boy, those trains are crowded! I got here, and it's all so dark. I didn't know what to do until I stopped to ask directions and I saw the sign says y'all were havin' a social tonight and servicemen were welcome. Been watching you from across the room, moving around, organizin' things like you're in charge. This your church?'

'Sort of, now I'm in London. I help out sometimes.' Watching her? Dismayed, Alice brushed hard at her uniform. She must look terrible. Perhaps it was a good thing the lights had been blown out. Why, oh, why hadn't she remembered her lipstick? She hadn't had a bath in days. And why couldn't she think of anything to say? She fell back automatically on to a familiar topic. 'My father came here when he was first ordained. Then they sent him to a country parish where –'

'Your daddy was a what?'

'A vicar. It's, um, what we call preachers in England.'

'So you're a preacher's daughter! Well, Alice, I come from a church-going family myself, where all the first-born sons are named Joe. Officially I was baptized Joseph Lee Lightfoot the Fourth. Don't know what denomination this here church is but my family's all southern Baptist. You bein' a church-goin' woman, I thought I'd better mention it.'

Alice had never heard of southern Baptists. 'Oh?' she said faintly.

'You feelin' better? I come from the country too, a little town called Goshen, Georgia. 'Bout a hundred miles from Atlanta. You've heard of Atlanta, haven't you?'

She nodded. She had no idea where it might be on the map.

'My family's had a farm there since before the Civil War. Daddy's branched out a little, has him some stores that sell feed and hardware. Had about ten in Goshen and Atlanta by the time I shipped out. Wants me to come back and help him run the business, seein' I'm the only boy. Promised me two hundred acres to build my own house when I do.'

What, Alice wondered, were 'feed and hardware'? And how much land would you have to own to give away two hundred acres? Just for a house? What *could* America be like? 'I'm rather hungry,' she said. 'I don't suppose any of the biscuits survived? I forgot to have lunch and I'm a bit light-headed. Usually I'm much calmer.'

'Sure. Here, have a cookie. Let's see, this plate looks the cleanest . . . Shame it's too late to invite you to dinner, but the officers' club is closed by now and probably most of the restaurants. You live near here? I was thinkin' maybe we could have dinner tomorrow, if you're not busy,' Joe said. He handed her a plate of biscuits that were somewhat the worse for wear. Alice ate them anyway. They tasted dusty but she didn't care: she was famished.

'They do some good steaks at the officers' club. Where do you live?'

Steaks? Alice almost fainted at the idea. 'Quite close to here,' she said, 'if the house is still standing. I'm billeted with two old ladies, who rather discourage callers.' It occurred to Alice that she was nearly twenty-eight and, aside from her father and boarding-school, she had spent her whole life living with older women, starting with her mother. She was uncertain what to say next. Should she agree to have dinner with him? He seemed nice enough but American servicemen were known to worm their way into a girl's good graces with charm, chocolate and cigarettes. She didn't want to give him the wrong impression . . . But on the other hand, she didn't want to put him off.

'They discourage callers,' she said again, without conviction.

Joe chuckled. 'That's OK. I know how old ladies are – real strict sometimes. Lotta old ladies in Goshen. I'll walk you home anyhow. They can't object to that when it's so dangerous out there. Besides,' he said, taking her hand, 'I need to know where to pick you up tomorrow so's we can have that dinner and I can see you in the light before my leave's over. Check that you're as pretty as you looked before the lights went out. Daddy says if a girl's pretty and knows her scriptures that just about covers all the bases.'

What on earth was he talking about? What bases? Then Alice caught her breath. Pretty? She hoped her face was clean at least. Never mind the scriptures right now.

'Oh,' she said, flustered, 'but I – I really ought to help clear up . . .' Across the hall Judy and Ellen were sweeping up broken glass and sending her resentful looks.

'Aw, come on. Quick.' He took her hand. 'Bet you clear up all the time.' He guided her outside firmly. She didn't protest: he was right, she *did* clear up most nights, and it was rather lovely to be rescued from it.

Outside, the rockets had destroyed an office building and a clothing shop, while a block of flats nearby was in flames. The fire watch were shouting and the pavements were covered with rubble, bricks and broken concrete, as well as slippery with water from the fire hoses. Alice tripped and half fell as she picked her way over broken masonry.

'Here, allow me,' Joe said. The next thing she knew he had picked her up and was striding easily through the

410

mess. She put her arms round his neck. What a night! After a minute she said, 'You can put me down now, we're past the worst. This is my square. The old ladies live on that far corner, next to the fish-and-chip shop.'

He set her on her feet, but she was oddly reluctant to let go of him. 'Fish and chips – that's like fried fish and French fries, isn't it? Will they be open? Everything looks kind of dark.'

'I can smell them.'

'Come on, then. You haven't eaten tonight and I can't have you fainting on me.'

Ten minutes later their hands were full of greasy newspaper and Joe was looking for a place to sit down. 'Do you have to go in right away? Or can we sit here on this bench and eat before the food gets cold?' he asked. 'Will you be chilly?'

'No, I'll be fine,' said Alice. Behind the bench the dark square was a mass of trees and shrubbery that usually rustled with courting couples or prostitutes and their clients. Although Joe seemed nice – very nice, in fact – Alice was anxious not to give him 'ideas'. Wasn't she? Suddenly she was unsure. What would she do if he did get ideas?

They fell on their fish and chips. Joe had wanted something called ketchup, whatever that was, but Alice had liberally doused everything with vinegar and salt. 'No ketchup,' she said. Afterwards she felt much better. Joe put his arm round her again and they sat for a while. Alice couldn't hear any courting in the undergrowth – the rocket, she guessed, and relaxed. She found herself smiling into the darkness. 'What *is* ketchup?'

Joe laughed. 'Tomato sauce.' He pronounced it 'tomayda'. 'I can't imagine life without ketchup. Everybody in America eats it!' He looked up. 'There's a few stars – not as many as back home though. I miss the night-time noises, dogs barkin', the cattle, owls . . . crickets. You miss livin' in the country?'

'I didn't think I would but I do. When my mother died I couldn't wait to get away, find different war work. I was a teacher and wanted to feel more a part of things – do my bit in a more active way. Oh, I don't know what I wanted.'

'Are you married?' Joe asked bluntly. 'Or engaged, or in love with some fellow in the forces?'

'Oh! Well . . .' Why beat about the bush? thought Alice. 'No, I'm not married. I was supposed to be, but the man I was engaged to went to America and came back married to somebody else. A complete surprise and rather dreadful at the time. His mother fixed up my job with the WVS. And here I am.'

'Lucky for me,' said Joe. He tightened his arm round her shoulders. 'Means I got to meet you. I wasn't sure if the reason you didn't say whether or not you'd have dinner with me tomorrow was because there was someone else. Just so you know right away,' he said, leaning closer, 'I'm not married either. But if this war made me realize one thing, it's that I'd like to be. Every time you go up in a plane you think, Maybe this time I won't make it back. Lot of pilots I knew haven't. I don't want to die without having been married, or had a chance to leave a child of mine on earth. And where I come from the two go hand in hand. So when I found a long-legged, pretty church-goin' gal I thought, Maybe this is the Lord's way of sayin', "Don't waste time, Joe, she's the one" . . .'

He had turned and his face was very close to hers. Alice wanted to say that this was all a bit quick for her but something told her to shut her eyes and *don't move*. Joe kissed her – in a nice way that left room for her to pull away if she wanted to, yet it was still a kiss that meant business. Alice felt breathless and wondered if he would think she was a shameless hussy because somehow she couldn't stop kissing him back.

Hours later a tired air-raid warden coming off duty passed the bench where Alice and Joe were sitting. He saw them nuzzling and laughing, holding hands, comfortable with each other, sweethearts, clearly. He saw the girl yawn and heard her say, 'All right, eight tomorrow night. Now I really must go.' But she didn't move.

The warden turned up his collar against the drizzle and smiled for the first time that day. Good luck to them, he thought. Good luck to us all.

Three days later, on Monday, the telephone rang in the Fairfaxes' hall.

'Evangeline, I can't talk for long but guess what? I'm getting married . . . Thank you. Next weekend . . . An American airman . . . Yes, it is rather sudden . . . Georgia, I think it's called. I'm going to live there after the war. You must show me where it is on the map next time we see each other . . . Very happy indeed . . . What? What did you say happened? Can't quite hear you, Evangeline . . . Burned down last Sunday? Gracecourt? Not another bomb! Oh, his cook's fault . . . I bet she went off to her sister's and forgot things on the stove . . . Sir Leander dead! Oh, how dreadful, poor old man. And Hugo? . . . I see. Yes, I shall certainly write to him in hospital. Unbelievable. Be sure to tell Frances, won't you? I've tried and tried to phone but can't reach her . . . In London again? You haven't seen her since the fire? . . . Well, when you do, tell her she was right about the dressing-case. I'm taking it on honeymoon and will think of her. Goodbye, Evangeline.'

Alice rang off. More bloody bad news! She squared her shoulders. She couldn't *wait* to marry Joe and go to America. Her life was going to start all over again in a brave new world where they would go to the southern Baptist church, people talked about 'tomaydas', ate ketchup and drank Coca-Cola. Joe was already asking what kind of house she'd like and talking about Joe the Fifth. She had an engagement ring with a cluster of diamonds that Joe had bought for her in Hatton Garden. He had insisted on a big one. She thought about her husband-to-be and smiled happily. She was pretty when she smiled.

33. Crowmarsh Priors, 8 May 1995

There were jealous mutterings at Albion Television when Katie Hamilton-Jones was promoted overnight from lowly researcher to presenter of the *Heart of England VE Day Fiftieth Anniversary Special*. She had been elated but when the big day arrived she was pacing the village green in Crowmarsh Priors and her confidence had evaporated. Her notes were a meaningless blur and her knees were shaking with stage fright.

While the crew set up their equipment she took deep breaths and tried to calm down. She walked around, checking angles for the best shots with Production in the studio. She wanted the older cottages with their low walls and front gardens, the Queen Anne mansion, which had been turned into a convalescent home during the war, set back behind a high brick wall, and across the green, the pretty Georgian terrace, the church and the Gentlemen's Arms, with its red, white and blue hanging baskets and bunting.

Behind her the lane, only one car wide, was just visible, twisting and dipping through the hedgerows. Beyond it the downs swelled, dotted with sheep. With a bit of manoeuvring the cameras could block out the row of ugly 1960s houses behind the pub so that viewers would see the quaint Crowmarsh Priors of fifty years ago.

'Testing, testing. Can you hear me in the studio, Simon?' she asked, for the umpteenth time.

'Don't worry, if you get stuck we'll talk you through it. Be professional. Five, four, three, two, one,' said Simon. 'You're on.'

Oh, hell! Deep breath. Big smile. Professional. 'Welcome, ladies and gentlemen, to this special edition of *Heart of England*! As the nation pauses in remembrance on the fiftieth anniversary of VE Day, I'm Katie Hamilton-Jones, for Albion Television, and we hope you'll stay with us as we report live all day from the village of Crowmarsh Priors in Sussex.' She made a dramatic sweeping gesture with her hand to indicate the village behind her.

'Stop waving,' said Simon and the editor simultaneously, in her earpiece.

Rattled, Katie clutched the microphone with both hands and continued, 'If London is the beating heart of Britain, country villages like Crowmarsh Priors are its lifeblood. Today, with the birds singing and sheep grazing on the hills above me, this peaceful village in Sussex looks like a picture-postcard, with its village green, its country pub and its cottages all basking in the early-morning sunshine. Throughout England countless villages looked like this when war with Germany was declared in September 1939.

'Today's special edition of the programme pays tribute to the people of Crowmarsh Priors and to villagers in all parts of the country who lived through England's darkest hour. VE Day marked the end of a terrible time and this fiftieth anniversary is a solemn reminder for those who lived through it. Today we will join the village in a special service of remembrance at the parish church followed, in the best English tradition, by a fête on the village green.'

It was going pretty well and Katie was feeling better. If she was this good on her feet, perhaps she should have gone to the Bar, after all. She tossed her hair back and spoke directly into the camera. She hoped her mother's friends were watching. 'We'll be speaking to a number of special guests about their memories and experiences. They include two elderly gentlemen from Crowmarsh Priors who will tell us about being in the Home Guard, and some of the residents of the Princess Elizabeth Convalescent Home for the War Wounded, here in the village.

'But today's programme is mainly about women. The women who stayed at home are the ones we rarely hear about, those who kept the home fires burning even while they added the burden of war work to a busy life. They were wives, daughters, sisters and mothers, who worried about loved ones fighting far away in the armed forces and, at home, braced themselves against the long-expected German invasion. Those women had a stiff upper lip, kept smiling and otherwise did their bit while they raised their families and were the mainstay of their communities. This programme pays tribute to those unsung heroines, and our featured guests today are four women who lived here in Crowmarsh Priors.

'Then they were four girls who became close friends. They were all wartime brides whose lives were shaped by the conflict. Now, they are elderly ladies, but today they are together in their wartime home for the first time in more than fifty years, to relive their experiences of England's darkest hour and reflect on the impact of the war on their lives. For many of our older female viewers, this will bring back wartime memories of their own.'

Behind Katie, the camera picked up a silver Mercedes turning sharply on to the green and parking at an angle. After a moment a woman got out of the driver's side and the door slammed with a solid 'thunk'. The camera homed in on her: short, tubby and elderly. She had on a purple-flowered silk outfit, with a large, glittering diamond spray brooch pinned to her substantial bosom, a many-stranded pearl necklace, mauve court shoes and matching stockings. She opened the car's back door and retrieved a picture hat of the same fabric as her dress, a silk handbag and lavender kid gloves.

The cameraman muttered, 'It's that Lady Whatsit, the one who paid for the church and everything.'

Katie squinted at her. The patroness of today's events, Lady Carpenter, was a dead ringer for the Queen Mother. 'Our first war bride has arrived! That's Lady Carpenter, Sir Bernard Carpenter's widow, who has just got out of her car. Lady Carpenter is the youngest of our four war brides, and it's thanks to her generosity that the historic parish church of St Gabriel's has been restored and that the celebration is taking place today. She's here bright and early to make sure everything is in place for this special day, this very, very special day, um . . . because she was . . . the special . . . um . . . arrangements. Um . . .' Shit! She was blowing it . . .

Back in the studio, Production were panicking too. Katie was losing it. 'Stay calm. Talk about the church, keep the flow smooth,' said Simon, firmly, in her earpiece.

Fortunately Katie was quick on the uptake and, despite her moment of panic, knew her stuff. 'Speaking of Lady Carpenter brings me to the parish church, which is just behind me,' she said, as the camera panned to a shot of it, 'the focus of today's ceremony. Elsie Pigeon was a girl when she was married there to Bernard Carpenter in 1942. A few months after their wedding the church was badly damaged by a stray bomb and has been closed ever since. After Sir Bernard retired from the Treasury he devoted himself to his hobby, wartime history, and on the rare occasions when he was interviewed, he reminisced fondly about the time he spent in Crowmarsh Priors when he and his wife were young. After his death, two years ago, Lady Carpenter heard that plans were afoot to demolish the ruined church, because of the cost of repairs, and decided to rebuild it in his memory.

'The church and the village of Crowmarsh Priors are closely linked to the de Balfort family. William the Conqueror rewarded his knight Giles de Balfort with land near the Sussex coast. Giles built a monastery to pray for William, and a fortress to defend him. They crumbled long ago, but the de Balforts have owned the property ever since. The last of the de Balforts lives near the village and we hope he'll speak to us today.

'Until it burned down during the Second World War, the de Balforts' ancestral home was Gracecourt Hall, dating from the reign of Elizabeth the First. The money to build it came from the wool trade, from inter-marriage with England's richest and most powerful families and, some say, even from the smuggling that flourished on this coast for nearly three centuries. Lady Carpenter furnished us with these photographs taken in Gracecourt's heyday in the 1930s. I believe they're on the screen as I speak.

'The de Balfort men made the Grand Tour of Europe and brought home many treasures from their travels. Over the centuries the house acquired a splendid collection of paintings, tapestries and silver. Until the 1930s the de Balforts' house-parties were famous. On the screen now you can see a picture of the croquet lawn and a picnic in the background . . . there are the tennis courts . . . that's a Chinese pavilion for tea parties, built just before the war, and here is the water-garden, laid out by a famous German landscape architect, which replaced the old-fashioned lake. The water-garden was art deco, very fashionable at the time, an elegant design of interconnecting rectangular pools. Sadly the house and its treasures were destroyed in a fire before the end of the war.'

'You're rambling! Get back to the Carpenters and the church,' ordered Simon. 'Interview Lady Carpenter.'

The camera followed Katie as she walked towards the Mercedes, speaking over her shoulder. 'But let's get back to the romantic story of the Carpenters and the parish church . . .'

Lady Carpenter was oblivious of the approaching TV camera. She was trying to chivvy someone out of the car's passenger seat. 'For God's sake, Graham!' she snapped, at a young man in a red and white striped shirt, navy blazer and flamboyant tie. The Cockney accent of her youth was no longer apparent.

Her thirty-year-old grandson, successful estate agent and party-going man-about-town, was horribly hung-over from a friend's stag do the previous evening. He sat slumped, ashen and carsick, wishing he had not agreed to drive down with his grandmother. His grandfather had always said he liked his motors and his women fast, and had kept several expensive cars, although he didn't like driving: they were for Elsie, who adored them even though she drove like a maniac. Bernard had enjoyed riding in the passenger seat, puffing one of his special Cuban cigars, encouraging Elsie to put her foot down. The smell of expensive tobacco still permeated the car.

If you weren't Grandpa, Graham thought, driving with Granny was terrifying, especially when she was in a hurry. He had tried to remonstrate with her, but the motorway had been a blur of lorries, overtaken at speed.

'Hurry up, Graham! Your grandfather never complained about my driving.'

Only because lung cancer got him before you killed him in a pile-up, thought Graham, but knew better than to say it aloud.

Lady Carpenter moved aside to let him out and her eyes narrowed as she squinted at a bent figure in an ancient Home Guard uniform, shuffling along, leaning on a cane and the arm of a girl in a long skirt. She was clutching a straw bag, rugs and a folding deck-chair. They stopped near the ladies' and gents'. The girl unfolded the chair and lowered the old gentleman into it. She settled a battered Panama hat on his head and, despite the sun, covered his knees with a plaid rug.

'As I live and breathe, it's Albert Hawthorne,'

murmured Lady Carpenter. She watched the girl spread a second rug on the ground and retrieve a paperback, a Thermos and sunglasses from her basket.

'Are you ready for your tea, Granddad?' the girl asked loudly, in the kind of voice people use with the hard of hearing. The old man nodded.

Graham's gaze followed his grandmother's. Then his mobile phone shrilled.

Lady Carpenter scowled. It was a particularly irritating sound.

'Sorry! I think we've finally got a punter for that wreck we haven't been able to shift,' he muttered to his grandmother, his hand over the phone's mouthpiece. 'Graham here,' he said smoothly.

Lady Carpenter took out her compact and checked her lipstick. One thing she'd say for Graham, he'd inherited Bernie's ability to wheel and deal. She listened.

'The Regent's Park property?' he asked smoothly. 'Yes, Park Village West. Enchanting house – Nash. Yes, Crown Estate, very exclusive. Indeed, they will be impressed back home in Dallas but you'll need to act quickly. Those properties are rare, snapped up the minute they come on the market on account of the big gardens at the back . . . Very unusual for London, yes. There was a canal behind the houses once . . . No, no, not any longer, you needn't worry about the little one falling in. It was filled in during the war because the Germans used it to navigate, and bomb the railway nearby. Monday at ten . . . Excellent. See you, then. Cheerio!' He pushed the end-call button. 'House needs a fortune spent on it and no one's interested except this American bloke, investment banker moving to

London. His wife's keen. Have to strike while the iron's hot. Since we're early I'll stretch my legs, see if there's any weekend cottages for sale. I never understand why people want them – who'd want to be in the country at the weekend?'

'Keep an eye open for Auntie Agnes and Uncle Ted,' Lady Carpenter murmured, through her powder puff.

Graham turned back, aghast. 'Bloody hell, Gran! You didn't invite *them*! Not bloody Red Ted! You know what he's like, and Agnes is worse. They'll drink too much and fall on the food like it's their last meal. Ted'll be button-holding people and haranguing them about how the Labour Party betrayed the working class. Agnes will pester people to sign some harebrained petition. And they'll drive the caterers crazy asking if they're unionized. I hope you told them no Socialist Workers' leaflets or whatever it is they distribute on the class war. And fat Cousin Trotsky will –'

'It's not Trotsky, it's Leon,' murmured his grandmother, brushing a bug off her silk-covered shoulder. 'I did tell them no leaflets, but you know your auntie Agnes . . . she's never got over things. Still, I couldn't very well leave them out today, could I? Blood's thicker than water. I owe it to Mum.'

'I just hope they don't unfurl any damned banners!' Graham put on his sunglasses and skulked off.

Lady Carpenter snapped her compact shut. Something Graham had said on the telephone about that house in London . . . What was it? A piece missing from the puzzle, even after all the research the private detective had done. She and Bernie had tried and tried to work out what it was. Then she said, 'I wonder . . .' very loudly. She pushed away the microphone Katie thrust at her, got back into the car, rang her personal assistant in London and asked her to find out more about the canal near the house that Graham was trying to sell.

A battered airport taxi pulled up behind the silver Mercedes. Lady Carpenter checked the time on her little diamond watch, a last Christmas gift from Bernie. Just gone ten a.m. She hoped they'd all be here soon. They had a lot to think about. She retrieved one last item, a leather dossier, from the back seat of the car, as a stout woman enveloped in flowing black jersey, feet bulging out of laced sandals, was helped out of the taxi by the driver, who reached back for her walking-stick. Her grey hair was coming loose from an untidy bun and she seemed hot and uncomfortable. Two teenagers holding McDonald's cups got out behind her, a boy in a baseball cap and a dark-haired girl in jeans and sandals. They bickered in some foreign language as the woman adjusted a large handbag on her arm and smoothed her clothes. Leaning heavily on her stick, she walked towards Lady Carpenter, followed by the teenagers. The girl raised her head and Lady Carpenter exclaimed. She was Tanni at that age, exactly.

Mrs Zayman looked bewildered. 'That's new,' she said, to her grandchildren, pointing at the housing estate beyond the pub, 'but otherwise, it's as I remembered it.' Perspiration beaded her upper lip and she looked back at the taxi, as if she was having second thoughts and might decide to get back into it. 'It's funny. Looking around I can remember so much – Evangeline working in the garden and all the vegetables, my sewing basket, Elsie and her poisons, Alice cycling past to school, Frances in her land-girl uniform. The only thing I can't remember is leaving. At the sanatorium they told me to rest, and not to worry, that the mind forgets what it needs to, that amnesia is nature's way of protecting us. Ah, well . . .' She shrugged.

The taxi's arrival took Katie by surprise. She signalled to the cameraman to catch the first minutes of the reunion, bound to be emotional. 'Handkerchiefs at dawn,' muttered the cameraman to the soundman. 'Here we go!'

The two women looked at each other, then bent stiffly and hugged.

'Oh, Tanni! It's been so long!'

'Elsie, my dear!' They rocked back and forth in their embrace. The teenagers stood back uncertainly. The taxi driver unloaded a suitcase and two backpacks, then drove off.

'We've just been watching the second war bride arrive,' Katie announced dramatically, to the camera. 'That's Antoinette Zayman with two of her grandchildren, Shifra and Chaim, who have flown in from Israel. Just before the war, she married Bruno Zayman, the distinguished historian, and came to England. Professor Zayman was unfortunately too ill to make the trip from Israel, so Mrs Zayman is escorted by two of her – let's see – several grandchildren! We'll go over and speak to the ladies now!'

Albert Hawthorne tapped the girl on her shoulder. 'What, Granddad?' she asked, looking up from her book.

He was pointing a shaking finger across the green. 'They was both slips of girls when they came – right when the war started, that was. All big eyes, scared to death. It was that Mrs Fairfax brought them here. Always meddlin', that woman.'

On the opposite side of the green a wooden door opened. It was set in the mellow brick of an old garden wall that surrounded the Princess Elizabeth Convalescent Home, with its fire escapes and ugly double glazing. A slim figure in a red dress and hat slipped out, letting the door bang carelessly behind her.

Katie whirled round. 'And that is the third war bride, Mrs Evangeline Fairfax, now making her way across from the convalescent home, which, before the war, was . . . was . . . the home of . . .' Katie checked her notes, but couldn't find it '. . . somebody in the village,' she finished lamely.

Mrs Fairfax was wearing a large straw hat with a bunch of fake cherries pinned to the brim, which wobbled disconcertingly as she walked. Up close, it was somewhat battered, like the worn leather clutch bag with a rhine-stone clasp and the open-toed shoes. Ignoring Katie and the cameras bearing down on her, she cried, 'Elsie! As I live and breathe!'

She threw her arms round Lady Carpenter, who said, 'Blimey!' as she was engulfed in a fog of cheap sherry and Chanel No. 5.

Mrs Zayman, breathing heavily and leaning on her stick, moved forward and threw her arms open. 'Evangeline!'

She hugged and kissed Mrs Fairfax, then wrinkled her nose. She stood back and prodded the two teenagers, who stepped forward and shook hands awkwardly.

'Chaim,' said the boy. 'Pleased to meet you.'

'Hello, I'm Shifra,' said the girl.

'You don't half look like your grandmother,' Lady Carpenter exclaimed. 'My grandson Graham's there somewhere.' She waved vaguely in the direction of the cottages.

Mrs Fairfax's head swivelled back and forth on her wrinkled neck. She had had a mild stroke, two years before, and the local doctor had warned her to stay off the drink unless she wanted to court another, massive one, but she hadn't paid any attention. Now she smiled broadly and said, 'Well, what nice-lookin' grandchildren you've got, Tanni. Anna's two youngest, aren't they? Hmmm?' She hiccuped. 'How's Bruno doing? I heard he wasn't well. And what's Johnny up to?'

'Bruno's about the same,' said Mrs Zayman. 'The surgery went well, thank God, but he has to keep quiet. Johnny's the same as ever, working hard, happy with his family.' She took refuge in frowning at the fluffy microphone that hovered over their heads. The soundman ducked back just in time as she raised her stick and aimed a swipe at him. Shifra and Chaim stared at their grandmother in amazement.

'Well, hasn't it been such a long time since we were together? Everybody's so scattered, what with Elsie and Bernie livin' abroad so much of the time, Tanni and Bruno in Israel and Alice in the States . . . but here we are together at last!' Mrs Fairfax struggled to regain her train of thought. 'My condolences about Bernie.'

Lady Carpenter's face became a mask. Evidently she was trying not to cry.

'Read his obituary when the papers came. Lung cancer . . . terrible . . . Those awful Woodbines he used to smoke, until the Americans came and he got all those cigarettes from the PX – made a fortune reselling them, remember? Never missed a trick, Bernie didn't. We'll sure miss him today, won't we, Elsie? I heard that rebuilding the church and this whole VE Day celebration was his idea, y'all having got married here and everything. He was a man of surprises, wasn't he?' The expression on Lady Carpenter's face told Mrs Fairfax she hadn't said the right thing. She changed tack. 'And look at your outfit!' She rushed on, like an express train going nowhere, unable to stop. 'I declare, it's so pretty . . . and that hat! Well, it's hard to believe it's been so long since we all lived here together. It's been, well, simply ages!' she gushed. The cherries bobbed and jiggled.

'Evangeline, pay attention! The Women's Institute said they'd leave refreshments for us in the new parish hall at the church. Nobody has been allowed in yet so we shall be private. As soon as Alice gets here, with some things she looked up,' Lady Carpenter muttered, 'I'll have something to show you. Oh, bloody hell, that girl with the microphone is a right nuisance!'

Lady Carpenter saw that the cameraman and the blonde woman babbling into a microphone were moving closer. 'Where do you suppose Alice is?' she interrupted, loudly enough for Katie to hear.

'That will be Alice Osbourne Lightfoot,' said Katie, forced to turn to the camera, as the old ladies had their backs to her again, 'who became a war bride when she married a US Air Force pilot in 1944 . . .'

Just then a grey Ford Fiesta with a hire-company sticker crunched noisily to a stop on the gravel. A moment later a tall woman with curly grey hair, wearing a beige trouser suit and clean white sports shoes, got out and fished an expensive cream leather shoulder-bag, a camera and a raincoat from the passenger seat. She looked at the sky, then folded the raincoat neatly and put it back. She locked the car and headed for the three women by the marquee.

'This is Mrs Lightfoot's first trip back to England since she left on a transport ship full of war brides bound for the USA in 1946,' Katie warbled, as the camera panned to a photograph of a liner with women crowded at the rails, waving handkerchiefs. 'And here are Colonel and Mrs Lightfoot on their wedding day!' The camera rested on a black and white photo of a smiling young woman in a matching coat and skirt, her hair in a victory roll. She was holding a bouquet and the arm of a tall man in uniform grinning down at her, with a carnation in his buttonhole and his hat under his arm. They stood on the steps of a dark Edwardian church, framed by an arched doorway. In the right-hand corner the hem of a vicar's cassock and his feet were visible.

Now another old man had wandered into the camera's field. He paused, and tipped his hat to Katie, revealing a lopsided face disfigured by old scar tissue, and partially obscured by a long shock of white hair. 'Forgive me. Hugo de Balfort,' he said. She knew immediately who he was: he had been badly injured trying to rescue his invalid father during the terrible fire that had destroyed Gracecourt. Katie's note told her that Sir Leander's body had been retrieved in his melted wheelchair.

'Oh, Sir Hugo, just the ticket,' Katie said gamely. 'You spent the war in Crowmarsh Priors, didn't you? You were medically unfit for the services but you were doing work that was just as important in farming the family estate. I'm sure most of our viewers know that feeding the country was crucial to the war effort. You also served in the Home Guard with Mr Hawthorne there. Can you tell our viewers about the Home Guard?'

Sir Hugo paused, leaning on his stick. 'All a long time ago, my dear.'

'Tell us what the Home Guard did.'

'We were supposed to drill, so we did for a bit – though, with so few of us, there didn't seem much point in marching up and down the green in formation. After a while we gave it up. Churchill ordered that we were to "fight them on the beaches" when the Germans came. Not sure what with. We started out drilling with broom handles. They promised us Sten guns. Teapots with a barrel. Jolly useless.'

'Now, I believe, Sir Hugo, that the Home Guard were also responsible for finding any German pilots who were shot down. Weren't there some camouflaged anti-aircraft-gun emplacements nearby on the downs?'

'Useless,' muttered Sir Hugo. 'There were, but they weren't usually manned. The gunners were needed on the coast, and we'd found in the Blitz that the ack-ack guns weren't very effective, you know. Didn't seem possible we could hold out much longer. Thought the invasion was a sure thing.'

'And did your Home Guard ever capture any Germans?'

'Bombers were sometimes shot down or crashed on the downs but the men in them were usually killed, I believe. We did find two chaps dead once, and the vicar insisted we buried them at St Gabriel's.'

'You probably saw the programme on television the other night, Sir Hugo, when they interviewed a retired air marshal who said that Military Intelligence knew the Germans had help from spies or Nazi sympathizers in southern England, who sent weather reports to the Luftwaffe – their bombing raids coincided remarkably with clear weather on this side of the Channel. Would that have been likely, do you think?'

'My housekeeper has the telly on at night so I did see a bit, but the air marshal's memory is probably not what it was, my dear. Would have been difficult to do anything like that secretly. Everyone lived so close together in those days, you see, everyone mucking in, doing their bit. We were all pulling together. There was a general paranoia about spies and German agents and so on. Ridiculous, really.'

'But the air marshal said . . . Ah, do please excuse me, our war brides are disappearing into the church hall, and I must try to catch them. Thank you for sharing your recollections, Sir Hugo.'

Interviewing old people was exhausting, Katie thought.

She wound up the first segment of the show as the cameraman filmed the war brides going into the church.

'So there they are, today's special guests, the four war brides. Antoinette Joseph Zayman, a refugee. Former land girl Elsie Pigeon Carpenter, who married her childhood sweetheart. Evangeline Fontaine Fairfax, an American who married a dashing English officer and followed her heart. And Alice Osbourne Lightfoot, a girl from this village who taught at the school while serving as an air-raid warden. Later she joined the Women's Voluntary Service in London, where she met her husband and was whisked away eventually to live happily ever after in the USA. Though time and distance have separated them, the ladies have come here today to share their memories and celebrate their enduring friendship, one of the happier legacies of the Second World War. Above all, this is their day and those are their stories.

'For Albion Television's *Heart of England VE Day Fiftieth Anniversary Special*, this is Katie Hamilton-Jones. Now we go back to the studio, because it's time for the news.'

The two teenagers who had got out of the taxi with Mrs Zayman were tossing a Frisbee back and forth. The pub had just opened and a blackboard outside announced that beer would be sold today at wartime prices. Lady Carpenter's grandson wondered if the pretty girl beside the old man in his Home Guard uniform would like a drink . . .

The girl with the microphone who had been yammering about war brides a few feet from his deck-chair had finally stopped. Through half-closed eyes Albert watched the

432

four women follow the vicar towards the churchyard, where the new parish hall stood next to the church. Someone was missing, but he was ninety-five now and his memory came and went. A musty smell rose as the sun warmed his old wool uniform, and in the distance, he thought he heard the whistle of a train . . .

34. Crowmarsh Priors, Midday, 8 May 1995

In St Gabriel's churchyard the new vicar gestured expansively at the shrouded tower. The old ladies shaded their eyes, looking up and nodding at what he said. Then he waved towards the overgrown churchyard. 'You probably can't imagine it, but things are much improved since the work started, Lady Carpenter. It was a dreadful mess, hadn't been touched since the bomb. It took ages to clear the area in front of the tower. The contractors said the graveyard is sinking in some places – they weren't sure how stable the ground was. The engineers decided it might be too dangerous to bring in heavy machinery at the back where the older graves are, so we had them trim the undergrowth by hand as best they could in time for the service. But the old knight's tomb is still over there.' He pointed towards the back of the church where a lichened stone sarcophagus lay half buried on its side.

The ladies could see the familiar helmeted figure. Its face was now entirely worn away except for the nose, but the crossed legs, a sword and a shield, with traces of the de Balfort coat of arms, were still visible. The vicar racked his brains to remember some interesting titbit from the newly printed church brochure, on sale for twenty pence. 'It's one of the de Balforts, of course. Bit of inscription still on the side. You see that his legs are crossed at the knee? That meant he went twice on the Crusades. Ankles crossed, once, thighs crossed, three times. The tomb's position is rather interesting, off by itself like that. Normally you would have expected a knight from the most powerful local family to be buried inside the church under the floor.'

Elsie turned to Alice and raised her eyebrows.

'So interesting to see it again. I'd forgotten exactly where it was,' murmured Alice, strolling towards it through the weeds and wildflowers, then leaning over as if to read the inscription.

'Do mind the nettles, Mrs Lightfoot,' called the vicar, as one stung his hand.

'It's all right, I'm in the Garden Club,' Alice told him inconsequentially. Out of sight, her age-spotted hand with the huge diamond engagement ring and a diamond-studded wedding band fumbled under the ivy. Where was it? She was sure it had been just about . . . there. She felt the knobbly skull on the corner of the tomb, then pushed it as hard as she could to one side. Nothing happened. She pushed again, harder, remembering to twist. The ivy rustled, there was a scraping noise and a small gap appeared as one side of the tomb shifted. She looked round to see if the vicar had heard but he was talking animatedly and hadn't noticed. She pushed again. There was a louder, grinding noise this time, of stone on stone.

This time Evangeline heard. 'Come look at this, Vicar. It's real sweet.' She pulled him away to the other side of the graveyard. The others joined her to look at a Victorian stone angel standing guard over three sunken gravestones. 'It's holding a smaller angel's hand.'

'Are you sure, Mrs Fairfax?' asked the vicar, batting at the creeper growing over the angel's wings to have a closer look.

'Bend down and you'll see it – there, under the right wing,' urged Evangeline. Sure enough, a little angel was peeking out.

'Wot I say is, let's go in and freshen up,' said Elsie. She knew that the last thing Tanni needed was for them to start talking about baby angels and wherever *that* might lead. 'We'll let you get on with things, Vicar. You'll want to be outside, waiting for the bishop.'

'Oh, Lady Carpenter, I'm quite happy to stay and –'

'Don't let us keep you. We'd like to put our feet up for a bit, have a cup of tea and a chat. It's been a long time since we saw each other,' said Elsie, firmly.

'Oh, quite. I'll just pop in and make sure the coffee things are there.' The others moved on but Evangeline slipped behind the angel's outspread wings, took a half-bottle of vodka from her handbag, unscrewed the top and had a big swallow.

'Let's get in out of the heat. It's quite comfortable in our nice new parish hall.' The vicar ushered Elsie and Tanni inside. 'Lovely new kitchenette, thanks to you, Lady Carpenter. Here's the kettle, just the ticket. No one's used it yet except the ladies who were decorating the church earlier – yes, good as their word, they've left coffee, sugar, cups, spoons . . .' he rattled on. 'And here's some long-life milk in the fridge and a plate of sandwiches! The note on top says, "Welcome Back to the War Brides! From the Women's Institute." Lovely!'

The vicar bustled about, rattling cups, asking about

milk and sugar, putting the kettle on to boil. 'Tickety-boo!' he chirped, as it began to hum.

'How nice,' said Tanni, lowering herself on to a chair. Elsie sat down too, still clutching her gloves, handbag and dossier. Her feet were swelling over the tops of her mauve pumps and the vicar was driving her crazy.

Evangeline came in and, hat now lopsided, drifted to the window that looked towards the downs. She pushed it open and leaned out. 'Here comes Alice,' she said.

'While this boils, I'd like to know more about the fellow who was vicar during the war – Hammet, his name was. You all knew him, I'm sure. Cambridge man, I understand. I want to mention him in today's sermon, but I'm not sure what to say. Haven't been able to find out much about him, really. The church records went missing in the confusion after the war. Was he married? Any family? I understand he died in 1947.' He looked at Lady Carpenter for confirmation. 'His heart, I believe? Strain of the war, no doubt.' He handed round mugs of coffee.

Evangeline murmured something that sounded like 'You could say it was his heart, yes,' as she took one. 'A heart murmur, we heard. You'd never know it to look at him, but his heart gave out, just like that, one day.' She walked over to the window and pointed. 'My husband is buried over there, next to his mother,' she told the vicar. 'After the church was hit they extended the graveyard into that field at the back. See the fence round it? Richard and Penelope, Nell Hawthorne, the Barrowses and I can't remember who else is back there. I plan on being buried there myself. Next to Richard.'

'Sandwiches, ladies?'

For a minute they ate in silence. Alice gazed at her surroundings in amazement, remembering how the old vestry had smelt of beeswax and mice. Now it smelt of new Formica.

The vicar had settled himself comfortably with coffee and his fourth sandwich and did not look like moving. 'I'm going to spend a penny,' said Elsie, decisively. 'Which way to the ladies'?'

There was a flurry of agreement.

'I might as well powder my nose,' said Alice clutching her handbag.

'Good idea,' said Tanni, heaving herself to her feet.

'Excuse me, Vicar,' murmured Evangeline, putting down her untouched coffee.

'It's just along that corridor,' said the vicar, leaping to his feet and pointing down a hallway that smelt of new carpet. 'I suppose I'd better get on with putting together a few words about this Hammet fellow. I'll be in the little room at the other end of the corridor.'

But the women's heads were together and they were no longer listening to him.

The ladies' had been done up with strawberry-patterned wallpaper, festoon blinds at the windows and pale green woodwork that matched the pale green wash-basins and lavatories. There was a small sitting room, with armchairs and a sofa with quilted covers, designed as an anteroom for brides and their attendants. 'Got it to ourselves. Good,' said Elsie, and sank down on the sofa. 'Now, we're all here because we want to know what happened to Frances.' She opened her dossier, and Alice reached into her shoulder-bag for a sheaf of notes. 'Alice and I've worked out bits, and maybe if we put our heads together we can figure out the rest. We all wondered how Frances could have disappeared without a by-your-leave. Even her father never knew what happened to her, and the police weren't interested. But my Bernie wouldn't give up. He fancied her, most men did, but it was more than that. He said it wasn't like her and his sixth sense told him something wasn't right. He said we owed it to her to find out what happened. For a long time he believed she must have had an accident, one of those wartime things, you know, people killed by bombs and never identified, or even foul play, and he put the word out with his underworld mates, offered a reward, even, but no one knew anything, not a dickie-bird.

'Finally he had to drop it, but he never forgot Frances. Later, after he'd made all his money advisin' the Treasury how to make banknotes and passports counterfeit-proof, he started lookin' for Frances again, only this time he could afford to hire detectives. They never turned up much, apart from her pictures in the paper when she was a débutante and got into trouble, and something about her being due to inherit a lot of money when she got married. Rebuilding the church was the best excuse he could find for excavating down the tunnel. He always wondered if she'd gone back another time after that night . . .'

'After what night?' asked Tanni. 'I don't remember what happened to the church. It was months later that I learned a bomb hit it. Yet if there was a bomb in the village I must have known about it at the time. Amnesia, the doctors say. It happens if you have a terrible shock.'

439

Tanni's face was suddenly pasty. 'But I feel there was something else and I don't know what it is. Why can't I remember?'

Alice exchanged a significant look with Elsie and Evangeline, and all three shook their heads. Bruno had rung them to say Tanni was coming, and to warn them that she had never recovered any memory of her dead baby, Rebecca, and the doctors were certain she never would. As far as Bruno was concerned, she had had enough grief to bear after the war, when she learned that she had lost her parents in Auschwitz and her twin sisters at a camp in France. Being unable to remember Rebecca was a blessing in disguise, he said. Tanni's friends must be careful not to mention her.

Alice and Elsie had put down the phone with a mixed sense of relief and guilt. If Tanni didn't remember anything about that time she clearly didn't recall their plan to rescue Lili and Klara, or that they were meant to be in the tunnel the night the bomb fell. That was a blessing too, more than Bruno realized. Since Bruno had never known about their rescue operation there was no point in telling him he must be wrong about the girls' having died in France. Any explanation would have been impossible after what had happened. Alice hoped Evangeline, who seemed unreliable now, wouldn't let something slip.

'Evangeline, you were the last one of us to see Frances,' Alice said quickly, before Evangeline could blunder.

The cherries bobbed as Evangeline nodded. 'It wasn't long after the fire at Gracecourt. She must have been catching the London train, because she wasn't in her land-girl uniform. She waved as she went past the house. I remember it clear as day. I never told anybody this but I had made her a promise that if anything happened to her ... but you knew Frances – you couldn't imagine anything happening to her and I kept expecting her to reappear. I'll tell you in a minute what I promised. You go on, Elsie.'

Elsie continued. 'A few years ago, when Bernie was sick with the chemotherapy, he liked me to read him the papers. One day, I spotted this.'

She reached into the dossier, took out a newspaper photograph and spread it on the vanity unit. 'Recognize anybody?' The caption said: 'Unidentified Wartime Photo of French Resistance'. The others crowded round to look.

'Who is it? I never saw any of those people before,' said Evangeline, after a moment.

'Can't say I have either,' said Alice, peering through her bifocals.

But Tanni exclaimed, 'Yes!' and pointed to a woman in a headscarf and rough shoes. She was talking to someone out of the frame, oblivious of the photographer.

There were gasps as the others peered more closely.

'It looks sort of like Frances, I guess, but ...'

'I'm sure it's her. Definitely.'

'It's Frances. I'd recognize her anywhere,' Tanni said positively, 'but she's pregnant.'

They looked at each other. 'What on earth was she doing in France? And who could her baby's father have been?' asked Alice. 'Some Frenchman?'

Evangeline shook her head, cherries bobbing wildly. 'Noooo ...'

The vicar knocked on the door. 'Ladies? Everything all right in there?'

'Fine, thank you. We're putting our feet up for a minute longer,' bellowed Elsie. She lowered her voice. 'No idea who the father was. But first things first. Bernie hired another detective right away, first time he'd taken an interest in anything since they made him retire from the Treasury. Even went into remission for a bit. The detective learned that the photo was probably taken some time late in 1944, near the eastern French border with Germany.'

'But how did she get there with a war on?'

'I know! Bernie and me asked ourselves that over and over again. It kept us awake nights. Then Bernie had an idea. He invited an old Treasury mate, who'd been in Military Intelligence during the war, to dinner, poured enough expensive wine into him to drown an elephant and showed him the photo. The mate hummed and hawed, pretended he had no idea, but that was because they weren't supposed to say anything about what they'd done in the war. We could tell he was startled but Bernie always got what he wanted. He kept topping up the bloke's port, and finally he said she'd been recruited for something under cover, because he definitely remembered the girl in the picture from one of the training centres, an admiral's daughter, he said. Stunning girl, but clever, too, very determined. One of the controllers, funny little man, was half in love with her. The woman in the newspaper photo looked plainer than he remembered her but he said it was probably a disguise and he was dead certain it was the same girl. So Bernie asked, "Was Frances Falconleigh 'er name?" and the man said, "That was it!"'

'A few days later the mate rang, said something'd

occurred to him. All the SOE agents dropped behind enemy lines were accounted for after the war, alive or dead, and he'd checked but there was no Frances Falconleigh among them. So she wasn't SOE, at least not in the beginning, but she might have been recruited for Churchill's secret home resistance thing, the Auxiliary Units. They went through the same training as the SOE, and by the autumn of 1944 a lot of SOE agents in eastern France had been betrayed and arrested, tortured and executed or sent to concentration camps. Someone like Frances, trained for an Auxiliary Unit, might have been parachuted into eastern France to take a captured SOE agent's place. He seemed to remember Frances was keen to be posted to France but she was young and they felt she might be a bit of a loose cannon.'

Elsie sighed and shook her head. 'And all that time we knew her, we thought she was on a land-girl committee! The detective found records of the training camps for the Auxis and the SOE where they taught all kinds of things, like surviving in the field, hand-to-hand combat, how to use explosives, dynamite and dodgy ones called "sticky-bombs". At one training centre the Shanghai Police trained them in interrogation. And silent killing.'

They digested this for a minute.

'Alice looked some things up too. Tell us, Alice.'

Alice opened her bag and took out a yellow legal pad of notes. 'After she found the photo, Elsie wrote asking what we ought to do next. Well, Joe's nephew was at the University of Georgia doing a PhD on something about wartime France, so I went to the university library in Athens and got him to help me. He was a little surprised that his auntie Alice wanted to know about resistance movements, but he was real sweet.'

She picked up the pad and read, ' "France was mostly liberated by the autumn of 1944, but there was a big push to the east by the Allies into Germany. On that border of France, however, collaborators were actively helping the Germans to save their own skins. The Allies wanted the French collaborators eliminated but they didn't want it generally known that they were using specially trained agents to assassinate them. Officially the British War Office disapproved of such tactics." Officially.'

'You don't think Frances –'

Evangeline interrupted Tanni, drawling, 'I don't know . . . but explosives? Maybe. After Alice left, remember the fire at Gracecourt that killed Sir Leander and put Hugo in hospital? I was the only one of us still here, and some people in the village said they'd heard an explosion in the direction of Gracecourt, and wondered if another bomb had exploded. Sometimes they didn't explode right away . . . Anyhow, it wasn't long after that Frances disappeared.'

'My wedding was on the thirtieth of August 1944,' said Alice. 'I rang Evangeline to tell her I was getting married, and asked her to let Frances know, because I couldn't reach her. I guessed she'd gone up to London, but she'd given me her pretty dressing-case and I wanted to let her know I was taking it on my honeymoon.'

'And none of us ever saw her again,' said Elsie. 'But our detective told us that by 1943 they were hunting for a spy network in southern England, with a centre of operations near the Sussex coast, where they expected the invasion to take place. It wasn't till Graham said something this morning about a house he's got for sale that a bell rang in my head – one of those missing pieces Bernie and I never could find. The house is near an old canal in London and Graham's client was worried about her child falling in. Graham said not to worry, it was filled in during the war because at night it reflected light so the Germans used it to navigate.'

'But, Elsie, what's that got to do with Frances?'

Elsie picked up another file with 'de Balfort' on the cover and opened it. 'This. Bernie let drop to the detective that Hugo de Balfort wanted to marry Frances, so he might as well look into the de Balforts. He came back and said they must have wanted Frances's money, because by the time the war came the de Balforts were ruined and unless Hugo married a rich woman, like his father had, they'd lose Gracecourt. But he also said the de Balforts might have been under observation. A lot of Germans and Austrians with Nazi connections had stayed at Gracecourt before the war, friends Hugo had made on his travels.

'I remember Leander de Balfort spending a fortune on one crazy scheme after another, landscaping, pavilions and deer parks and so forth, to impress his friends. Lady Marchmont disapproved of it all,' said Alice. 'Aesthetes annoyed her. Hugo's mother had been an heiress and Lady Marchmont could never understand why Sir Leander had wasted his wife's fortune so irresponsibly. It was one continuous house-party for years, a frightfully smart and glamorous set.' She sighed. So many years later the memory of the shooting lunch to which Lady Marchmont had dragged her still made her cheeks burn. 'The women were that rather brittle society sort, with marcelled hair and rouge, all flirting madly with each other's husbands.'

'Lady Marchmont didn't know the half of it,' Elsie told her. 'The detective said he had a hunch he wanted to follow and asked if we'd pay for him to go investigating in Germany. Bernie agreed, and a month later the detective was back with a pile of letters from Sir Leander he'd unearthed in a German archive. Got 'em all copied, and guess where he got the money to do all that building Lady Marchmont disapproved of?'

'Where?'

'According to the letters, his German friends had persuaded him that a Nazi takeover in England would be good for toffs like the de Balforts, that it was the only way to save Gracecourt. They paid Sir Leander a lot of money in the years before the war, laying the groundwork, like, for marching into England. But he spent it all. Those pools, that water-garden thing? They were designed by a famous German architect, big Nazi supporter, as it turned out. But the Germans didn't take over in England as fast as Sir Leander'd expected. So he was desperate for money and depended on Hugo to marry Frances, for her fortune, like he'd got Venetia's.'

'You mean Leander de Balfort was one of the traitors we were supposed to watch out for?' Alice was appalled. 'To think that anyone in our midst . . .' She was overwhelmed.

Elsie snorted. 'There's worse! Sir Leander's Nazi friends knew he was desperate to carry on the de Balfort line. To string him along, they let him into a secret, that they were doing experiments – all that nonsense about breeding a master race people didn't hear about until after the war. He wanted the de Balforts to benefit from that. And here's a copy of a letter he wrote them, about how he'd found "a perfect specimen of womanhood" for his son. He goes on about how as an "artist" he wanted to design a master race of de Balforts by breeding his son and Frances and, if the Nazi doctors were right, they'd have twins over and over again. He got quite excited about Frances having twenty or thirty de Balforts, who'd each go on to have twenty or thirty, and so on till England was crawling with the little buggers. Makes you sick, it does. And here's the copy of that letter.' They passed it round in silence. Then Alice noticed that Tanni looked as if she might faint and forced her head between her knees.

The vicar knocked again. 'Ladies? Everything tickety-boo in there? It's nearly time for the service and the bishop's car has just pulled up.'

Elsie glowered at the door and lowered her voice. 'So Hugo was under a lot of pressure from his father to get Frances to say yes. I don't know whether he knew what his father was doing. The letters don't say anything about bombing the church or the tunnel . . .'

'What tunnel? You said something about a tunnel before,' said Tanni. No one knew what to say. 'Let's get back,' she went on. 'Shifra and Chaim will be worried.' She felt ill and breathless – another anxiety attack. The room began to close round her so she did her deep-breathing exercises as she had been taught, but her heart was pounding: she had to get out of there.

'Ladies!' bellowed the vicar, rapping sharply at the door. The bishop was a stickler for punctuality.

They stood up, smoothed their clothes and picked up their handbags.

'We'll finish later,' said Elsie. 'Now we've got this ruddy service to get through.'

Outside St Gabriel's a procession was forming. Two acolytes holding crosses fidgeted, while the bishop, the vicar, the churchwardens and twenty elderly residents of the Princess Elizabeth Convalescent Home milled at the entrance. The men all wore their old uniforms and some had medals. Several of the women were in service uniform. Those who were not wore hats and gloves. They all stood as upright as they could. All had walking-sticks or Zimmer frames.

Everyone was waiting for the four war brides to walk down the aisle and be seated.

At the door of the church Elsie closed her eyes and remembered her wedding day, Bernie fidgeting at the altar, his look of relief as she came towards him in the splendid wedding dress, step-pause-step-pause, on Albert's arm. Watching Bernie's eyes widen at her appearance, then him taking her hand from Albert and hanging on to it for dear life. Saying, 'I will,' too loudly. She bit her tongue hard to stop the tears spilling over. 'Gran, come on, now,' whispered Graham, giving her arm a little tug.

Tanni took her place between her grandchildren, followed by Evangeline and Alice, who had chosen to walk together.

*

448

'Thought they'd never make it,' muttered Katie, to the cameraman, as the war brides and their escorts moved slowly down the aisle between the pews, which were draped in red, white and blue bunting. 'But what a great shot.'

35. Crowmarsh Priors, Evening, VE Day 1995

The service was over, the bishop had blessed the new buildings, there had been a lavish tea on trestle tables in the marquee on the green. Several elderly inhabitants of the Princess Elizabeth Convalescent Home sat together, walking frames behind their chairs.

Out of the corner of her eye Katie saw Elsie and Alice walking across to Evangeline, who was heading for the parish hall. Then the three turned, came over and spoke to Tanni, who took money from her handbag and gave it to Shifra and Chaim. 'But not too much to drink,' she told them. The teenagers grinned, then set off towards the pub where the young people had collected and were busily eyeing each other.

Katie moved in quickly to get her interview.

Elsie answered her questions, wishing the girl would stop tossing her hair about. 'Yes, my husband would have been pleased the church was rebuilt,' she said, not really concentrating, just agreeing to what Katie said so she would finish the interview and go away. It was so annoying when she was trying to concentrate on putting the last pieces together. Her big hat nodded steadily. 'Yes, he died two years ago. Yes, it was a great pity. Yes, good to hear the bell ring again. Yes, brings back memories. Romantic gesture, yes, it was, my husband was very romantic. Oh, yes, rags to riches, you could say that. Yes, yes . . . The war feels like yesterday, just like yesterday. You put it so well, love.'

Katie gushed her thanks and moved on to the large woman in black.

'My memories?' asked Tanni bleakly. 'What do I remember?' She sounded astonished to be asked.

'Tell her about the wedding dress for Lady Carpenter, Bubbie,' prompted Shifra.

'Ooh yes!' gushed Katie, flashing a wide-eyed 'oooh' look at the camera. 'The ladies will want to hear about *that*!'

Tanni warmed to her subject, explaining where they had got it and a little more about clothes rationing, how they'd made new clothes out of old ones, and how she had sewed for the village. When she'd finished, Alice and Evangeline looked up from their tea to see Katie and her microphone hovering. 'Now, I want to hear all about our last two war brides! Tell our viewers how you met your husbands and what you did in the war!' Katie burbled. 'What are your most lasting memories of those years?'

Alice looked thoughtful, as if she had trouble remembering. 'Um, well, rationing, of course. Food and clothes were in short supply and most people were terribly patriotic and tried to make a little go a long way. Make do and mend, you know. Victory gardens. Anderson shelters in the gardens. Evacuees. Trying to keep morale up, not let the side down . . . quick weddings. Like mine.'

Katie said, 'Ooooh!'

'Not what you're thinking, dear. It was just that you had to make up your mind quickly with the war on. No dawdling.'

'How long had you known Colonel Lightfoot before he popped the question?' asked Katie.

Alice smiled. 'A weekend. We met on a Friday night and married a week on Monday, at a church near my husband's air-force base. I pulled strings and got leave. He pulled strings and found a chaplain.'

'I remember the music,' said Evangeline, dreamily. Her handbag was open and Katie saw a bottle of vodka.

'Now, there's something no one else has mentioned!' said Katie. 'The music! Those jolly sing-songs! "Roll Out The Barrel", "We'll Meet Again", Dame Vera Lynn . . .'

'No, I hated singalongs. I'm talking about swing and jazz,' said Evangeline, looking off into the distance. 'The lindy-hop. Jazz clubs in Soho. Glenn Miller.'

'Oh, yes, Glenn Miller!' said Katie.

'Yes, I've got a big collection of records. I knew someone . . . a musician in Paris . . . always wanted to play with Glenn Miller. He used to send me records . . . All the records he played on . . . My husband, Richard, loved listening to them. Richard was torpedoed and . . . was never very well after that, and the thing he liked best was those records. I had to play them for him every day . . .'

Simon prompted Katie through her earpiece and she turned to the cameras. 'For those of you too young to remember, Glenn Miller was a famous American band-leader who used to travel to entertain the troops, just like Gracie Fields and Vera Lynn. Unfortunately his plane disappeared over the English Channel in . . .'

'December 1944,' said Simon.

'In December 1944. Tragically some of his band were on the plane too,' finished Katie.

Evangeline nodded.

'Excuse us,' said Elsie, and the four women moved away.

The fête was in full swing. The caterers had finally cleared the marquee tables of the tea things, replacing them with huge tubs of ice holding bottles of beer and white wine, corks drawn and replaced; the red wine was left open along the tables, with an array of plastic glasses, and squash for the children. A huge barbecue had been lit. Trays of sausages and kebabs had been brought out of a refrigerated lorry, and there were mountains of rolls and pitta bread, and vast bowls of salads. Young mothers in summer dresses sipped white wine and agreed on the impossibility of a school run all the way to Tunbridge Wells, while their husbands held plastic beer mugs and asked each other if they had talked to the fellow in the tie who was big in property and thought prices in Crowmarsh Priors could only go up.

Albert Hawthorne's pretty great-granddaughter brought Albert a half-pint of stout from the Gentlemen's Arms. 'I know wine doesn't agree with you, Granddad. The barman wouldn't let me or Graham pay for it when he heard it was for you,' she said. 'It's because you were in the Home Guard with his grandfather.'

'You're a good lass, Lizzie,' murmured Albert, taking a long drink. He'd need the lav soon, and that young man in the navy blazer and fancy tie hanging around Lizzie like a fly round jam could help him get up. He settled back in his deck-chair and wondered why stout didn't taste as it used to.

'Why are they going back to the church?' said Lizzie. 'They must have forgotten something.' The four war brides were walking away in a little group. The vicar didn't see them go because he was talking animatedly into Katie Hamilton-Jones's microphone about the crisis of faith today.

Katie was looking desperately over his head, hoping for a glimpse of her mother's friend, the event's patroness, to interview next.

'That old man's joined them, the one with the scarred face, Sir Hugo de Balfort,' said Lizzie to Graham. 'I guess they must all be a bit emotional, like you said your gran was, walking into church. They probably want a quiet chat away from the cameras. You can't get a word in edgeways with that woman bouncing around, sticking her microphone into your face. They look a bit tired, now they've all got canes to lean on. I heard your gran asking some of those people from the home if they could borrow theirs for a bit. She thinks of everything, doesn't she?'

'Just a quiet chat, Hugo,' Elsie murmured to Sir Hugo as they gathered round him, 'because you must have noticed an omission in today's service.'

'Frances Falconleigh,' said Evangeline.

'Oh, yes, Frances,' he said. 'What became of her? I was quite smitten by her at one point. Dashing girl, rather.'

'We want to show you something,' said Tanni.

'Ask you a question, actually,' interrupted Alice.

'At your service, naturally, ladies.' Sir Hugo bowed.

They reached St Gabriel's. They were out of sight of

the green now and in the shadow of the restored tower.

'Come with us,' said Elsie. 'It's back here.' She leaned on her cane as she walked. Her feet were killing her and it had been a long day. 'Come round the side here.'

'Ah, the old knight's tomb,' said Sir Hugo. 'Interesting story about that . . .'

'First let's talk about Frances. She found out that you and your father were signalling to the Germans during the war,' said Elsie, flatly. 'They always knew someone near the south coast was doing it. And that the signals were coming from the vicinity of Gracecourt.'

'I beg your pardon,' spluttered Hugo. 'Preposterous! How would I – or Father, who was an invalid – signal to anybody?'

'Your father spent a lot just before the war, money he didn't have once he'd run through your mother's fortune. The estate was in debt, on the verge of being sold. It would have been the end of the de Balforts at Gracecourt. Bernie checked. But suddenly there were new tennis courts, new stables and the water-garden. And if anybody knew how to get money from crime it was Bernie but even he, with all his contacts, couldn't trace how you'd managed it. But on your travels, you made friends with some Germans who later visited you at Gracecourt and offered your father a great deal of money in return for some favours.'

'Ridiculous!'

'It wasn't till today that I knew what you'd done. I worked it out from something my grandson said. Those long pools in the water-garden. Your father built them to German plans so the Germans could navigate by them.'

'Nonsense! How on earth could you navigate on a little bit of water?'

'On a clear night water reflects light, especially moonlight. Those long narrow pools pointed the way for the German planes. And you were the one who sent the weather reports so they'd know when it would be clear.'

Sir Hugo's eyes narrowed.

'Meanwhile Frances was bored with being a land girl, and her father's friends agreed she could train as an English resistance agent, but they decided to send her back to Crowmarsh Priors with instructions to watch you and your father.'

Alice stepped closer and Sir Hugo fell back a pace. 'The net was closing round you, wasn't it? Traitors and spies were shot. By then the German money was long gone and Frances wouldn't marry you. You thought she was sweet on Oliver Hammet so you started watching the church, to see how often she went there. But you also needed something else to sell to the Germans and, watching the vicarage, you discovered what we were doing, and you remembered the smugglers' tunnels, the ones I'd told you about when I lunched at Gracecourt before the war – Lady Marchmont dragged me along. I had too much sherry and started babbling, as I always did, because I never knew what to say to men. You were a terribly polite listener,' said Alice, 'and kept asking me questions. I told you all about it, reminding you that the de Balforts had had a hand in the smuggling, and that there was said to be an underground passage with an entrance in the churchyard.'

'Rubbish!'

'It occurred to you that you could sell that information to the Germans. It would have been valuable, knowing a secret way into the country for German troops. Your father was determined you should marry Frances and made you feel inadequate because you had not persuaded her, so before you sold them the location of the tunnel, you persuaded your German friends to jettison a bomb over the vicarage to eliminate your rival. They bombed the church and churchyard instead, on the night we were waiting for a rescue party to arrive with some children smuggled from France. Tanni's sisters.'

Alice suddenly realized what this information would do to Tanni and stopped. Elsie and Evangeline were looking horrified. But Tanni said, 'No ... I have always known there was something about that night, something very terrible. Now I remember. We tried to save them. We tried to save Lili and Klara ... but ...'

'Tanni ...'

'We all tried ... There was no other way. We had to take the chance.'

'Tanni ...'

'It's better that I know at last. I must see this through to the end,' said Tanni. Her voice was very calm.

'It was a long time ago.' Sir Hugo's voice had sunk to a whisper. 'And she preferred him to me.'

Elsie took over. 'Frances had been watching Gracecourt for some time. She went back there shortly before she disappeared, found your father alone, she thought, and forced the truth out of him, that Gracecourt was the centre of a British Nazi network. You were hiding and

457

overheard, but Frances was armed and you couldn't do anything. We don't know what happened next or how the fire started, though people say there was an explosion and Frances had access to sticky-bombs. They didn't expect you to live. But you did and you'd heard from Frances herself that she was an agent. And you got word to your superiors.'

'She went to France in the last months of the war,' Sir Hugo said.

'When you got out of hospital you sent the Germans her description,' Alice went on, 'and told them she was working for Military Intelligence, was dangerous and might turn up in France . . .'

Sir Hugo looked directly at her. 'The fool! She should have married me when I asked her,' he hissed. 'Father practically begged her. With her money we would have had no need of the Germans. How else was the family to survive? I offered her a chance. The de Balfort name would have reached new glory. The German scientists were perfecting genetic experiments . . .' His eyes glittered. 'When I think of what might have been! But now,' he made a terrible noise, half sob, half shout, 'it's all over! None of it matters now.'

The four old ladies had backed him against the tomb. 'Tell us what happened to Frances. How did you have your revenge?'

'The Germans shot her, of course,' he spat. 'Records are never secret if someone is determined to find them, even in wartime, and our supporters were at all levels of the government here. I became certain she was sent to eastern France. Many of the SOE circuits had been broken up and agents arrested there. The British sent replacements and, as I suspected, Frances was among them. The Germans found her in 1945 – February, near Ardennes. They sent me a message. She was discovered hiding in a maternity hospital, posing as a Frenchwoman who had just given birth. Normally they would have sent her to a prison camp. But with the Allies approaching they shot her at once.'

The four old women surrounded him. Then Elsie raised her cane and hit him as hard as she could. Tanni struck him from behind. Evangeline caught him hard across the knees and Alice on his head. There was a crack and he stumbled and fell to the ground. In fury they hit and prodded him with all their strength. The old man curled into a ball, trying to escape. He fought back until he hit his head on the tomb and lay stunned.

They looked down with loathing.

'Oh, Frances,' said Alice, breathing hard, 'to think of your being shot!'

'For Mum and Jem and Violet, and all the others you helped to kill,' panted Elsie.

'My family, Lili and Klara,' said Tanni, breathless too, 'and . . . all the innocent people, all the deaths . . . and . . . and . . . I remember now!' she cried. 'I had a baby, and it died . . . That night! I always knew it was something horrible, but I could never remember what. Oh, God!'

'Richard's convoy,' said Evangeline, swinging her cane like a woman possessed. 'He suffered, for twenty years I watched him suffer!'

'Frances!' said Alice. 'And Mummy! You helped kill them all, you fiend.'

'Push him in the tunnel and leave him!' Evangeline ordered.

'No, no no,' he wailed feebly.

'Push him in!'

Alice tottered backwards. She twisted the skull at the side of the tomb and the hinge swung open.

'Quick,' said Elsie, puffing. They all bent to roll him into the entrance beneath the lopsided knight. There was just room in the dark, narrow space. The old man fought back, scrabbling at the ground, but he was no match for their combined strength and anger.

There was a cry from the huddled figure as it disappeared into the black hole. Then something thudded at the bottom of the narrow steps. Alice swung the door shut. After all the years they had waited, it had been almost too easy. The four old ladies bent over their canes, breathing hard. Tanni was sobbing and moaning incoherently. Evangeline put her arms round her. 'Bruno tried to protect you, you know. He loves you.'

'Bernie's lawyers said there was never a chance of putting him in jail,' wheezed Elsie. 'We agreed he should pay,' she said, looking at the others for confirmation. 'We agreed?' The others nodded and smoothed their clothes. 'We'll go back now.'

'I wonder,' said Alice, 'what happened to Frances's baby?'

'You know, when I said we should look for the dad, Bernie got that ferrety look that always made me suspect something, but he said maybe Frances wanted that to be a secret,' said Elsie, leading the way. 'For an awful moment I thought, Surely it's not Bernie! But he saw the look and said no, before I could ask him. Then he said something else about how you had to keep promises, if that was the last thing you were asked. I don't know what he meant.'

'Great shot,' muttered Katie, to the cameraman, spotting the four ladies walking towards them from the church. Obviously tired, poor old things, especially Mrs Zayman, and looking their age in the twilight. Dishevelled too. 'Let's close with a shot of them and then the fireworks,' she said, as a loud bang filled the sky with sparkles.

She raised her microphone. 'Do you ladies have any final words for the viewers?'

'No, dear, we were just talking about war crimes. A bit tired now, I think. Excuse us.'

'Oh,' said Katie, not sure whether to pursue them.

'Get ready to wind up,' said Simon.

The microphone picked up the voice of the old man in the Home Guard uniform, wailing that he wanted another pint, he didn't want to go home yet. He was saying to no one in particular, 'There's only four. One's missing.'

'Who's missing, Granddad?'

'The one married the parson – Oliver . . . What was his name? I were a witness. Sudden, it was, in Tunbridge, church there. Bernie drove us. Oliver said something about a husband can't testify against his wife. Bernie laughed and said, was Frances planning on becoming a safe-cracker, then? Oliver told him sometimes you took things and people on faith, but he was lookin' at Frances when he said it. Bernie and me was sworn to secrecy, not to ever tell anyone, not Elsie or Nell or nobody. They

461

looked happy as Larry when it were over. Then they carried on in the village like nothing had happened. Frances kept coming and going, then she was gone for good. Left a letter with me for Oliver, told me to look after him if she didn't come back. Nell saw her before she disappeared and said if she hadn't known Frances wasn't married she would have sworn she was in the family way. Said you could always tell. Course, bein' sworn to secrecy, I couldn't say anything . . .'

'What a story, Granddad! What happened?'

'Don't remember, except we never saw her again after the last time. I finally gave him the letter, but he never said what was in it. Turned out he had a dicky heart, poor chap. Nobody knew, he looked right as rain. Died in 'forty-six or 'forty-seven. Nell said . . . Well, it were a long time ago. Long time ago.'

The barbecues were just hot ash. The sun was setting and the caterers were rattling empty bowls, trays and bottles back into their vans. The flowers drooped and the over-excited children, with ice-cream on their faces, were handed Union flags to wave in the background while Katie signed off and the credits rolled. The war brides posed with the vicar while the local paper snapped a picture. Fireworks exploded festively across the village.

'It's been a memorable day. And that's it from me, Katie Hamilton-Jones, for Albion Television. As we end this special edition of *Heart of England*, we hope you've enjoyed being with us at this poignant memorial celebration. We've heard mostly from the older generation today, so we'll let the next generation have the last word.'

The camera panned to a mob of children bobbing in

the background behind her, clutching ice-creams and flags.

'Have you all had a lovely day?'

Behind her the children jumped up and down, waved their flags frantically and shouted, 'Yes!'

The credits rolled.

Epilogue: 12 May 1995, London, Missing Persons' Helpline

'Missing persons helpline, Lily speaking. Can I help you? . . . Yes, let me get a form. There we go. Now, I need to get some information from you. Name of the person missing? Sir Hugo de Balfort. Address? . . . Thank you. Age? . . . Eighty-five or so you think . . . No, that will do. And when was the last time you saw him? At breakfast in the bungalow . . . Where did he go missing? . . . Never came back from a VE Day celebration near his home in – where was that? Spell Crowmarsh Priors for me. On the bank holiday, was it? . . . Yes, a lot of places celebrated over the weekend.

'And you are? . . . Miss Pomfret. Annie Pomfret. Housekeeper. Any family? . . . No, right. Did he seem confused, Miss Pomfret? Does he need any medication that you know of? . . . No, I appreciate you don't snoop in his medicine cabinet, but sometimes people are more observant than they realize. Would there be a photo of him you could send us? . . . I do understand that you don't feel it's your place to make free with his possessions, but if we're to put out a bulletin, the public will need to know what Sir Hugo looks like. And your contact telephone? . . . I *quite* understand your sister does not wish to be rung at all hours.

'Miss Pomfret, we do work closely with the police but unless you've any reason to suspect foul play . . . Yes, we'll put out a bulletin right away. Usually elderly people are simply confused and wander off. We find them safe and sound and only lost because they've forgotten where they're supposed to be . . . Yes, we'll do our best. Thank you, Miss Pomfret. Try not to worry. We'll be in touch as soon as possible, when we know something. Goodbye.'

Lily hung up, put the completed form in her out-tray and stretched. 'That's the fourteenth elderly person to have gone missing last weekend,' she said, to her co-worker. 'Good thing the weather's been warm. Did I tell you they found the old lady from Herne Hill sitting behind an old air-raid shelter? VE Day triggered some kind of memory and she was convinced the siren had gone off. She was waiting for the shelter to open.'

'They've gone overboard with this thing,' said her colleague. 'I mean, my grandfather says if you went through it once you don't want to relive it. He was in Italy and then at the Normandy landings. He and my gran took their holiday to get away from it all – went to Florida. Your family in the war, Lily?'

'On Dad's side they were Quakers and conscientious objectors, so my granddad was a medic. Don't know much about Mum's side.'

'Oh? Why?'

'My grandmother and her twin sister were raised by a foster-family in Manchester. We never knew where they came from, but there was some mystery about them. They both spoke French and German, even the twin who was brain-damaged or something. My mother said her mother remembered a big house with a pink bedroom where a girl who might have been her sister read stories to her.

Then she remembers being on a train with other children, and a farm and some old people and then men talking in the dark, and my grandmother being terrified that what she called 'the big men' were going to kill her and her sister.

'Years after the war was over, her foster-mother finally told her that one night a serviceman with a big duffel bag came knocking on their door to ask if he was in a Jewish neighbourhood. He believed he was because he'd lived in Manchester before the war. They'd thought he was looking for lodging and as they had an extra room they let him in. Instead he told them some story about being shot down in France, then being rescued and helped to get back to England. He put his duffel bag on the floor, opened it and there were two little girls asleep inside. He disappeared before they could ask him more. Strange, isn't it?

'All the girls knew were their names. My grandmother and her sister remembered hearing their foster-parents argue in English, then they had to put on black clothes and were told not to say anything in the streets. They were used to keeping quiet so it didn't seem strange at the time.'

'What a story!'

'I know. When my grandmother married, my great-aunt lived with her but she died young, when my mother was a child. My mum said she looked exactly like my grandmother and they were both really pretty, only my grandmother was clever and did a university degree after she married, then became a teacher like her husband. My mother remembers her great-aunt being sweet and gentle, and looking after her while my grandmother went to classes. She said my grandmother never got over her death. I'm called Lily after her.'

'Amazing! I guess there must be a lot of stories about the war that you never hear. Someone ought to write about it. 'Scuse me, Lils, there goes the phone again. No, you're due for your tea break. I'll get this one. Hope your wandering old man turns up.'

He just wanted a decent book to read ...

Not too much to ask, is it? It was in 1935 when Allen Lane, Managing Director of Bodley Head Publishers, stood on a platform at Exeter railway station looking for something good to read on his journey back to London. His choice was limited to popular magazines and poor-quality paperbacks – the same choice faced every day by the vast majority of readers, few of whom could afford hardbacks. Lane's disappointment and subsequent anger at the range of books generally available led him to found a company – and change the world.

'We believed in the existence in this country of a vast reading public for intelligent books at a low price, and staked everything on it'
Sir Allen Lane, 1902–1970, founder of Penguin Books

The quality paperback had arrived – and not just in bookshops. Lane was adamant that his Penguins should appear in chain stores and tobacconists, and should cost no more than a packet of cigarettes.

Reading habits (and cigarette prices) have changed since 1935, but Penguin still believes in publishing the best books for everybody to enjoy. We still believe that good design costs no more than bad design, and we still believe that quality books published passionately and responsibly make the world a better place.

So wherever you see the little bird – whether it's on a piece of prize-winning literary fiction or a celebrity autobiography, political tour de force or historical masterpiece, a serial-killer thriller, reference book, world classic or a piece of pure escapism – you can bet that it represents the very best that the genre has to offer.

Whatever you like to read – trust Penguin.